SCARS OF THE LEOPARD

AN EPIC AFRICAN ADVENTURE

DAVID MARK QUIGLEY

This book is dedicated to my beautiful wife Rhonda.
Thank you for all your love and support. I love you.
Q XOX

ABOUT THE AUTHOR

A native New Zealander, David Mark Quigley worked variously as a farmer, vineyard owner, clinical hypnotherapist, and serial entrepreneur. Travelling extensively chasing adventure across Europe, Australia, and Africa, he has been obsessed with animals and nature ever since. Inspired by his travels, he decided to tackle his dyslexia by writing a book, *Scars of the Leopard* and unexpectedly discovered his love of writing, and wrote two further action adventures, *White Gold* and *African Lion*. He is a sculptor and produces striking wildlife sculptures cast in silver, alongside running an international environmental consultancy. He is also the innovative architect of Hashbooks, the multi-layered publishing platform where life-changing anecdotes and insights meets adventure. He lives in Naples, Florida, with his wife and numerous furry freeloaders, in a home he built in his spare time.

FOREWORD

Most characters depicted during this text are imaginary and bear no resemblance to any known, living persons. Also, the establishments of de Lout Investments and Network have no known equivalents in real life anywhere in the world.

However, as a number of the events portrayed in this book actually happened, the main characters' names have been changed to protect their identity. Also, inasmuch as research for the book would allow, certain world events described throughout the book actually took place.

Scars of the Leopard is a blend of fact and fiction. Which is which? You decide.

DAVID MARK QUIGLEY

PROLOGUE

Utter disbelief; that's what I felt. Not necessarily at the words of the assessment in front of me, but at the emotions it provoked. Hurt, bewilderment, numbed incredulity at what she'd said and was still saying. The plush interior of the office faded from my mind as I tried to focus on her words.

'Dave, look, there's good action and attention to detail in the manuscript, but some of the critical scenes... will just have to be rewritten.' She shook her head sadly. 'Even though it's just a story –' she made air quotes – 'you're doing your readers a great disservice.'

I eventually found my tongue. 'So, Miriam, you're saying the book lacks credibility.'

'Exactly.'

Jesus! I'd spent fifteen months writing the so-called novel, only to get it blasted down in a shower of flames. And after all I'd been through, I never thought for a minute that her words could evoke such a flood of emotion. Was a literary agent the right way to go, I had to ask myself?

She was speaking again. 'Look, Dave, I'm not saying it won't find a publisher, but it needs an awful lot of rewriting and tightening. You've got a talent, most of the manuscript proves that, but why not use it for something that's, say, a little less dramatic? Plausible, even.'

I stood up without another word and stripped off my suit jacket and tie. It was obviously the last thing she expected. She began to protest when I started to undo the buttons on my shirt.

'Honestly, Dave, I really think that... oh my god!' she gasped, looking at my chest.

She stared, dumbfounded, as I re-buttoned my shirt. I'd done up the last button when it finally sank in. This was the first time I'd heard her lost for words.

'You mean it's... those scars... the manuscript is... Oh god. It really happened. It's not fiction at all.' she stammered.

I shrugged. 'Miriam, I never said it was. Perhaps you should read it again.'

'Yes. Yes, I think I will.'

She looked down at the title page on the desk in front of her. It read: SCARS OF THE LEOPARD.

CHAPTER I

OMUMBO

To the east the sky glowed violet-pink, but the land stretching out to the horizon was dark and ominous. The only visible features were the black distorted shapes of trees and bushes, thrown into sharp relief by that smouldering incandescence. The crisp, cool air smelt, belied the fire of the day that was soon to come. The land seemed to wait in breathless silence for the dawning of a new and exciting day.

Then with the suddenness that only happens in Africa, the sun came crashing over the horizon, shattering the veil of darkness that hid the harsh desert. With it came a cascade of colours that seemed to pierce the eye: greys, reds and browns, with a smattering of living green in stark contrast. Minute sparkles reflected the clear, unyielding sun, mere fragments of brilliant light that signalled the beginning of the end for the brief dewy African dawn.

The flaming sphere rose, rimed in reddened gold, sweeping away the darkness from horizon to horizon. The pre-dawn silence fled, and a stark, cloudless blue sky spread over the desert, aptly named by its native inhabitants the Great Thirstland.

A staggering scene unfolded, teeming and flowing with radiant colours. This unique stretch of the Kalahari Desert was inappropriately named a wasteland; deep fertile sands were covered with grass, an abundance of bush, and clumps of trees. Antelopes, birds, lions, and of course leopards roamed free.

For centuries on this particular spot had stood an ancient baobab tree. An Arabian legend said: *The devil plucked up the baobab, thrust its branches into the earth, and left its roots in the air.* This one, with its grotesque, barrel-like trunk and stunted, twisted limbs, looked out to the east over a small undulating plain towards low, rust-coloured hills.

The plain was paved with brown time-weathered sand, and studded with hardy clumps of stalky desert grass, stunted bushes of thorns and an occasional green umbrellas of acacia.

No visible greenery had clung to the baobab's ancient contorted limbs. It had nestled in an outcrop of weather-beaten rock, and the mythology of the

Herera people, who once called all of Namibia their home, told that their tribe had risen from this very tree.

Traditional Herero beliefs held that the one benevolent, omnipresent supreme being – *Ndjambi Karunga* – created the first man and woman of their tribe by causing them to emerge from an omumborwnbonga tree. The legend claimed that this baobab was that tree, and the surrounding area was the birthplace of their tribe.

Over the years, as the legend slowly seeped southward, it had been perverted. Stories of an abundance of treasure came to the ears of greedy white men. The only things that had protected this Herero shrine in those early colonial years were the vastness of the Kalahari, and its furnace-like heat.

As the temperature began to soar, an eddy of wind tumbled in from the east. The peaceful desert morning was shattered by a sound that reminded anyone listening that the Herera shrine had long ago been destroyed: the metallic slap of metal on metal.

Where the ancient baobab tree had once stood, there was now only a remnant of an extinct frontier mine. The headgear's dull, pitted metal, abandoned in a state of disrepair, was all that remained of the once sacred site.

Behind the weathered headgear, derelict buildings of galvanised iron, the sheets originally studded together like wings of a plane but now curled up at the corners, flapped in the dry desert breeze. But it wasn't the buildings or the head-gear, standing like a skeleton of some prehistoric dinosaur, that marked man's titanic struggle with the earth and elements; it was the dumps, the mine's tailings towering to the sky, that seemed to symbolise the mountainous endeavour that had destroyed this once fiercely beautiful place.

Hanging drunkenly from an open doorway was a painted, barely legible sign. It simply read, OMUMBO MINE. The man who discovered and pegged the mine had not only destroyed the Hereros' sacred tree; he had also bastardised its name.

There had indeed been an abundance of wealth hidden directly beneath the ancient baobab. From its beginnings, the tree had sat directly above one of the richest volcanic diamond-bearing pipes in the world. At the height of the mine's production it had produced nearly twice as much as the next richest, but its reserves had rapidly pinched out, and the mine was left to stand as a monument to man's greed, and his triumph over oppressive nature.

As this pillaged and plundered place had once shaped the history and the convictions of man, as a new sinister and evil presence grew in influence and power throughout the world it would continue to shape the thoughts and endeavours of man, but this time on a far grander and global scale.

CHAPTER 2

As the twilight of the Transvaal highveld faded through crimson to a deep rich indigo, its beauty was lost on Avril van Nel as he headed south in his rented van en route from Pretoria.

Van Nel was a big man, heavy in the gut with a high-coloured complexion from years of heavy drinking. He had recently turned off the M1 from Pretoria to Johannesburg, and was now on the N1, Johannesburg's Western Bypass. The further south he drove, the more anxious he felt. His stomach was knotted with tension, his palms clammy with sweat. Every time he thought about what was in the van, his stomach coiled even tighter, and he had to wipe his hands on his trousers.

'Oh god,' he groaned miserably. His destination was now in sight.

Van Nel never even saw the vast complex of the Crown Mines on the left. His eyes were riveted on South Africa's largest city and biggest ghetto: Soweto.

A haze of smoke like the devil's cape shrouded Johannesburg's satellite city, just fifteen kilometres to its south-west. Van Nel's tension solidified into fear. As if it knew of his deplorable act, the low-rise, high-density city seemed to wait in grim silence for his arrival.

Van Nel had never been into Soweto before. God forbid: he was white. He had heard it described as the murder capital of the world. He cursed again for agreeing to the rendezvous.

He could picture it in his mind. The sprawling urban slum of shacks and hovels with its narrow potholed dirt roads. The sidewalks littered with rotting garbage and discarded junk, and countless derelict, burnt-out cars, abandoned as if symbolising the anger and hatred of the city's black populace. And of course, the smell.

The sun had already sunk like a red, angry ball into the leaden skyline. It had seemed to reflect the smouldering anger and brooding emotions of the city. In its place a repressive darkness, compounded by the lingering smog, slowly enveloped the city for another cheerless night. Van Nel turned in to Diepkloof Extension, the first of Soweto's many suburbs. He was surprised to see neat, upmarket houses; black doctors, lawyers and businessmen had chosen this suburb as their home. 'Soweto isn't supposed to be like this,' he mumbled. But as he travelled towards the adjacent suburb, Orlando East, everything changed. Diepkloof was a ruse, a façade, that the Johannesburg City Council had helped create to soften the rest of the city's misery and anguish.

'Christ,' van Nel breathed in desperation, thumping the steering wheel. He was hopelessly lost and very close to panic. His first impression had long since passed; Soweto was definitely the slum he had first imagined.

In the back alleys of Orlando East, he was seeing the real Soweto in all its glaring poverty. He had locked all his doors for fear of being attacked; on every street corner were groups of unruly looking youths. They were *tsotsi*, street thugs, he was sure; he felt hopelessly conspicuous, and it intensified his fear. He felt eyes like steel probes boring into him from every quarter, but thankfully he had not been approached.

'Damn it,' he cursed again. 'Soweto. Why Soweto, of all places?'

For endless minutes van Nel drove in aimless circles, through countless neglected streets. He didn't have a clue where he was. He tried retracing the route he came in by, but everything looked the same: row upon row of tiny dingy homes, each accompanied by its *Mkhukhu* — a dilapidated backyard shack which housed rent-paying tenants.

As if a gloved hand from heaven was slowly descending over the city, it was growing even darker. Van Nel cursed and peered longingly through the windscreen for any recognisable landmark. As thousands of coal-burning stoves were fired, the hazy smog became more oppressive. He realised with sickly dread that even if he wanted to leave the city he couldn't; he was helplessly lost. He thumped the steering wheel again.

The first evening lights had begun to flare, but their glow gave van Nel no joy. He needed to find the rendezvous, or at least a way out of this godforsaken place. The youths on the street corners were growing more menacing, and the darkness compounded his fear.

In desperation van Nel changed direction. He nearly cried out in joy as he recognised the railway line that carries droves of commuters to Johannesburg's Central Park Station each working day. Follow that and I'm home free, he thought, elated. Forget the money; I'm getting the fuck out of here while I've still got the chance.

His heart missed a beat as he recognised another landmark: one of the few two-storey buildings in Soweto, the Pelican Club, opposite the Orlando railway station. An absorbing greed began to override his fear as he identified

Orlando's soccer stadium a little further on. This close to the rendezvous, he decided, he might as well keep to his lucrative meeting after all. His days as a security guard would soon be over.

The weather-beaten Elephant Trading Store in Orlando East is one of the oldest shops in the district. Van Nel didn't know which was worse: the deserted oppressive silence outside the store, or the wary watchful eyes in the rest of the suburb. But as he sat waiting in the van, he felt relieved. He was now back in control, or so he thought.

'Christ!' Like a startled cat his fear leapt again, and he jumped a foot off his seat at a light tap on the window. A big blond white man was staring through the glass.

'You van Nel?'

He nodded.

'Well, open the door and get out. You're late.'

The man wasn't just big; he was huge. Van Nel wasn't small, but the blond guy towered above him. All the same, he needed to hold his own. 'I got lost. So what? Why the hell Soweto anyway?' he demanded, with an aggressiveness he wasn't feeling.

'You agreed to the meeting, so spare me the heartache,' the blond man retorted in unaccented English. He stabbed a finger at van Nel's chest. 'Did you bring it?'

'What the hell do you think...' van Nel began. He found himself brutally bundled up against the side of the van, with a vice-like hand clamped around his throat.

'You've been paid half already for this, so make it easy on yourself and shut the fuck up.' The man spoke quietly, yet like the quiet swish of a whip, the words lashed about his face. The blond man released him. 'Show me,' he demanded.

Scowling as he rubbed his neck, van Nel led the way to the side door. Inside was a large, dull metal trunk. 'This is a two-man job,' van Nel said. 'I only just managed to get it in by myself. It's mostly solid lead.'

'And you're sure this is the right stuff?'

Van Nel, still indignant from his earlier treatment, snapped back, 'Of course it is! It's stamped on the top and side. See for yourself.' He pointed to the two impressions stamped on the lead casket. 'See here, and here. U235.'

'Good.' The blond man nodded, satisfied. 'And the van is rented, as you were asked?'

Van Nel immediately became suspicious. That didn't sound like a simple query, more like a damning verdict. 'Yes,' he hesitantly replied, as he began to back away.

'Good, very good.' The blond man nodded again. 'We won't be needing you again then, will we?'

The penny began to drop. Van Nel cursed his own stupidity. The blond man raised his hand and snapped his fingers. Van Nel cursed again. He had left his 9mm FN 35 under the seat in the van. He turned to run, but he hadn't gone a couple of paces before he was encircled by black youths. They didn't try to attack him, they just stared, standing menacingly still, between him and the handgun and the sanctuary of the van.

The blond man pushed his way through the circle of bodies. He stood a full head taller than most of the youths, and though he was white he obviously commanded their utmost respect.

He looked into van Nel's stricken face and swept an arm around the youths. 'These are what you would call the Comrades, Soweto's young radical activists. If you were African, they would call you an *Impimpi*, a sell-out. Now, for selling out your country – not that they really care – they have a gift for you. Scream all you like.' He shook his head sadly. 'People may even hear, but I'm afraid nobody will come to your aid. Enjoy your Sowetan necklace.' As he turned and walked through the circle again, his words were simple, but their intent very clear. 'He's yours.'

Before van Nel could react, he was swamped in a rough and tumble of bodies.

The big man stepped back and watched the proceedings with interest. A car tyre filled with petrol was forced over van Nel's head. He began to scream before it was set alight.

As the pathetic screaming figure tried desperately to dislodge the burning tyre over his flaming hair, a smell similar to roasting pork filled the air. Slowly van Nel began to lose co-ordination as he staggered aimlessly around in front of the jeering youths. Eventually his charred and blistered hands fell to his sides. With his head and upper torso consumed with flames, he dropped lifelessly to the ground.

As the blond man stood indifferently watching the burning spectacle, his attention was eventually drawn away from the human torch by one of the black youths who came to stand at his side. He held van Nel's wallet in his outstretched hand. The blond man took it and spoke. 'You and the Comrades have done well.' He opened the wallet and pulled out a thin wad of notes. He quickly counted it: two hundred and twenty rand. He handed it to the youth. 'Make sure nothing remains of the white man. I don't want the police asking any questions.'

Carrying the wallet, he turned his back on the charred and still burning figure. He stepped into the rented van, started it and without looking back, drove away to the east.

As he drove out of Soweto, he rifled through the wallet, the last trace of van Nel. Nobody would ever know of the gruesome fate that had befallen him. He held up the card he was searching for; it identified Avril van Nel as a security guard at a South African government installation called Valindaba.

'This I'll have to get rid of myself,' he said. It was too sensitive to fall into the wrong hands. He slipped it into the breast pocket of his shirt; he would burn it later. 'One down, one to go. First stop Natal, the Valley of a Thousand Hills, then halfway across the world to New Zealand.'

CHAPTER 3

It was cool and dark inside the small New Zealand country pub. The sweet smell of alcohol and stale cigarettes turned his stomach slightly; a light blue haze of smoke lingered in the air like a faint polluted mist, stinging his striking golden eyes. It was blowing again today, from the north-west, hot and very dry, the sort of day that sapped a man's energy. As he walked up to the long single bar, he carried himself with a relaxed air of confidence, a man who had experienced life.

'Gidday, Jack,' he said. 'Jug of DB, thanks.'

The bartender, overweight with the ruddy complexion of a heavy drinker, looked up. 'How are ya, Dave? What's been happening? You're in early for a Friday evening.' He reached down under the bar and pulled up a glass jug, which he placed under the beer tap. As it began to fill, looked expectantly at Dave.

'You know what they say about mad dogs and Englishmen – well, it's too hot out there today.'

As he waited for the bartender to finish, he causally glanced down at a copy of the Christchurch Press, sitting beside him on the bar. The newspaper was open at the business section; the article that caught his eye was a recap of legislation, potentially the most historic executive decision of 1985 that Ronald Reagan had signed in the White House on December 12th, a day ago. A quick scan of the article told him the bill was supposed slice the US federal deficit to zero. 'Not likely,' Dave muttered. He knew it was a stop-gap measure implemented to try and bolster North America's weakening balance of trade.

'Sorry, what?' the bartender asked.

Dave was about to respond when he looked up and noticed a reflection in the tall mirror behind the bar. 'So, they've found me at last. Damn it!' His mind was racing. 'I knew it was too good to last.' He pushed the newspaper away.

He had woken early this morning and his sixth sense had told him today was going to be different. It hadn't let him down in all the years of his former profession. He had learnt to trust it and use it, for when he hadn't it had normally cost him dearly. Could you really call it a profession? he mused, as he started going over the events of the morning.

He was lying in bed trying to put his finger on it. Something seemed to be fluttering, like a butterfly on the wind, just below the surface. He knew not to force it, it would come if and when it was ready.

Clay was lying at the foot of the bed, curled up quite contentedly. One of those golden eyelids popped open but snapped shut as soon as he knew Dave was watching him. No way was this Labrador going to wake until he had to.

The sun was just bursting over the hills on the eastern horizon. Fragments of rich golden light danced about Dave's room, but the beauty and tranquillity of the moment was lost as his unease persisted. It was a small bedroom, impersonal, decorated in gold and brown. A double bed, functional chest of drawers, nothing more. A room that hadn't yet been accepted as a permanent sleeping place.

'Come on, *cheri*, rise and shine,' a woman's voice sang in French from another room. 'You've got that mob of ewes to shift off the face this morning, before the wind gets up.'

'Yeah, yeah, keep your hair on, Anne,' Dave yelled back in the same language, though he was still deep in thought. Clay was yawning now, staring up at him. The dog seemed to know what would happen if he didn't rise. It might be his house, his farm, and his day, but that was his mother's voice and that made a difference.

Dave had never known his father. His mother, using some eloquent French colloquialisms, had described him as a free spirit who had walked out on the family when he was too young to remember. They had met in France, and after a whirlwind romance, married and settled back in New Zealand on the family farm. Five years and four children later he left; apparently that was the longest he had stayed in one spot. Dave's mother was of hardened French farming stock, and she ran the farm and raised the family on her own. It was partly this tenacious French blood that had led Dave to where he was today.

'What are you looking at?' Dave demanded of the Labrador. Clay casually turned his head and looked out of the window as if he hadn't heard.

Dave swung his legs over the edge of the bed. The uneasy feeling came back twice as strong. 'Something's not right,' he said softly. He looked over at Clay. The dog had now picked up his sense of disquiet. Ever since he had rescued him as an abused puppy, not only was he fiercely protective of Dave, but an intuitive link seemed to exist between them. With his head slightly cocked, he was staring intently at his master. One of his supple ears drooped to the side, and his eyes sparkled with a curious, half-expectant look. Dave knew Clay wouldn't be leaving his side today.

Dave stood up and crossed to the door leading to a cobbled patio outside. The door had been hooked back for the night. The morning was still and very mild. He raised both his arms above his head and rested his hard-callused hands on the architrave, leaning to his right. As he thrust his hip to the side, his head dropped forward, deep in thought.

Clad in nothing but red briefs, his body had a certain presence. He stood well over six feet and was deeply tanned, with the physique of a highly trained athlete.

He dropped both arms to his side and stepped lightly down onto the patio. Three long strides carried him to the edge of a well-kept garden. That brief movement would have shown any onlooker his body was indeed well-proportioned and far from over-developed.

The gentle fragrances carrying from the garden normally relaxed his soul, but they gave him no peace today. Dave thrust his hands on his hips. The gesture emphasised the width of his shoulders, but clearly showed the scars that criss-crossed his back. Some stood out proudly, as sharp, shining ridges, others were sunk into his skin as if hiding from the world. They gave his body a primeval air of suffering.

He stared out, his eyes unfocused, into the distance. There was a norwest arch forming above the hills to the west. The wind would blow from that quarter today, hot and dry. It was notorious in this part of New Zealand, the Canterbury plains.

Dave turned and walked back inside. He had short sandy hair, and a creased brow typical of a man in authority, or one who worried a lot. His nose was slightly crooked from several breaks, and a small pale scar ran horizontally just below his left eye. He had a large honest mouth and when he smiled, which was rare these days, it showed even white teeth. The face you couldn't really call handsome, but like his body, it had a certain engaging presence.

Like his back, his chest and stomach showed well healed scars. Very few people outside his family had seen those scars, he had made sure of that, but he did have an occasional unconscious habit of playing his fingers over four parallel ones running down his chest and stomach. At those times unmasked suffering clearly showed in his fierce eyes.

'Yep, something's not quite right,' he repeated to himself. The feeling rarely surfaced nowadays; for the last two years that part of his life had been over.

So, they've found me at last, he thought. Damn!

No one in this small country community knew about his past. Not even his family. Of course they suspected something, what with the change in his personality and the scars. But nobody here had ever seen him raise his voice in anger. To the locals, Dave Old was just a thirty-five-year-old farmer, who had been home a couple of years after a long stretch overseas.

Dave looked around the bar, which was busy for an early Friday evening. He recognised all the faces; at least his back was secure then. But he felt something akin to premature grief for the peaceful life he had slowly begun to develop, which he had a premonition was about to be destroyed.

After paying for his jug of beer, Dave grabbed it and a glass from the wooden counter and made his way towards the man whose reflection had disturbed him. His name was Kane van der Zwet, and he was a big man, handsome, with long blond hair, a smooth face and distinctive high cheekbones. He flashed a friendly smile as Dave approached.

Kane was sitting behind a low table. He was alone; the locals were keeping their distance from the stranger. One well-tanned hand rested lightly on the tabletop; the other hand must have been at his side.

Kane spoke first, in relaxed, unaccented English. 'Hello, Dave, it's been a long time. You're looking well.'

Dave was standing before him. He placed his jug on the table. 'What do you want, Kane?' he said impassively.

'Well, it's good to see you too,' Kane replied sarcastically.

Dave waited for Kane to answer his question. It didn't take long. 'Vulcan sent me.'

Vulcan. The Roman God of Fire.

The name filled Dave with loathing, but he managed to keep it from showing on his face. 'Did he now?' he replied with an edge of bitterness.

As he looked into Kane's ice-blue eyes, Dave felt his anger and desire for revenge, like a violent storm, begin to build against the tyrant and self-styled god who had caused his scars. But it was imperative to appear to remain indifferent, so without another word he turned and walked from the hotel. He was going home. If Kane had tracked him this far, he'd know where to find him. His brutal past and Vulcan's baleful influence over him had returned.

It was another mild morning; dawn was just breaking over the horizon. The clouds to the east were tinted red, and the dark hills surrounding the wide valley gave it a solemn air. The dry shape of the countryside wasn't yet apparent in the half-light, its sins hidden to the human eye.

The sweet scent of freshly cut hay floated on the morning breeze as the birds sang their praises to the new day. The morning had a sense of tranquillity about it. This, Dave thought, was the magic time of the day.

The light was strengthening now. The valley before him was a blend of different shades of brown; another drought had begun. November had been dry, and the beginning of December had given no reprieve. Today was going to be hot and dry again.

Dave could now make out the distant hills to the west. A black scar was evident to the naked eye; there had been a recent scrub fire in one of the rugged gullies. But this morning he paid scant attention to the scenery unfolding before his eyes. What did catch his attention was a pair of magpies, the black and white crows of New Zealand, harassing a solitary hawk. They were playing a game of chance, which they very rarely lost. They were skilfully diving and swooping at the predatory bird, just short of its outstretched talons. Dave envied their freedom.

He was sitting on the steps of the cobbled patio, beside a pool of blue-tinted water, crystal clear to show off the perfect white cement. A lush green lawn swept from the patio down to a haw-haw at the bottom of the garden. The uninterrupted view of the valley gave the illusion that just beyond the sunken fence it dropped away to nothing. But there was a stream down below the garden, a sluggish trickle sacrificed for the benefit of the parched land. A host of green willow and poplar trees studded its banks. These and the pampered gardens formed a hidden oasis in the thirsty farming terrain.

Behind Dave stood a rambling old Summerhill stone house. Its windows, doors and the exterior panelling were sand-blasted cedar, giving the characterful house a rustic look. It perched on a slight terrace, boldly showing itself as the homestead of the property that swept out before it. Well established evergreen shelter trees were cunningly positioned to ward off the prevailing winds, yet still allow a magnificent view towards the eastern hills.

The farm was six hundred hectares of semi-productive farming land. It was profitable wool and fat lamb country. Both farm and house had been in Dave's family since the turn of the century; it was the place he called home.

Clay, Dave's ever faithful companion, sat on his haunches beside him. His hand rested easily on the dog's shoulder, showing the comfortable bond between them. Clay was staring out towards the valley at some scene that had captured his imagination.

The back of Dave's neck began to bristle as his intuition flared, and he felt Clay stiffen as his hand began to tremble against the dog's shoulder. Clay, his chest rumbling, turned his head and let out a barely audible growl. Dave silenced him with a low growl of his own, but the dog continued to watch warily over his shoulder.

Kane had arrived silently and stood poised behind Dave in the open French doorway leading from the homestead's living room to the patio. Kane began to stalk softly forward again as Dave, without turning his head, asked, 'How did you find me?'

Kane froze, shocked at being detected, and an ominous silence descended upon the scene. Even the birds stilled their morning chorus, waiting in silent anticipation for what was to come. Then the tension evaporated as Kane replied, 'You know Vulcan, he has tentacles spread throughout the world.' He took an extra couple of paces and sat on the step next to Dave. 'I received the airline tickets and instructions in the usual fashion. I was told to approach you at the hotel.'

He looked unseeingly over the countryside. It was obvious he had more to say. Dave glanced at his face with anticipation.

Kane noticed the look. 'Vulcan wants us both back again,' he said, looking seriously towards Dave.

Dave snorted a humourless laugh. 'Is it really worth it, Kane?' he asked, frowning.

Kane met his gaze squarely and replied in an impatient tone, 'You know damn well it is.' He lifted his hand and made a sweeping gesture towards the land before them. 'You can't deny it has been profitable for you in the past. I'd hazard a guess that you could buy this place of yours freehold five times over with what you what have, shall we say, *acquired* working for Vulcan over the years.'

Yes, Dave had to admit he was very wealthy by the average man's standards, both here and overseas. But he made no comment, just shrugged and rested back upon his elbows on the step.

'We'll both be involved in the same operation. He wants us to work together if the need arises. I think this is the big one.'

That quickened Dave's interest; he sat up and cocked his head to the side, surprised. He was about to speak but thought better of it.

It had taken Dave a year to wind down after closeting himself at home, and the next year had been hard too. He found himself dwelling on the past during periods of inactivity, though he knew it served little purpose. Yes, he had to admit, this was what he had been waiting for: to strike at the source of not only his emotional and physical wounds, but also at the devious architect of the current economic chaos swiping the world.

During the last two years he had ignored the worsening plight of the world's economy and instead concentrated on developing the farm to a point at which it required very little effort. He now occupied most of his time keeping in shape and disciplining his mind, but he knew he needed the challenge that now lay ahead. He had made a pledge to himself never to be active in his country of birth. So far he had lived up to that promise, and instinct had told him he would be soon venturing overseas again.

'I leave on Friday with your reply,' Kane said. 'What are your thoughts?'

Dave knew what he had to do but gave no indication. 'You'll have my answer by Friday.' He turned his head and looked out across the valley, trying to hide what must surely show in his eyes. He was already marshalling his thoughts, planning his activities and the clandestine contacts he would have to make, readying himself to stalk his prey once again.

Both men fell silent. Dave knew Kane would be feeling as he did: excitement, fear, anticipation. Emotions that charged your veins and set you free, while still making you a prisoner of your soul.

'I'd like to stay if I could, even if you choose not to return. I'd like to spend some time with you here, if I may?' Kane appeared sincere.

Dave was startled, caught totally off balance. Yet before the feeling took hold, he realised with a twinge of disappointment that Kane was still doing his job, for no warmth registered in his eyes. He would be well paid for bringing Dave back into the fold.

Is this all we've become? Dave wondered. But he didn't let the realisation show in his face. Instead he rose to his feet, and with a light backhanded gesture tapped Kane on his chest and said, 'Well, come on, ya big ox, if you're staying with me, you'll be earning your keep. Let's have some breakfast.'

CHAPTER 4

She was dressed in black, the grief evident behind her veil. Yet even in mourning she carried herself with dignity. Her emerald green eyes were awash with tears, and as they overflowed down her face, she made no attempt to wipe them away. She stood alone, and to the side, accompanied only by her sorrow.

She was tall and broad-shouldered for a woman. Her black dress hung just above her knees, revealing elegant well shaped calves. Her hands were strong, the fingers long and tapered, each nail meticulously covered with a shade of deep rich ruby; the same colour coated her lips; strangely, it seemed to heighten her air of loss. She lifted her head and looked over at the group assembled around the newly dug grave. As she did, she took in a long deep breath which revealed a glimpse of her even white teeth. Her brow was knotted in pain, or perhaps in anticipation of the events to come.

Her skin was lightly tanned and smooth, glowing with vibrant health. She had lightly touched her cheeks with rouge, which emphasised her beauty. Her long brown hair was tied severely behind her head, the ponytail falling to the base of her graceful neck.

The small crowd around the grave began to disperse; she noticed most of them were too embarrassed to offer their condolences. She was glad, for she wished to spend some time alone as she bade a silent farewell to her newly departed husband.

She didn't notice the small group of mourners approach her from the side, until a hand touched her lightly on her upper arm. As she turned towards the touch, she was met with a look of undisclosed resentment. She looked past a short stocky man to see the same look clearly evident on the two women's faces, his mother and sister, standing behind his shoulder.

'I do hope you realise, Karen,' the man began, 'that it is necessary to read the will as soon as is practicable.' Karen had only ever known him to be distant and controlled, so was surprised to see him wringing his hands together as he made the comment. He swiftly arrested the movement when he noticed her scrutiny.

'Yes, Peter, I am sure it is in the best interests of the company. Your brother would want us all to know who will hold the reins.'

Despite himself Peter bristled with anger.

His mother laid a restraining hand on his shoulder and said in a condescending tone, 'I am sure Thomas has made the correct decision for all of us, even you, Karen. Come, Peter.' She turned to leave. 'We will expect you at our solicitors at four. Until then, Karen, goodbye.'

The threesome turned in harmony and walked towards the waiting vehicles. As they left, Karen lifted her chin and set her green eyes in determination. As she watched them walk away, pain, outrage, loathing and resentment compounded her grievous feeling of loss.

Once their vehicle had departed, she turned and walked alone to the side of the grave. Tears again began to stream down her face. She looked down at the beautifully presented mahogany coffin and closed her eyes tightly, her mind numb with fear, for she was now alone again.

It took quite an effort to break the sense of devastation that seemed to grip her; she felt she could easily end it all. But it was that very thought that worked as the catalyst to break the morbid spell.

She stood motionless for many moments. Then she lifted her head and, as if now forged in stone, her whole body took on a determined cast. Her eyes were fierce, staring unfocused into the distance. She quickly stooped and took a handful of the newly dug earth and dropped it on the coffin's polished lid. She swiftly turned away, and brushing the soil from her hands, purposefully strode towards her car.

A tall African held the door of the black Mercedes limousine as she approached, 'Thank you, Moses. Please take me to my office.' He inclined his head and gently closed the door as she thankfully settled back into the padded leather seat.

As the limousine glided into the stream of heavy traffic, she began to feel secure in the cocoon of comfort. Karen was deep in thought, and her chauffeur broke that train. 'We will all miss him, *Nkosikazi*.' The Zulu form of address for royalty. 'He deserved a longer life.'

'Thank you, Moses. I will still carry his name,' she said with pride.

She was alone as she ascended in the lift, now wearing a charcoal grey business suit with matching shoes and briefcase, which she clutched at her side. Knotted at her throat was a burgundy silk scarf. Her hair was severely pulled back and coiled on top of her head.

The lift opened on to a magnificently decorated reception area, tastefully furbished in natural wood and soft pastel shades that set the wood alive. The decorator had been able to capture such a rare mood that this vestibule heightened one's anticipation of success. As she turned to her left, this was the feeling that she carried with her to the office at the far end of the passage.

After she entered the office and respectfully closed the door, still holding the handle behind her she leant back against the burnished wood. Rich dark panelling lined the walls of the large office and before her stood a huge, intricately carved rosewood desk which commanded the attention of the room. Karen walked past the furniture and bookshelves of the office's informal discussion area towards the work of art. She ran her hand along its edge with what seemed like religious awe, then moved to stand behind the desk, in front of an enormous plate glass window. She stood transfixed, staring out at the view she had seen many times before. It was then the full enormity of her situation came crashing home. She spoke quietly towards the scene before her: 'Thank you, Tom.' The gratitude was evident in her eyes.

Before her spread the vast city built on gold; Johannesburg. She must now be one of the richest women in the southern African republic. Thirty years of age, she would be able to mould an empire that would continue to change the fortunes of her country. Her husband's will, in essence, had read, "I bequeath all of my assets to my loving wife Karen. The rest of my family I leave in the care of her determined generosity."

She quietly opened the connecting door from the office into the company's boardroom. A group of men were crowded around a central figure who was reading from the Johannesburg Star: 'Tom de Lout was buried yesterday after a brief private ceremony, attended by his family and close friends. Mr de Lout was seriously wounded while hunting in Zimbabwe. He later died in intensive care in a private hospital here in Johannesburg. Mr de Lout, the founder and president of the multinational property and mining concern de Lout Investments, is believed to have...'

Karen walked unnoticed to the head of the long oak table. She smacked the red folder she was carrying down onto it. 'Let the press chase the stories, while we concentrate on the facts, shall we, gentlemen?' She looked across at Peter de Lout and demanded, 'Mr Chairman, please bring the meeting to order.'

'Yes, of course, Karen,' he said with barely disclosed contempt, his attitude vastly different from the previous day. The other board members quickly took their seats as Peter promptly executed her request.

All heads turned expectantly towards the head of the table as Karen stood and arranged the notes before her. She looked up, her face a mask of steely concentration. 'I have called this extraordinary meeting in the light of the death of my husband.' Inwardly she winced, but nothing showed on her face. 'As you will all by now be aware, he left all his controlling shares to me.' She paused to assess the mood of the room. It was thick with tension, as if shrouded in a cloak of darkness. 'I have had an agenda drawn up for each of you.'

She handed the single sheets to her secretary who now stood at her side. As the sheets were placed before all those present, she sat down and let the gravity of the situation impress itself on them all.

The first item was simply headed: Nomination and Election of New Company President. The second item was Appraisal and Discussion of Existing Board Members. Karen wanted the members to fully accept who was now in control; the first test was about to come.

All heads were turned towards her again. She spoke, staring at Peter. 'I accept my unchallenged nomination as president of de Lout Investments. Peter, please call the vote.'

For now, Peter's normal cool reserve was gone. He sat dumbfounded at the foot of the table, his head bent forward and his mouth hanging open. Twenty-four hours ago he had felt invincible, but now his dream seemed to be crumbling before his eyes, his hopes of gaining control of de Lout Investments in tatters. He broke the morbid feeling with a visible effort and numbly did as he was told.

Karen inclined her head in satisfaction as the vote was passed and recorded. 'This brings me to the second item on the agenda.'

Some of the board members, Peter more than most, were now visibly perplexed, restlessly stirring in their seats. She looked up at the chairman, who could barely hold her gaze. 'I have disagreed with many of you in the past.' She paused, holding her audience captivated; the atmosphere she had created hung like a Sword of Damocles. 'But I see no reason to change any of the positions on the board.'

There was an audible release of tension. The shock hit Peter like a physical blow, but Karen continued without acknowledgement. 'And unless, gentlemen, we have any objections, I would like to move on to item number three.' She had now created the atmosphere she desired.

Four and a half hours later, Karen locked both doors leading into her new office. She walked over to one of the dark green leather settees and collapsed thankfully onto it, holding her head in her hands, and visibly shaking. She had only just been able to hold her fragile resolve throughout the entire meeting, but she had done it. And she had seen the respect slowly rise in their eyes.

She had compiled her own research on all the board members. They were all leaders in their fields, tough and uncompromising professionals. She had ruthlessly exploited her one and only advantage: their uncertainty. She had challenged them and won their approbation.

There had been looks and comments of complete astonishment when she presented her strategy for the coming financial quarter. She had put forward deft and cunning motions, bullying and harassing them until she had complete agreement. The skilful concepts and submissions she proposed rocked even their professional stability. At the close of the meeting she had seen recognition and respect twinkling in their eyes. She had thrown them a challenge and they had adopted it as their own. As a team, they had begun to forge the way for a new and exciting direction for the company.

Karen had worked long through the previous night to prepare for the meeting, and she was now firmly in control. Thankfully, nobody had exposed her inner fear. She sat back and bit down on her lower lip to control her trembling. She now knew that in the business realm she could meet and overcome any challenge, any hurdle that stood in her way. She stood up and laid aside the terrors she knew she would face again in the small hours when she was home alone.

CHAPTER 5

It was Sunday afternoon and Kane was sunning himself beside the pool, an arm draped over his head to protect his eyes.

Dave spoke as he passed the prone figure. 'I'll be back in about an hour.' Kane barely grunted an acknowledgement as he walked around the edge of the pool and through a small wooden gate in a short hedge.

Once Dave had gone through the gate, Kane quickly rose and watched him walk down towards the small stream below the house. He cursed inwardly; he had been told to watch Dave's every move. He justified his rare lapse of vigilance by assuming Dave was about to perform some menial task on his farm.

Kane was now alone; Dave's mother had also left early this morning. He decided to make good the opportunity by searching the house. He crossed the patio to the door leading into Dave's bedroom, but before he walked in, he saw that damn Labrador lying on the bed, its eyes fixed like glue upon his face. He tested its resolve by taking a step into the room. The dog's hackles rose along the length of its ridged back as a deep growl rumbled from its throat, its quivering lips exposing long white pointed fangs. Kane found his own resolve wanting. 'Just don't want to create a situation that needs explaining,' he told himself. He stepped back and quickly scanned the interior of the room, but nothing caught his eye. He would wait for another opportunity, if it ever happened to arise.

He was quite confident Dave's decision would be positive, but he did acknowledge one of the principal reasons Dave had been so effective in the past was his unpredictability. Even Kane was impressed with some of the results Dave had achieved.

Dave walked through a cutting that had been widened to allow the stream below the homestead unrestricted access in times of flood. The cutting had exposed the dark greenish-yellow clay that kept the surrounding land dry in summer and wet in winter. The track he was walking on, just above the stream, led to his brother's neighbouring property. It was coated with a fine yellow powder, characteristic of the pliable silt-loam that was found here in the Omihi Valley. The walk gave him a chance to think through the recent turn of events.

Dave was blessed with an inquiring mind and he tired quickly of most mundane activities. Consequently he searched for constant mental as well as physical stimulation. His memory was almost photographic, and his mind still managed to keep its creative flair. He was an accomplished linguist, fluent in half a dozen languages with a smattering in as many more, which made it easy for him to past as a national in any number of countries.

Figures also fascinated him and could hold his interest for hours on end, which allowed him to wisely invest the money he had accumulated over the years. Some people might have called a number of his investments bizarre speculations, but most had paid him handsomely.

All his five senses were sharply honed, each complementing the others when the need arose, but far and away his most remarkable talent was his intuition. It had served him well in all areas of his life, both personally and professionally.

Walking up the slight hill just beyond the cutting he eventually arrived at his brother's weatherboard house. It had been constructed just after the turn of the century, in a time of great affluence in the farming community. It had once been a show-home, but its state of disrepair suggested that was many years before. The boards of the verandah that surrounded the north and west aspects of the house were buckled and twisted with age, the façade was badly in need of paint, there was no garden, and the only remnant of a long-forgotten tennis court was the sagging netting fence that once surrounded it. There was very little shelter left around the building; for the last few years it had remained in phase one of his brother's planned development strategy.

Dave stepped up onto the porch and walked towards a sliding door recently added to the home. As he placed his hand on the handle, he looked around cautiously; satisfied, he slid it open and stepped into the darkened interior.

He knew his brother would be down at the local hotel, so he wouldn't be disturbed. Walking through to Frank's bedroom he soon found himself smiling and shaking his head. The focus of the room was a king-size water-bed, which he knew from his brother's graphically described exploits got plenty of use. He had described it once as his sea of passion.

Dave prodded the bed and tried to visualise what his brother had said he had actually done during his last adventure. No, he thought, shaking his head. The little bugger has to be lying.

29

He laid the thought aside and reached for the phone beside the bed, which undulated as he sat on it. He attached the scrambler unit he had brought, placed the receiver to his ear and dialled a London number. As the number began to ring, he casually glanced at his watch: 3:15 pm. They'll be twelve hours behind, he thought, but the English voice which answered didn't sound sleepy.

'Dave Old,' he responded. 'Rewind the tape, Johnny, and turn it off.' There was a click, a gentle high-pitched whine and another click, followed by a brief silence.

The man spoke again. 'Tape's off, scrambler's on, ready to receive. How can we help?'

'Information concerning Kane Van der Zwet. Dutch descent, American resident, Miami, Florida. Last five years' movements, intelligence requested. Stop. Information concerning real name unknown, code name Vulcan. Place of birth unknown. Residence unknown. Suspected co-ordinator of illegal and subversive economic activity. Suspected operations; southern and northern Africa, western Europe and north America. Last five years' movements, intelligence requested. Stop. End of message.'

There was a slight pause. 'Right, got it. We'll see what we can do.'

'Thanks, Johnny.' Dave broke the connection, unhooked the scrambler unit, and left the room.

CHAPTER 6

As Dave broke the connection and left his brother's bedroom, the man called Johnny was still scribbling on an office pad as he fumbled the receiver back on its cradle. The code he was using was indecipherable, and Johnny was the code name he'd had since he became involved in the information gathering business.

He was a nondescript man, prematurely bald with a round fleshy face and an out of shape body. His round-shouldered stoop and inquisitive expression were the marks of his trade. Johnny had spent countless years hunched over a large desk cram-packed with recording equipment, computer screens and terminals, phone systems, and radio devices. He was quite simply the best in his field. His network of contacts on both sides of the law numbered hundreds. If the information was available, Johnny had the resources and the contacts to collect it.

His base was a top-storey flat in west London, part of a small red-brick complex situated close to the M4 leading into the heart of London, and not far from Heathrow Airport and the London Underground. The nearby park was an advantage as well; anyone following one of Johnny's infrequent visitors would easily be spotted in the open green.

However, the main reason for the flat's location was its cover as a residential dwelling. It was well known among the neighbours that the nondescript man and his flatmate were keen ham radio operators; that explained the complex system of aerials behind the building. The place's real function as an intelligence gathering centre had so far gone undetected by any subversive factions.

When Johnny had finished scrawling his message, he walked along a small hallway to another room, where his so-called flatmate was seated behind a desk piled high with files and paper. He laid the message on the desk, and the man looked at it with interest which quickly turned to confusion. He raised his hands and sighed.

'What's going on, Johnny?'

'The Leopard is active again.'

There was a pause. 'You'd better give me all the details. Any idea where the call came from?'

'Sorry, all I can tell you is it was international.'

As Johnny was about to leave the room, Richard Black leaned back in his chair and thoughtfully rubbed his chin.

'Hmm, this'll be interesting,' he murmured, as he leant forward and reached for the message. 'You'd better give him what he requests, usual channels.'

They were a most unlikely team, dedicated to a cause both men were prepared to go to extraordinary lengths to further; very little sleep was just one of them.

Richard was born in South Africa, but he was a British subject. He and Johnny were employed by the British Secret Intelligence Service, but with no affiliation to any specific branch. They were something of a law unto themselves.

Richard ran a close-knit team, simply called Network. It specialised in information gathering for the SIS, and anybody else that requested it, for a price. To the outside world, their service appeared to be run by an independent organisation, an elaborately cultivated front which provided an excellent cover to keep prying eyes away from its real function. For the right price, as long as it never jeopardised Britain's security, anybody could use it to gain access to a wealth of information.

It was also unique in another way; it never had been subject to budgetary restraints or cutbacks, since it was financed entirely from its own revenue. Other western security services dealt in laundered money to finance part of their covert operations; Network appeared to be above board. In fact, it had vast capital reserves to draw from.

The organisation's apparent autonomy meant the team was able to maintain intimate connections with all major security organisations throughout the free world. This supposed independence also opened normally closed doors in eastern Europe, and other destabilising influences around the world. Consequently on a number of occasions potentially disastrous situations had been averted quite anonymously. But Richard's main area of concern and specialisation was in the country and continent of his birth.

He was forty years of age, quite a handsome man, his brown hair cropped short, clean-shaven with a strong jaw and humorous probing eyes. Laughter lines framed his eyes; his was a face that could quite naturally break into a smile. He stood just under six feet tall and was well built, but best suited to using his mind. His congenial nature and keen intelligence had helped him build one of the most successful organisations of its type in the world. In different circumstances, he might have enjoyed international recognition as one of the best in his field.

After Richard had studied Dave's request at length, he sat stock-still for quite a while, staring at the request without seeing it. When the spell eventually broke, the corners of his mouth tugged upwards in a smile, but this time it wasn't mere congeniality that made him grin.

CHAPTER 7

The next few days were uneventful for Dave. He felt as though he was marking time, though a sense of urgency was developing. Kane helped him on the farm; they erected a fence line down one of the hilly ridges facing north-west, Dave's last phase of development on the property. He hadn't planned to complete the job until late autumn, when the ground wouldn't be so hard, but it was a good way to put Kane through his paces and reacquaint himself with the quirks of the other man's personality.

They spent the evenings sitting up late, engaged in long, roving discussions. Dave found it exhilarating to be in company that was both intelligent and articulate. They probed and tested each other's convictions and lines of thought, casually searching for any weakness or hardened view. They were so similar in nature, yet galaxies apart.

It was in the middle of the afternoon. Both men had just sat down for *smoko* – New Zealand's version of afternoon tea. It was sweltering, not a breath of wind, and the sky was cloudless. They were sitting on the ridge beside the partly completed fence; all that remained to be added was the bottom two strands of high tensile wire.

They had dug the posts in by hand, about one every three metres. The going had been tough; Kane's hands were raw and blistered, but not once had he asked Dave for a reprieve. This had given Dave a brief glimpse into his stoicism.

They were both stripped down to the waist, wearing only shorts and work boots. Kane sat in front of Dave, staring out over the valley and New Zealand's main trunk highway which ran through it. A heat haze rose from its dark surface. There was very little movement: just wandering stock and the occasional vehicle.

The valley was divided into uneven rectangular paddocks. Even from this height, the ground looked brown and thirsty. The only green was a few stands of lucerne, and the willow and poplar trees clustered along the banks of two small streams.

Dave looked over at Kane again, now able to observe him unnoticed. His blond hair fell to a point between his shoulder blades. His legs, arms and shoulders were a mass of muscle, with one small neat scar on his shoulder the only noticeable blemish. Probably from a cholera shot, Dave surmised.

A light sheen of sweat coated his back and shoulders, and the waistband of his shorts was soaked through. His skin had darkened to a richer brown in the last few days, from its exposure to the New Zealand sun, and his body clearly showed his dedication to his cause – which Dave was sure included himself.

Dave looked down at the dregs of tea left in his enamel mug and asked, 'What time do you leave on Friday?'

'Sorry, what?' Kane looked over his shoulder. 'Oh, I fly out from Christchurch at 5.30 pm.'

Dave was impressed with Kane's little charade. It required great mental stamina to stay on guard and appear to be miles away. Perhaps his observation of Kane had not gone unnoticed after all. There was clearly more to the man than met the eye.

'I'll take you down if you like.'

'Thanks,' Kane replied, leaning back on his elbows and turning his head.

His hair was plastered to his brow, emphasising a deep intelligent forehead. His eyebrows were virtually white, bleached by the sun, and his pale blue eyes seemed to search for something in Dave's face.

'I know how you got some of those scars, but what about the rest?' he asked, pointing at the four parallel ones scribed in his chest and stomach.

Dave's face remained impassive, but his eyes flashed. Kane knew he had struck a chord, but he couldn't fathom the tune that now echoed from the past. Kane watched him, fascinated by the way the simple question had produced such a reaction.

Dave was silent for several moments, then he turned his head, and looking squarely at Kane, replied simply, 'On a job.'

Something in Dave's eyes sent a pulse of excitement through Kane's chest. Was this man a far deadlier adversary than he had ever known, or an unworthy opponent to be crushed and left to die like a crippled animal?

The moment was shattered as Dave got up, brushed the soil from his shorts, and said in his usual deliberate manner, 'Come on, we've got a fence to finish.' He was firmly in control again.

It was Friday morning; the day Kane was due to leave New Zealand with Dave's reply. The rural mail service had delivered early, and Dave was standing at the breakfast bar with the morning's edition of the Christchurch

Press open at the classifieds, totally absorbed in its contents.

Kane walked into the kitchen unannounced, and Dave looked up with a guilty start. Kane noticed, but immediately dismissed it; Dave's mother was standing nearby at the kitchen sink, and she didn't turn around or acknowledge his presence. Kane knew she disliked him. Woman's intuition, he had told himself; she clearly sensed there was some nefarious bond between him and her son. It wasn't lost on Kane that Dave had a close relationship with his mother – something he wouldn't hesitate to use if the need arose.

'What's happening?' Kane asked.

Dave's attention was already back on the paper. 'Just looking to see if there are any worthwhile auctions. Want to replace one of the shearing machine motors before the autumn,' he replied casually.

His mother turned around. She was middle-aged, with dark wavy hair, slightly overweight, with laughter lines permanently etched across her face. The look of contempt she threw for the blond man in their presence didn't suit her attractive face.

'You know Friday morning's paper is no good for auctions,' she retorted, her French inflections still evident. 'The better ones are advertised on Wednesday or Saturday.'

Dave closed the paper, and as Anne turned back to the sink, he pulled a face behind her back and threw the paper into a wastepaper bin beside the breakfast bar. He moved towards the fridge, asking over his shoulder, 'Do you want some breakfast, Kane?'

'Sure,' came the reply.

The moment had neatly been forgotten.

Dave wanted to inspect the boundary fence between him and a neighbour, so he and Kane ventured to the back of his property in his Toyota Land Cruiser.

The farm ran to the east and was bisected by a steep north-west lying face which from a distance created the illusion that it was part of the receding hills further to the rear. At the top of the face, a wide plateau made up of grassy paddocks stretched to a deep rugged gully, which eventually rose into the dark forest that climbed the distant hills. It was the gully they were travelling to.

They left the vehicle in the lane; the gully's sides weren't quite sheer, but they made the going difficult. Exercising caution, they made their way down into the bottom along a well-marked sheep track. The vegetation was different here; it faced away from the weather. The grass was lush and green, while native trees and shrubs peppered the ground. There had been no stock in the gully for quite some time; it was due for grazing.

At the bottom of the gully a small stream trickled, and above it towered radiata pines like row upon row of soldiers reaching for the sky. The stream, the setting, and the sun's warmth cascading down gave the gully an air of untroubled well-being. It felt like a special place. Kane turned to Dave and commented on the soothing atmosphere.

'Yeah, it's a place you could stay forever.'

Kane raised an eyebrow. 'I wouldn't go quite that far.'

Dave lifted his chin. 'That tool pouch that's hanging in the tree, could you get it, please? I want to repair a floodgate down around the corner in the stream.'

Kane looked over at the tree; a brown leather pouch was suspended from a small branch, across a tangled overgrown grassy area. Dave was already down beside the stream walking towards the bend, so shrugging his shoulders Kane began to walk through the long grass. He paid no particular attention to where he was walking, preferring to absorb the sense of tranquillity the place exuded.

Suddenly he found himself walking on air. He lunged wildly to one side, but he was fractionally too slow. As he dropped, his ribs slammed against the edge of the void that had opened up. He grunted as the air was driven from his lungs. He frantically grasped for a hold, but the grass came away in stalky clumps as he fell into the dark cavity below.

As he began to fall, a sickly feeling clawed at his gut. Time seemed to slow down, and his mind was racing. As a surge of adrenalin coursed through his veins, long forgotten thoughts began flashing before his eyes. The fall seemed to continue forever, and he found himself wondering if this was what it was like just before you died.

But no sooner was he airborne than he fell heavily to the ground. His head snapped back, and stars burst before his eyes as his skull cracked against a massive unyielding body of rock. He lay still, his old training flooding back, and his senses began to clear. It was dark and cool, and the air smelled damp and of rotting vegetation; the ground was littered with small rocks and bones. He quickly assessed his body; a slightly twisted ankle, extremely painful ribs, and a head that throbbed like hell.

Sitting up, he dismissed the injuries and looked about him. He was in some sort of deep hole; he looked up and saw light pouring in. He rose gingerly to his feet and placed his hands on the facing wall; as his eyes grew accustomed to the gloom, he saw smooth rock covered in a brown greasy slime. He found he was at the bottom of a bottle-shaped hole. He wiped the slime off his hands on his shirt, looked up again and saw how he had fallen through. A mat of thick grassy roots had intertwined, giving the illusion of solid ground; he had stepped onto the mat and fallen through.

The chamber was about two metres wide at its base, and approximately five metres deep. It began to narrow about a metre above his head. Any attempt to climb out would be futile; a man on his own could easily die down here. He raised his head, cupped his hands around his mouth and bellowed. Almost immediately a dark shadow fell over the opening.

Dave had always known that several limestone sink-holes ran parallel to the stream. They were formed centuries before, when the stream's bed was a lot higher than it was at present.

His grandfather had discovered a number of them, when he had been losing stock in this area, much to his disgust. He had suspected theft until he found one of the holes, nearly dying in the process. After a short search, he discovered several more. For nearly eighty years, to some degree or other, these sink-holes had been fenced off.

Straight after Dave had called London the previous Sunday, he grabbed a tool pouch from his brother's workshop. Then he ran to the back of the farm and crossed the boundary onto his own property well out of sight from the homestead. It hadn't taken him long to find the sink-hole he was looking for. He carefully lifted the metal standards and wire netting that surrounded it and hid them around the bend in the stream. At a brief glance it wasn't obvious that it had been cordoned off for so long; he was pleased he hadn't grazed the block for quite a while.

Testing the opening of the sink-hole with one of the metal standards, he felt it was perfect for what he planned for Kane. His grandfather had told him the holes were quite deep.

Now, Dave sat back on his haunches with his forearms resting on his knees. He could see Kane clearly, at the bottom of the hole. Kane himself could see Dave's dark shape outlined against the opening, but was initially puzzled by his apparent lack of concern. Then the truth washed over him as Dave's earlier comment echoed through his mind: 'It's a place you could stay forever.'

Kane quickly realised Dave must have prepared the trap during that hour on Sunday afternoon. He had to admit he walked into it, literally. Damn, he thought, I was too self-confident by far. He was at Dave's mercy.

He looked up and spread his hands. 'Well?' he asked.

Dave's voice carried down to him easily. 'It's nothing personal, Kane. I just can't let you ruin this life.'

'Come on, Dave, you'd be doing the same. I'm just following orders. He'll come for you again, but next time there will be no warning, and it won't be a friendly visit.'

'Sorry, pal, can't accept that. Like I said, it's nothing personal,' Dave replied. 'We were the only two working in the African sector.'

'Maybe, but next time he'll bring somebody in from outside to get you back.'

So his hunch had been correct. He had always suspected they were the only two.

'Well, he'll have to now, won't he? As for the mission, now we're both unavailable. So long, Kane.' Dave began to rise, but Kane's next comment stopped him.

'Dave, he can't, not for this mission. We're the only ones he's got capable of infiltrating the company he's going up against.' Kane was pleading now.

So it's a big one, Dave thought. And he seems to know a hell of a lot more about Vulcan's operation than I've ever been able to find out.

'How the hell would you know that?' he asked Kane, his tone implying he wasn't expecting an answer. This time he did get to his feet.

Kane swallowed hard. He had a real dilemma. He certainly didn't want to rot down here, but he was reluctant to give Dave any more information. It might save his life, or it could seal his fate. After a few moments he took the only option available to him. 'I've met Vulcan.'

Dave's gamble had paid off, but the comment startled him all the same. He maintained his poker-face, even though he knew Kane could only see his outline. The full implication struck him like a piercing note. 'Only a very select few have ever seen Vulcan,' he murmured. As the thought resounded in his mind, his intuition snapped into focus and he looked down at Kane. There was no trace of deception on his face.

Dave slowly lowered himself back onto his haunches. 'I find that very hard to believe. Tell me more.'

'Help me up and I'll explain,' Kane tried.

Dave snorted humourlessly. 'Sorry, pal, no deal. Information first.'

Dave's senses sharpened as Kane began to talk. 'It was last northern winter. I was sent on a job in southern France. I was to pick up a package from a courier at the ski resort at Tinges. I'd been there a full week before anyone turned up. Only problem was there were three of them waiting for me at the rendezvous. I was summoned to a meeting down the valley at Val d'Isere, and introduced to him in one of the private chalets there.' He paused.

'Go on,' Dave demanded.

'Well, those three and one other must have virtually lived with him. While I was with him none of them let me out of their sight. I was sure one wrong move would've been my last. He was a short guy, and I'm pretty sure he was American.'

'Why?' Dave flicked the question like a missile.

'Just a hunch; his mannerisms, the cut of his clothes, other small things. He hardly spoke. One of his companions did all the talking.'

Kane began to rub the tension out of the back of his neck. His fate now hung in the balance.

Dave's intuition told him what he had heard was the truth. He already knew Kane had an exceptional eye for detail, and would have acquired far more information at the meeting than was given willingly. He had no need to question his judgment.

Dave never intended to kill Kane; all he wanted was answers to a number of questions in the most painless way possible. But now, as he rocked back on his heels, he realised the man had far more information than he had ever anticipated. A queasy sense of duty transformed the situation completely.

Kane thought he could make out a change in Dave's expression. He had gambled and lost. But what other choice had he had? He resigned himself to his fate as Dave reached for something to his side.

The seconds seemed to drag for an eternity; only the manner of his death was not yet plain.

As his mind explored the possible ways he might die, he couldn't help but be impressed at the simplicity with which it had been arranged. His body began to shake with dread, and his skin felt cold and clammy. He certainly didn't want to die. His heart pounded and a sickly feeling began to well up inside him, threatening to escape his lungs in a roar. But the cry never left his mouth; a rope dropped in front of him.

It took long seconds for Kane to take in what had happened. Then relief sank through his body as if somebody had pulled a plug. With his teeth clenched in rage, he flew up the rope, not bothering to check how it was secured, and as he perched on the edge of the sink-hole he fixed a murderous glare on Dave.

Dave was expecting the attack, but he knew a man thinking rationally would nearly always beat a man consumed with rage.

Kane began to stalk his prey, but before the situation erupted in a blaze of seething anger, Dave let out a short, sharp, two-toned whistle. From behind Kane a vicious growl exploded.

Clay was standing as if cast in stone, his massive chest thrown forward; the only evidence of movement was the quivering of his throat and the twitching snarl of his teeth. His eyes gleamed like polished coals.

The presence of the dog effectively defused the situation. Kane slowly stood upright and dropped his fists, but his eyes still held the sparks of burning fury that Dave knew would flare at him again one day.

Kane let out a breath of suppressed rage and whispered, 'Your time will come.' He turned and stalked away up the track.

Dave walked over and knelt before his dog. He grabbed Clay's face affectionately and looking into his eyes, realised that his time would indeed come. His violent past had returned.

CHAPTER 8

I t had taken Karen about a week to feel fully comfortable with her new role as president of de Lout Investments. Although she had taken an active role in decision making in the past, it had never been with anything like the influence she now commanded.

Before she was appointed to the main board of de Lout Investments, her late husband had given her seats on some of the lesser boards with de Louts' subsidiary companies. She had made a terrific impact with all of her placements, but they all felt hollow; she had always been looked upon as Mr de Lout's wife, as if her natural talent was purely the result of the marital link.

Tom de Lout had always sought her opinions on all major decisions and the direction the corporation was to take. On several occasions even his vast experience and intelligence was left reeling by the options she seemed able to put forward so effortlessly.

They had been married for three brief years before Tom met with his death; he was twenty years her senior, she his second wife. He was big in many ways; his physique, his bearing, his whole aura gave him a presence larger than life. His mind and body had been strong and solid, and these were the vessels he had used to carve out his titanic success.

They had first met soon after Karen graduated with honours from Witwatersrand University in Johannesburg, receiving an MBA in marketing and passing out at the top of her class. She took a position with a small but highly productive marketing company, and met Tom when she was thrust, virtually uninformed, into presenting a marketing proposal to the board of de Lout Investments. Although she hadn't even had the opportunity to work on the final brief, she closed the deal single-handedly, with apparent ease.

As it turned out, the company she worked for was a subsidiary of the de Louts marketing arm. It had been a setup from the start; someone at de Louts had recognised her potential and covertly plucked her fresh from university, but it wasn't until that board meeting that she had come to Tom de Lout's attention. Because of her remarkable presentation skills and unmistakeable other abilities, he immediately had her placed amongst his personal staff.

Within a year Karen had become indispensable to him. She travelled the world at his side, adding a completely new dimension to the now thriving corporation. It had taken another year before they became romantically involved. To him she was like the favourite niece he had always wanted; to her, he was like the father she had never known. Tom's power and quest for life had given her the opportunity to blossom, while her ingenious solutions and creative bias led him to use his own talents to the full. Their marriage had been satisfying for them both, but in entirely separate ways.

The loss of Tom still clawed deeply at Karen, but her new-found responsibilities enabled her to immerse herself in her work. Karen had been told that time was the greatest healer of all.

Thomas de Lout had laid the foundation for his company before he was twenty-five years of age. His mother was born into a wealthy mining family whose enterprises had been built up by two brothers, in gold and diamond mining. Neither brother had sired a son, and their three daughters were thought lacking in the business aptitude required in the fierce economic times. The brothers eventually sold their holdings to larger mining concerns.

After the death of both brothers, the inheritance was split between the daughters. One remained a spinster; the other two married, one to a lawyer, the other to a young man who was affable, but ignorant when it came to investments. Her inheritance was eventually frittered away over the decades.

Tom was their first-born son. His father had also studied law but had never practised. All the same, he eventually bumbled his way to a well-paid position in the Republic's parliamentary system. His career peaked when he became under-secretary to the Minister of Minerals and Energy Affairs.

Tom's family lived above their means, and he soon saw he wouldn't be left with much of an inheritance. Fortunately, he showed business acumen beyond his years, and by the age of nineteen was already a successful entrepreneur. Within two years of leaving school he owned a fleet of delivery vehicles, which he sold for a massive profit and began to invest in property. His rapid rise in the business world didn't go unnoticed by his spinster aunt.

Tom had a sister and a brother, who he never had much time for. His sister was pleasantly attractive but witless; his brother was clearly ambitious, but from youth showed a petty, bitter type of arrogance. Their mother was always busy with social engagements, and paid them little attention. Tom got on well enough with his father, but his real confidante was his unmarried aunt. He spent countless hours listening to her relive the triumphs of his grandfather and great-uncle, and how they had built up their mining concern, and found that the family's mining blood coursed through his own veins. His aunt had made some wise investments, so her original inheritance had grown colossally, but never once was Tom able to entice her to invest a single pound with him.

By the time he was twenty-three he had already acquired a substantial property portfolio through his own efforts. He was often invited to dine with his family, and one night, tired of aimless arguments and petty gossip, he went to wait for his father in his study. On the desk was stacked all the correspondence that crossed his father's boss's desk. From then on, he made a point of developing a close relationship with his father, who took great pleasure in Tom's visits. Tom's guilt at taking an unfair advantage decreased each time the information he covertly acquired helped him to even larger profits; his property transactions, and now his share trading activity vastly increased his wealth.

This was how he stumbled onto the information that led to his greatest success: a set of documents outlining a strategy to address South Africa's shortage of natural oil reserves. It was ironic that the Republic was well supplied with virtually every usable mineral bar this one.

There were two proposed options; the first was a little-known process which produced usable fuel from coal, something the Republic had in abundance. The second, which really quickened Tom's interest, was a proposal to purchase derelict mines and turning them into underground storage bunkers to be filled with imported crude oil.

Tom realised this was where he could break into the big league. He researched the mines in the report, mortgaged himself to the hilt and purchased as many options as he could. Stretching himself to the limit but still leaving him woefully short of his mark. The report itemised a time frame as well as the mines themselves; given the meagre horde he had managed to amass, the government would snap up the others and force him to sell, or worse, wait for his bankruptcy.

In the pits of depression, he turned to his aunt for advice. Tom poured his heart and soul out to her, and piqued her interest; some of the mines had once been owned by her father and uncle, and she had an opportunity to bring the past back to life. She lent her nephew every pound he needed.

The outcome was by no means certain, but he soon shed his guilt when he found he had many millions of pounds at his disposal. He was able to secure every single option, and negotiated the deals before the government realised what he had done.

A bizarre situation ensued; the young man was holding the South African government to ransom. The longer they waited, the firmer he stood. The government threatened, cajoled and persuaded, but week by week he increased his asking price. Their desperate need to implement the program meant the impasse was discussed at cabinet level, fixing the name of Thomas de Lout firmly fixed in their minds. It came to a head when he was politely invited to attend a meeting with his father's boss, the Minister for Mineral and Energy Affairs. A deal was concluded, and Tom walked away with many millions of pounds. He retained the options on the family's old mines, paid his aunt back in full, and with this one transaction had the means to found de Lout Investments.

Another lucky break came several years later, resulting from his sentimental gesture to his aunt. It transpired that the old family mines were the sites chosen for military oil storage bunkers, largely because of their remoteness. The government didn't bother to negotiate the purchase of his options, but came straight in with the offer of a joint venture, beginning a long and profitable association that was still breaking new ground when Karen took charge.

Karen realised, with a nostalgic pang, that Tom had always been able to attract luck to himself. She mused that the truly dedicated ones, committed to a worthwhile cause, usually did.

Tom was certainly one of those, she thought.

She was familiarising herself with one of the mammoth projects that had needed her attention, Pump Station Omumbo. It wasn't that it hadn't run smoothly since its inception; the problem was the calibre of people she had to deal with.

The reports that now lay in front of Karen showed the true significance of those early agreements. The company, in association with the government, owned or controlled all the military storage bunkers. Initially the government and, to a greater degree as the years passed de Louts, were able to stockpile vast oil reserves that they had relentlessly purchased on the world markets. She knew that the Republic already had a thirty-year supply of crude oil to keep her war-machine running, even if the world's oil supplies were closed to her country that very day. She also knew that, because of this association, there was a twenty-year supply of crude oil for normal public consumption if a blockade ever took place.

De Lout Investments was thoroughly intertwined with the energy needs of South Africa; the company also had vast tracts of coal reserves, and had had the foresight to invest in the oil companies' processing expertise. This enabled them to economically produce high-quality engine-grade fuels and oils from both their own reserves and the country's.

Again, de Louts profited from a joint venture, this time with the government and the oil companies. They had perfected such a radically superior method that now all of the petrol consumed in the Republic was a blend of fifty per cent refined imported crude with fifty per cent processed coal. De Lout Investments was now so heavily involved with the economy of South Africa that the country's survival depended to a large extent on Karen and the decision-makers of this one company.

Karen had been fully vetted by her late husband's company security arm when she first began to work by his side. She was again more rigorously investigated just prior to their marriage, this time by the country's National Security Service; she had of course come through the investigation unscathed. When she became heir apparent to the head of the giant corporation, it had been the Republic's President himself that had sanctioned her appointment.

The company was by no means going to suffer because of the death of Tom de Lout. In fact Karen felt certain that the ensuing years would prove to be the most profitable of all. Financial activities in the Republic were certainly going to increase enormously, for this is where Karen intended channelling her energies. Most overseas investments would, for the time being, command little of her attention.

This was the passion that now gripped her: the desire to help create a stable and secure economic state. It enabled her to hide, and even suppress, her emotional wounds.

CHAPTER 9

Neither man had spoken for the last twenty-five kilometres as Dave's Land Cruiser rumbled to the south, the whining of the heavily lugged tyres carrying into the cab. It was an unspectacular drive down from Dave's farm towards Christchurch, the largest city in New Zealand's South Island. The land either side of the main trunk highway was flat arable farming country, normally fertile for grain and grazing, but at this time of the year dry and thirsty. The only standing vegetation was the dry grass on the verge of the road, the occasional golden-brown fields of grain, and the sparsely scattered trees.

As they travelled closer to the city the breathless heat of the day lost some of its intensity, now that the plains fell unrestricted to the cool waters of the Pacific Ocean in the east. Even though the heat from the blazing sun was no longer trapped by surrounding hills, the slight dips and hollows in the road that were barely visible on cooler days shimmered with the illusion that they were filled with water. These tricks of nature danced and played about before the approaching vehicle, and the two men travelling together were also locked in their own forms of subtle manipulation.

Kane needed Dave's answer to take back to Vulcan, but Dave had chosen not to show his hand until he was sure he had as much information as he could draw from Kane.

Both were ruthless men, but in their own individual ways; Kane had brute strength and brains, Dave his own skills. If necessary, each would kill or prepare to be killed, but for what reason only they could tell.

There is no name that could be laid on their profession; they were far more than highly paid assassins. They were a new type of mercenary; using their own skills and the solid resources that backed them, they had become adept at extorting vast sums of money from their chosen prey. They could not only orchestrate the downfall of a vulnerable country, but also arrange the collapse of huge and secure corporations, whose power would then fall into the hands of their employer. Dave and Kane were professionals who stood apart, using whatever means available to achieve their objective.

As they travelled south the temperature began to cool outside, but a different sort of heat rose within the cab: a kind of intensity both men had called on before. Kane sat slouched, one foot casually resting on the four-wheel drive's metal dashboard, staring ahead motionless and giving off an air of nonchalance and relaxation. Dave's posture was similar to Kane's, but a faint hint of tension, like a subtle fragrance, slowly drifted from both men. They each felt it, but chose not to acknowledge it. It puzzled Kane, for he felt he should be the one at a disadvantage; he still needed Dave's answer before his current job was complete.

On arrival at Christchurch International Airport, Dave parked the Land Cruiser on the road outside the international departure lounge. He didn't even bother turning the engine off; it seemed to growl impatiently. Kane had pulled up his carry-all from behind his legs and placed it on the seat between them, with one hand on the bag, the other clasping the handle of the door. He switched his gaze to Dave for the first time since they had left the farm.

'Well?' he asked.

'Well what?' Dave replied.

Kane swallowed hard, his eyes gleaming. But the pride and fury that he swallowed soon leapt back to the surface, as it recognised Dave's masterful playing of his emotions. He smiled and shook his head in reluctant admiration. 'You haven't lost it, have you? Are you prepared to accept Vulcan's offer?'

'I don't know what the offer is. But yes, I am interested.'

Kane reached into the side pocket of his carry-all and extracted a thick brown manilla envelope. 'When you've read that you'll know just as much as me. The same conditions apply as always: no copies. And you've got a free hand to run the operation as you choose. If the need arises, I should be available to help.'

Without a second glance Kane opened the door, and with his bag clutched to his side, he walked through the automatic doors into the departure lounge.

Dave gently snorted and shook his head. A frown of annoyance skipped across his face; it appeared Vulcan had always known he couldn't stay away for long. The envelope was typical of his planning; it was obvious Vulcan thought he had his measure.

However, this time, as he weighed the envelope in his hand, the expression that flickered across his face wasn't annoyance, but cunning. Finally, the wait was over.

As Dave slipped the envelope unopened into the vehicle's glove-box to read later in private, he knew his self-imposed exile had come to an end.

Later, as he parked his Land Cruiser in the lean-to attached to the farm's woolshed, he sat for several minutes deep in thought, focusing his mind on the manilla envelope. He still hadn't opened it and again gently weighed it in his hand. Then he seemed to come to a decision. He left the vehicle and began to walk the short distance across the yard towards the homestead.

Before Dave was halfway to the house, he noticed Clay sitting patiently beside the small wire-mesh gate leading through a macrocarpa hedge into the grounds. The permanently wrinkled frown on the dog's forehead seemed more pronounced than usual. Faithful as ever, Dave affectionately thought. 'Come on, he's gone now,' he said in a reassuring tone. 'Get that worried look off your face.'

Clay, as if understanding Kane had left, bounded forward excitedly. He picked up a stick on his way, and playfully pranced about in front of Dave.

'Come on, you're a bit old for that, aren't you?' Dave wrestled the stick from the dog, then pretended to flick it back over his shoulder.

Clay went racing off in the direction he assumed it had been thrown, but soon began to twist and turn in puzzled circles, trying to see where on earth the stick had landed.

'Gets you every time.' Dave laughed. The antics of the dog seemed to lift his own spirits.

Clay trotted back to his master, realising he'd been deceived. This time he waited until he had actually seen Dave throw the stick before bounding headlong after it.

Dave watched Clay with a warm affectionate smile. He reflected how quickly an animal can sense a change in a person's mood. He realised only dimly that he had used a similar sense himself in the past, and it had helped save his life.

Inside the house, Dave locked himself in his study and remained there for some considerable time. It didn't take him long to absorb the contents of the envelope; what took most time was organising a plan to prepare himself adequately for the forthcoming mission. What was more, he had to compile a lengthy message to send to London, to request all relevant information for the tasks that lay ahead.

Johnny coughed politely, and Richard Black woke from his cat-nap on the office couch.

'The Leopard,' Johnny began, standing just inside the office door, 'has requested all available information on the top thirty companies in South Africa.'

Richard was instantly awake. 'Everything?' he asked, amazed. 'Subsidiaries, the works? Even overseas interests? Hell, that's one mountain of information.' Richard stifled a yawn as he moved from the couch to sit behind his desk. He retrieved a pen from among the files littering the desk-top and began to scribble notes on a legal pad. 'When has he asked for it? And how does he want it?'

'He's asked to have it all on disks, to be left at Heathrow Airport to be picked up in about four weeks' time.' Johnny answered, watching his boss intently.

Richard leaned back in his chair, thoughtfully tapping the pen on the front of his teeth. 'OK, put it all together. This feels like the break we have been waiting for.'

Johnny groaned and rolled his eyes in mock distress as he left the room.

Richard gazed into space, a look of triumph, or possibly apprehension, etched across his face.

Dave had begun to build up quite a dossier of his own on most of the thirty companies, from memory and the resources of New Zealand's public library system. Some details were thin, but the likes of Barlow Rand, Anglovaal and de Lout Investments proved easier. De Louts, he knew, even had subsidiaries here in New Zealand. He was beginning to enjoy the thrill of a challenge again.

In the envelope Kane had left with him was a brief outline of the assignment. It was written in a code unintelligible to most people, but Dave soon had it deciphered. The essence of the message was that he would be spearheading the infiltration of one of South Africa's most important companies, because for some reason it held prime significance to Vulcan and his global economic coercion. It didn't specify which company, so he began his own inquiries to get the feel for the work ahead.

Along with the outline was a one-way plane ticket to Melbourne, Australia, and an address where he would pick up the next set of instructions. Dave knew Vulcan was always very careful; there was no reason to think this time would be different. He expected to have to go to many drop-off points before he had a complete picture of the mission.

When he collected the next instruction in Melbourne, a substantial amount of money would be transferred to a numbered bank account in Switzerland. The size of this figure alone was enough to indicate the magnitude of the operation.

Dave planned to arrive at the address in Melbourne on the due date, but not in the way that had been arranged; he had already begun to run by his own rules. He had six weeks before he was due there: probably just enough time to do what he had planned.

The Leopard had begun to roam.

CHAPTER 10

As Kane settled back in his seat in first class, he was a satisfied man. He would remember the two days he had spent in Sydney for a long time; they had topped off a successful mission. He had completed his primary task, though he had to admit not quite as planned. All the same, the humiliation and awkwardness he'd endured were worthwhile in the end.

Kane didn't exactly hold a grudge against Dave, but he was determined to even the score one day. He would bide his time, and felt confident Dave Old wouldn't even have a chance to rue the day he had crossed him.

He settled back in his seat and drifted off to sleep with a conceited smile on his lips. Next stop Los Angeles.

On his flight from Christchurch to Sydney, Kane had gotten on exceptionally well with one of the stewardesses. It didn't take him long to persuade her to show him the sights of her native city. When she called for him at his hotel suite in the Hyatt Kingsgate, she brought a friend just as stunning as she was. They were both true blondes, one long-haired, the other short, and had exceptional figures: full-bosomed, with narrow waists and flaring hips.

Kane and his companions never quite managed to leave the suite until it was time for him to leave for the airport, forty-eight hours after he had arrived. Both girls had an insatiable sex-drive, almost an addiction. Their bisexual tastes didn't deter him in the slightest, they in fact increased his own animal lust.

Kane's huge sexual appetite and his tendency to bear a grudge were his two major failings. But like most men with a fragile ego, he never saw them as weaknesses, or something he might have cause to regret.

Dressed casually in Levis and open-neck shirt, Kane stared out of the window at the Theme Building, soaring above the ground and constructed in parabolic arches as the Boeing 747 completed its final approach into the third busiest airport in the world.

Like an environmental mugger waiting for another victim, a dirty-brown haze hung over the airport and the surrounding city, but Kane never noticed it; he was too busy compiling the report he would have to give in just over an hour.

The pilot of the huge jet executed a near perfect landing, and the passengers hardly felt the wheels touch down. Kane was among the first to leave the aircraft; he always travelled light, and only had the carry-all he had taken on board with him, and once he produced his United States passport the immigration officer rapidly lost interest in him.

As he stepped out into the California sunlight, a dark maroon Cadillac Fleetwood glided into the kerb beside him. Perfect timing as always, he thought as he opened the front passenger's door and took the seat beside the driver.

The vehicle eased back into the traffic towards the main San Diego freeway towards Newport Beach. Kane settled back in the cushioned leather seat and savoured the sense of anticipation that settled over him like a cool breeze.

'So, a successful trip.' More statement than question from the chauffeur.

'Yes, thank you. Most successful.'

Kane spent most of the journey deep in thought, and before he realised, they were driving down Newport Boulevard, through Costa Mesa. At the Pacific Coast Highway at Newport Beach, they headed south towards Laguna Beach. Just after they passed the Ruben E. Lee, the magnificent old paddle steamer turned first-class floating restaurant, the Cadillac veered right and followed Jamboree Road around to a narrow bridge leading onto Balboa Island.

The island only had one short road, servicing the twenty-three houses perched on this prime spot of real estate. Each home had its own private jetty and craft; most were character homes, sedately fringing the island's cobbled road. Behind their majestic façades, the properties swept down to their own stretch of private beach.

The Cadillac gently manoeuvred into the garage of a superb work of architecture. Every brick and granite block had been tumbled to age them; the roof was grey slate, the walls imported oak and white plaster. The stone sills matched the Tudor façade.

Inside it was palatial. Artworks lined a huge sweeping staircase; Kane recognised Picasso, and the German old master Lucas Cranach. At the top of the stairs was a computer room housing some of the most sophisticated computer systems in the world.

This was the first time Kane had been into Vulcan's study. Three walls were covered with books, each individually rebound in dark green morocco.

In one corner were two leather-covered chesterfield sofas, and a huge antique oak desk dominated the other side of the room.

Vulcan stood beside the desk, hands clasped behind his back, staring out through the lead-lights at the harbour view. He wore a freshly pressed tan Pierre Cardin suit.

'Well, was our trip successful?' he asked without turning around.

The 'our' irked Kane, but he didn't let it show. 'Yes, very successful.'

The sense of anticipation that had been building all day reached its climax. Would Vulcan be generous with his praise, or would Kane have to prove his worth yet again?

Kane was addicted to his own internal narcotic; the greater the fear or anticipation, the stronger the craving for it became. This was one of the reasons he excelled in his chosen profession. The monetary rewards were great, but it was this adrenalin high that really drove him.

It was as if Vulcan was able to read his thoughts; he stood motionless before the window, letting Kane's yearning build to a crescendo. Then he turned and spoke. 'Well done, Kane, this time you have outdone yourself.'

Kane's sense of triumph was an almost physical release, as if a syringe of morphine had been injected into his vein. Vulcan was a master of anticipation, and also a scholar of the opposite; with a few words he could bring soaring emotions tumbling down around a man's ears.

'Yes, Kane, but at what cost?'

Kane's world caved in.

Vulcan indicated one of the sofas. 'I would like you to tell me about it.'

Kane's mind was reeling. He had expected to report on his trip, but not to Vulcan himself. Experience had shown him that exaggeration or reconstruction of the truth was impossible; this man had a remarkable ability to ferret out the truth. He would have to use all his negotiating skills to prevent his humiliation at Dave Old's hands from being revealed.

But he needn't have bothered.

'Tell me, Kane,' Vulcan asked, 'what information does our Mr Old now have that he lacked before?'

Kane was shocked, but made himself think carefully before replying. Partial honesty, he felt, was his best defence. 'He knows I have met you. but not the extent of our association. He also knows there are no others working in the African sector.'

'Hmm, I see.' Vulcan paused, and slightly inclined his head, 'Again Kane, I commend you. You have done better than I had expected. Even you cannot doubt the calibre of our Mr Old.' Vulcan paused again. 'But I am intrigued to know how he gained this information?'

So far during the short meeting Kane had felt he was on an emotional rollercoaster: one moment euphoria like a pauper winning the lottery, the next grovelling in the pits of despair, then again the heights of acclaim.

He chose his words carefully again. 'It would be best to say, Dave Old's mental agility now equals his physical prowess.'

'Perfect, just perfect. His unscheduled rest has made him invaluable for his next assignment.'

This was the first time Kane had seen Vulcan show emotion. His eyes had glazed over, and he was rubbing his hands together. Normally he remained detached from whatever task he was effortlessly co-ordinating. It was as if this mission had some personal vendetta attached to it or maybe it was just its magnitude. Kane dismissed the thought as Vulcan began to speak again.

'Now you have seen him in his home environment, there will be other details to add to his file. Have them included before you leave.'

Kane's first thought was the close relationship Dave obviously had with his mother.

For the next hour Kane was given his next set of instructions. This time the sense of anticipation carried him to heights he had never imagined. He would have the fate of powerful men resting in his hands, and their death upon his conscience.

CHAPTER II

Dave stood at the back door to the homestead in jeans and blue checked shirt, his bags packed beside him. The solemn mood of the overcast morning seemed to match his own, as if a shadow had fallen over his departure. He was travelling light, just one suit and a small hold-all.

Clay sat on his haunches looking up at him affectionately. His tail was gently sweeping the ground clean. This was going to be the hardest part; the dog had been his constant companion for the last two years.

Dave knelt and hugged the dog to his chest, tears prickling his eyes. Clay had sensed his mood, and gently nuzzled his ear.

'Now, Clay boy, I am going away. I'll be back, but I want you to look after Anne for me, OK?' Clay rose and dejectedly walked the few paces to sit beside Dave's mother, solemnly peering at his master from beneath drooping eyelids. It was as if the dog had understood every word.

His mother's usually merry face was wet with tears. For days he had been avoiding her, but now he had to face her. 'Come on, Mum. I'll be back.'

'But what will happen to you this time?' She stifled a sob. 'At least last time I got half my old son back.'

Dave drew her into a hug and gently kissed the top of her head. 'Yes, but this time I hope to bring back what I lost.'

Dave didn't look back as he walked to the waiting vehicle, though the suppressed sob that followed him pierced his heart. It was all he needed to strengthen his resolve; this time he would come back for good.

The Boeing 747 was packed at this time of the year; Dave had been lucky to get a seat.

The stewardesses did their rounds, and the meals and the rumble of the engines lulled most of the passengers into sleep. The odd cough did nothing to disturb the peace; Dave settled back, closed his eyes, and drifted back to the time when it all began.

Dave had always been driven by a determination to make a success of his life. He realised at an early age that this meant he must either do something better than most people, or find something different. He intended to do both.

He wanted to use the talents he possessed, but by the time he left school he hadn't worked out what those talents were. But in the tales of successful men he had studied, one quality kept glaring back at him: self-discipline. If a person could discipline their mind and body, virtually anything was possible. He decided to invest the next five years in acquiring that quality.

Just after his nineteenth birthday, he told his mother he wanted some overseas experience. Armed with her grudging support and a long list of relations, he headed straight for her home country. A few weeks later, he stood in front of the gates of the Old Fort in Vincennes, in Paris. A plaque on the wall read: *Bureau d'Engagement, Legion Etrangère*. Recruitment Centre, Foreign Legion.

After he had signed lengthy documents, he was taken to Aubagne, near Marseilles, the Legion's main base. He went through the three-week selection process and emerged with flying colours.

He was assigned to the *4ième Regiment Etranger* and shipped to a base at Bonifacio, at the southern tip on the island of Corsica. Three hundred and fifty new recruits were put through an initial training by the Instruction Group of the Foreign Legion; Dave found those fifteen weeks the hardest he had ever experienced.

After four weeks, the recruits were issued with what would become their most treasured possession; the white *képi*, the cap that identified them as Legionnaires the world over. Two days later after 5.30 reveille there was an inspection. The duty sergeant saw that Dave's *képi* had a light smudge on its peak. Dave would have accepted his punishment without question if he hadn't noticed the sergeant put the smudge there himself. Sergeant Pique had already earned the nickname the Sadist, and for some reason he was particularly brutal towards Dave. A Legionnaire is able to request an Individual Contest against a corporal or sergeant instructor. Dave was granted his the same evening.

It was the first time anybody had dared to request a contest against Pique. He was tall and well built, and years of Legion training meant he was superbly fit. When the fresh nineteen-year-old recruit faced the hardened fighting man, the onlookers knew the outcome. The contest was laughable; Pique's first punch caught Dave square on the eyebrow and cut him to the bone. For the next couple of minutes, with blood streaming down his face, Dave appeared to take a pummelling, and the officer overseeing the contest intervened. Few watchers noticed the smile that flitted across the officer's face; the fierce golden eyes that met his gaze were cold and calculating.

Pique had been lulled into a false sense of security. He landed blows effortlessly, and began to show off – until he found himself on his backside, gently swaying from side to side. He had regained his feet fighting mad, and for the first time he really looked at his opponent. Dave was half a head taller, and his bloodstained smile was the most menacing the sergeant he had ever seen. He looked around for an avenue of escape, too late. The young soldier danced forward and let fly a flurry of blows. Sergeant Pique was unconscious before he fell, and did not come around for three days. None of the new recruits had trouble from him again.

After Dave completed his training he was posted to *2ième Regiment Etranger de Parachutistes*, the Foreign Parachute Regiment. Most of the regiment had already flown out to Chad in northern Africa, where the government had requested help with rebel activity. But before Dave joined them, his next phase of training began at the French Army parachute training school at Bilda. Then his military career began in earnest; a year in Chad taught him the true meaning of discipline. And during that year, Dave fell in love with Africa.

His physical dexterity and intelligence marked him out, and he was transferred back to Corsica and attached to the *2ième Regiment Etranger d'Infanterie* as part of an élite counter-espionage unit. Their first few missions served two purposes: to protect France's interests, and to assess the abilities of the recruits. Dave performed well under pressure, and later, in the classroom, he soaked up lessons which programmed him into a weapon of covert activities.

His well-tuned ear and superb memory enabled him to learn languages with astonishing speed, and by the end of his first year with the Legion he could pass as a native Frenchman and as a national from any number of countries.

In the autumn of his second year, Dave was singled out for intensive planning and training for a top-secret mission. Nine years earlier, the then president of France, Charles de Gaulle, had foiled a plot to topple him. Memories were long in the army, and now the senior officers who had staged the Generals' Revolt, as it was called, took their revenge. The former president's death certificate claimed he died of a heart attack. The killing machine that Dave Old had become knew different.

The success of this momentous operation meant that his superiors now looked upon Dave as their protégé. He was given complex and dangerous assignments, and soon began to live for the thrill of the adrenalin high. He was also serving the apprenticeship he set himself, acquiring the self-discipline he needed.

When his five-year service as the Legion's most gifted recruit was drawing to a close, he found his superiors expected him to continue to serve; he had become indispensable to them, and knew too much to be set free. General Alain Marcet, best described as a wily old gun dog, rarely missed a trick, but two attempts made on Dave's life two months before he was due to leave proved feeble, and both times the would-be assassins found their roles reversed. Dave took the opportunity to consult a lawyer, who made some simple arrangements which ensured his safety.

A few days later, in an office at the Legion's base at Aubagne, General Marcet studied the contents of a brown manilla folder. He paled as he realised how incriminating the information was, especially to him. Perhaps it wouldn't stand up in a court of law; but that wasn't what concerned him. The file explained in detail every operation Dave Old, had carried out for him and his cronies: the orders, the plans and of course the outcomes.

He absent-mindedly fumbled for the light switch, and muttered a curse as the room remained dark.

The general, unaccustomed to things going against him, thumped a clenched fist on the desktop. He slumped down in his chair, his mind racing. He would have to make a deal. He thumped the desk again.

'Yes, General, you trained me well,' came a voice carried from a dark corner of the room. 'Perhaps too well.'

The general jumped to his feet, frantically tugging at the top drawer of his desk. To his horror, it was empty.

'I hope you don't mind, I took the liberty of borrowing your revolver.'

Like a ghost, Dave stepped out from the pitch-black recess, himself clad in black.

'General, you look a little pale. Some distressing news?' Dave stood in front of the desk, arms folded across his chest, the General's Colt .45 revolver in his hand pointing towards the ceiling.

The general took in a short sharp breath, but managed to look at his uninvited guest with some of his old composure. 'No wonder you have been such a success.'

Dave ignored the comment. 'I've come to make a deal. The only trouble is, you have no trump cards. Please close the door and take a seat.' He waved the revolver at a pair of comfortable armchairs.

For a man unaccustomed to taking orders, the general proved remarkably co-operative. After he had closed the door, the two men sat in the gloom facing one another.

Dave hooked one leg over the arm of his chair, swinging it casually as he assessed his most senior commanding officer. He pointed to the desk with the revolver.

'I have the originals deposited safely with a man whose instructions are to release them to the press if I meet with an untimely demise or go missing for an extended period of time.'

The general swallowed hard and looked decidedly ill. He hadn't said a word since they sat down.

'What you will do to ensure these documents don't, aah, become public knowledge is this: first, ensure I live a long and healthy life. Second, give me a high-security clearance with army intelligence, describing me as an expert security advisor. Third, I need a French identity that can be substantiated. And of course, fourth, a substantial sum from your budget in recompense for past inconveniences. For these meagre requests, General, you will have my silence.'

The hard-nosed general nodded his head to each of Dave's demands. 'I'll put everything in place right away.' He was still nodding as Dave collected his files and merged back into the night, leaving him sitting in the gloom.

At the end of his five years' service Dave was discharged at a Ceremony of Liberation. He left a very wealthy man, with an impeccable reference and top-level clearance for future security work throughout the world, and a dual identity that would protect his origins. With these resources and the abundance of skills he had acquired, he had secured his future success.

CHAPTER 12

'Richard? Sir Colin Bleach here. Are you free to speak?'

The call had come over Richard's priority line. Only a small, select number of callers used the line, all with top security clearance. 'Yes, Sir Colin. Speak away.'

Pleasantries over, the caller's tone changed, and he became upper-class and patronising. 'Look here, Black, something has to be done about this Vulcan fiasco. If none of your agents can come up with the goods, we'll just have to take the whole business over ourselves.'

Richard pictured the pompous little man, short and round, practically bald, with red cheeks and jowls that wobbled whenever he spoke. A man with an inflated ego.

'Sorry, you've lost me on this one, Sir Colin. What fiasco are you referring to?' Richard replied calmly.

'Oh, for god's sake, you know jolly well what I'm talking about. You haven't done a thing about this case since it first came up. I've got all sorts of people breathing down my neck, you know. The Prime Minister for one.' Richard could almost see the spittle leaping down the phone.

'Stretching the truth a little, Sir Colin?' Richard felt anger rise, but he took great care it didn't reach his voice. 'The PM is just anxious about the problem, as we all are. That's why I'm in regular personal contact. We discussed the matter only yesterday.' As an afterthought, he added, 'Among other things.' That would rile the little man even more.

'Huh,' came down the line.

'You know I have full control over this business, with a signed directive to confirm it. And I am making headway.'

'Headway? Damn it, Richard, I'm the chief of the SIS and I demand some proof of this headway!' Sir Colin's voice rose to the point of hysteria.

This time he had gone too far, and Richard finally erupted, something he'd never done since he had known the man.

'Hold your tongue, you pompous ass! You have no authority over me or my organisation. How dare you speak to me in such a derogatory and condescending manner. I run an independent organisation financed from non-government sources. In future, all information could very well be cost-related.'

Richard fell silent. They both knew it was a hollow threat, but the stunned silence on the other end of the line made him smile.

When Sir Colin spoke again his tone was soothing. 'Richard, Richard, I am merely concerned to know how I can possibly be of assistance. We do have a huge network of contacts we can draw on.'

Richard's blood was still boiling, but on the outside he had reverted to his normal unflappable self. 'Thank you, but no thank you.' No way was he going to let Bleach know he probably already used those contacts, probably with a lot more success than the SIS.

Sir Colin sighed. 'It's just that Brendan Oechsli and Uri Ferkatovich have been in contact again. You can see my position; I need some sort of response to give them.'

The Deputy Director of the CIA, and the Head of the KGB's Foreign Intelligence. So that was the reason for the call. Richard replied in his normal business-like tone.

'I think it's time for another meeting. Please organise it and send me the details. Yes, a neutral country. No, I'll be going on my own.' Richard broke the connection and leant back in his chair, pondering the sequence of events that had led to Bleach's call.

It had to be the most significant meeting of the three superpowers since the end of the Second World War, yet it was never recorded or publicised. If any reporters had investigated the sudden appearance of three high-ranking officials in Geneva fourteen months earlier, their stories had never been published.

The British SIS, the American CIA and the Soviet KGB had formed an alliance to track down and destroy one of the most highly organised and ruthless villains the world had ever known. The man known as Vulcan was effortlessly undermining their countries' power and influence throughout the world, disrupting their economies, so that eventually they would be unable to resist his final push towards his ultimate goal: the domination of the power structure of the world.

All three countries, and many of their trading partners and allies, had begun to experience restraints of trade, and tariffs which affected their exported goods; even their imported raw materials had begun to be affected by price hikes and limits on supply. Reluctant trading partners caused difficulties for Britain, the USSR and the United States, and their own economies began to boom as the north African and Asian markets started to absorb the excess materials.

During the last few years vast sums of money had been changing hands throughout the world, starting with huge amounts paid into Swiss bank accounts. Of course, the transactions were untraceable, but rumours inside Switzerland suggested that these sums were going to politicians in the countries which were causing the most difficulty for the three super-powers. This unebbing flow of money had eventually become self-generating, but the puzzling thing had been, and still was, where on earth it had originated.

Another equally distressing development was that third world countries frequently refused to meet interest payments on their loans from the west. There appeared to be a subtle switch of influence throughout the world.

The Armures Hotel, near St Peter's Cathedral in Geneva, a small first-class establishment dating back to the seventeenth century, had been evacuated a day prior to the meeting and teams of surveillance experts from all three countries had worked together to sweep the premises clean. In an unprecedented show of co-operation, the three security services organised a meeting that to the outside world never existed. No records were kept, no written information passed; the meeting relied on verbal exchanges between the American Brendan Oechsli, the Russian Uri Ferkatovich and Richard Black. Exposing himself to his country's old adversary, the Soviets, had been a risk, but the risk of Vulcan far outweighed it.

Richard relived the meeting in his mind, recalling the uncharacteristically frank and open discussion with the other two security chiefs.

'My friends... Let me be the first to say I never thought I would ever speak those words... My friends, we have a problem. A rather large problem. The Soviet Union is having difficulty maintaining the influence she would prefer to have over some of her closest allies. It is our fear that our influence in Eastern Europe is beginning to crumble, to be replaced by something fuelled only by greed.'

Uri Ferkatovich spoke excellent English. He was a bear of a man; his head and shoulders, his rumbling voice, every aspect of him was huge. He was a man who could dominate any company. He had a square face with a heavy muscular jaw which was blue with stubble even so early in the morning. His dark hair was swept back over his head, and hairy fists punched the air to emphasise everything he said. He was the most brilliant security tactician to come out of the Soviet Union in the 20th century; part of his success was because he preferred a hands-on approach.

Richard remembered how the Russian's frankness had etched an expression of what looked like amazement on Brendan Oechsli's face.

Oechsli was the shrewdest western security chief in decades. He had come up through the ranks, a real fighter for what he believed in. A tall, dapper man, always immaculately groomed, he had short-cropped brown hair, a long thin face and hypnotic eyes which would make the average man quail.

Ferkatovich was still speaking. 'This, this, Vulcan is threatening our trade with these allies. And if it is happening to my country, it must be affecting yours, and yours.' He stabbed a sausage-like finger at each of his companions.

The Russian spoke the truth. Richard's own sources had informed him that Moscow was experiencing unrest, not only from Eastern Block but also from within its own borders. Unease was building in a large proportion of Soviet republics. Some were even starting to hint at independence.

For several moments after Ferkatovich's opening address there was stunned silence.

'Well, I must say, Uri, I never thought I'd ever hear such candour from a Russian,' Brendan Oechsli drawled. 'Come to think of it, I never thought I'd call you Uri to your face.'

The American got up and began to pace the room, his brow creased.

'My state department was been on my tail now for near on six months because of this character Vulcan,' he began. 'We're also beginning to lose trade and influence, a lot of which appears to be going to the Arab nations, or those insatiable markets in Asia.

'Gentlemen, it appears this Vulcan has us over a barrel. We may even need to ask your countries for aid.' The American stopped and raised his arms. 'Treasury have dubbed it a substantial budget blowout.'

It was Richard's turn to speak. 'Gentlemen, my country's situation is as precarious as yours. We have just received a report from Europe that some countries are starting to question the trade alliances they have with Britain. I fear your countries will soon receive similar reports.'

The Russian and the American turned their full attention on him.

'I feel we must put our differences aside, at least for the time being, not only to protect our current positions, but to make up the ground we have lost.'

'Right, my friend, where do we begin?' Ferkatovich growled.

The CIA man also looked expectantly at Richard. It seemed he had been elected as their leader.

'A question first, if I may. I realise you are on different sides, and I have no wish to compromise either of your positions, but what about your nuclear influence? Surely you can influence your allies by threatening to take that protection away?' he asked.

Brendan answered for both of them, which at the time Richard thought was a little strange. 'Our need is as great as theirs. We could threaten to take away our missiles and leave them with no protection, and some countries might even be glad of it, but most know we need to be there just as much as they need us. We may be on different sides, but we're both experiencing a stalemate.' He turned to the Russian. 'Correct, Uri?'

The Russian's impassive nod was confirmation enough, but the deference he gave to the American seemed out of character. Yet Richard let it go, as his next comment confirmed his new appointment as leader.

'I have infiltrated Vulcan's organisation.' He held up his hands to stop the barrage of questions. 'But I stress, gentlemen, it may take time to get my man to the heart of his organisation. It has to be played with extreme caution. I can't tell you anymore.'

For the next six hours they had hammered out a strategy to beat their hidden enemy. Naturally there wasn't total agreement, with some heavy-handed diplomacy on the Russian's part, and some subtle tact from Richard and the American they eventually reached a workable accord. The only brief interruption was when their respective bodyguards brought in refreshments. Brendan's man asked if there was any more he could do, and left without further comment when his offer was declined.

Now, why had that insignificant moment stuck in his mind, Richard wondered. He forgot about it as he began to prepare for the meeting that now loomed.

'Gentlemen, we have a leak.' Richard's words opened the second meeting between himself, Uri Ferkatovich and Brendan Oechsli.

Pandemonium struck. The other men began to rant and rave, and accusations and threats flew about the room like predatory hawks. Brendan could hardly be heard above Uri's bull-like bellow.

'Your western security has always been so easy to penetrate,' he roared. 'This operation is failing because of your undisciplined security services. Mother Russia will never stand for this. If this was our operation, such incompetence would never have occurred.'

Uri's head of steam began to blow itself out, and Brendan was able to cut in. 'You Commies couldn't operate your way out of a wet paper bag. Jesus George, you've been feeding hogwash to your peasants for so long, you're starting to believe your own fairy tales!'

Uri found his voice again and began to bellow even more loudly. Richard placed his hands in his lap and watched with interest, storing the scene away in his mind for future reference. But both the Russian's and the American's vehement reactions didn't seem to ring true with him; there was more to this than met the eye. However, he did concede the pressure on them was probably reaching unbearable proportions; for every small victory they won, another defeat crashed down on them. It was like trying to hold back the Atlantic Ocean with a wall of sand.

The uproar slowly subsided as both Uri and Brendan blew themselves out and sat down sheepishly, trying to avoid the gaze of their British colleague.

'Gentlemen, we're all under an enormous amount of stress,' Richard began. 'At present we are the only allies we have, so for our countries to pull through we must continue to pool our resources.'

He breathed a silent sigh of relief as the volatile atmosphere seemed to disperse. Finally, they could get down to work.

It was the KGB man that spoke first. 'You mentioned a leak. How do you know of this?'

'Uri, it's like climbing a huge mountain of sand. We never seem to be getting anywhere, let alone able to see the summit.'

'He's right,' Brendan chipped in. 'Vulcan seems to have the jump on us. The whiz-kids in Treasury are getting awfully jumpy. On the outside we may look fine, but internally the cracks are starting to show. We're having to rely increasingly on support and funds from Japan and China. It could shape up to be even worse than the Depression.'

From the intelligence he had gathered Richard knew Brendan was correct. The growth in the United States' trade deficit, together with a rising trend in federal government's expenditure, meant she was becoming the world's largest debtor, with her balance of trade completely out of kilter. Only recently their President had had to sign legislation that effectively raised the federal budget's ceiling, yet on the other hand to mask this had signed a contra law that was supposed to slash the federal deficit to zero. The apparent mismanagement of their economy, the depreciation the US dollar and Congress's failure to abide by the recent legislation to contain the deficit led Richard to believe that Vulcan's power had started to influence the decision makers of the United States.

'Yes, I fear Soviet Union is no different,' Uri rumbled dejectedly. 'We are encountering widespread protests within our borders and beyond. My country is plagued by unrest.'

'Unrest.' Richard laughed wryly. He knew the USSR was in a state of near economic siege. Reports he had received and detailed satellite pictures that had come from the States indicated that throughout the Soviet republics there had been fighting and looting. Strikes and rioting were breaking out throughout most of their major cities. But one thing Richard was still having difficulty comprehending was how Vulcan had disrupted the Soviet government's carefully developed ideology, and her staunch internal security. The only explanation for its escalating dilemma was that Vulcan had one or more high-ranking Soviet officials doing his bidding.

All three countries' trading positions had grown worse since their last meeting. Their deficits were growing as outlets dried up, and it didn't help that each super-power was covertly trying to take advantage of the others' weakened state. Like grave diggers looking for gold, they were just digging themselves in deeper.

'OK, gentlemen, I don't need to tell you how Britain is faring. You will know that the government is selling off assets, and you have probably guessed it is because the country is becoming increasingly short of cash. You'll have also received my report on last year's unsuccessful attempt to assassinate the British Prime Minister, and the majority of her Cabinet during the Conservative Party's annual conference. It has been confirmed, it wasn't an IRA bomb in Brighton. It was another demonstration of Vulcan's power, similar to the influence he exerted during the coal miners' year-long strike.

'We would have trouble enough combating Vulcan if the British government was unified,' he continued. 'But as things stand... well, you can see we're no better off than either of you.' Richard blew out a breath, glad that part of the meeting was over. He looked at the two faces in front of him. 'What progress have we all made?'

No answer came from either man.

'Very well, I'll begin. My agent has made contact. I don't expect to hear from him again until he has either succeeded or failed in exposing Vulcan.' Richard calmly laid his hands on the tabletop and waited.

'How can I help?' the huge Russian asked.

'I'd like you to withdraw all but your most trusted men from the field. They must only be accountable to you, and you alone. They need to go over every contact, follow every lead, resort to whatever means they have to, to get the smallest clue.' Richard looked at the American. 'Exactly the same with you, Brendan. And no reporting back to your superiors if can get away with it. We can't afford to trust anyone. We may not like it, but we've got to assume even our top government officials could be at his beck and call. We have to stop this leak, whatever the cost.'

The meeting had lasted less than an hour, but there was no more to be done. But they all seemed reluctant to leave, as if one of them might remember something they had forgotten to relay.

The question thrown in by the American as they were all rising from the table was deceptively casual. 'How long has your agent at the centre of this hunt been active?'

'A couple of years now,' Richard replied offhandedly. 'Why?'

'No reason,' the American replied, looking away.

Several days later, an international phone call was placed and a gravelly voice spoke in an unmistakable accent.

'He has been active for several years now. I suggest the person responsible is found and taken care of.'

CHAPTER 13

He stood naked before her beside the large double bed in a sparsely furnished hotel room. A thick mass of dark body-hair covered his chest and shoulders, and his massive penis hung limp before him.

He spoke for the first time, his accent distinctive. 'Did you bring it, the information?'

Bereft of speech, she briskly nodded her head. Her large round blue eyes hadn't left his face since he began undressing.

'Come.' He held out a huge spade-like hand. She trembled.

He undressed her, and her desire intensified with every item of clothing he casually discarded. Still her eyes hadn't left his face.

She had a beautifully clear complexion and a well-developed body, full-breasted, heavy-boned and solid. Her quivering need for him grew as she stood naked before him.

'You have done well,' he said and tenderly kissed her on the mouth. She shuddered as he began to guide her towards the bed.

She lay on the bed looking for the first time at his body. It was colossal, and gave off an animal magnetism.

A sob left her lips as he pushed her knees towards her ample chest and knelt before her on the bed, his member now a steely rod. She moaned as he guided it slowly inside her, up to its hilt.

As he drew his pelvis back for another tender stroke, he leaned forward and pinned her knees against her chest. She was entirely helpless, at his mercy. She threw her blonde head back and cried out as he began to take her to heights of pleasure she had never dreamed of.

The last words she remembered were, 'You have done well, Susan, very, very well.'

Karen stood looking through the huge picture window behind her desk, transfixed by the sight of Johannesburg. She never bored of this scene. Ant-like people scurried back and forth below her on President Street; but it wasn't the people that held her gaze, it was the vast cauldron of wealth and power that boiled before her. She winced as a movement behind her broke her enchanted mood.

'Oh, I'm sorry, Mrs de Lout, I didn't realise you were here.' Her secretary. The young woman stopped halfway to her desk.

'It's fine. What are you doing in so early?' Karen glanced at her watch. 'It's only just half past seven.'

'Oh, I enjoy my work. Some people work to live, I live to work. I hope you don't mind?'

'Well, of course not.' Karen changed the subject. 'What have you got for me?'

'I've received the final itinerary and your booking confirmation from Afro Ventures. I managed to book you on the twenty-four-day safari through Namibia, Botswana and up to Victoria Falls in Zimbabwe.' She placed a brochure and some papers on her desk.

As excited as a child, Karen skipped forward to rescue the information before it became entangled with the paper jungle already needing her attention.

Karen and her secretary had an excellent working relationship. Unlike many successful and powerful women who only kept male assistants, Karen didn't feel threatened by other women, even the most competent ones. She liked a feminine touch to her organisation.

'Gosh, I feel like a schoolgirl playing truant,' she said with a beaming grin. 'Twenty-four days. I don't know if I dare. What do you think?'

'What I think doesn't really matter, but if anyone in the company deserves such a trip, it's you.'

'Of course what you think matters,' Karen said sincerely. 'Thank you for the compliment. If you can hold the fort, maybe, just maybe, I might be able to justify such a long absence.'

As the young woman turned to leave Karen called her back. 'How was your trip to Zimbabwe last weekend? You'd been looking forward to it for so long?'

The secretary turned bright scarlet and brought her hand up to cover her mouth. Karen was amused. 'It was an enjoyable trip then?'

The blonde girl giggled and stammered, and Karen let her off the hook. 'If Peter de Lout asks if I am available today, please give me some warning. Thank you, Susan.'

'Mr de Lout is on his way up.'

'Thank you, Susan. Please send him in when he arrives.'

Karen knew exactly why Peter was coming to see her. By now he would have found out about her proposed safari trip. As she began to plan her strategy, she reached into her top drawer and pulled out the information Susan had given her earlier. It was madness, but she just had to get away and mix with some real people for a change. Since she had become president of de Lout Investments it had been absolute bedlam and she had been living in a bubble.

Her transition into the role of president of the giant corporation had gone smoothly enough, but so many meetings and introductions had to take place for diplomacy's sake, and she still had to manage her increased workload: reports to peruse, documents to complete, contracts to sign. If she could have operated on two hours' sleep a night, there still wouldn't have been time for everything. Until a few weeks ago, her workload had felt like shovelling sand into a bottomless pit; only now did the pit appear to be filling, allowing her to take some time for herself.

Karen looked again at the brochure on her desk. 'Twenty-four days,' she whispered guiltily. Was it the holiday she kept telling herself she needed, or just a desire to escape her responsibilities?

She had seen much of the region before, so how long she stayed would depend on the company. She could cut the safari short if pressing matters needed her attention back in Johannesburg. But it could still be the trip of a lifetime.

She was still totally absorbed in her thoughts when a tap at her office door brought her back to the present.

'Susan suggested I come right on in. I hope wasn't interrupting anything important?' There was no sarcasm in Peter's tone, but as she gathered up the information about the safari and slipped it into the top drawer of her desk, she knew his calculating eyes had seen what she was doing.

They had never been close and never would be. Theirs was a totally professional relationship and an extremely good one in that context. She kept him on as chairman of the board because he was probably one of the best accountants in southern Africa. His top priority was the company's profitability, which had increased since they had jointly implemented Karen's plans.

'By all means take a seat.' Karen indicated one of the padded leather settees in the informal discussion area. 'Can I offer you a coffee?'

'Ah, no thank you, I've only just had one. He clearly didn't want to get too comfortable; was something unpleasant on the way. Karen wondered. 'I hope you don't mind if I do; my throat's parched.' Before he could answer Karen walked to the door and asked Susan for a coffee. Her simple ploy worked; Peter was thrown off his stride. He fidgeted with his tie and flicked an imaginary speck of dust off his neatly pressed pinstriped trousers.

Susan and Karen had both used this gambit before, and Peter hadn't yet cottoned on. Karen had learnt he needed a set pattern to work to; any variation and he quickly lost track. It never took him long to adapt, but Susan's arrival with the coffee would disrupt him again.

'Now, how can I help you? I noticed you hadn't made an appointment.' Another ploy to put him on the back foot.

'Yes, well, ah, it has only just come to my attention. It's about this proposed trip of yours, two matters regarding it really. It's quite a while to have you out of action, after all you are an intrinsic part of this company. Without you, well, anything could happen.' Peter sat forward; he had turned on his most persuasive manner, and Karen couldn't help but feel his the charisma. With an effort she hardened her resolve.

'Peter, you must agree we both need a break. You've already planned yours, as part of your next tour of our European offices and plants. I need to be here while you are away, and since I haven't been up to our office in Namibia yet, I thought I'd work it into a break of my own.'

Peter conceded the point with a slight inclination of his head. Round one to Karen.

But only just; he wasn't finished. 'Yes, I take your point, but…'

Here it comes, she thought.

'… twenty-four days, hell of a long time to be out of touch.'

'Not quite. I'll be in touch at Windhoek, Maun and Victoria Falls.' Not the best counter-attack, Karen thought, but that round's probably even. 'And if need be, I can cut short the trip.' A lot better, but a hell of a concession to give away.

He tried a different approach. 'A public safari? It's not as if the company's short of a rand or two; we even have our own game concessions up north.'

How could she tell him she just wanted to get amongst some real people and let her hair down, be Karen, and not Mrs de Lout. She knew what his answer would be: 'But Karen, that is just what you are.' Best to say nothing; she had learnt early on in her career never to show weakness.

Karen was stuck for words, but right on cue Susan entered with her coffee, giving her a chance to think. As she waited for Susan to leave the room, she began to feel sick inside at what she was about to say. But she had no other choice.

She looked up, staring evenly at Peter's calculating gaze, the spoon stilled in her hand. 'The reason I prefer not to use the company concessions and the other exclusive game resorts should be quite apparent to you...' She let the statement hang, but Peter was at a loss until she dropped the next comment like a grenade. 'He was your brother, after all.'

'Oh god, I am so sorry, that was thoughtless of me. Of course, it'd bring back memories.' Peter sounded sincere. Round three to Karen.

She regretted having to use the memory of her late husband in such a way, but Tom would have done the same in her position. Peter was persistent, however. He used the one argument she had no answer for.

'Security, Karen. What about your safety?'

She winced, knowing he was right. To the corporation she was invaluable, but to the criminal world her worth could be measured in millions. It was bad enough when Tom was alive but now it was sometimes unbearable; bodyguards accompanied her everywhere. The only places her wolves, as she had grown to call them, weren't visible were her home and the office. That was the price she had to pay for the position she held.

He had her cornered, and he knew it. She told herself he only had the good of the company at heart, but at times like this she hated him and the life she had to live.

Karen stood up, indicating that the meeting had come to an end. Peter thought she'd finally seen his point of view, but as often happened he had underestimated her.

'Peter, you look after the security arm of de Louts, so you'd better figure it out and ensure my trip is kept a secret. Also, could you please run a check on all the other people booked on the safari, including the company running it.'

Peter pursed his lips angrily, but didn't say another word. He rose stiffly from the settee and stalked out of the room.

Karen was intrigued; why such a show of annoyance? It looked as if this wouldn't be the last she'd be hearing on the matter.

CHAPTER 14

As the Boeing 747 kissed the runway at Charles de Gaulle Airport in Paris, Dave knew he would be in for a long and tedious wait. The routine, every time he passed through Paris, had never changed in the twelve years since he had been discharged from the Foreign Legion.

He had flown the most direct route possible to France. When there had been a stopover, he had made sure he'd waited in the transition lounge, so there was no record of him going through any passport control. He presented his French passport for the first time since leaving the south Pacific. The immigration officer fed his information into a computer, looking cautiously at him, and indicated that a colleague should take him away for questioning.

He had to wait for nearly two hours, under guard in a small starkly furnished room, before a smartly dressed lieutenant was ushered into the room and pulled up a chair. He had dismissed the armed guard and sat across the table from Dave.

'Congratulations on your promotion, Lieutenant,' Dave said in French. Two gold stripes adorned the man's uniform.

'Thank you, Monsieur Old, and welcome home,' Lieutenant Le Droff replied affably. 'Will you be staying in France long, or are you just passing through?'

'You may tell General Marcet I am only passing through this time. And I regret I am unable to meet with him on this occasion.' A light smile creased Dave's lips.

The lieutenant's whole body began to shake with laughter. 'I am sure the general will be most disappointed,' he managed to say eventually. 'I don't know what you two have in common, but you are certainly a thorn in his side. He prances around like a cat on a hot tin roof whenever you're in France.'

'Nothing much changes, does it?'

Lieutenant Le Droff was disappointed; he would have loved to know the source of his general's distress.

'What's my security clearance?' Dave asked after a brief pause.

'Still as always.' The lieutenant was serious again. 'Your file is for the general's eyes only. I am the only other member of his staff who knows of its existence.'

Dave had been sure nothing would have changed in that regard either, but he was still relieved to hear it. Without the clearance, he would have had to rethink all his plans.

'You are free to go, Monsieur Old. Your entry into France has been wiped.' The lieutenant pushed Dave's passport across table. 'If I can be of any assistance, now or in the future, I am at your disposal.'

Dave had never accepted help from the general's aide in the past; he knew it would be reported straight back to the general. He liked having the wily old bird where he was: useful as a reference, but not a man to owe favours to.

'Thank you. One day, perhaps. But for now, I've a boat to catch. Oh, and give the Stork my regards.'

The lieutenant winced at Dave's use of his boss's nickname. 'You can count on it. Until we meet again.'

Dave shook the lieutenant's outstretched hand and was quickly ushered away, the meeting already forgotten. He had a boat to catch to England.

From Dover, he caught the train through to London Victoria. He made a short excursion, then took the Piccadilly line to Heathrow Airport, dressed as a backpacking tourist. All he carried was a scruffy old rucksack; everything else was in a room in a quiet hotel near Hyde Park. His only task in Britain was to pick up some computer disks from a drop-off point in a storage locker at Heathrow. It was here he almost made his last mistake.

He felt decidedly uneasy as be approached the row of lockers, and decided to follow his intuition. He took a seat from which he could observe them, and pretended to read a newspaper.

He spotted the watchers right away, loitering in small groups with a clear view of the lockers. He didn't attract attention to himself by leaving immediately, but when he did stand up his planned itinerary had just been blown to smithereens.

It was a dark night, and the pavements were coated with ice. Richard Black felt uncomfortable, and not just because of the cold snap.

He was heading back to his base after a brief meeting with the Prime Minister on the Vulcan issue. The country's trading position was growing more precarious by the month. He was told in no uncertain terms, 'We need results!'

Ever since he had left Downing Street, he had felt uneasy, he thought because of the unpleasant meeting with the PM. But as he left the Underground all his alarm bells began to ring.

He was positive he wasn't being followed; he was using all the tradecraft he had learnt as a field agent. He had stopped for a pint at the local pub, and no one had entered or left while he sat there. He left by the rear door as a precaution, and was certain nobody followed.

Walking towards the flat, the sense of impending doom abated but didn't disappear. He lingered in the last shadow of some overhanging trees before he crossed the road, and still didn't spot anyone. He studied the stairs leading to the only door into the flat. The grey beads he had placed on the steps hadn't been disturbed. He climbed the stairs and took out his keys, puffing slightly and telling himself it was time he to do something about his flagging fitness.

The door pushed open easily and he stepped into the hallway. Johnny must have been out; the flat was in darkness. He groped for the light switch in his office, just off the hallway, and was rewarded with a pop and flash.

'Oh Christ,' he mumbled, feeling his way towards the desk.

His only warning of an intruder came too late. He heard the metallic click as the gun was jammed into the base of his skull.

'You bastard, you scared the living daylights out of me,' Richard swore, rubbing the back of his head.

A smile danced across Dave's face. He perched on the corner of Richard's desk, the picture of relaxed innocence as he swung his foot back and forth.

'How did you find me, and what've you done with Johnny?' Richard demanded indignantly.

'So many questions.' Dave tapped the side of his nose. 'He left on an urgent call about thirty minutes ago. I think he thought it was from you.' He smiled again.

'OK, what is it you want? You know it's dangerous for you to be here,' Richard said wearily.

'Not a bit of it. Who else knows about this place?'

'One too many now.' Richard raised a hand despairingly.

Dave suddenly became serious, and Richard stiffened.

'Richard, you have a leak.'

'Oh no.' He didn't question Dave's claim; he knew him too well. 'What's happened?'

'There were three teams of watchers at the airport lockers when I went to pick up the disks. I figured one of them was yours; them I could've handled. But three. Sorry, pal, you've got problems.'

Richard was back on form. He jumped up from the couch and slid behind his desk, his mind worrying at the problem like a terrier with a bone. 'You're right, one team was mine. But the others...' He shrugged. 'I'll have to send in a decoy to lead them off the scent, and try and find out who they are. Any thoughts on that?'

'Well, one'll be Vulcan's. As to the other, I wouldn't have a clue.'

Richard stared up at the big man. 'I know you've told me before, but to help clarify my thoughts tell me again: how does Vulcan operate? How did he start gaining so much power?'

Dave threw Richard's Browning down on to the desk and flopped down on the couch. 'How he started I wouldn't like to hazard a guess; if you can find that out, you'll probably have him nailed. How he operates: he has the world split into different territories and runs them independently. He'll have small groups of freelance agents operating in each; at least, that's what's happening in Africa. Each group is active in its own sector, and only there. He'll choose a target, normally an influential company, and send one or more of his agents in to destabilise it to the point where one of his shelf companies can take it over. The assets he controls must be in the multi-billions if the other sectors are half as successful as the African one. He must be one of the wealthiest men in the world.' A thought occurred to him. 'How have you got on with that list I gave you, of the companies I've worked on for him in the past? Their ownership must eventually lead back to him.'

'No luck so far; he must have one hell of an accountant working for him. Johnny's still trying to untangle the maze of shareholders and dummy corporations involved with the first one on the list. He's nowhere near finding out who really owns it.' He paused, but Dave made no response. 'OK, you'd better give me everything else you've learnt about Vulcan since we last spoke. I'll give you copies of the disks before you disappear.'

In as precise terms as possible Dave described Kane's visit, his instructions and the information he had acquired from him. He also told Richard about his suspicions regarding the mission he was embarking on.

Richard absorbed every scrap like a sponge. As soon as Dave had finished he threw out his next question; he wanted Dave's gut feeling before he had time to think.

'Is Vulcan one man or a group?'

'One man,' Dave replied without hesitation.

Next day Johnny was still miffed about his boss sending him on a wild goose chase halfway across London. Sometimes he didn't understand Richard at all.

The phone rang; he answered it and scribbled a brief message on a notepad. As he was about to take the message through to Richard, the phone rang again. He frowned as he scribbled another note and took them both through to his boss.

'I don't know what's going on, but I get a call to say the disks have just been picked up, and then I get another from passport control to say Dave Old left Heathrow about an hour ago. Who picked up the disks, where the hell's Dave been, and what on earth's going on?' Johnny asked, scratching his head.

'I'll get on to it. Leave it to me.' Richard smiled to himself.

The Leopard was on the prowl.

CHAPTER 15

'Please take a seat, Mr Pearson.' Karen indicated one of her green leather settees in her office's informal discussion area. 'Coffee?'

'Tea, if you wouldn't mind.'

James Pearson rested his ample buttocks on the seat. He was overweight, and the type of man that didn't wear clothes well. His suit was ill-fitting, and the knot of his tie was pulled so tight it looked as if hadn't been undone for months. His hair was bushy and unkempt, and always looked untidy. But as he sat with his hands neatly clasped under his comfortable paunch, he was the picture of rumpled tranquillity. He had a merry glow about his face, and quick, intelligent eyes. He never set out to draw attention to himself, but once he had gained it, it would rarely waver.

After the tea and coffee had been served, Karen crossed her legs and rested her hands in her lap. 'You said on the phone that you have your final report for me.'

Pearson ran his own private investigation company, staffed only by himself and a part-time secretary. He saw no need for a fancy office and horde of staff, so he worked from home. He had left the South African police some years before, disillusioned with its structure and methods. He went out on his own and did the two things he was good at; talking to people, and investigation.

'One question first, if I may?'

Karen nodded.

'Why did you hire me when de Louts have one of the best security and information systems in South Africa?'

'I needed somebody entirely impartial, separate from the company.'

'Hmm, I see.' He took a sip of tea.

Karen saw that she had told him far more than she had intended. She'd have to take more care in future.

Pearson leant down to the briefcase he had propped up against the settee, extracted the report and placed it on the coffee table. 'My findings.'

Karen didn't move. She fixed her gaze on the private detective. 'I'd rather you told me in your own words.'

Pearson would have been disappointed if Karen hadn't asked him to do so. He felt he had sized her up quite well; she hadn't reached her position in de Louts by hiding behind reports. But there was a quality about her that he couldn't yet fathom. He had the impression that she was somehow deeply disturbed by something. Maybe it was the position itself? He dismissed the thought and began to speak.

'As you are aware, I have been investigating the death of your husband for the last four weeks. I have spoken to numerous people here, and in Zimbabwe and Zambia.' He paused briefly as he noticed Karen's interest quicken. 'Until a week ago I would've said your husband's death was an accident.' He stopped speaking as Karen sat forward, eyes wide open. What he was about to say was even more shocking; he hoped she was up to it.

'Initially, everything pointed to an accident. I won't go into all the grim details; you know, he supposedly shot himself in the early hours of the morning, alone in a viewing hide waiting for a leopard to take the bait that had been left. At first I found it hard to believe that a man with your late husband's reputation and hunting experience would shoot himself accidentally, yet everything in my original investigation repeatedly confirmed it. But what did intrigue me was the disappearance of two of his senior trackers shortly after the event.' The investigator's eyes took on a faraway look.

'I eventually tracked both of them down to a small village north of Livingstone, just across the Zimbabwe border in Zambia, near the crossing at Victoria Falls. Both men were petrified once they found out why I was there. One, I was never able to persuade to talk, but once I got the other on his own he went to pieces. It transpired that your husband had been generous with support in a time of need, so he wanted to repay that debt, in part at least.' He fell silent and took another sip of his tea.

'I would like you to be entirely forthright,' Karen said. 'I didn't hire you to play theatrics, Mr Pearson.'

James made a show of composing himself and put down his teacup. 'From what the tracker told me, there were footprints going in and out of the hide, and they didn't belong to any member of your husband's party. He is a man who can read signs on the ground better than you or I can read a book; it wasn't hard for him to unravel what took place.'

James Pearson paused and took a deep breath. 'Apparently, the impostor was a big man; he wore combat-type boots, but was light on his feet. The tracker thinks he was of European descent; the prints left by his boots were similar to ones he's seen worn by American hunters in the past. The man stalked your husband in the early hours of the morning, when any shot would've been put down to your husband firing at the leopard. There was a brief struggle and your husband was killed with his own rifle. So what I thought would be a simple case of accidental death had turned into a calculated murder.'

Karen was visibly shaken.

It took her several moments to realise the detective had stopped talking. She sat back and deliberately relaxed her shoulders in an attempt to still her racing mind. Part of her had suspected it was murder from the start. Now her suspicions were confirmed,

She felt like a pressure cooker about to blow. She fought to control the tremble in her voice, and asked, 'Is this all the tracker said?'

'In relation to your husband's death, yes. But he did make a couple of other comments.'

'Go on.'

'It was something like, "To Vulcan I am now dead", and then, "Beware of the Leopard".'

Pearson looked nonplussed. Karen was equally puzzled, but she made a quick decision.

'Mr Pearson, I would like to retain you on a full-time basis until you've solved this mystery. Of course, I'll meet your usual fee, and cover all expenses. I'd like you to follow every lead no matter how small or seemingly unrelated, and for security's sake I believe we should keep no more written records. I'm relying on your complete discretion until we have enough evidence to take to the authorities.'

Once James Pearson had left her office, Karen told Susan she didn't want to be disturbed for the rest of the day, and locked both doors into her office.

She slumped down on the settee and dropped her head in her hands, whispering softly, 'What have they done to us, Tom?' Tears streamed from her eyes and her whole body shook as grief for her husband consumed her all over again.

James Pearson was only vaguely aware of the short well-dressed man he passed in the hallway. He was pleased he had been retained to unravel the growing mystery; he knew he would have been unable to leave the case alone.

He decided to contact Network in London, to see if they could shed any light on the tracker's mention of Vulcan, and the Leopard. He had used their services in the past with great success and knew the cost would be horrific, but with a client to pick up the bill, that didn't concern him.

As he stepped into the elevator, it occurred to him he could also approach his old contact in the CIA here in South Africa. They hadn't kept in touch since he left the police force, but he was sure somebody in the bureau could assist him.

Peter de Lout took his role as head of the security arm of de Lout Investments seriously. 'Who was that scruffy fellow that I passed in the hallway?' he asked Karen's secretary.

'A Mr Pearson. He's a private detective working on a personal matter for Mrs de Lout.'

'Oh, I see. And what matter would that be?' Peter tried to sound casual, and Susan didn't notice the probing look in his eyes.

'She hasn't told me, Mr de Lout, but I suspect it's about the death of her... your brother. I do worry about her at times.'

Peter was thunderstruck. 'I believe there is enough concern within our family to meet our needs, thank you,' he snapped. 'Is Mrs de Lout available?'

Susan's glacial smile did not match her respectful tone. 'I'm sorry, she is unavailable for the rest of the day. May I give her a message?'

Peter made no reply. He left the room swiftly; there was something urgent he needed to do.

James Pearson had booked into a beach-front hotel in Durban, and was in his suite planning his investigation. All the information he had gathered since Karen de Lout hired him was laid out on the bed.

He was a man who thought best on paper. As his old boss in the police force used to say, 'Best way to explain a problem to yourself is write it down. You can't write something down without explaining it to yourself.'

He went over the facts in his mind, ticking them off on his fingers one by one.

'One: Tom de Lout was murdered by an unknown man in Zimbabwe. Two: the murder was made to look like an accident. Three: our tracker friend said two things that at the time appeared unrelated: "To Vulcan I am now dead", and "Beware of the Leopard".

'Right, no go on both counts with Network and the CIA, but...' He tapped his fingers together, recalling both conversations. He was sure both parties knew more than they were letting on.

He had concluded that Vulcan and the Leopard must be part of an operation, or code names for something or somebody. A week of footslogging in the less desirable areas of Johannesburg had thrown only a flicker of light on his investigations. The Leopard was definitely a person, and the public library had shed a little light on Vulcan. Apparently he was the Roman god of fire. James had gone back to Network and the CIA with the definition, but his reception had been even frostier. He was on his own with this one.

He walked over to the window and stared out at the beach-front and the Indian Ocean. His most successful contact had taken place four days ago.

James had been scraping the bottom of the barrel; nobody knew or wanted to know about Vulcan or the Leopard. Even his most reliable sources clammed up tight as a shell, and no amount of money could persuade them otherwise.

Then a stroke of luck while he was out in his hire car. A van bearing the logo *Oxlee's Slager, Butcher*, stopped at some traffic lights a couple of cars ahead of him. 'Of course. Joseph.'

The van stopped at the next shopping centre. A slightly built black man was leaving the vehicle as James parked beside him.

When the pudgy private eye stood in front of him, Joseph's eyes darted from side to side looking for an avenue of escape. A firm grip on his shoulder halted him.

'Now, now, Joseph, all I want is a few words. Still in the same job, are we?'

Joseph made a sort of whinnying sound and gave a sickly smile.

'I have a few friends at John Vorster Square who may want to talk to you.' One mention of the Johannesburg police station made Joseph wriggle nervously,

'Please, *Baba*, I am now an honest man. As you see, I have a steady job that keeps me from trouble.' He meekly indicated the van.

Joseph was a petty crook with some scam or other always in progress; this was why he was so useful. Whenever James was able to find him, which was rare, he was a wealth of information, and invariably prepared to trade it for his continued freedom.

They had stopped not far from the Wimpy Bar. It was almost empty at this time of the day, so James led him to a seat there.

Joseph's face was ravaged with old scars and pock marks and his expression was permanently surly. His dark yellowish eyes looked everywhere except at James.

'Joseph, don't make me play games. I can take you straight to John Vorster Square, or, you can answer a few questions.'

Joseph whinnied again, and James sat back with his arms folded.

'What is it you would like to know, *Baba*?'

Much better. 'The owner of de Louts was killed in Zimbabwe. Who did it?'

The black man's mouth drooped, and he raised his hands and shrugged. Either he genuinely didn't know, or he had been taking acting lessons since their last meeting. Probably the former, James decided.

But he wasn't about to decrease his stranglehold on the rogue. 'They say the cells at John Vorster are quite comfortable nowadays.'

Joseph wailed, 'I only know what I've seen on TV. Honest, *Baba*, I know nothing.'

James shot his next question out before Joseph had a chance to compose himself. 'How are Vulcan and the Leopard linked?'

The African's face drained to a bloodless grey, and he took refuge in one of the oldest and most effective defences black African men can employ: a blank facial mask that hides all emotion and thoughts. James had seen it used many times, but the sallow hue of Joseph's skin told him the true story. The man was terrified.

'One name, Joseph, just one name,' he said almost tenderly.

Joseph's whisper was barely audible. 'It is more than my life is worth to tell you this thing.'

James reached into the inside pocket of his jacket and laid a thick wad of bank notes on the table before him. 'How much is your life worth, Joseph?'

The colour quickly returned to the African's face, and his eyes began to dart from side to side. He was clearly torn between two distorted loyalties: his love of money, and the fear something had instilled in him. One of the two would soon overcome the other. James hoped it would be the money.

'More than this,' Joseph whispered, his hand creeping towards the pile of notes.

James knew he'd made his decision. They just had to settle on the price.

He whisked the money away, and Joseph's mouth dropped open, and he uttered a moan of protest. Before the moment was lost James produced another wad just as thick as the first, and laid the two side by side.

Joseph licked his lips. His fingers slowly reached towards the prize, but John's hand came crashing down upon them. Joseph let out a little yelp, more in fright than pain.

'Tell me what I want to know.'

This time greed overcame fear. 'For this amount of money there is a lot I can tell. There is a man you can talk to here in Jo'burg, and I have a cousin who works in Natal…'

A permit was required for travel into KwaMashu, one of the large black South African locations in the north-western outskirts of Durban, but James thought that piece of legislation was ridiculous. Laws were there to be broken, he decided with a twinkle in his eye. He only hoped the directions Joseph had given him were accurate; he certainly didn't want to get lost out there. He had a quick shower and shave, then ventured out. He soon wished that he'd hired a less conspicuous car; the nearly-new Commodore looked decidedly out of place in the township. He laid a pistol, a 9mm Star, on the dashboard in easy reach; he wasn't taking any chances.

As he drove along the deeply rutted dirt road, he passed a number of Zulu women in clean but scruffy cast-off clothes. They carried forty-litre plastic drums of water on their heads effortlessly and without shedding a drop; their legs seemed to glide over the ground as their upper bodies remained motionless. James marvelled at the grace and ease with which they balanced the substantial load.

He had been to many similar locations throughout South Africa, but the poverty appalled him. Shanty town was not the right word; it implied something temporary. These shelters may have been crude, but their inhabitants had obviously made them their permanent homes. He passed row upon row of shacks built of anything their owners could lay their hands on: packing cases, mud bricks, plastic, corrugated iron. Only the lucky ones had solid roofs, and there was no running water, sanitation or electricity.

James peered down one rough alley where a middle-aged woman, her dress pulled up above her bared buttocks, was defecating. She stared back at him uncaringly. Words failed him; he shook his head and looked away.

The crudely drawn map indicated the next turning left.

He bumped along an even rougher track and found the shack he was looking for. He took his pistol off the dashboard and secured it in its leather hip holster.

As he locked the car James sensed a movement behind him. Heart pounding, he swung around and grabbed for his gun. Gathered at the edge of the track was a group of pot-bellied Zulu children, staring wide-eyed at the white stranger. Most wore only in grubby t-shirts and baggy shorts, their callused feet bare.

'Who speaks for this *impi* of young warriors.' James asked in fluent Zulu.

Their mouths dropped open in amazement, then turned upwards in beaming smiles. The tallest of the group took a pace forward, his chest puffed proudly out.

James reached into his trouser pocket and pulled out a handful of change. He sorted through the silver and copper, chose one of the largest coins and flicked it towards the lad, who caught it deftly. His eyes opened round and huge and his mouth fell open as he saw what was in his hand. A rand coin. He had never held this much money in his life. He stared in wide-eyed wonder at the smiling white stranger.

'I need an *impi* of brave young warriors to guard my car. Do you know of such an *impi*? For their loyalty they will be rewarded with another coin such as you have in your hands.'

The little urchin quickly nodded his head.

'Well?' James demanded. 'Where is this *impi*?' He made a show of looking around.

'We, *Baba*, we will be your *impi*.' The little urchin beat his fists against his chest.

James was having trouble suppressing a grin. 'You?' he questioned dubiously. Then he continued on, 'I will trust you, but if you fail me...' He wagged an admonitory finger at the group, who were already scurrying to surround the car.

James shook his head, still smiling as he walked towards a white-headed Zulu who sat propped up against the shack he'd come to visit. The old man had been watching the procession with interest.

'May I sit beside you, *Madala*?' James asked respectfully, again in Zulu.

The man nodded towards a wooden box beside him. James sat, and dug into his jacket pocket for a packet of cigarettes. 'I have no use for these. Maybe you know of somebody who would like them.'

The Zulu looked at the packet, then at the boys strutting importantly around the car. He nodded again, and James dropped the packet beside him.

'They say it may rain,' James began.

The two men talked around in circles for the next hour. James never tried to push the pace; he didn't want to offend his host. But he could see the old Zulu was becoming intrigued as to why he was here.

They played a subtle game of verbal hide and seek, covering a wide variety of topics and sizing each other up.

Eventually the white-haired man said, 'It is spoken by fishermen of a lesser tribe that the white shark will swim lazily amongst a shoal of peaceful fish until they are used to his presence, then he will attack the shoal to feed. Is this not so, my friend?'

James suppressed a grin. '*Madala*, somebody as wise as you must surely know it is the shoal that lured the shark into their presence, so that the bright and nimble ones, once he has eaten his fill, may feed more plentifully.'

The old man stared in astonished silence. '*Hawu!*' he guffawed with glee, slapping his knee. He had finally accepted his uninvited guest. 'How can a humble old man such as I help a learned one such as you?'

'It is said by a cousin of yours to the north, that one of your sons is a worker of metal.'

'It is so.' The old man nodded proudly.

'It is said that he works for a man here in Natal.'

'This is also so.' The man was becoming suspicious.

'I would like to talk to your son. Your cousin in the north says he may help me.'

'Who is this cousin you refer to?' the Zulu asked suspiciously.

'He is a butcher's apprentice. He is called Joseph,' James revealed, inwardly tensing. Had he used the right approach?

'*Awu*, that rogue.' James clenched his teeth; had he said the wrong thing? But the old man continued, 'If you have come all that way on that rascal's say-so, you are a desperate man.' He fell silent for endless moments, his eyes never leaving James's face, then, 'I believe you can do no harm to my son. The Valley of a Thousand Hills is where you will find him. He will know of your coming before you arrive.'

The tension left John's body in a rush. The old Zulu gave him directions, and as he stood up to leave, he decided to take one more chance. He looked down at his host. 'Vulcan and the Leopard, what do you know of them?' he inquired.

The old Zulu answered without hesitation. 'I am an old man and I have had a fruitful life, but, my friend, I still have some living to do.'

James understood. He nodded. '*Ngiyabona* – I praise you.' He turned and headed back towards his car.

Walking away, he wondered for the first time how much living he himself had left.

James's trip to the Valley of a Thousand Hills was a brief one.

He stopped at Bothas Hill and asked for further directions. The engineering shop where Joseph's cousin worked was only a couple of kilometres up the road.

It was the size of two football fields and one of the most sophisticated he had ever seen; the tools alone must have been worth a king's ransom, and he couldn't begin to imagine what some of them were for. He identified row upon row of piping, huge metal gate valves and a plethora of other pumping and drilling equipment. But it was the name on the door that gave him his first clue.

He sought out Joseph's cousin and asked a few pertinent questions. The answers told him who to question next; between this and the information he had gathered in Johannesburg, he was certain of his next move, but first he needed to report back to Karen de Lout.

No one appeared to be supervising the black African workers, so he took the opportunity to look around the cavernous engineering shop. Right in the back he came to a large enclosed workroom. One brief glance was enough to show him the most sophisticated equipment of its kind he had ever seen; now he knew what was being manufactured here. He quickly strode away from the shop, unable to fathom why they hadn't locked the workroom door. What he had to tell Karen de Lout was explosive. Literally.

CHAPTER 16

Waiting was always the worst part of any job, but Dave was a patient man. He slumped comfortably behind the wheel of a rented Toyota, reading the daily paper, the *Melbourne Age*. The story that had caught his attention was about a murder in Gaborone, the capital of Botswana.

He had picked up the car at Melbourne airport and settled into his hotel before driving out to the comfortable suburb of Armadale where he was to pick up his next set of instructions at a boarding house. He wasn't due to arrive in Melbourne for another week, but was exercising his usual caution and waiting to see who dropped the information off.

It was the second morning of his vigil, and he was in luck. A taxi slowly cruised by and stopped outside the boarding house. The man who alighted was none other than Kane Van der Zwet. The big blond-haired Dutchman carried what looked like a courier's satchel into the house, and reappeared within moments, striding back towards the waiting taxi, which glided off towards the city centre. Dave followed at a discreet distance.

Kane's vehicle took a leisurely route to Melbourne's international airport.

Dave parked his car as Kane paid off the taxi, and swiftly followed the Dutchman into the terminal. He spotted him striding towards a row of ticketing counters and followed, merging easily with the crowd despite his size. Kane's visit had clearly been timed to the minute. No sooner had he presented his ticket than the public address system announced the final call for passengers on a flight to Papeete and Los Angeles.

Kane showed his ticket and passport at the entrance to the international departure lounge and disappeared. Dave was left staring into space, but in possession of another clue to the growing mystery.

During his drive back to the boarding house, he began arranging every snippet of information he had gathered, about Kane, South Africa's current situation and Vulcan's organisation into chronological order. After reading the article in the *Melbourne Age,* he was sure he was close to making a breakthrough.

Almost before he realised, he had stopped the car outside the boarding house.

The courier pack was clearly marked with his name and nobody asked any questions. He waited until he was in his hotel room before he opened it.

The satchel's contents were typical of Vulcan's approach to security: tourist brochures for Perth and the old port of Fremantle, completely innocuous if it had been intercepted. The only clue to the next drop-off point was a scrawled message on the back of one of the brochures: I'll forward your mail to the American Express Travel Service in Perth. It was simply signed V.

He was still a week ahead of schedule. A thought struck him and he reached for the phone. As he waited to be connected to a number in Perth, he was sure he had just uncovered another clue.

'I knew it!' Dave lifted a clenched fist in triumph.

He had arrived early in Western Australia, but the information he needed was already waiting for him at the American Express Travel Service's office. The attractive brunette receptionist was happy to divulge that it had been dropped off before he had picked up his package in Melbourne. 'Yes, come to think of it he did have long blond hair, and he was rather a big man,' the helpful girl had said.

Kane again. The man certainly got around.

Now Dave was walking back from the middle of Perth to his hotel. It was the most inconspicuous place he could find, a few minutes' walk from the city centre. With a wait of seven days before moving on to his next destination, he needed to make sure his activities during that time went unnoticed.

He was pretty sure he now knew where Kane had been and what he had done before dropping off both sets of instructions. And that was important.

CHAPTER 17

ane had arrived five days earlier in Gaborone, Botswana's largest settlement and capital, in the south-east of the land-locked state and just under twenty kilometres from the border with South Africa. Because of the politically sensitive nature of the meeting he had organised and arranged the details himself. He sat at the head of a long wooden table, in a private conference room in a large hotel. Around the table were seven men, potentially the most powerful in southern Africa.

They were all black, proud, intelligent, and handsome, the Inner Circle of the UDF, the United Democratic Front. Over the last few years these men had been given enough financial backing, resources, and above all direction to turn them into one of the most formidable political organisations in South Africa.

On 20th August 1983 the UDF was launched at the Rocklands Civic Centre in the Western Cape. Although not officially endorsing the doctrines of the African National Congress, the new organisation adhered closely to them, and in so doing had successfully created a national multi-class movement with the emphasis on non-racialism.

It quickly achieved a groundswell of popular support and huge increases in membership despite attempts by the South African government to disrupt and hinder it. It was helped by mass resistance to the government, and offered an alternative to the popular ANC.

Ironically, what was probably the UDF's greatest break came in 1984 when their high-profile leadership in Natal and the Transvaal were detained by the authorities. In a skilful manoeuvre, six senior UDF leaders sought refuge in the British Consulate in Durban, creating an ideal platform to present their case not only to South Africa, but the rest of the world, which of course massively increased their support. From then on there was a conscious and successful effort to expand its influence through all levels of the Republic's communities.

The UDF was still a legal organisation in the republic, but its huge success exposed it to an increasing number of detentions and treason trials, and general harassment from the white run, minority state. The threat of detention forced its leaders and activists into hiding. Regional and national executives had to resort to meeting in secret and using clandestine networks to pass on information.

Possibly for strategic reasons, the South African government continued to tolerate the UDF's existence, but the organisation found itself with a foot on either side of the law. From necessity it functioned at a semi-underground level. What the South African government had helped to create was an unseen enemy: the UDF's Inner Circle. Those seven men now controlled a massive organisation affiliated to many other resistance groups, which continued to achieve substantial victories in its struggle against apartheid and the white governments tyrannical rule.

Kane's gaze locked with the other dominant figure in the conference room, seated at the foot of the long table: Jaunus Zamba, the UDF's recognised leader. Like his companions, he was dressed in a dark lightweight three-piece suit. The cost of what these men wore on their bodies alone would have fed for a year the average African family they were fighting for. A crisp white shirt contrasted with Zamba's purple-black skin; his hair was cropped close to his skull, and his eyes were dark and rimmed with perfect whites. The gleam of power that sparkled in his eyes clearly marked him out as their leader.

Even though the Inner Circle had written into its constitution that there was no one leader, it was an undisputed fact that no decision was ever made or action undertaken without the approval of this man. He was well over six feet tall and in prime physical shape, with an intelligent forehead and an unblemished face that did not give away his age,

His hands rested lightly on either side of a single sheet of white paper on the table before him, and he returned Kane's stony gaze effortlessly. Behind Zamba stood his bodyguards, wearing the standard garb of the modern-day African enforcer: mirrored aviator sunglasses, and business suits with the inevitable bulge under the left armpit.

The meeting had only just begun, and not a word was uttered until the other men had finished sweeping their gaze from the foot to the head of the table.

A shaft of unrestricted sunlight pierced a crack in the heavy net curtains that hid the group from prying eyes. This shimmering ray seemed to symbolise the glimmer of hope South Africa's poor black and coloured communities placed in these men and their organisation. As the reflection from the light danced about the seven faces, Kane began to speak, his eyes never wavering from Zamba's face.

'I would like to thank you gentlemen for accepting Vulcan's invitation to attend this meeting.'

In response Zamba raised a clenched fist, slammed it on the table and spoke in a deep rich voice, with a hint of malice. 'It was no invitation, it was an undignified summons. In future we will not be directed or controlled as if we were children.'

There were nods and murmurs of agreement from around the table. This was the mood that Kane had hoped for. In an even, unemotional tone he challenged the black man.

'Would you not agree that the UDF is now in a far more formidable position, and much better equipped to claim its rightful place as the government of South Africa?' The steely silence did not deter him; he continued, 'And would you deny that this situation is directly attributable to the finance, resources and strategies that have been made available to you from Vulcan?' This time there were reluctant murmurs of agreement.

Zamba's eyes flared like flaming torches. He replied impatiently, 'We concede Vulcan's generosity and resources have been most useful. But the UDF now feels we would serve our people's needs far more effectively by using our own resources, without greedy help from outside.'

That's called biting the hand that feeds you, thought Kane.

Approximately three years previously, the UDF was an organisation with no leaders, limited financial backing and no effective structure. It was no more than a hollow mouthpiece for unorganised men with a dream. Vulcan's injection of finance, guidance and planning had enabled it to evolve into a potent force that threatened the power base of the South African government.

'This is one of the very reasons you have been asked to attend this meeting.'

But before Kane was able to continue, Zamba cut him off.

'We thank Vulcan for his initial support. He will be properly rewarded.' Despite the words. no gratitude showed in his face.

Kane lifted an expensive briefcase which he placed on the table. 'I feel, gentlemen, I may be able to change your point of view.'

Each of them except Zamba leant forward in hungry anticipation. They had all received similar cases in the past, filled to the brim with money.

'Do you think, Mr Van der Zwet, that we can be bought again? And for a pittance?' Zamba paused and slammed a clenched a fist on the table. 'When now we have within our grasp the country that can give us and our people back our rightful wealth, wealth beyond our wildest dreams. We thank Vulcan for his assistance, but the people of South Africa will control their own destiny.'

It was turning out even better than Kane had hoped. As the other men, and even the bodyguards, broke into spontaneous applause with the lust for power blazing in their eyes, Kane flicked open the catches of the briefcase. None of the members of the meeting noticed the deft movement as he snatched up the object the case concealed. Before the applause had stopped Zamba's bodyguards were sliding to the ground, dead. Kane had in his hand a 9mm Beretta. A wisp of smoke slowly curled from the silenced barrel, making it appear grossly deformed; he had shot both men between the eyes.

Kane now aimed the weapon directly at Jaunus Zamba, causing total confusion amongst the Inner Circle. Some were halfway out of their seats, craning their necks to peer at the fallen men. Zamba himself had screwed his upper torso around to look at his stricken bodyguards. Kane shot him through the point of the right shoulder and his arm hung loosely at his side. All heads swivelled towards the noise, and the only sound came from the foot of the table.

Zamba was clutching his smashed shoulder, moaning pitifully. He turned to look at Kane, his eyes already sunken and haunted as blood gushed from his ruptured brachial artery. His once proud face was a mask of pain, but because of the swiftness and brutality of the attack, no one had yet gone to his aid.

Kane fixed his aim on the black leader's forehead and he calmly said, 'I'm sorry, gentlemen, we cannot accept your refusal of our support.'

Zamba's head was thrown back and his uninjured arm flopped lifelessly into his lap. Once more the UDF was without a leader. Zamba remained sitting upright in his chair, his head thrown to the side. The last sound he made was the watery evacuation of his bowels.

The room fell silent. The other men around the table stared in wide-eyed horror; their eyes darted from Zamba's lifeless figure to Kane's deadly pale blue eyes. As a drop of blood dripped from the neat hole in the dead man's head and made a cushioned splat on the carpet, Kane reached into the briefcase once again. Their horror changed to unalloyed fear, and each man began to cower in his seat. Kane produced a small glass jar filled with a clear fluid, suspended in it was what looked like a long, fat, brown slug. He rolled the jar to the man on Zamba's right; the man gagged when he recognised the contents.

'That, Mr Gamon, is the index finger of your youngest wife.' There was an audible gasp from the group.

Kane turned his head and directed his next comment to the man on Zamba's left. 'Mr Tombo, you will now find your youngest niece will walk with a permanent limp.' The man's mouth hung open.

The tentacles of Vulcan had reached out far and wide, weaving an intricate web of fear and persuasion around each of the men around the table. The brutal execution before their eyes, and the barbaric injuries inflicted on two of their immediate family, had shown them they were now forever at Vulcan's beck and call. Kane waited in silence as the ghastly reality of their plight took hold.

'Gentlemen, in the near future South Africa will have a government of the people. We plan to ensure that those of you who choose to will head that government. There is only one prerequisite: that you seriously consider having your current benefactor as your closest advisor.'

Kane carefully placed the Beretta back in its foam rubber support and snapped the case closed. He stood, grasped its handle and headed towards the door, stopping as his hand gripped the knob. He turned to look at his stunned audience and said, 'There will be no reprisals against today's demonstration. Somebody will be in touch with each of you in the near future. Thank you.'

He didn't look back as he left the room; his mind was already on his next assignment. 'One down, two to go,' he murmured as he walked away.

Two days later the world's press heard of a callous act of violence by the South African security forces, a hit-and-run raid in neighbouring Botswana. Of course, the security forces denied the accusations, but the UDF vowed to retaliate for the death of one of its most prominent members. The Botswana government was demanding an apology from the South African Republic.

CHAPTER 18

James Pearson replaced the phone in its cradle. He had just organised a meeting at Karen de Lout's office. He felt he was beginning to make some real headway after his trip to Natal. It was a far bigger matter than either he or Karen had imagined; it appeared her husband's death was just a small piece of a huge puzzle which could affect the country, maybe even the world.

He had told her this, and she had asked him to explain, but all he was willing to say was, 'It's best I tell you in person; even those close to you may prove to be a risk.'

James lived on a peaceful avenue in a suburb of Johannesburg. His home was his sanctuary. He had friendly neighbours, and a calm setting in which to spend time on his hobby when he wasn't working. He rarely had visitors, so a knock at the door came as a surprise.

He went to answer it, tucking the note he had referred to while speaking to Karen into the pocket of his shirt and gathering up a newspaper which he had left by the phone. He hoped the interruption wouldn't take long; he would already have to rush to get to their appointment.

The sun was behind the figure at the door as he opened it. All James could see was a big man with flowing locks of blond hair and blue overalls with what looked like a tool belt slung around his waist. A tradesman looking for work, he decided.

'I was wondering if you could help. I'm looking for 3 Villa Doro?' the man said in unaccented English.

'Yes, that's me,' James replied.

'Ah, so you're Mr Pearson?' the man asked, drawing something from his tool belt.

It was the lack of accent that alerted James. He threw the newspaper at the visitor, and tried to slam the door in his face. But a large spanner caught him a crushing blow to the wrist; the bones graunched and snapped like a dry twig. His hand hung useless as he tried to spin around and escape through the house.

As he turned, a crashing blow glanced off the side of his head and he fell heavily to the floor. A sharp pain from his damaged wrist made him cry out, but he tried to drag himself to his feet. He heard the door close behind him, and his broken hand prevented him from pushing himself up. He felt a heavy foot stamp down between his shoulder blades, driving the air from his lungs. Something rammed into the back of his skull, and a hammering void of darkness smashed through his head.

That was the last thing he felt.

The big man with blond hair tucked the silenced Beretta back into his belt. Leaving James's lifeless body where it lay, he pulled on a pair of soft leather gloves and quickly searched the house. He never looked back at the body as he let himself out the way he had entered, saying to himself, 'Two down, one to go. Next stop Australia.'

CHAPTER 19

Dave's instructions were to take a bus from Perth to a town approximately three hundred kilometres to the south. From there he would be taken to his final destination. He had left at nine in the morning, and after six hours bumping and juddering through the brown, eucalyptus-studded countryside, he could think of better ways to travel.

Finally, the bus pulled off the street onto a large shingle parking area, across the road from an old wooden trading store that obviously served both the town and the rural community. Relieved the trip was over, Dave pulled his luggage down from the carry-net above his seat and alighted.

The bus swayed out of the uneven car park in a billowing cloud of dust, which settled to reveal a single vehicle, an old HQ Holden with a thick coating of red-brown dust. Its rear suspension had seen better days; the rear bumper was only a few centimetres from the ground. A scrawny middle-aged man leaned against the side, oblivious to the dust clinging to his clothes. He looked at Dave and raised a hand.

'You Old?' He pushed himself off the car, and swiped at the dust on his backside. 'I'm going to have to pat you down and search your bags.' He took a couple of paces towards Dave. 'Orders is orders.'

Dave dropped his luggage, and as the man reached out to him, he grabbed him by the shirt and hauled him off his feet. As the man hung suspended in the air, his legs paddling back and forward. With their eyes only centimetres apart, Dave hissed in a menacing whisper, 'Let's make ourselves clear; you don't touch me or my property.'

The man cowered, and he emphatically nodded his head. Dave gently placed him on the ground and stooped to pick up his bags.

Straightening his shirt collar and trying to restore his dignity, the man produced his car keys and unlocked the boot. As Dave approached, he saw him throw a hessian sack over a rectangular nail box in the corner of the cavernous boot. Before the box was completely covered, he spotted something written in bold black ink: *Wemyss Est, Gnowangerup*.

Dave had studied a map of Western Australia before he left Perth. They weren't far from Gnowangerup; that must be where he was staying.

Gnowangerup was no more than a single, wide gravel road, lined with shops and amenities to serve the large surrounding farming community. Stock and station, supermarket, clothing store and of course the post office. Few people were about, and the town had a sleepy feel. The man parked the Holden in front of the largest building, the supermarket.

He spoke to Dave for the first time since leaving the car park. 'I've gotta pick up some supplies. You wait here.'

Dave raised an eyebrow at the departing figure. As the man disappeared into the supermarket, he reached into the breast pocket of his shirt and extracted a thin, folded aerogram. He took a pencil from his wallet and quickly wrote a message on the sticky folding flap. He left the car and strode quickly towards the post office, licking the flap and sticking it down as he went. If anybody intercepted the airmail, all they would find was an account of an enjoyable holiday in Australia.

He returned to the car and looked at the reading of the speedometer. He was just settling back into his seat when his driver, weighed down by the boxes he was carrying, walked on bowed legs towards the car. Now he could concentrate on the job at hand.

They had travelled thirty-two miles, according to the old HQ's dashboard, from Gnowangerup when they turned off the blacktop onto a long gravel driveway, past a sign for Wemyss Estate. They had arrived.

At least sixteen kilometres closer to Ongerup: still too far to walk there and back in a single night. But he knew approximately where he was; he had been right to send the letter.

As always, Vulcan had made it extremely difficult for anybody to interfere with his plans. Dave was on his own. The prospect didn't worry him; he preferred it that way. The planning stage of his mission was about to begin.

Just over a kilometre and a half down the driveway they turned right past a huge area of covered sheep-yards and a wool shed towards a large plantation of tall eucalyptus trees. The driver had opened up since they had entered the property; he even vouchsafed his name. 'Ya c'n call me Collin,' he drawled.

Dave learned the estate was ten thousand hectares of farmland, five and a half thousand under cultivation and seventeen thousand merino ewes. The property employed eight married couples and one single man: by most standards a big operation.

They drove into the eucalyptus plantation towards a compound dominated by a large T-shaped building which normally provided accommodation for the shearing gangs, designed to sleep thirty-four, with living rooms, kitchen, laundry and shower block. The surrounding trees would hide it from prying eyes; it was a perfect base for Dave. He would feel like a walnut rattling around in a tin drum, but looked forward to the solitude. He helped Collin carry the supplies into the kitchen. The interior walls were covered with painted cement board, and the only natural sunlight shone through two louvred windows. His own room was stark, with a grey iron cot in one corner and an old wooden dresser for storage.

'Sheets and blankets in the laundry. I'm at the far end, but you'll probably never see me,' said Collin as he left.

Dave hardly heard him; his attention was taken up by something that looked out of place in the basic room. On a table opposite the bed stood a desktop computer. Just as he had expected, all the information on the forthcoming mission would be on disk.

He walked over to the machine, turned it on and pressed the help key. A menu began to scroll up the screen. He pulled the chair out and adjusted the keyboard and screen to the best position.

He tapped some keys and brought up the file menu. It was blank; the computer's memory was clean. He would have to wait.

A little while later, his belongings unpacked and stored away, he sat at the computer again, sorely tempted to take out the disks he had received from London. But some instinct stopped him; he decided to wait until he received more information.

He felt the hair on the back of his neck prickle. Somebody was stalking him; good thing the disks stayed hidden, he thought. He rose from the chair and squatted under the window, all his muscles taut, senses honed to a cutting edge. It was deathly quiet, as if the wind and birds were watching.

He smelt the man before he saw him.

A dark shadow fell over the door. Dave's body was wired with pent-up energy. A short samurai sword appeared around the door; his heightened vision took in its lustrous shine and engraved razor edge. Next to appear was a pair of hands clasping a perfectly bound handle. As a small, neat foot stepped lightly over the threshold, Dave exploded into action.

In a lightning blur of movement, he swept out one hand and hooked it around the intruder's ankle. The other grabbed the hands holding the sword. The assailant began to topple backwards, and Dave wrenched the sword towards his exposed throat. He released the ankle and jumped to the

SCARS OF THE LEOPARD

man's side. With his free hand he grabbed a handful of hair and twisted the attacker's chin. The tip of the blade touched the intruder's skin and a feather of blood sprang from the nick. There was a strangled cry, and stricken eyes darted from the blade to Dave and back again.

All this had taken less than ten seconds. Maintaining the pressure, Dave said, 'What will it be, Sammy, death or dishonour?'

Another strangled cry erupted from the helpless man's throat. Dave released him and rose to his feet. He looked down with his hands on his hips and began to laugh.

The man on the floor responded, 'Is no joke, no joke at all.'

The man stood up. He had Asian features, and the top of his head barely reached the middle of Dave's chest. His eyes matched his jet black hair, his face was smooth and it was impossible to guess his age.

'You pay for that,' he said, dabbing at the blood on his chin.

Dave was still laughing. 'I expected somebody, but not you, you little rogue. I thought they'd killed you long ago.'

'*Hmph*. You just lucky. Sammy still the best. I exercise you until you drop for this. Big overgrown piece of French cheese.'

'That'd be *Gruyère de Comté*, to you Sammy; the hardest you'll ever come across. And you exercise me just as much as you like. You haven't beaten me in the past, you won't in the future.'

'*Hmph*. We see about that. Tomorrow morning, early.' He waved his hand and began to stalk away. 'You find out. Sammy not soft anymore, you'll see.' He disappeared around the corner of the laundry block, leaving Dave still laughing.

Sammy had been his fitness instructor on three separate occasions. He was good; Vulcan only used the best. Dave would be driven to the very limits of his endurance; Sammy would make sure his body was performing at its optimum level. Before any of his agents went into a mission, Vulcan ensured they were in peak physical condition. Sammy would be well rewarded for his expertise, but mainly for his silence. He ran a small martial arts dojo in Honolulu. He was a master of his craft, an expert at training, teaching and moulding men to be the best they could. And unless things had changed, Dave was quite sure Sammy had no idea who was paying him.

The next three weeks for Dave were unmitigated hell. He was dragged out of bed at four thirty each morning. Sammy invariably appeared as fresh as a daisy. 'Come on, you lump of muscle, time to work,' was his reveille.

Dave had forgotten how intense the physical preparations were, second only to his basic training in Corsica, with the Foreign Legion. Each day began with a run to the other side of the station and back: thirteen kilometres as the crow flew, but Sammy chose the main farm track, which added another three. This was only the warm-up.

After the morning run came a substantial breakfast, which Dave couldn't enjoy because of the nausea he felt. Sammy cooked and prepared all the meals: highly nutritious, but most of the time Dave chose not to ask what he was eating.

The rest of the morning was given over to martial arts, beginning with meditation. 'To quieten the mind, and get the mind and the body flowing as one,' Sammy explained.

For the first few mornings Dave didn't care; it just gave his exhausted body a chance to rest before the unarmed combat commenced. 'Now you pay,' Sammy would say gleefully. On the first three mornings Dave was beaten black and blue by the nimble little Asian. It wasn't until the fourth day, when Dave landed a telling blow to Sammy's midriff, that the little teacher offered anything resembling praise. 'I think we may have break now, to let you rest,' he wheezed.

For two hours after lunch Dave practising on a makeshift firing range beside the complex. Sammy had supplied him with a semi-automatic handgun with a silencer; he disliked firearms, so was glad to leave his pupil on his own.

The first afternoon Dave never fired a shot. He lay in a wasted stupor, and only snapped out of it as he heard Sammy approach.

'Why you make no bang bang?'

Even in his depleted state Dave was able to counter. He pointed at the silenced barrel. 'Very quiet, so the neighbours won't hear.' Sammy didn't want to know about such things, so the matter was quickly forgotten. He clapped and rubbed his hands together. 'More exercise.'

The rest of the afternoon was taken up with sprints and weight training. Dave plodded through what were meant to be sprints, glad to move on; the weight training was the easiest part of the routine. He worked four days on and two days off, alternating between chest, shoulders and triceps and legs, back and biceps. Sammy saved the worst till last: abdominals. At the end of each session Dave lay curled up on the ground with his stomach muscles burning like fire, hating Sammy all over again.

As the days went by, the more he was able to do, the more Sammy asked of him. He was perpetually tired and sore, totally exhausted at the end of each day. The only way he was able to shower at night was propped up on a kitchen chair, letting the scalding water cascade over his body. Before he retired, Sammy massaged his weary muscles to release the toxins that built up, so the pain remained bearable. At night he slept like a dead man. For the first time in many years he didn't wake lathered in sweat and shaking with fear from fighting the demons in his mind.

The beginning of the fourth week brought a change in routine. Instead of dragging him out of bed for his early morning run, Sammy thumped a thick sheaf of documents and computer disks on the table beside his bed. They contained every detail of his mission.

CHAPTER 20

'He's been where? Australia! What the hell for?'

How the hell would I know? Brian Westcote kept the thought to himself and said respectfully instead, 'You asked me to have his movements tracked, sir, and that's where he went. I have no other information. I'm sorry.'

'OK, what did he do in Australia?' was the next demand.

'They followed him to Sydney, then they lost him.' Westcote spread his hands apologetically.

'Blast.' Brendan Oechsli thumped his fist into his other palm. 'What about in Britain?'

'Sorry, sir, they only picked him up leaving Heathrow.'

Brendan was an expert interrogator, and knew when to throw in a question which would keep the subject guessing. 'Have you sent that report off to London yet?'

You know damn well I have, Westcote thought, thrown slightly off balance. 'It went in the diplomatic bag two nights ago,' he replied.

Again, Brendan changed tack. 'You haven't located Network's base?'

'Ahh, no, not yet, sir. But the feedback I'm getting is they're not far away.'

Westcote hated taking the flak for the field officers, but this was the only way up. Stick close to the boss through thick and thin, and his paper-pushing days would soon be over.

'Crap!' Brendan retorted. 'If they haven't found it by now, they never will. Richard Black's too damn good and his movements far too slick; losing him in Australia clearly shows that.'

He stood up and walked over to the window. He didn't see the flat, wooded countryside on the banks on the Potomac; he was too deep in thought. Hell, I need to get out there myself, he told himself, instead of hearing it from some mealy-mouthed clerk.

He came to a decision. 'I'm going back in the field. This one's too big to be screwed up by a bunch of amateurs.'

Westcote began to shift his weight nervously from foot to foot; he had heard what the officers had to do out there in the field. He found his voice.

'Does that mean, sir... I, err... who will look after the office?' he stammered.

Westcote in the field, heaven forbid, was Brendan's reaction. He opted for tact. 'Sorry, Brian, probably best if I have somebody I can trust back here at base.'

Relief flooded man's face. 'If you think it's best, sir...'

Poor guy; he was trying his best to sound dispirited. Brendan struggled not to smile. 'Believe me, Brian, that would be best for all of us.' And that, he thought, effectively covers my butt if anything goes wrong back here, but gives me the excuse I need to be away from meddlesome eyes.

CHAPTER 21

As Richard walked into the flat he heard Johnny noisily shuffling paper in the computer room, making it known that at least one of them had been at the office and busy. He continued into his own office, and threw a brief glance at the piles of documents that had accumulated on his desk in his absence. He groaned inwardly. All this work, and a crisis brewing.

He slumped on his chair and began tackling the mountain of paper. The crisis would have to wait. At least his trip had brought about some progress with that.

Richard made a point of handling each piece of paper only once. A key ingredient of his job was the effective use of time. He frequently asked his agents, 'You can gather information efficiently, but were you effective while doing it?' This was why his information collecting agency was the most effective in the world.

He scribbled his own notes and memos on the originals, rather than generating even more paper. Some people who that received their own letters with Richard's reply on them thought it rude, but it saved time: one of the reasons Network produced such outstanding results.

Richard had already made a huge impact on his paper-mountain when Johnny walked in. 'Enjoy the trip to Australia?' he said in an irritated tone.

'What trip was that?' Richard inquired.

Johnny was aware he shouldn't have known of his boss's movements. He looked blankly at Richard.

'Why did you have me followed?' Richard asked, keeping his voice even.

'I admit I kept tabs on you, but I didn't have you followed. You didn't even tell me you were going.'

Richard stared up at him. He had a way of making Johnny feel inferior.

'Johnny, we have a leak, and I can't rule out any possibilities.'

'Heavens above, you don't think it's me? We've been a team from the start,' Johnny exclaimed in a wounded voice.

'I'll ask again, why did you have me followed?'

'I only used the watchers at the airports. Just to see where you were going,'

Johnny said awkwardly.

'For Christ's sake, do you think those watchers only work for us? Why do you think we always use more than one? Shit, Johnny, you don't know what your petty, small-minded meddling might have done.'

Johnny looked suitably shamefaced. Richard knew he was inquisitive; he always needed to know what was going on – one reason he was so good at his job. But Richard had to seek out all possible sources of the leak. Since the investigation into Vulcan had begun, a pungent air of deceit had lingered. He had set himself up, and somebody had taken the bait. But if Johnny was telling the truth, who were the other two teams that had followed him from Heathrow to Sydney? And why?

Richard dismissed Johnny with an abrupt reprimand. He flicked on the switch under his desk that duplicated all the recordings of incoming and outgoing calls and activated the hidden computer program that copied and stored all recently processed data. It took another three hours of solid work to clear his desk.

Johnny remained subdued for the rest of the day. Late in the afternoon he knocked politely on Richard's door. 'I've just cleared the box; a report of some sort has come in from Langley, and an aerogram from Australia. What do I do with them?' he asked.

Richard looked up. 'Johnny, what I said to you earlier was necessary, but it's still business as usual. Stamp and file the report as you've always done, and all airmail letters come directly to me.' He held out his hand. 'But you may as well give them both to me now.'

Johnny looked down and muttered, 'Thanks, boss. And... sorry again.' He left before Richard could reply.

Richard held the aerogram up to his desk lamp. Ingenious, and simple; typical of Dave. He examined the edges of the letter; nothing showed through.

He took the letter into the kitchenette and put the kettle on. When it boiled, he peered down the hall to Johnny's room, closed the door and held the edges in the billowing steam. 'Wemyss Estate,' he murmured. It meant nothing to him.

He burnt the letter in an ashtray, took the ashes to the toilet, and flushed them down the pan. The postmark was Gnowangerup, he remembered. That was meaningless too; he'd have to look it up.

As he walked past Johnny's office, he poked his head round the door.

'When you've a minute, bring the file we received last week from Ferkatovich.' Johnny waved a vague acknowledgement; he appeared absorbed in his computer screen.

Back to normal, Richard thought wearily. No doubt the guy would be checking up on him again tomorrow.

Back at his desk Richard swallowed heavily. I have to find out one way or the other, he told himself. For Dave's sake if nothing else, he hoped Johnny was clean.

Johnny had just walked into his office. Richard took a deep breath. 'Everything you can give me on Wemyss Estate.' He spelt it out. 'The works. And an update on the file on Kane Van der Zwet. The one Dave recently requested.'

They were making some headway at last. Richard had two reports in front of him, from two very different parts of the world: one from the head of the Soviet Foreign Intelligence and the other from the deputy director of the CIA, both couched in brash terms. He had to admit they had something to crow about, given the progress they were making.

It had been a very different couple of months since their last meeting. Because of the crackdown in security, they all had been able to win back some of the support and trade their countries had lost. It was psychological warfare, and the battle of nerves was just about to heat up.

Vulcan's tactics of buying politicians and influential figures throughout the world had proved remarkably effective to date. But as some countries experienced the instability that invariably accompanied trading with new partners, their balance of trade had suffered. They started renewing tentative links with their established, secure markets of old.

But a bombshell hit just after Johnny walked into Richard's office.

'I have the information on Wemyss Estate. Wasn't hard to track down.'

Richard had just finished absorbing the reports. He closed them, looked up at Johnny and slipped them into the top drawer of his desk.

'At the turn of the century the government of Britain nationalised a coal mine that a chap Wemyss owned. They paid him a million quid for it, hell of a price in those days. Anyway, because of this chap's shrewd investments, his estate now has quite a few interests throughout the world.'

Richard leaned forward, chin resting in his hand, committing Johnny's account to memory. 'It owns a brick works in Glasgow, a tea plantation in Kenya and two farms in Western Australia. There may be more – that's all

I've uncovered so far.'

'OK, get me the exact locations of them all, and everything on whoever runs the estate. Anything else?'

'Just the paper. *Daily Mail*. Forgot to bring it in earlier.' Johnny laid it on the corner of the desk and left the office.

'OK, Dave, I'm as near as dammit to knowing exactly where you are. It's your job to let me know who's being targeted. All I have to do is figure out why,' Richard muttered ruefully.

He looked at the paper in front of him, and his expression changed to horror.

Snowflakes floated down, disappearing on the wet pavement, and a heavy quiet seemed to hang over Paris. Piers Lassere's bones ached, his feet were cold, and he wished his chauffeur would hurry with the car. He was tall and thin-faced with flowing white hair, though not quite as old as he looked. After France was liberated at the end of the war, he was a young man with a mission: to see France prosper so it would never be dictated to by a foreign power again. He had never intended becoming involved in politics, but his heroism in the Free Army of France and his fierce convictions meant he was the type of man men followed. He was now a highly regarded minister on France's Council.

His mind turned to the most pressing issue he had faced for several years, and he recalled a conversation two days previously with his press secretary. 'The English may be pompous and pretentious, but in heaven's name, why stop trading with them? It's sheer lunacy. A powerful faction in the government is being motivated by factors other than our country's needs. But at least now I am winning back support.'

Lassere was a pivotal member of France's government. He had gathered a group of followers who supported the shift of trade back towards its old trading partners. He'd fought for it tooth and nail, for France and France alone; never, if he could avoid it, would he see his country's well-being suffer again. Every day his support grew stronger, but one stumble could see all his work come crashing down.

'Come on, where are you?' he muttered to his missing chauffeur, stamping his frozen feet.

As the silver limousine finally glided around the corner, a man on an ancient moped began to pedal towards the vehicle. The moped's tiny motor was running as it skipped up onto the pavement; the rider reached into his pocket and drew out an egg-shaped object. The chauffeur was leaning through the open door of the limousine, arranging a rug around the old man's legs.

Something hard hit the chauffeur on the elbow and fell into the lap of the minister. It looked like a small green pineapple. They both stopped what they were doing and stared at the metal globe. The last sounds they heard were the whining of a small motor, then a faint metallic click just before the grenade exploded and turned the limousine and its occupants into a fireball.

'Hilda, switch the wireless on please,' the grey-haired lady said to her daughter-in-law.

'Yes, Mother, I know what time Helmut is speaking. We have a couple of minutes yet,' the fair-haired young woman replied.

'I am so proud of my boy, and your steadying hand has helped him so much, Hilda.'

The younger woman turned away from the radio. 'Thank you, Mother, you are most kind. But he is only the Assistant Minister of Economics. He has far to go.'

'Go on with you.' The older woman waved a wrinkled hand.

Hilda affirmed twiddled the knobs of the radio and sat down beside her mother-in-law.

The announcer began to speak. 'Good morning, this is Deutschlandfunk transmitting throughout West Germany and the rest of Europe. We have great pleasure in welcoming to our Köln studio this morning the Assistant Minister of Economics. Welcome, Minister Ernst.'

'Thank you.'

The older woman beamed with pride, and Hilda sat forward, listening intently. This interview would have a major impact on her husband's progress within the government of the Federal Republic. A large percentage of West Germany's most influential people would be listening.

The announcer was speaking again. 'What you are proposing will have a major bearing on the trade markets of our country. Surely it is better to continually expand these markets?'

During the brief silence Hilda pictured her husband composing himself to respond.

'Would it not be better to establish new markets while retaining the stability of existing ones? Where would it leave us if these new markets were inadequate for our country's needs?'

Brilliant, Helmut, Hilda thought. Always leave them with a question to answer. '

'Yes, I concede that, Minister,' the announcer responded, 'but surely these old markets only exist because of the preferential treatment that prevails?'

'Import and export incentives existed in the past, but as you know, we are now moving into a free market situation. Is it not better to establish growth on a strong foundation, instead of building a completely new structure?' her husband declared in a clear, decisive voice.

'So sensible, so practical. I'm sure Helmut will gain the support he needs,' said Hilda proudly.

Her mother-in-law wasn't really listening to a word of the broadcast; she was just proud of her son.

It was warm in the small studio; Helmut knew the thermostat had been set to make him feel uncomfortable. The interviewer was scanning his notes to plan his next assault. He looked up. 'The economy of West Germany is very stable, wouldn't you agree, Minister?'

Before the Minister could reply, the door behind him opened. The announcer's head snapped up; the red light indicated they were still on air. He glared at the intruder and mouthed, 'Bugger off.'

The intruder raised a dark object and briefly touched it to the back of the Minister's head. There was a sound like muffled thunder, the Minister's head contorted out of shape and he collapsed over the console.

'Christ!' the announcer screamed. 'Go to commercial.'

Hilda's head jerked up as a smothered boom echoed from the radio and the announcer screamed. Somehow she knew her husband was dead.

Why the hell was it up to him to sort out this fiasco? He looked up at the hostess. 'Could I please have another drink, Miss?' he asked in well-educated Dutch.

'Certainly, sir,' She stooped to retrieve his glass.

Once the hostess was out of earshot, the grizzled man turned to his private secretary in the next seat. 'Who requested I fly to Brussels and tee up these trade talks?' he asked.

'Sorry, sir, I'm not sure. You received the memo yourself.'

Hendricus J. Pelser, retired Minister of Foreign Affairs for the Netherlands, was on board a specially chartered executive jet. He was retired, but those who mattered said he still wielded more influence than most of the Council of Ministers.

'Why doesn't our government just reverse the trade restraints themselves, without having to hold our bloody neighbour's hand?' he demanded.

'Perhaps because neither country wants to lose face,' his secretary replied respectfully.

'You mean those wimps in Parliament don't. Ridiculous. Somebody has been receiving backhanders.'

There was nobody else in the cabin, so they could speak freely.

The secretary was about to speak, but the hostess appeared. When she had served Pelser's drink and moved away, he said, 'It might be wise, sir, if you sought the help of the right authorities.'

'Rubbish. Once I expose that band of hypocrites, there'll be more than trade talks.' He waved his glass and spilt some of the drink down his shirt.

The other man suppressed a smile. 'I still think at least you should let somebody else know of your investigations, sir.'

Pelser stirred restlessly. He knew the risk he was taking, but who could he trust? 'I fear, Vaughn, it's far bigger than we suspected. I have made discreet inquiries, and there appears to be a switch in the balance of power in Europe. In fact, I wouldn't be surprised if it affected the whole world.'

Both men knew they were fighting an enemy they didn't know. It was like trying to track a blood-borne cancer.

'I suppose we must have allies somewhere, if both Holland and Belgium wish to discuss lifting these outrageous trade constraints,' Vaughn observed.

The sky outside was crystal clear now they were above the clouds. The plane flew like a predatory bird, its landing gear neatly tucked into its silver belly. The two men failed to see a small plastic-wrapped package strapped to one of the wheel struts, the size of a small tape recorder with a small clock attached; a miniature arm was ticking slowly towards a red mark at the top.

The jet began its descent. 'Not long now, sir,' said Vaughn.

That was when the plane shuddered, and something erupted at Pelser's feet. His legs were driven towards the cabin roof, and he was sucked through a gaping hole as the pressurised cabin was breached.

'Well, Olof, did you enjoy the film?' said a woman to her companion.

The hook-nosed man chuckled. 'Yes, Lisbeth, I did. Again, another wise choice,'

Olof Palme, Prime Minister of Sweden, was not as relaxed as he appeared. A few hours with his wife at a downtown Stockholm cinema had only given him a brief respite. Known as a true democrat, devoted to peace and non-violence, Palme was seen as a friend of the poor and oppressed, but tonight he felt inadequate. He no longer commanded the same influence among his cabinet colleagues. Huh, trade restraints, he scoffed to himself. It has gone on for far too long.

It was answer enough. 'Come,' Lisbeth said affectionately. 'Let's go home.'

Olof pulled up the collar of his jacket. 'I think we'll walk,' he decided.

He dismissed his bodyguards, proud to be able to walk safely about the Swedish capital, unencumbered by an entourage of gun-wielding guards. As the couple walked along Sveavagen, Stockholm's well-lit main thoroughfare, he found he could lay aside the dilemma that gripped his country and enjoy the peace.

He didn't see the man in a ski jacket produce a handgun and fire two crashing shots. One bit him in the back, the other wounded his wife. As the booming echo faded away, Olof Palme slowly crumpled to the ground. At six minutes past midnight in Sabbatsberg Hospital, the shrewd, compassionate Prime Minister of Sweden was declared dead and the country's political innocence came to an abrupt end.

'*Oh my god!*' Richard Black stared at the newspaper. The front page headline of the *Daily Mail* glared up at him:

BLACK DAY FOR EUROPE'S POLITICIANS.

It was the four names that had caught his attention; Piers Lassere, Helmut Ernst, Hendricus J. Pelser and Olof Palme. He began to read the article. *In what appear to be unrelated terrorist attacks, four of Europe's most influential men have died. It is a day all Europe will mourn.*

Richard skim-read most the of the article, which confirmed his worst fears. The four dead men were the driving force behind Europe's renewal of trade with his country. As yet the press had not linked the deaths, but Richard knew it for what it was: a demonstration of Vulcan's power, and a warning to everyone of influence in the world. The macabre display simply stated, *Support this new power, or face the consequences.*

With these deaths all the progress Britain, the United States and the USSR had made in the past few months had turned to dust. There would be no more support from the four men's countries.

CHAPTER 22

On her day, Karen de Lout could be the most ruthless, perceptive business negotiator anybody would have to face. It didn't come naturally to her, but when her mind clicked into focus her skills were awesome.

Today was not such a day.

She strode from the boardroom, outwardly the picture of composure, but inside the wrath of hell would have had trouble matching her fury.

'Three bloody amendments.' She slapped the red folder on her desk and placed her hands on her hips, her aggressive posture highlighted by the sunshine pouring through the picture window behind her.

'Karen, it was necessary,' Peter said in his deliberate way, following her to her desk. 'We haven't even had the final surveyor report yet, and you are proposing extending the field. I think it wise...'

'Peter, shut up, you made yourself clear in the meeting. You know bloody well what the report will say. You've just lost us over three million rand.'

'I'm sorry, Karen, but I may have saved us over a hundred and fifty million if the field is dry.'

With a huge effort Karen controlled herself and sat down in her high-backed chair. She calmly placed her clasped hands on the desk and in a sweet voice laced with venom, she said, 'Thank you Peter. I have work to do.' She stared at him until he left, making no attempt to hide her fury.

As soon as her door was closed and she was alone, she quietly rose from her desk and stood before the picture window. No, she definitely was not having a good day. But she needed to dissipate this anger somehow, or nothing useful would be done. She walked back to her desk and pressed the button on the intercom. 'Susan, I'll be in the gym for the next hour and a half if there's anything important. And make sure it is important.'

The company gymnasium was situated on the top floor of de Lout House. Years before, her late husband had done extensive research into corporate health and fitness. He had found that company-run health promotion programs that included diet, exercise and stress management reduced absenteeism by as much as forty per cent. Every rand spent on corporate fitness gave a return of three rand. When the gym was first built, all the executives were advised most strongly to take advantage of the facilities. and the full-time staff who ran them.

The gym was neat as a new pin. The mirrors that lined one wall were spotless, the red and black striped carpet that covered its floor blended well with the tasteful furnishings. The equipment was state of the art, and updated yearly. There was a steam room and sauna, and a dietitian attended every week to advise on good eating habits. De Louts' executives were probably among the healthiest and fittest in the country, and interestingly, also among the most productive.

Karen chose the bench press machine, and soon her whole body was drenched in sweat. She wore a light grey tank top with a white sports bra, baggy white shorts and Adidas trainers. Her muscle definition showed she was a woman in peak physical condition.

She finished her set, sat up and looked at herself in the mirror. She didn't see the beautiful intelligent woman with broad shoulders, a narrow waist and long shapely legs; just a lonely widow trying to drive her pain away.

Even before marrying Tom she had been driven by a need to protect herself. While at university she had gained a black belt in karate, but a sense of insecurity persisted, and still did, even though she was one of the wealthiest women in South Africa, and probably one of the fittest. She had begun to realise she was a woman who truly didn't know herself and was too afraid to start looking.

As she picked up her towel she saw Susan open the door at the far end of the gym. What now? she thought despondently.

'Sorry to disturb you, Mrs de Lout, but there is a policeman waiting to see you.'

'A policeman?'

'Yes, ma'am. He's been there for quite some time. He insisted on waiting until you were free.'

'I'll be there in a moment.' Karen hoped her instincts were wrong, but something was certainly amiss.

Half an hour later, showered and immaculately dressed again, she was back in her office.

'James Pearson. Yes, it does ring a bell. I believe he worked for my late husband occasionally. Why do you ask?' Outwardly Karen was the image of calm. Inwardly she hated herself; it felt as if she was betraying the private detective.

The police inspector looked uncomfortable in the presence of the most powerful woman in South Africa. 'I'm sorry to tell you he's been found murdered at his home.'

She felt a stab of guilt in the pit of her stomach, and it began to churn and twist. 'I'm dreadfully sorry to hear that,' she heard herself say. 'Is there anything I can do to help?'

James Pearson had never turned up for their meeting and Karen had tried in vain to locate him. Their clandestine arrangement made more than a few phone calls difficult, though it was probably one of those that had brought the police here today.

'We found this in the breast pocket of his shirt.'

Karen took the piece of paper from his outstretched hand. 'That's my private line here at the office.'

'But you have had no contact with the man. Is that correct?' The inspector looked decidedly awkward.

Karen's mind was racing. What on earth could she say; that Pearson had discovered her husband was murdered by some mysterious man in the Zimbabwean bush? Or that he had uncovered something far more sinister, but had no opportunity to tell her about it? She was all too aware how preposterous it would sound to the inspector, and besides, she had no proof of either allegation.

Her thoughts clicked into focus. 'That's right, no contact at all. But that was also my husband's private line. When I took over this office, I saw no need to have it changed.'

A visible wave of relief washed over the man. 'Yes, of course. You understand we are following the only lead we have.'

The phone number wasn't the only thing on the folded sheet of paper, but Karen had no desire to be questioned about the others. She stood up. 'Well, if I can help you no further, I'll ask my secretary to show you out.'

'Of course, Mrs de Lout. I have taken up enough of your valuable time. You won't be bothered again.'

She showed the inspector to the door and watched as Susan escorted him to the lift. When the secretary returned she said, 'Cancel all my appointments until tomorrow. I don't want to be disturbed.'

Karen slumped in her chair behind her desk, sick with guilt and feeling entirely responsible for the poor man's death. The other items on Pearson's note seemed to chase each other round her head. *Watch those close to you.*

Beware the Leopard. U235. Valley 1000. Reflecting shield. Hot and Cells. What on earth did it all mean? Some intuition told her it was imperative she found out before it was too late. But how? And too late for what?

CHAPTER 23

The morning was still and clear, the dew quickly evaporating as the sun pitched over the eastern horizon.

'Hell, this is even worse than the early morning runs,' Dave grunted. Sammy was chirping a few metres away, harassing him into greater effort.

Dave squatted on his haunches in front of the huge round boulder, the thick corded muscles in his forearms bulging. With all his considerable strength, he lifted the rock onto his bent knees, beads of moisture leaping out as his face clenched into determined concentration. His knees creaked, and he threw his back and buttocks into the lift. With his mouth open in a soundless cry, he slowly straightened his powerful legs. Below his shorts, his tanned skin quivered and twitched as his leg muscles forced the gigantic weight upwards.

'Come on, you great heap of heaving muscle, run, run faster to other end of clearing.' Sammy did a little jig beside Dave as he staggered in a fast walk towards the trees.

This was Dave's new morning exercise. They still occasionally ran to the other end of the station, but it was now pretty infrequent. There was little imagination involved; the exercise consisted of man-handling each rock from one end of the makeshift pistol range to the other. Sammy had helped build Dave's stamina, now he was working on his strength.

There had been quite a row when Dave had suggested five rocks instead of four. When he dropped the fifth rock in line with the others, Sammy had hopped up and down in anger, but knew Dave had won.

Dave's daily routine had changed drastically since the arrival of the information on the forthcoming mission. He spent the mornings with Sammy, refining and honing his fitness and physical skills, and although Sammy never said a word, Dave knew the little Asian was impressed. In the afternoons and evenings he locked himself away in his room. Sammy would respectfully knock and leave trays of food outside his door. This pattern had continued unbroken for six weeks.

Dave was in his element; working alone, he unravelled the financial structures, assessed the key personnel and probed for weaknesses of the huge corporation he would help bring to its knees. Most of the information he needed was on computer disk, the rest as photographs and layouts of the company plants and buildings. Not for the first time, Dave marvelled at the extent and complexity of Vulcan's resources. He wondered if the company knew this much about itself.

Dave leaned back in his chair and whistled; he'd finally figured it out. With the data Network had supplied and what he'd received from Vulcan, he had been able to piece together a hugely detailed picture of the company.

'Somebody's taking you for a ride.' Dave spoke aloud, and looked up guiltily at the window. But there was no one around to hear.

He went back to the keyboard and began tapping the keys. It would only take him a few days to recheck; he was sure he was right, but he had to be certain. It would probably have a major bearing on his mission. Other people's weaknesses were strengths that Dave could use against them.

On the surface, it appeared Vulcan had supplied him with everything he needed. It was the additional data from Network that made the difference; without both sets of information, he would never have spotted the discrepancies. Comparing the detailed financial statements from each source revealed that huge amounts of cash was being siphoned from the European and North American interests. Dave's next question was where was it going to? Something very odd was going on at de Lout Investments.

It was in the middle of the afternoon, and Dave was making far greater progress than he had anticipated. Then something alerted him, and his fingers fell motionless. There was a faint vibration, not yet a noise. He grabbed the semi-automatic, locked his room and ran out into the middle of the pistol range. He stood motionless, the pistol dangling at his side, scanning the pale blue sky.

He caught a flash of movement to his side. In a blink he had extended his arm, the gun pointing at the middle of Sammy's chest.

'Move and you die.' His voice was steady and his eyes were still fixed on the horizon.

Sammy stood still as a statue; Dave's deliberate manner told him the big man was serious. He had seen the same look in his eye briefly several weeks before, when he had nearly pushed Dave too far. For the first time in many years Sammy had actually experienced fear. And now here it was again.

Dave could hear it now; his acute hearing homed in on a faint speck in the far distance. A light aircraft was coming in from the north. As it approached the whine of its engine rose and fell, distorted by the gentle breeze.

When he was sure it was flying directly at the complex, he flicked the pistol barrel at Sammy. 'Move. Inside, and stay away from the windows.'

Left alone in the small clearing, he tucked the pistol inside his belt and at the last possible moment darted for cover as the aircraft roared overhead.

He watched from the shadows thrown by the blue gums as the plane departed. He was sure the pilot must have seen him. He wondered why he had miscalculated.

Dave's room looked like the advance planning headquarters for a war. Little of the original walls still showed; stuck to the asbestos sheets were photographs, diagrams and schemes. If the directors of de Lout Investments had seen the amount of detail displayed there, they would have been horrified. There was no way they could counter everything Dave had planned to destabilise their company.

One facet of Vulcan's research that wasn't included in Network's were detailed personnel reports on all of the key executives. Two names stood out: Karen and Peter de Lout. If one or both of these were neutralised, the whole empire might not fall right away, but the ensuing uncertainty would create enormous cracks in the company's normally solid foundations. There must have been previous attempts to undermine the corporation's structure; for instance, Dave didn't believe for a moment Tom de Lout's death was accidental.

Dave picked up the letter that had accompanied the information on de Louts. One passage stood out: *It is required that you use whatever means necessary to place de Lout Investments in an uncompromising position, so a takeover of all its assets and resources may be orchestrated.*

Once this had happened, the unsuspecting company would hold the key to the power structure of the world.

Dave put the letter aside and looked up at a photograph on the wall. 'Karen de Lout,' he murmured. He already felt he knew her well; she was the real key to his mission, he was sure. 'Will I have to destroy you along with your company,' he mused, 'or will you give me the answers I need?'

In the package of information on de Louts was a large black and white photograph. Karen was staring defiantly at the camera. It was a head and shoulders shot, with her hair pulled severely back from her face. The face was clear and strong, with high cheek bones; her chin jutted forward. A striking face, with eyes that drew his attention. The lids were slightly hooded, and suggested a keen intelligence, and something more besides.

'What are you trying to hide?' Dave whispered, tapping his lower lip. He hadn't met the woman and yet already knew she had weaknesses. But what were they?

He had decided on his strategy.

CHAPTER 24

The moment of truth. 'Come in, Johnny, and close the door.'

'What is it, Richard? You look a little on edge.' Concern was carved across Johnny's face.

Well, either you're a damn good actor, or I've done you one hell of an injustice, Richard thought.

Richard reached for his letter opener and slit the letter he was holding. It had been re-addressed from a PO Box in Perth, Western Australia. With a certain amount of trepidation, he drew the contents from the envelope and scanned the pages. He relaxed and blew out a sigh of relief. Johnny was clean.

Richard felt foolish for ever doubting him. He looked up guiltily at the faithful man in front of him, still peering at him with concern. What could he say? How could he tell him about the trap he had set?

He found his voice, and said humbly, 'OK, you can go now.'

Johnny stood for a moment, clearly puzzled, then he shrugged and left the room. Richard sighed, letting the tension flow out of his shoulders, then smoothed out the report before him. It had been laboriously typed on a portable typewriter, and some of the words were smudged and blurred. It was the name at the bottom that first caught his attention. Scotty McLeod, Katanning, Western Australia.

The few pages were quite detailed, but one paragraph in the middle was of special interest to Richard. *The only addition of any note to my previous recce of Wemyss Estate several months ago was a row of five large boulders in the clearing beside the shearers' quarters. I also noticed a tall, sandy-haired, well-built man run for cover just before I passed overhead.* So Dave was alive and well. Another sigh of relief. Two pieces of good news, then: the leak hadn't originated from his organisation and Johnny, or Dave wouldn't have been seen alive.

The thing that worried him was where the devil it was coming from.

The five boulders rather intrigued Richard; he was glad his telegram to McLeod had instructed him to report on *all* changes and irregularities.

On Richard's brief visit to Australia not long ago, he had ended up for a number of days in Perth. Without Johnny knowing, Dave was able to pass a message to him, summoning him to the Western Australian capital. It had been tricky to lose the trackers who followed him from Heathrow, but he'd managed to give them the slip.

He had booked into at a budget hotel in Perth – budget being the kindest word – and registered under an assumed name. He had met briefly with Dave, who told him how he would get the location of his training camp to him: the aerogram technique. It was up to Richard and his contacts to find him, so he could pass on information about his mission for Vulcan.

Between the two of them they had worked out ten of the most likely candidates; de Lout Investments was number five. Dave would need to find a way to communicate from the training camp, and let Richard know which company he was instructed to infiltrate.

Richard remembered the conversation well. They were sitting in a cramped, sparsely furnished hotel room with a single bed, a night-stand and nothing more.

'Well, how the hell do I do that?' Dave had asked, throwing his hands up in bewilderment.

'I'm sure you'll find a way. Just put up the appropriate number of markers to indicate which company it is. I don't know, cut down ten trees if you have to.'

'Huh,' Dave had snorted. But Richard knew he would find a way.

'So it's de Louts.' Richard walked through to the computer room, where Johnny was ensconced as usual, bent over a keyboard peering at the screen before him. 'Update everything we've got on de Lout Investments, worldwide, as quickly as you can, please.'

Johnny raised a hand, still staring at the screen. Richard knew it would be on his desk in next to no time. 'Also, have we heard from Oechsli yet?'

'Not a whisper.'

'Hell, that's nearly two months now. Put out a priority message to all the watchers, circulate his photograph. I want to know what he's up to.'

Richard returned to his own office and stared up at the map of the world he had just pinned on the wall. He would need to share his thoughts with somebody at this delicate stage of the operation, and who better than Johnny? Another reason to be relieved he wasn't the source of the leak.

It was a detailed map with a number of pins embedded in it, to represent the main players in the operation. The most prominent pin, a bright red one, was in the south-west corner of Western Australia. It was the key to the success of the mission. Oechsli's pin had yet to find a home; Richard was sorely tempted to place it right in the middle of London, though heaven knew why. Ferkatovich's was placed firmly in Moscow; Richard had heard from him regularly for the past couple of months.

He had just finished shading in all the countries that had either wound down trade with Britain or were proposing to introduce tariffs when Johnny brought through the updated material on de Louts.

He whistled. As he scanned the pages. 'Trade restraints, huh. Hell, half the world is covered.'

It was an exaggeration, but only slightly. Richard stood back and stared at the map again. 'No, it doesn't look good. The PM is rather concerned; quite frankly the balance of trade looks pretty sick. There's a hell of a lot riding on us.'

'Those assassinations were a bit of a turning point.'

Richard swung around and stared at Johnny. 'Was it that obvious?'

'You had your reasons for not confiding in me. But I've been in this game just as long as you.'

Richard felt another stab of guilt. He would probably have made a lot more progress if he had trusted Johnny. Oh well, what was past was past.

'Hey, a thought has just occurred to me.' Johnny pushed past Richard and gazed up at the map, his eyes twinkling. 'I'd have to check it, though.'

'Come on, Johnny, give.' Richard knew that expression too well. Johnny would lead him a merry dance if he was given half the chance.

'I can't be sure—' which meant he was pretty positive '—but while you've been putting this together, I noticed their strongest subsidiary companies are in the countries you've shaded.' He waved the thick de Louts dossier in his hand.

It was Richard's turn to push past his colleague to stare at the map. 'That has just added a completely new dimension to this operation.'

'You mean it places much more emphasis on the Leopard succeeding. All the same, I'd better do some more research on those subsidiaries.'

Richard breathed deeply and closed his eyes. Yes, it was good to have his confidant back. Johnny's perceptiveness would be vital if they were to succeed. And most of that success would be in the hands of Dave Old: the Leopard.

It had been a surprisingly mild night for February in London all those years before.

Richard had just boarded the underground at Earls Court.

He was in the middle of investigating the apparent suicide of a British member of Parliament in Miami Beach, Florida. It looked as if John Stonehouse had killed himself after allegations of theft and forgery. But there was no trace of his body, and Network had been unable to come up with any leads.

Just as the automatic doors were closing, a big sandy-haired man slipped into the compartment, holding a large manilla envelope. Though the carriage was nearly empty, he sat down beside Richard, but seemed to ignore him. As the train glided into the next stop, the big man rose from his seat and placed the envelope on Richard's lap. He didn't look back as he stepped onto the platform and left the station.

Richard was dumbfounded at the casual way the information had been passed to him. He began to wonder if the man had been a figment of his imagination; but no, there was the envelope, lying on his lap. Normally he wouldn't have opened it until he had returned to base, but his curiosity got the better of him.

Inside the envelope was every detail of the investigation he was currently running, with one major difference: it included the current location of the MP who was presumed dead. Within a month John Stonehouse was arrested in Australia on charges of theft and forgery.

This was Richard's first contact with the man he came to know as the Leopard. It worried him initially that he might have been exposed; until that night he had been quite confident that no other security organisations in the world knew of his existence. He carried the nagging doubt with him for some time, but as it turned out, the fear was unfounded.

Richard would have loved to call the Leopard his agent, but the man, who years later introduced himself as Dave Old, worked with him and Network only when he chose.

Until the current operation, he had known little of Old's past beyond his exceptional results. At times, however, he suspected Dave had accepted the mission for personal reasons. He hoped he was wrong but even if the man's motives were questionable, Richard was sure the bond they had developed over the years, coupled with the enormous fee he was charging, was enough to ensure Dave remained on the side of the angels.

Inside Charing Cross Station, Richard opted not to take the Underground;

he was sure he was being followed. Before he left the station, he made a quick call at a payphone, then ran up the steps out onto the Strand, into the bustle of the city. He had no trouble hailing a cab, and as he settled down in the back, he was satisfied he had shaken off the tracker.

'Where to, guv?' the cabby inquired.

'Turnham Green Tube station, please.'

As the taxi pulled out, something alerted Richard to a man with a limp who was making surprisingly good speed towards another taxi he had hailed. No matter, Richard thought, settling back to enjoy the ride; plenty of time to worry about that when he left the cab.

He had first noticed the man with the limp as he passed South Africa House on the Strand. He had lengthened his stride without appearing to increase his speed, and when the other man maintained the same distance behind him, he was sure he was being followed.

His black cab pulled in beside the entrance to Turnham Green station. A stream of early evening commuters was pouring out onto the pavement. This was panning out even better than Richard had hoped.

He paid off the taxi and was reaching for his change, when the cabby spoke. 'None of my business, guv'nor, but we've been followed ever since we left Charing Cross. He's stopped just up the terrace.'

Richard had noticed the cabby's quick eyes in his rear-vision mirror. 'Probably just a coincidence,' he said offhandedly. 'Thanks all the same, squire.' He left before the cabby had time to reply and walked into the station.

The last of the commuters had trickled out of the station. He flicked his Travelcard at the bored attendant and turned towards the stairs, throwing a casual glance down the exit lane. The man with the limp was entering the station. At the top of the stairs, he turned back on himself and walked to the far end of the platform, which was virtually deserted. He pulled his hat down over his eyes and flicked up the collar of his overcoat; it was quite chilly up here at rooftop level; the Underground had long ago left its warren of tunnels.

From his vantage point he was able to observe unnoticed as his shadow stepped onto the platform. The man casually looked around; he reminded Richard of somebody, but he couldn't think who: unusual, as Richard rarely forgot a face.

The man had not spotted him yet, but he caught a brief glimpse of fiercely hypnotic eyes. Now he knew exactly who his shadow was. Interesting, he thought.

A train pulled in and disgorged a surge of bodies Richard waited until the last of the them had disembarked before boarding, and didn't bother looking for a seat; he was getting off at the next stop.

Minutes later the train glided into Chiswick Park. Out of the corner of his eye he noticed the other man leave the train in his wake. Right, he thought, let's see how good you are.

He walked back toward Turnham Green, his gait loose and slightly slumped, to make him look shorter. As he turned onto Chiswick High Road, he could feel the man behind him. Opposite Town Hall Avenue, he stopped, and peered into the entrance of a shop. He looked left and right, and entered.

The limping man was suspicious, but he'd come too far to lose his quarry now. He quickened his pace, and no sooner had he stumbled a couple of paces than his target reappeared in front of him.

With the hat still pulled low over his eyes and the collar of his overcoat hugging his ears, the target swiftly crossed the road and followed a path to the far side of the green, where he stopped and sat down on a park bench., The limping man was mystified; what was he doing? All he could do was sit on an adjacent bench and wait.

Richard grinned from his vantage point in the shop doorway. Good call, phoning Johnny from Charing Cross. Years behind a desk makes you rusty, he thought, looking at the man with the limp.

He duplicated Johnny's route and sat down on the bench beside his shadow. 'I like your new attire, Brendan. It suits you.'

Brendan Oechsli's head snapped around, his piercing eyes riveted on Richard's face. Was it shock or pure rage that registered in his eyes? Richard couldn't tell; the glimmer was extinguished as swiftly as it appeared.

'I knew you were good, Richard, but I honestly thought I had you beat.' Brendan removed his tattered old coat and wig and dumped them in a nearby rubbish bin at the green. His clothes underneath were surprisingly neat and tidy.

Richard gestured 'all clear, stand down' to Johnny, and led the way to a pub on the edge of the green. He bought drinks at the bar, and they moved to a secluded corner table, away from the band playing quietly and the locals who had stopped in for an evening pint.

'Never did get used to this warm, flat beer of yours, 'Brendan said, peering into his glass.

127

Richard remained silent, waiting for the Deputy Director of the CIA to tell him why he'd followed him.

Oechsli looked up. 'This leak.' He threw his hands in the air. 'The President's right down my throat. I just don't know who to trust. For the last couple of months, I've even been spying on my own guys, and no go, can't dig up a thing.' He shook his head in disgust and looked directly at Richard. 'I'm not gonna spy on Ferkatovich on his turf, am I? So you're the next best thing. First I had to locate your base. I must say you've done one hell of a job of concealing it.'

'Thank you for your honesty. If it helps, I have just proved the leak's not from my organisation.'

'The Russians, then?' Brendan raised an eyebrow. 'What do you think?'

'Brendan, I have no more idea than you do. We each need to cover our own backs. We've got to trust each other, and the Russian too.'

'Yeah, yeah, but who do we usually blame for this sort of crap? Goes against the grain working with them.' He shook his head again.

Richard took a sip of his bitter as he considered what Brendan had just said. But before he could draw any conclusion, the American asked his next question. 'How's your boy doing on the inside?' He leant forward, his brow heavy with concern.

Richard's antennae twitched. That question didn't sound right. 'Could be dead for all I know. Lost contact with him around the time of our last meeting.'

'I hope to hell he's not, a lot's riding on this boy of yours.'

To Richard the American's concern didn't ring true, but he couldn't pinpoint why so he let it go. 'What's your next move?' he asked instead. 'We've got to force Vulcan into some sort of mistake. He must be vulnerable somewhere.'

'Come on, Richard, we both know those assassinations in Europe mean he's got us by the short and curlies. I'm baffled, and I'm doing the only thing left to me; I'm staying in the field until this is resolved one way or another.'

But what are you really up to? Richard thought as he finished his pint. You'll bear watching, and at least I've got the teams to do it.

CHAPTER 25

The training and planning stage was over. At times in the last two weeks it appeared even Sammy's strenuous exercise programme was unable to slake Dave's thirst for physical exertion. It wasn't that his body could take limitless physical punishment; rather, a combination of sheer pig-headedness and mental control that allowed him to endure the gruelling regime. Both Sammy and Dave himself judged he was ready.

He was standing in the laundry beside an old coal-burning boiler, watching the flames caress the twisting sheaves of paper he'd thrown in. He squinted as a burst of heat wafted skyward and the reflection of the flames danced like playful demons around his eyes. He threw in the last of the information he'd compiled since his arrival months before. It was time to leave.

The walls of his room were bare, the only evidence the tatty bits of sticky-tape left behind when he cleared them. The computer stood in the corner, the screen staring into the empty room. Dave's bags were packed, the mattress folded in two on top of the metal cot; the room was as he had found it.

Sammy was leaning against the old HQ Holden. Collin was slumped behind the wheel; like a will-o'-the-wisp, he had reappeared to take them back to Perth. As they wended through the archway of eucalyptus trees, neither Dave nor Sammy looked back.

It took five and a half hours to reach Perth International Airport. For most of the trip Dave and Collin were silent, but as usual Sammy chattered away like a playful monkey, never expecting a reply, conveying his joy at being alive.

In the airport car park, Collin handed Sammy and Dave their tickets. Dave's was a return to Johannesburg, Sammy's a direct flight to Honolulu. Not for the first time, Dave grudgingly acknowledged Vulcan's superior planning; he had just over an hour to check in and board the flight to Africa.

Inside the airport terminal Sammy never left Dave's side; if there had been a chance to pass on information, Sammy would have done his best to prevent it or at the very least reported his actions.

They walked up to the South African Airways counter, and Dave presented his ticket and passport.

As the attendant completed the formalities, Dave began to flick through Perth's daily newspaper, the *West Australian*, starting at the back and casually thumbing through the pages.

When the ticketing procedure was complete, he closed the paper and left it as he'd found it. Sammy was none the wiser, but that cursory act had told him Richard Black now knew of his destination and his mission; confirmation delivered courtesy of a cryptically worded classified ad Richard had placed in the paper.

Tickets and passport in hand, Dave made his way towards the departure lounge.

At the entrance he stopped and placed a friendly hand on Sammy's shoulder, and said with a smile in his eyes, 'Good journey, my friend, and I hope we meet again.'

Sammy bobbed his head, and with a beaming smile he watched his finest protégé disappear.

CHAPTER 26

'I'm fully aware of the implications, Comrade,' Uri Ferkatovich bellowed, 'but I won't let a bunch of half-wits jeopardise this operation.'

'In all fairness, Comrade Ferkatovich, I feel calling our best agents half-wits is a little harsh.' Vladimir Beria, Ferkatovich's deputy, was one of the few people in Moscow who could talk to him like this without fear of retribution.

Beria looked more like a banker than deputy to the Head of the First Chief Directorate of the Committee of State Security. His fine crop of dusky hair was swept back across his head, and he always wore a slight frown, though his eyes were alert and clear. The intelligent head on top of his narrow shoulders had taken him to a highly respected position in the KGB. He was of average height, but beside Uri he looked tiny. He tried to shrink still further at his superior's next onslaught.

'Harsh? You say harsh!' Uri yelled even more loudly. 'You call the fiasco with the UDF a well-run operation? By all that is sacred, man, we are losing control. They have given us no productive leads whatsoever on Vulcan.' He paced heavily back and forth across his office, emphasising each point by crashing a beefy fist into the other palm. Uri appeared not a happy man.

The Head of the First Chief Directorate of the KGB's office was on the second floor of the twenty-two storey headquarters, in the south-west of Moscow in Yasenevo. It was a spacious office by Russian standards, but modestly furnished by choice. The walls were lined with maps from all over the world, each with shaded areas indicating which of Uri's twenty departments was responsible for them.

His deputy sat awkwardly in one of the uncomfortable wooden chairs in front of the large wooden desk, his body twisted around to watch his superior. He tried another tack. 'If you became involved with this mission yourself you could easily be recognised, with disastrous consequences.' He raised his hands in a gesture of appeal.

Uri wasn't listening. 'Beria, how long had we been nurturing our relations with the UDF? One year, two? And this, this Vulcan, whips them out from under our nose. First trade restraints, now this; it was the only high point that we had to focus on.'

Beria forged on. 'Again, Comrade, with all due respect, it appears it was Vulcan who turned them into a political force in the first place. However, I believe all is not lost, we can repair the damage.'

'Forever the optimist aren't you, Comrade,' Uri said scornfully. 'While that Dutchman, Van der Zwet, is terrorising those natives we haven't a hope. And don't give me your crap about neutralising him; somebody would take his place, even if your dim-witted agents could get close to him.' He stopped to turn an icy stare on his assistant. 'Did you hear what he did? Right between the eyes, in front of everybody. No, Comrade, the only course of action left is to find Vulcan and destroy him.'

'But Comrade, that's what we have operatives for. It's not your job.' Beria rose from his chair and faced Uri. He had to stop him; if anything happened to his superior, he would be held responsible, and Siberia wouldn't do much for his promotion prospects.

Uri appeared not to have heard him again. He turned and stared out of the window at the massive head of Lenin on a granite block overlooking an ornamental lake and the gardens. 'What of Vulcan's other operative, the Leopard? With him and the Dutchman on the rampage, things will only get worse.'

At least this time Beria felt confident he had some good news. 'We suspect he is dead. There has been no word of him for over two years now. I think we can safely assume we won't be bothered by him again.'

Uri swung around and raised an eyebrow 'Really? I'm glad to hear such confidence.'

Did the chief know more than he was letting on? If he did, how, for goodness sake?

Uri was speaking again, planning his movements. 'Going in through Angola then down through Namibia will be my best route.' He flopped down in the ancient swivel chair behind his desk and looked dispassionately at his deputy.

Long ago he had taken an active role in this current operation, something he was sure Beria knew nothing about. But now things were moving into a critical stage, it was time he involved himself on the ground again. But he needed to cover his back in case things went wrong. He actually liked Beria, but this wouldn't be the first time he'd used somebody he liked as a scapegoat. Sentiment certainly hadn't got him where he was today.

'Draft my order of release and countersign it,' he ordered.

Beria was appalled. He certainly didn't want the Head of the KGB's First Chief Directorate taking needless risks, and he saw no good reason for the chief to embark on active service. Having to countersign his order for release made it far worse than he'd imagined. Beria slumped down in his chair and stared dully at the man who was supposed to secure his prosperous future, not mark him for life.

He realised Uri had been staring at him for many seconds, and said the first thing that came to mind. 'Why Africa? Surely Europe would be a better place to start, what with the trade embargoes?'

'I feel it in my bones. Africa, more precisely South Africa, is the key to the success of this operation.' Uri rubbed his hands together. 'As you are aware, our grasp on Africa appears to be slipping away, but I ask you who is the real architect behind this slide?' He didn't wait for an answer. 'Some would say it's the CIA, others the South Africans. But let's consider what has recently happened in the last few years, especially in the light of the subtle shift of power throughout the rest of the world.' Uri licked his lips. 'Three African countries we had within our grasp; one is lost, the other two slipping away.'

He walked over to the map of Southern Africa and stabbed the three countries with a meaty finger. 'Angola, Mozambique, Zimbabwe.' He began pacing the office again. 'Firstly, Angola. We installed the MLPA as the legitimate government there, with Agostinho Neto as president after the end of Portuguese rule. What happens?' Uri threw both hands in the air. 'Neto dies, and all of a sudden we find a once uncoordinated bunch of Angolans, UNITA, has established solid control in the south of the country. Even with Cuban troops present. I ask you, where did the financial backing and organisation come from all of a sudden?'

He shoved two sausage-like fingers at his deputy's and face. 'Secondly, Mozambique. We put in Samora Machel as president and his crowd, what are they called again?' He flicked his fingers impatiently.

'FRELIMO.' Beria was fascinated by Uri's astute reasoning. 'The Marxist Front for...'

'Yes, yes.' Uri waved his hand for silence. 'And what happens there? The economy is in ruins, the legal system and local government in disarray. But we find another splinter group, RENAMO or whatever they are called, gaining control. Sound familiar?' He stopped in the middle of the room and combed his fingers through his thick hair.

'Are you saying, Comrade, that this has been co-ordinated by...'

'In a minute, Beria.' Uri held up three fingers. 'Thirdly, Zimbabwe. We were correct to back Joshua Nkomo and his ZAPU party during the bush war in Rhodesia, but what happens after we have poured years of support and arms into the struggle? I'll tell you. Robert fucking Mugabe and his ZANU party swept in. But I ask you, how did ZANU gain so much support and control? And how much help did the Chinese and Koreans really give him?' Uri sat down again and peered at Beria from under bushy eyebrows.

'Are saying Vulcan orchestrated all this?' Beria was on the edge of his seat.

'Theorising, that's all, and I haven't even mentioned the fiasco in Ethiopia. I've had my suspicions for some time. It's the speed, you see. One moment no sign at all, then all of a sudden a country, or as in Europe a market, is lost to us.' He stopped and folded his arms across his barrel chest. 'What you must understand is this: even though we poured over six and a half billion roubles into those African countries in arms alone, we still had to appear to abide by international laws no matter how ineffective they are. We also have a power structure here in Moscow we answer to, so progress can be slow. But somebody that is tied to no governing body can use whatever means suits their end. Beria, I believe that is Vulcan.

'Good lord, Comrade, if that is the case, he could be taking over control of the world. But with what aim?'

'Two of the most powerful motives in the world: *greed and power*. Now, do you see why I am a little concerned at the lack of progress from our agents?'

'I take your point. I never suspected Vulcan had such deep historical roots, or was turning into such an enormous problem.'

'And that, Comrade, is why I'm here and you're there.'

Beria pretended not to hear the dig. 'So the same pattern has emerged with the UDF. One moment we have them, the next they're gone.'

'Precisely, and that's why I believe everything points to South Africa. Vulcan is planning something big down there. That's why I need to be there without anybody knowing. He has to be stopped.'

'What about the co-operation with the British and the Americans? Surely, they, well, shouldn't they know?' It was Beria's turn to pace the room.

'Maybe, maybe not. I believe this agreement we have with them may be the first of many. Remember the USSR wasn't a well country even before the trade restraints. I believe it can go one of three ways. Vulcan may succeed, and influence the world's power structure. Or we can destroy Vulcan with the help of our eager friends and be forced into a freer world.'

Beria had stopped, and was trying to say something. Uri held up a hand to silence him.

'Or lastly, we can find and destroy Vulcan ourselves and continue his crusade as our own, quickly and decisively achieving the domination that the KGB has always striven for.'

Beria was silent for many minutes as he sought to absorb the full implications of what his chief had laid out. It pained him to say it, but he had no choice. 'Now I understand, Comrade, why you're sitting there and I'm sitting here. When do you propose to leave?'

CHAPTER 27

He smelt the familiar aroma as soon as he stepped from the air-conditioned body of the Boeing 747. How many times had he arrived at Jan Smuts Airport and tried in vain to identify that elusive smell? Dave recognised it as the smell of Johannesburg; nowhere else in the world smelt quite the same. It wasn't offensive, but there was something unique about it; almond oil, mixed with the smell of industry? Or was it the highveld? Again, it eluded him.

Dave was one of the last to leave the aircraft. It had been a rather satisfying flight; the woman in the next seat had served a useful purpose. She was an Australian, travelling down to Cape Town to meet up with her fiancé, who had gone on ahead a month earlier.

Dave had been virtually celibate since he had gone back to his self-imposed exile in New Zealand; there was no opportunity to foster long-term relationships. At a personal level he felt the lack, though professionally it wouldn't make the slightest difference. But Dave always did what was necessary to achieve his objectives; remove emotion from the equation and anything was possible.

He looked down at the dark-haired woman walking beside him. She had linked her arm with his. and had indicated she hoped he would look after her for the night.

Once the 747 had left Perth Dave had found it quite easy to strike up a conversation with the woman; she had warmed to him from the onset. The conversation that flowed during the fourteen-hour flight had been entirely one-sided. Dave had learned a great deal about her: strengths and weaknesses, likes and dislikes. He had a number of reasons for choosing a woman to practise his indirect interrogation skills on. Women were generally more sensitive to subtle forms of deceit, and Dave intuitively knew Karen de Lout would be one of the most perceptive women he could ever choose to deceive. He had been out of action for so long that he felt he had to practise, if only to be sure he still was able to apply the delicate means of persuasion he'd been taught years ago. And what better target than an attractive woman, engaged to be married?

In the terminal building, instead of going through passport control right away, he disengaged her arm and said he would meet her on the other side. She shrugged as he walked up to the South African Airways counter, produced his French passport and asked the attendant to call security. Within five minutes he had been ushered away into a small, guarded interview room somewhere in the depths of the terminal building. With a certain amount of regret he knew he'd miss his date with the attractive Australian.

It took another five minutes before a short, brown-haired man walked in and closed the door behind him.

'Athol,' Dave greeted him.

'Man, have you caused a stir. Thank god you got the pilot to radio ahead. Damn, but it's good to see you, Bot.' Athol Jansen took a couple of paces towards Dave and shook his hand. 'I thought you were dead. Not a word for two years. What gives?' He may have been short, but Dave knew he had a heart like a lion and the muscle to match. The crooked nose and the pale scars weaving through his thick eyebrows showed that he had once been a boxer, and a good one. But the gold-rimmed glasses gave him a scholarly look.

'Your government hired me to track down Vulcan. I went one better and waited for him to come to me. I have more information on him now than I've ever had, even more than when I was supposed to be working for him.' Dave sat down and crossed his arms over his chest.

'What do you mean, *supposed to be?* You did more damage in those few years than I care to remember.' Shaking his head ruefully, Athol pulled up the only other chair in the small room.

'Look, Athol, the deal was my way or not at all.'

'OK, OK OK.' Athol held his hands up. 'I suppose you'll want a weapon?'

'No, you just make sure all the paperwork is in order. By the way, who else knows about me?' Dave asked.

'No one but me. I've had a hell of a job keeping your file alive this last year. The Minister isn't a happy man.'

Athol told him what resources were still at his disposal; as usual they amounted to next to nothing. That suited Dave; the less input he received from the South Africans, the fewer people would know he was there. He knew enough about Vulcan's influence to be sure that the country's national security service would have been breached.

'Athol, I'm going to have to bring you up to date with what I know, and why Vulcan hired me again. But first, I have to make a call.'

137

Dave reached over to the phone on the table and dialled a local number. When the call was connected, he swore softly; answerphone. He hated leaving any record of his activities, no matter how innocent they appeared to be. But needs must. He quickly left his message.

'Sandy, Dave Old. I'm at Jan Smuts. I'll be here for the next hour. Time 11:45pm. Otherwise, pick me up at the Holiday Inn tomorrow, early.' Dave broke the connection and looked at Athol. The South African looked rather sheepish.

'Sandy,' he said with a half-hearted laugh.

Dave grinned. 'Yeah, right. I take it, it was only Sandy that kept my file alive. So much for your faith in me.'

'Well, come on, man, it was two years, and Vulcan is resourceful. Even you are human. Do you know, she hassled me every week for those two years? Surely that's worth something.'

She heard the phone ringing, but it was like some sound way in the distance. All that mattered to her at that moment was to quench the fire that raged in her groin. Her denim shirt was unbuttoned to the navel, and one rose-tipped breast had escaped from the support of her bra. She tugged wildly at the man's jeans, soft frantic moans escaping her lips.

He was having a lot more success. She arched her back and lifted her buttocks, and he began to glide her jeans down over her narrow hips. The ringing stopped and the answerphone clicked on, and the voice that spoke penetrated the depth of her passion. She froze, though above her the man worked blindly on, oblivious.

'Sandy, Dave Old. I'm at Jan Smuts,' was all she heard.

With a hefty shove, Sandy dislodged the man. He fell, startled, on his backside, looking up at her like a child who had just dropped an ice-cream cone. She stood up, quickly zipped up her jeans and re-cupped her exposed breast, and began to herd him to the door.

'What the...'

'Go on, shoo, *voetsek*, out.'

He was spun around, and a hand heaved him through the open door.

'Don't call me, I'll call you,' were the last words he heard.

'So, where did you get to, anyway?' Athol asked, trying to break Dave's frosty mood.

Dave replied with a question of his own. 'Tell me, what happened in

Botswana with the UDP?' He leant forward and rested his chin in his hand.

'We still haven't quite figured it out, not that it really worried us,' came the answer. 'We can only surmise it was an inside job. But shit, we got a hell of a lot of unfavourable flak; most of the world's convinced we had him killed. Zamba was rather a prominent figure. Mind you, I don't think we're going to have too much trouble from the United Democratic Front until a new leader emerges.'

'On the contrary, if I don't succeed that's where all your worst nightmares will come from.'

'What's that supposed to mean? They're now in complete disarray, back to where they were a couple of years ago.' But a look of alarm flashed behind Athol's glasses.

'Athol, I can't prove it, but I believe Vulcan had him killed. The reason you hired me was because Vulcan was the author of the UDF's rise to prominence. We know he financed them and gave them direction. Whether you've pieced it all together or not, I'm telling you it's because his long-term aim is to install a puppet government here in South Africa, to create a secure base he can work from. He's covertly, and quite successfully, turned the UDP into a force the world recognises as stable enough to control your country's wealth.'

'Are you trying to say a takeover of South Africa is imminent?' Athol sat forward, pushing his glasses up onto the bridge of his nose.

Dave remained silent for many moments, assessing how much to tell the national security agent. 'I suppose it depends on what you mean by imminent.'

'Oh no,' Athol groaned. He'd learnt long ago it was unwise to second guess Dave. 'You'd better continue.'

'What came out of Vulcan's influence was a leader the rank and file of the UDF could respect and look up to. With finances, direction and leadership the organisation began to build momentum and outside support. They found there were other parties prepared to give them the same as Vulcan, but with fewer strings attached, so they tried to push Vulcan out. Believe it or not, this worked in his favour. It identified Zamba as the leader; killing him gave Vulcan an extraordinary opportunity to brand the organisation as his own once and for all, while neutralising the only significant opposition.'

'Hence the cold-blooded way it was done,' Athol chipped in.

'Precisely. I'm even pretty sure I know who did it.' He held up a hand as Athol began to ask who. 'No, I can't tell you. I need him back in the country.'

'OK, let me get this straight. Vulcan's now got the UDF in the palm of his hand, their Inner Circle being some sort of government in exile for the republic, right?'

Dave nodded.

'But how the hell is he going to get rid of the current government? Our national security, army and even our balance of trade are stronger than they've been in years.'

'Exactly. South Africa is one of the few western countries that hasn't been affected adversely by the worldwide trade restraints. It also has every necessary resource and mineral, bar one – oil. And you already make half of what you need from coal. South Africa is virtually self-sufficient, except in oil. But once a government that is acceptable to the world is in place, even that will no longer be a problem.'

He paused briefly. 'Athol, what could be a better country to use as a springboard from which to dominate the rest of the world? I have no idea how he's going to dislodge the government, but you can be sure it'll be well planned and totally effective.'

Athol just shook his head, dismay engraved on his face as he started to appreciate the magnitude of the problem. He and his superiors had always known about Vulcan, but they hadn't really believed his activities would affect South Africa. They viewed the current happenings in the rest of the world with little more than a passing interest. Their balance of trade was steadily increasing, and they had one of the finest security organisations in the world. Vulcan's activities had always seemed far removed.

Admittedly, he'd been a minor problem in their neighbouring countries, but it was only when he helped turn the UDF into a formidable force that his actions became any kind of threat. That threat was the reason Dave's services had been secretly engaged. But what Dave was now saying showed Athol that South Africa had been lulled into a false sense of security.

Dave was speaking again.

'Something else you need to be aware of: with the economies of the western world and the USSR on shaky ground, South Africa will be able to dictate the price of gold. Athol, what are the world's currencies based on?' There was no need for Athol to answer. He went on, 'Also, Britain has over four billion dollars in investments in South Africa, and the United States about three billion. Another source of instant wealth if those investments were nationalised. Can you see why it's so important to destroy Vulcan, before he destroys us all?'

Both men fell silent. Dave knew Athol had begun to grasp the extent of Vulcan's plans, but he needed him to comprehend the masterful intellect behind those plans.

Athol shook his head as if trying to clear his mind. 'OK, Dave, so why are you here? That has to be the key to his plan.'

Dave wasn't yet prepared to answer that. 'Tell me this. If you were setting out to execute such an enormous plan, how would you go about it?'

Athol stared towards the ceiling and bit his lip. 'I suppose I'd use a well-known organisation with offshoots throughout the world. But surely that would be the tricky part? I can't see any of the big subversive organisations being willing to work together.'

'Organisation? Or company?' Dave asked. 'Truthfully, how many terrorists have achieved long-term results in the past?'

'None.'

'But use another form of terrorism, the economic kind, and the effects are far more debilitating and long-term.'

Athol blew out a long breath. This was turning into a nightmare.

'Which South African company has huge vested interests in southern Africa, and solid foundations throughout the rest of the world as well?'

Dave barely had to wait for the answer. Athol tapped his hand on the table. 'De Louts... Oh god, is that why you are here? Is it de Louts you are after?'

'Exactly. Vulcan wants de Louts undermined. He wants to bring their leadership down, so he can take over the corporation.' He stabbed a determined finger at the South African's chest. 'If that's what I have to do to get him, I'll do it. Remember, my way or not at all.'

Dave and Athol spent the next half-hour or so talking around the complications and intricacies of the mission and the problems it would entail. Dave had already decided on a course of action and intended to stick with his decision; he'd just spent months planning it, after all. At one stage Athol blurted out in exasperation, 'You could be wrong.' But deep down he knew Dave was right; he just felt trapped.

'Look, sunshine, if you want me to get close to Vulcan, this is the only way. I can leave the way I came; the choice is yours.'

'Yeah, OK. Without you we would never have come this far, and what's more, we would've blundered into a trap that was obviously set years ago. All I want is to make sure de Louts is the best option.'

'We've been through it. Take it or leave it.' Dave spread out his hands, palms upwards.

Before the South African was able to answer, angry shouts carried from the corridor outside. A woman's voice penetrated the ruckus.

'Touch me, buster, and you'll be sorry.' A meaty blow, followed by a painful yelp.

Dave's first thought was that the Australian woman had come to find him. The next outburst told him exactly who it was. Athol was at the door, and wrenched it open.

'You self-righteous prig, get your paws off me.'

A tall, slim, blonde-haired woman in her late twenties, dressed in denims, was beating a uniformed security guard with a night-stick she'd obviously relieved him of. He cowered under a rain of blows as he backed down the corridor.

'Oh my god,' Athol whispered, then bellowed, 'Stop that this instant.'

The woman's arm stopped in mid-air and she looked startled, like a child caught in mischief.

'I'll handle this, thank you, Sergeant,' Athol said, dismissing the security guard. He looked at the woman. 'Give him back his stick, Miss Thomson.'

With a huff the woman handed back the guard's stick and stood in front of Athol with her arms folded, one slender hip thrust out and her head cocked to the side. He had moved out into the corridor, and Dave had stepped back into the interrogation room out of sight.

'Is there some way I can help you?' Athol asked.

'I know you've got him here somewhere, and I'm not leaving until I've seen him.'

Athol moved to the side and Dave stepped from the interrogation room.

'Hello, Sandy. Having fun, are we?'

Her whole posture changed. She stretched out her arms, gave an excited hop and launched herself at him.

Dave was acutely aware of her supple body pressed tightly against him. The Australian I could've handled, but this is a little too close to home, he thought.

'Come on, Sandy, you'd think I'd come back from the dead.' Dave had to use surprising force to break her stranglehold.

As Dave untwined her powerful arms from around his neck, she deliberately looked over at Athol, who was watching the spectacle with undisguised amusement. She said, 'At least one of us knew he was alive, right, Captain Jansen?' Her stare cut him to the bone. 'Also, before I forget,

Dave, ask him when the last deposit was transferred into your account.' Athol lost his grin.

'OK, Sandy, I think we'd better be going.' She still had a firm hold of his upper arm and wasn't letting go. He turned to Athol and raised an eyebrow. 'Well?'

'The money will be deposited tomorrow.'

'I take it you agree to my terms?'

Athol threw his hands in the air. 'What choice do I have?'

'I'll be in touch. We'd better not be seen together. Come on, Sandy.'

As they began to walk away, Sandy caught Athol's eye. With a haughty flick of her head she huffed and turned away, looking up adoringly at the big man.

Athol heard Dave say in a resigned voice, 'Don't look at me like that, and let go of my arm.'

With a look of undisguised delight, Sandy impishly pressed up closer still.

CHAPTER 28

The nightmares had started again in earnest. He was consumed with dread, his whole body drenched in a cold clammy sweat. He trembled violently with every terrified scream, and only woke when a gentle, soothing hand touched his shoulder.

Dave's haunted eyes snapped open, his body taut, ready to strike out at the demons. He sat bolt upright in bed, recognising Sandy just in time; the killer punch flew high and wide of her anxious face.

'Hush, now,' she lulled. She retrieved the towel he had left at the foot of the bed and gently pushed him down. He fell back unresisting, and she began to dab the moisture from his scar-ravaged torso.

Despite his harrowed state, Dave couldn't help noticing her firm, striking form. Then, like a malaria victim racked with fever, another fit of trembling gripped his exhausted body.

Eventually Sandy rolled him on his side and pulled up the duvet. She looked down at him with concern and bit her lip. She had always known him as a strong, independent man, but now all she saw was a tormented figure consumed by a private hell he had chosen never to share. Her heart felt about to break; all she could do for him was use her own body to provide some comfort.

She lifted the duvet and slipped in behind him. Her warmth shocked him, but her stroking fingers began to quieten his over-active mind. How long had it been? he thought. Certainly not since he left New Zealand. The complete exhaustion he experienced in Australia had ensured his body was too weary.

No one else knew the reason for the nightmares that had plagued him for so many years. Some mornings he would wake totally drained, the few hours of untroubled sleep he had managed quite unable to counteract the mental exhaustion.

His mother and Sandy were the only people aware of his ordeals; they both knew how to wake him from the horror and soothe him back to sleep. For this alone he was infinitely grateful, but he hated himself for the wounds to his soul. Vulcan had caused the wounds, and in so doing had created a dangerous enemy.

When Dave woke in the grey half-light of dawn, he was alone. He dressed and walked into the kitchen, where Sandy was already busy.

Yesterday evening Sandy had taken him straight from Jan Smuts Airport to the house he owned in a suburb of Johannesburg. She had looked after the house and his office in his absence. Dave had spent a lot of time in southern Africa, and the continent had got into his blood. Despite the night's ordeal, it felt good to be back again.

'You've been training for a mission,' Sandy accused. 'You're in the best physical shape I've seen for years.'

Dave perched himself on one of the stools at the breakfast bar.

'How's business been since I've been away?' he asked.

'Fine, no thanks to you,' Sandy said. She turned placed a bowl of fresh fruit in front of him, a mischievous grin on her face.

Dave recognised that look. Either disaster was imminent, or she had performed one of her feats of business wizardry. 'OK, what the hell have you done this time?'

She laid his current financial statement next to the bowl of fruit, and he breathed a sigh of relief. At least he wasn't bankrupt; in fact, he was surprisingly solvent. He quickly flicked through the report, which Sandy must have compiled during the night. The totals didn't make sense. The figures seemed to be correct, but the huge profits exceeded any of his previous years. At the very best he had expected to break even during his absence.

'I got a bit bored, so I went out and brought in a little more business.'

'*A little?* I'm glad you were only a bit bored. What on earth did you do?' Dave asked in amazement.

'Well, mister hotshot security consultant, you're not the only one that can sign your name,' she said playfully.

Dave closed his eyes and groaned. Sandy continued, 'You did say not to let anybody know you were away. So I attended all the meetings, and some more that I organised myself, then I negotiated and signed the contracts. The companies were all very impressed when I implied you were unavailable because you were working on a top-secret defence contract for the government. It even enabled me to put up your fee. Wasn't I clever?' She beamed at him, and he was impressed against his will.

With his reference from France, his experience and a natural affinity for exploiting security, Dave had found it easy to establish a first-class reputation with many security-conscious companies of South Africa. When he first moved there, before his intermittent work around Vulcan, he spent several months researching the companies he had chosen to work for. His initial approaches had been much as he expected; they were quite happy with their current security arrangements and didn't require any additional advice. But they all had the good fortune to have Dave's name fresh in their minds when their security was breached a little while later. His second approach met with more success.

At the time Sandy was working as private secretary to the chairman of one of South Africa's top twenty companies. She was the only person perceptive enough to realise Dave himself had breached her company's security. She waited until he was on the brink of securing his most lucrative and long-term contract, then presented her own report to him. It itemised all the breaches of security experienced by the companies he was working for, and the dates they had occurred: invariably just prior to his landing his contracts. It also laid out how he had breached her own company's security, and proposed a plan almost identical to his own that would remedy the situation. What really astounded Dave was the conclusion: it gave him an ultimatum – hire her, or be exposed. It puzzled him why she would want to leave a stable and well-paid job, but all she said was, 'I'm bored and looking for a challenge.'

Working with Sandy proved something of a challenge for Dave. She soon became far more than a private secretary; she drew up his contracts, looked after his office and house, and because of her good looks was able to open doors that remained closed to even him. In all ways but one they were like chalk and cheese; he was taciturn and calculating, she was bubbly and direct, but their determination and disciplined natures meant they made a formidable team and achieved exceptional results.

Sandy used her forthright manner to push Dave far more than he would have himself. She bullied him, and demanded results to ensure her own healthy share of the profits. Dave made sure she earned that share, exploiting her talents to the full. He discovered very early that she possessed excellent investigative skills. She could be unbearably irritating until the desired information was forthcoming, or she could subtly persuade the most secret information out of a client with effortless ease.

If it hadn't been for her remarkable results, Dave would probably have dispensed with her services many times; she not only extended him professionally, she also challenged him personally. When he was in South Africa they lived and worked together, but he remained aloof, and froze out all her advances and plays for attention. He was determined to keep their relationship on a professional footing, and Sandy was unable to lure him to step over the line.

Sandy threw piercing questions at him throughout breakfast; she screamed and yelled, sweetened and coaxed, and when Dave remained obdurately silent she threw her hands in the air and stormed from the room.

He took the opportunity to walk outside and survey his property. The house sat perched on top of a sloping hectare of immaculate lawns and garden. It was large, single-storey and T-shaped; he smiled at the thought that he had left one T-shaped building for another.

Nestled into one of the angles of the T was a pool, sparkling in the early sunlight. He chose to take some time to sit on a bench, savouring the tranquillity. He had only been there a few minutes when Sandy found him, still nearly beside herself with curiosity.

He moved along the bench and she sat beside him. 'You said you thought I had been training for a mission, and you were correct. This is the one I've been waiting for. It'll be more dangerous than anything I've been involved with in the past, so whether or not you help is entirely up to you – I'm not going to ask.' Dave stopped, and looked straight into her eyes. They didn't waver.

'Dave, if this is to do with Vulcan we both know this is the one we, and I mean we, have been working towards. Don't expect me to opt out now,' she said decisively.

Dave nodded. 'As you've obviously figured out, Vulcan has hired me again, but this time the stakes are huge. We were right for me to disappear, and heaven knows what resources he used to track me down. That alone tells us how huge his plans are.'

He recounted most of what he knew: everything he had gathered since Kane had approached him, what had happened in London, Melbourne, Perth and Western Australia, right up to the meeting he had with Athol Jansen the previous evening. She sat attentively, hands clasped between her knees. Only when she was sure he was finished did she speak.

'So de Louts is the key. You think we can expose Vulcan while we probe the company for weaknesses?'

'I'm sure of it. He wouldn't have tracked me halfway round the world if I wasn't vital for his success, and because of the scale of his plans, he'll be prepared to take risks. One too many, and it'll be his last.' Dave's eyes flared like a hound baying for blood.

Sandy asked quietly, 'Tell me why you've developed such an obsession with Vulcan. You're normally so objective.'

Obsession. Objective. Dave had never looked at it like that before. He sat in silence, contemplating his answer. Yes, he had to admit she was right, he was obsessed. 'Sandy, you're one of the few people I've grown to trust. You know every facet of my business, including my quest to stop Vulcan. But there are a few aspects of my past you'll never know. All I'm saying is this: you know about the nightmares and you've seen my scars. It was Vulcan who caused them and Vulcan who will pay.'

By this time it was mid-morning, and surprisingly hot. Sandy led the way into the cool of the house, over a small enclosed cobbled courtyard and through the separate entrance which led to the office. Only the two of them ever used it. 'The standard of help is appalling. I'll handle it myself,' was always Sandy's reply when Dave suggested they employ a receptionist.

They shared the main office, a spacious room with one wall covered with books on simple wooden shelves. One half of the room held three two-seater leather settees surrounding a large rectangular coffee table. Two desks faced each other in the other half, both with keyboards and computer screens. Sandy had kept up with the latest developments in technology; Dave saw that the equipment had recently been updated.

Once Sandy entered the office she dropped her playful guise and became serious. He swept the room for bugs, and they sat facing one another across the coffee table. Soon the table was littered with her notes, on the information Dave had gathered, his orders from Vulcan, and his theories. Dave knew that Sandy would use her deductive genius to glean some extra insight that might even change his own perception completely.

'So you're saying this de Lout woman is the key.'

'As I told Athol, I'll do what is necessary to get close to Vulcan.'

'OK, point taken, but have you considered that the rake-off of funds from de Louts' European companies could've been Vulcan's initial source of capital? I bet you'll find de Lout Investments is one of the few companies throughout the world that hasn't been unduly affected by trade constraints. Just be careful the gazelle you stalk doesn't turn out to be the hunter waiting for you.'

Sandy's shrewd perception had thrown an entirely different light on the mission. Dave was obsessed with reaching Vulcan, and hadn't seen this connection. 'So you're saying de Louts could actually be contributing to

Vulcan's war-chest?'

For the next hour they hammered away at these new implications, though all they could do was conjecture until they could prove de Louts' European subsidiaries hadn't been affected by trade embargoes.

'Look, I think we have to proceed as planned until we know for sure Vulcan's initial money has come from de Louts,' Dave said. 'Then we can look at planning an alternative strategy, if necessary. Is that fair?'

Sandy agreed. 'OK, but you'll have to contact Network. They'd never give that sort of information to me.'

'I'll do it this afternoon, but not from here. We'll have to be very careful how we use the phones.' Dave reached for a sheet of paper listing de Louts' directors. 'Meanwhile, I want you to find out as much as you can about these directors, but especially the president and chairman. He's her brother-in-law, Peter de Lout. Where they live, their movements, the works. But be careful.'

'And what are you going to be doing while I'm being careful?' Sandy demanded.

'There's a friend I have to see.'

Sandy knew that was all the answer she was getting. 'Dave Old, sometimes you infuriate me,' she huffed, throwing down her pen.

As Dave entered the alley, adrenalin flowed like a euphoric drug through his veins. His heart pumped like a locomotive as he approached the three black youths who had pushed themselves off the wall. One remained in front of him, and as the other two circled behind, he heard the swish of a switchblade. Never once did his eyes leave those of the youth in front of him.

'I am looking for a man,' he said in fluent Zulu. Surprise flitted behind the youth's gaze. 'A man you will know. Timot Ngema. Where will I find him?'

The youth's shifting eyes darted back and forth; he certainly knew the name; it was one to respect, and protect from prying strangers, especially white ones. He signalled with a curt nod, but the attack died as swiftly as it began.

Dave skipped sideways and lashed out with a powerful back-heel which caught one of the two youths behind him a crashing blow to the chest. The boy collapsed, wheezing, and Dave slammed the point of his elbow into the face of the other one, just as the edge of the switchblade slashed through the air where his kidney should have been. The second youth fell to his knees, dropped the knife and covered his face with his hands. Dave deftly scooped up the knife and turned back to the one in front, who stood wide-eyed and bewildered.

Dave spun the knife in his hand. 'Do you know where I may find this man?' The youth's eyes flicked to the two stricken youths, and as if in accord they all turned to flee; but Dave leapt forward like a predatory cat and caught the first one's neck in a grip like a boa constrictor. 'I'll ask again, where will I find my friend?'

The youth pointed to a battered door at the far end of the alley. Dave released him, and without looking back, walked towards the door.

There was no sign above the door, which stood ajar. Dave pushed it open and stepped over the threshold. To the patrons of the shebeen he was no more than a shadow in the doorway. All talk froze as they stared at him.

He spoke in fluent Zulu. 'It is said there is a man among you who was once as swift as a gazelle, yet as fierce as a lion. It is also said this lion is now past his prime.'

The shocked group gasped. Through the thick haze of tobacco smoke Dave made out a tall black man rising from his seat by the bar.

'What jackal that lurks in the shadows and yaps at the heels of his king says these things?' the man bellowed.

Dave remained silent as the thickset man approached him, hammer-like fists clenched and cannon ball head tilted slightly to the side. Dave spoke again, 'No jackal, only a man a friend once called the Leopard.'

The thickset man stopped as if had hit an invisible brick wall. 'You!' he said, a grin tugging at his disfigured face. He accepted Dave's extended hand and they shook in a reverse grip, as was the African fashion.

'I see you, friend. But I fear it is unwise for a man even of your talents to be seen in a place like this.' He turned and flicked his head.

Dave followed him to a door behind the bar, silence lingering in the rancid smoke and piercing eyes drilling into him like tiny harpoons. Compared to the rough surroundings they had left, the room they entered was surprisingly well furnished and tidy.

'I use this place as my humble office,' Timot said. The humorous twinkle in his eyes belied the submissive posture he adopted.

Timot was probably one of the wealthiest black men in Johannesburg. Staring at his bowed head and clasped hands, Dave's mouth began to twitch, and a full-blooded roar of laughter burst from his lips.

Timot's shoulders shook uncontrollably, and fat tears of ran down the creases in his scarred face.

It wasn't until Dave began to stagger and slap his thigh that Timot's own laughter escaped. The two men hooted and snorted in harmony, re-establishing their bond of friendship.

Dave eventually fell silent, hugging his sore ribs, as Timot continued to laugh for the sheer joy of it. As he waited for his friend to control himself, he recalled the beginning of their friendship.

Dave found the year after he left the Foreign Legion the most boring he'd ever lived through. He stayed on at Aubagne, but the security contracts he was given were little more than highly paid errands. General Marcet wanted Dave well within his sights.

But four years of action left him yearning for more, like a pent-up lion hungering for the open plains. He even considered signing on for another five years. But at the end of the twelve months he packed his bags and left for Africa.

It was by chance that he found himself in a bar in Salisbury. His flight had been delayed, and he decided to investigate the night-life. A group of drunk and rowdy white Rhodesian servicemen accosted him, demanding why he had dodged enlistment to help rid their country of the black scourge.

Half an hour later, the military police found a bruised and battered man staring savagely about him, and five comatose off-duty servicemen littered around him. It took three MPs and several bleeding noses to bundle him into a Land Rover and to the military stockade. By the time the army had established Dave was a foreigner, his plane had left. He hadn't really decided where to go next, and he craved action. He enlisted.

Assigned to the Rhodesian Light Rifles, he found himself fighting an enemy that never really warranted the name. His first leave saw him again alone in a bar in Salisbury, wondering what on earth he was doing. Nettled by an obnoxious white Rhodesian, he ended the night in the stockade again.

Next morning he learnt to his disgust that the man was an officer in his own regiment. He was charged with insubordination, and sentenced to three weeks in the Box, the Rhodesian equivalent of the Legion's *la pelote*. He was the only white man; the purpose was to instil discipline into the hardiest of blacks. Which was when Dave met Timot.

They struck up an instant rapport, and became running mates; when most other detainees had faded, they uncovered reserves of energy. Timot was never formally educated, but he had a shrewd and perceptive mind. He taught Dave Sindebele, the spoken language of the Matabele tribe.

Timot was a Zulu of royal descent. When Dave asked his new friend what on earth he was doing fighting in the land of his traditional foe, Timot said simply, 'I had trouble with a man's wife. And heaven help me if she ever finds me.'

They left the Box with a friendship of solid gold. Within a week of their return to their separate regiments, they were both called up for something which proved to be a gruelling physical trial for the legendary Selous Scouts. Dave was one of the few foreigners ever to join the trial.

A dozen men started and by the end only three potential recruits remained. They completed what they were told was their last test, a sixty-five-kilometre forced march through rugged African bush, and bone-weary, literally fell on the waiting Land Rover. They had already endured a sleepless weekend of physical hell when, dispirited and utterly exhausted, they heard the sergeant tell them to return to the starting point.

Without hesitation Dave and Timot staggered to their feet. The third man declared, 'No way, pal. You can stick the Scouts.'

Dave and Timot hadn't stumbled a hundred metres when an officer appeared from behind a bush and said, 'Welcome to the Scouts.' They had passed their final test: following orders unquestioningly.

They developed a bond closer than brothers, fighting and laughing together, and losing count of the times they saved each other's lives. But later, Dave's indebtedness to Timot went far beyond the boundaries even of such friendship.

Timot struggled into the chair behind his desk, wiping away the tear smudges that glistened around his eyes. Dave was still waiting patiently for him to gain some semblance of control.

In the uneven light of the office the Zulu's scarred scalp shone like a bright coin. Normally the first sight of his war-ravaged face could make the bravest of men quail, but it betrayed the intelligence that prowled beneath the hard-bitten façade.

He could trace his ancestry back as far as the legendary King Shaka, and in his younger years he had been expected to exert his physical dominance. The scars that adorned his face and skull were worn with pride, for they were the product of tribal traditions.

'I take it business is going well,' Dave said.

The comment brought Timot to the verge of hysterics once again, and Dave's mock groan of distress did nothing to calm him. 'It goes well,' he answered, then added, 'Hell, it's good to see you again.'

When Dave and Timot first left the rapidly declining Rhodesia and moved south, Dave bankrolled Timot into business. Making use of his natural instinct for survival and his astute intelligence, Timot found his true calling. Like everyone who thirsts for success, he found the business world treated him kindly. The profits on Dave's original outlay were phenomenal; within a few months Timot had paid him back in full with a full year's interest. Timot used weakness to his advantage; it was the motivation that drove him beyond others' meagre efforts. What he lacked in schooling he made up for in shrewd business acumen. His business tentacles spread into virtually every area of the black community in Johannesburg and Soweto. He would have been at home in any boardroom in the country.

'Timot, I need to ring London. Do you mind if I use that?' Dave asked, pointing to the office phone.

With an acknowledging wave, Timot said, 'Sure, would you like me to leave the room?'

Dave shook his head and dialled the familiar number. His call was picked up straight away.

Timot listened to the brief but enlightening conversation with interest. His call completed, Dave settled back in his armchair to tell of the events that had led to his leaving and returning to Africa.

At the end of the long explanation, Timot moved to the window and stared through the heavy net curtains at the alley. The corded muscles of his neck stood out, and he clasped his hands comfortably behind his back.

'If what you say is correct, and I'm not questioning your judgment, both black and white men have much to fear from this tyrant,' he rumbled, moving to sit facing Dave, his face heavy with concern.

By the country's government of his birth he was regarded as inferior, but Timot was also a realist. He fiercely opposed the white minority's apartheid regime, but given the complexities of the current power play, allowing the UDF to gain control as a puppet government for Vulcan definitely wasn't the answer.

'I'll need your help if I am to succeed.' A statement of fact, not a request; there was no question of Timot not offering his support. He was the one man Dave knew he could rely on, to the death if necessary.

'Of course I assume you'll need somebody on the inside at de Louts.'

Dave and Timot were already thinking along similar lines; it had only taken this first brief meeting for their minds to click into harmony once again. 'That would help, yes.'

'I already have a cousin there, working as a chauffeur. His name is Moses. He'll do as he's asked.'

The size of Timot's extended family was a constant surprise to Dave.

Timot shrugged. 'What can I say? My grandfather was a busy man.' He frowned and continued, 'There are some things you should know. They'll help us to track down this Vulcan.' He paused. 'It didn't surprise me when you arrived today. There've been questions asked about you recently.'

Dave's interest quickened.

'That police inspector, James Pearson, the one that caused so much bother, has been asking questions about you and Vulcan. It was to do with the death of Tom de Lout.'

For a moment Dave was surprised to hear that James Pearson was involved, but that didn't last long. The man was crafty, and too perceptive.

When Dave had first set up his security consultancy in South Africa, Timot had helped with his unique method of canvassing for business. During those early ventures only two hiccups arose; the first was Sandy, the second was a lot more irritating and potentially disastrous. James Pearson had proved a lot more astute than the companies.

Dave and Timot had just completed their most ambitious and successful drive for business yet. After extensive planning they executed a near perfect rocket attack on a massive chemical installation, established by none other than de Louts and the South African government, in the coal-rich area of the northern Free State. The plant was built to convert coal into gasoline-related products, and because of its national importance and sensitive nature, the response to Dave's approach after the attack was overwhelming. His future in South Africa looked secure – at least until James Pearson started investigating.

How he discovered that Dave launched the attack he'd never know, and nothing was ever proved. Dave eventually secured his contract, but decided his methods had become too precarious. Afterwards he solicited work in more conventional ways.

It didn't surprise Dave that Pearson's name had come up. This time he hoped they would be allies.

If the detective was investigating Tom de Lout's death, he could safely assume his theory was correct: Tom de Lout was murdered by Vulcan. Everything seemed to point to de Louts as the key to Vulcan's success.

'How did he come to question you?' he asked Timot.

Timot shrugged. 'He knew de Lout was murdered, that was plain. But when he asked about the Leopard, he didn't know it was you.'

'Sorry, you've lost me.' Dave was bewildered now.

'He asked me what I knew about Tom de Lout's death and if I knew anything of the Leopard. Then he asked how the Leopard and Vulcan were connected. He never mentioned your name or referred to you in any way. I also don't think he's a policeman anymore. He wasn't interested in my business here.'

'So he gave no clue about how he came to talk to you. Surely he never knew you were involved in the attack on the chemical plant?'

'He spoke as if he didn't know me at all, but the questions he asked, well, he appeared to know half the answers already.'

Dave remained silent for several minutes.

'What exactly did he ask?' he asked eventually.

'He wanted to know about de Lout's death in Zimbabwe, and he mentioned two places in Natal. I couldn't see where his questions were going, so I couldn't follow them up. Then as you know, he asked about you and Vulcan...'

'Do you know anything about Tom de Lout's death?' Dave cut in.

'Nothing. It never concerned me.'

'What about these places in Natal? Do they mean anything to you?'

'Zululand is my home, I know the places well. It'll be easy enough to find what we need to.'

Dave knew his influence spread far and wide. There existed in Africa another world which few white men ever came to understand.

'Two more things I'll need to find out.' Dave flicked a thumb in the air. 'How Pearson made contact with you—' he raised the adjoining index finger '—and who he spoke to in Natal and why.'

James Pearson had added a completely new dimension to Dave's mission. He hoped it would be a productive one.

He prepared to leave, but what Timot said next made him sink slowly back into his seat.

'Pearson also asked a lot of questions about the activities of the UDF. He made it sound important, so I followed it up. Dave, judging by what you've told me and what I've discovered, there's big trouble brewing.'

Fingers of dread whispered down Dave's spine. If Vulcan was moving into politics as well as trade, his plans to control the economies of the world were far more advanced than he could have imagined. He felt as if he was entangled in the intricate web of a spider, whose threads were only now becoming visible.

CHAPTER 29

It would be unfair to call Kane a racist, but he was certainly a bigot. He was intolerant of anyone he regarded as inferior to himself; the colour of their skin was immaterial.

His first day at his hotel in the northern Transvaal had been unproductive. He was livid, and quite prepared to throttle the black idiot that was supposed to meet him the night before.

The room he had booked was a rondavel, set apart from the rest of the hotel complex. The small circular thatched building consisted of a living room and spacious bedroom with en suite facilities, and the roughcast exterior was painted brilliant white. The outlook was magnificent; a lush green valley of native bush swept away from his doorstep towards a vista of fertile bush-clad hills and valleys as far as the horizon.

A warm breeze licked about Kane's face, bringing with it the untainted smell of nature and the sounds of Africa, the peace and serenity protected by the secluded location.

The unspoilt view was lost on Kane. He had given up pacing and was slouched in an armchair, going over the preparations he had to make before taking up his final post in Johannesburg, which would see this current mission completed. This was one of three staging posts for the storage and the distribution of arms that were being trekked in from Angola and Mozambique. The arms were for a small, highly-trained groups of UDF dissidents, who were being trained in secret by Cuban and Soviet fighters from Angola and Mozambique, and located in various parts of the country. The men had been relatively easy to relocate, but the weapons were proving a little bit more difficult.

The plan was to use these small groups of men as strike forces to capture and annex the country's radio and television stations and key government offices. It had been a mammoth task to organise the training camps and the targets they were to attack. Whether the groups succeeded or not didn't matter; they would provoke the country's twenty-five million blacks into an uprising which would sweep the decimated minority government from power.

The extent of the government's destruction hinged on that rogue agent Dave Old and his assignment with de Louts. Kane bridled at the thought of Dave; he would enjoy settling that score.

The storage depot in northern Transvaal was very near the hotel, and only a hundred and fifty kilometres from the border with Mozambique, but the consignments had been arriving via a longer and more complex route through Zimbabwe. Not for the first time, Kane cursed the strict security of the Kruger National Park; it was in place to protect the world-renowned wildlife, but also effectively barred the shortest and most economic route for arms from Mozambique.

There was a loud thumping at his door.

'You Van der Zwet?' A heavy-gutted white man spoke in accented Afrikaans.

Kane was surprised; he had expected his UDF contact to be black. The man had unruly red hair, unkempt clothes and a casual attitude to personal hygiene. He didn't wait for Kane to reply. 'I've come to show you the stuff.'

Kane was of Dutch descent and understood the language. He stared at the man slack-jawed.

'Well?' the Afrikaaner asked with a surly glare.

'Sorry,' Kane replied absently.

The man grunted, 'Up at reception they said you were Van der Zwet.' A hint of doubt shadowed his face and he began to turn away.

Kane slowly rose from his chair and approached the man. 'No, by all means, come on in,' he said amiably, giving him no choice. He took a quick look over his shoulder through the open door to check nobody was about, then slammed it, making the Afrikaaner jump.

'Look, I'll have to be going. I've gotta meet somebody,' the man said tentatively.

The guiding arm around his shoulders tightened as Kane spoke. 'Oh, by the way, my name is Van der Zwet. *Mister* Van der Zwet to you.'

The man suddenly found himself caught in an unyielding headlock, his neck savagely twisted and his windpipe slowly crushed. He began to choke and gasp for breath, until a hammer-like fist caught his ruddy face a crashing blow. His body hung like a sack of flour in Kane's grasp.

Kane swore venomously. He hadn't intended to knock him out; he wanted to inflict more pain, to teach the idiot a lesson. He released his grip, and the unconscious man slumped heavily to the floor. There was no satisfaction from the kick he administered to the man's soft, unresisting belly; the prone figure was comatose and never felt a thing.

The darkness slowly began to recede. The Afrikaaner felt himself drifting, slowly at first, then with vastly increasing speed, until the light hit him like a solid rock. Pain pounded through his head as a hand slapped his face.

'What the...' he managed groggily as his vision cleared. A big blond giant was standing above him, his cold eyes blazing in rage.

Kane reached down and grabbed a handful of his greasy hair. 'Get up, you animal,' he hissed.

He gave a half-muted cry as he was hauled to his feet. Kane dragged him by the hair to one of the armchairs and threw him into it. He stooped, only centimetres away from the Afrikaaner's cowering face. 'Show such disregard for security again and I'll kill you. And where the hell were you last night?'

The man cringed to the back of the chair. As Kane pulled away, he spluttered, 'I was... we were... we had trouble with the last batch of guns. One stupid black broke his leg. I had to send the others back for him and his load. It took all bloody night...'

'I don't care if the whole damn bunch of them broke their legs, never stand me up again,' Kane barked. 'Anyway, what the hell's your name?'

'Du Preez, Jan du Preez.'

'Well, du Preez, you'd better show me what I've come to see.'

The guns and ammunition were stored on the Afrikaaner's own farm, a few miles away. Both men were silent as du Preez, hunched over the wheel of his Datsun *bakkie*, drove them to the dump.

The storage sheds were well back off the road. Kane would never have admitted it, but he was impressed with the skill and care with which they had been concealed. Everything was stored in long rectangular boxes, each with a cryptic stencilled label. Du Preez had hidden them near the back of a long, enclosed barn, surrounded by hundreds of twine-bound bales of hay. It took half an hour for his porters to open a berth wide enough for Kane to inspect, a random selection of the boxes. He was well pleased with what he saw.

There were no sophisticated weapons; the guns were Czechoslovakian AK 47s and Soviet TT-33 Tokarev automatic pistols. The AK 47s had been chosen because they were sturdy, reliable and practically indestructible. The pistols would be used by the section commanders.

The only other weapon type in the cache was Soviet RPG-7 rocket-launchers, which would be used against more intractable opposition. With all this fire power, Kane thought, there was certainly going to be some damage.

He swept the straw from his trousers and spoke to du Preez. 'I'll give you the orders for shipping them out myself.'

'When will that be?' du Preez asked hesitantly.

'Soon. Very soon,' was all the answer he received

CHAPTER 30

Richard placed the receiver carefully back in its cradle and blew out a long breath.

'Trouble?' Johnny asked.

'What? Oh no, nothing I can't handle. Just Sir Colin pain-in-the-arse Bleach, trying to put pressure on us again, says he's concerned about the state of the economy, as if that's anything new. It looks as though News International is about to cause ructions, the word's out five thousand workers may lose their jobs.' He snorted a humourless laugh. 'The way he spoke, you'd think it was my fault. God, Rupert Murdoch's a meddling old prick.'

The pressure from above was beginning to tell on the boss, Johnny thought. He wasn't often so caustic.

Richard rolled his shoulders and pointed at the piece of paper in Johnny's hand. 'What have you got for me?'

Back to business, then. Johnny was relieved.

'We've just had a call from Dave Old. He's looking into de Louts' European and North American connections. He wants you to fly down and meet with him.' He laid the single sheet on Richard's desk.

'Sounds like he's following a hunch. How did he get there?'

Johnny was about to answer, but Richard had clearly been asking himself. He looked up, his attention on his colleague again.

'Have you finished compiling those financial statements for de Louts yet?'

'It's a mammoth task, but it should be done in the next couple of days. Suppose you'll want to take them down with you to the meeting with Dave? If you're going?'

'No choice. At present he's our only lead on Vulcan. We have to give him all the support we can.'

For the first time that day Johnny looked properly at Richard's face. It was drawn and haggard, with blue-grey smudges under his bloodshot eyes, and the frown creases were a lot more pronounced than the laughter lines.

Richard was still speaking. 'By now you must have some idea if de Louts' overseas subsidiaries are channelling funds elsewhere?'

'Well, going by the figures so far, and you must understand the investigation is by no means complete, I would say they're guilty as charged.'

'Are you sure?' Richard demanded.

'No, Richard, I'm not, I just said so. For the moment it's an educated guess. But the figures I've come up with so far indicate that funds have been siphoned off. I can't tell you to where.' Johnny hated conjecturing. He felt far more comfortable reporting on conclusive evidence.

But he had actually been prepared to speculate. Richard knew Johnny very well; it was safe to assume his colleague was right. It appeared de Louts was Vulcan's major backer.

'What did Dave say about the meeting?'

'The Holiday Inn at Jan Smuts, as soon as possible. Same code name as in Perth. He'll be checking at the hotel daily.'

'You'd better book me on the next available flight. And...'

Johnny raised a hand. 'Yeah, yeah, I know, finish the report on de Louts.' He turned to leave, then whirled around and punched the air in frustration. 'I must be going senile. What I came to tell you was that I just heard Ferkatovich is trying to disappear, and he was also spotted in Africa a number of months ago. Zimbabwe to be precise.'

'What?' Richard exclaimed, rolling his eyes. 'I knew his reports were too regular. How did you find out?'

'An Aeroflot steward on our payroll reported a man of his description trying to get back to Africa under an assumed name, by a rather devious route. He remembered the same man on a flight into Europe, then on to Africa, several months back. He's only just passed on the information. Not one of our braver recruits, I'm afraid. I followed up with some contacts in Africa.'

'Hell, what a shambles. That means both Oechsli and Ferkatovich are out there on their own. My bet is the Russian is heading for South Africa and Oechsli won' t be far behind. They know something's happening down there. South Africa seems to be where everything is pointing – probably just as well I'm flying down myself.'

Richard now knew there was no hope of finding out where the leak that had plagued the joint operation with the CIA and the KGB had originated. The trilateral agreement was obviously defunct, Network were on their own again.

He sat in silence for a few moments, trying to decide whether to take Johnny into his confidence. He too hated making assumptions without facts to back them up. Normally he would keep his own counsel, but with something as important as this he needed a sounding board to help him clarify his thoughts. He wanted to be sure about his theory concerning Oechsli and Ferkatovich before his meeting with Dave.

He took a deep breath and put his thoughts into words. Johnny's silence and nods of reluctant agreement only confirmed what he suspected.

Sergei Ivanovich Doblin had to admit it wasn't the easiest posting he'd ever received. He was the KGB's Resident, or head of station, in South Africa. A man of average appearance, his only distinguishing quality was his remarkably perceptive mind. After spending a short time as the head of Illegal Support in Australia, he had been promoted and transferred out to Pretoria several years before.

Instead of spending most of his time trying to de-stabilise South Africa so that it was ripe for Russian control, he was instead busy with something most of the world would consider contrary to the KGB's principles and methods. He was arranging top-secret meetings between Pretoria and Moscow. Meetings so sensitive that if they became public knowledge, it would provoke outrage and condemnation throughout both the western world and the black African countries that were at present sympathetic towards Moscow.

Because the USSR and South Africa between them had something approaching a world monopoly with gold, diamonds, platinum and other precious minerals, they had chosen to work covertly together to attempt to regulate those world markets. So Doblin's activities with regard to co-ordinating espionage operations in South Africa were limited. In these troubled times every cent of foreign exchange was vital to Moscow, and the Kremlin certainly didn't want to disrupt the lucrative arrangement they had with Pretoria. The agents under Doblin's control could best be described as idle.

Doblin was preparing himself for bed when the phone began to ring. Irritated, he consulted his watch; eleven thirty, and an hour later in Moscow. Who on earth could it be at this hour? He picked up the receiver. 'Hello.'

'Is this line clear,' demanded the caller in Russian.

The voice sounded familiar. Doblin didn't hesitate. 'It is swept daily. Who is this?' he demanded angrily.

The answer struck him like a blizzard, chilling him to the bone.

'Ferkatovich.' Without waiting for a reply he continued, 'Beyond the Botanical Research Institute here in Pretoria, there is a row of Lombardy poplars. Meet me there in thirty minutes. I will be in a beige BMW.'

The connection was broken before Doblin had a chance to respond.

Doblin was perturbed, to say the least. He had only once met the Head of the KGB's First Chief Directorate, and that was at a ceremony of honour in the secret Memory Room, where the intelligence agency commemorated its heroes. He had been overawed by the man's dominance, and had subsequently heard many stories about how unpredictable Ferkatovich was, but never in his worst nightmares had he expected to see him here in South Africa.

Driving east past the Botanical Research Institute, he spotted the poplars in the distance, and *oh no*, there was a beige BMW at the side of the road in front of him. He slowed his car and stopped just in front of it. A dark silhouette was slumped behind the wheel. He wondered if he should flash his lights, but decided that only happened in the movies. As his uncertainty began to build, there was a flash of headlights from across the road.

Doblin climbed out of his own car and crossed to the BMW. A large, bearded man leant over and unlocked the passenger door. The man looked like a South African, a born and bred Afrikaaner. The weather-beaten uncompromising face, the clothes, even his demeanour. Doblin hesitated as the door was flung open.

'It is wise to be wary, Comrade, but get in.' The thick accent identified the man immediately.

Doblin had a bad feeling about this. He had hoped the phone call was a hoax; even a trap would have been better than this. In stunned silence he slid into the seat beside his chief.

Without a word Uri Ferkatovich started the vehicle and drove west. Both men sat in silence, staring intently at the darkened road; it didn't take Doblin long to work out that they were heading towards the Hartbeespoort Dam.

The deep rumble of Uri's voice cut across the quiet, startling Doblin. 'You are obviously wondering what I'm doing in South Africa, alone and unannounced. Officially, Comrade, I am still in Moscow. You are the only member of my staff to know I'm here. It will remain so.'

If I'm so privileged, why do I feel as if you have just signed my death warrant? Doblin thought. 'You have my complete discretion,' he answered respectfully.

'How many men do you have operating here in the Republic?'

'Taking into account registered agents and illegals we have twenty-six. Including myself.'

'Good. It will be enough. I take it they are inactive at present?'

Doblin was unsure how to answer this. Was his competence being called into question? Surely not; his orders came directly from Moscow. How to put it delicately... 'I admit the agency force is a little large for the assignments that are passed on from Moscow,' he said slowly, 'but yes, they are rather inactive at the moment.'

Uri began to chuckle, a sound like muffled thunder which Doblin found most disturbing. 'Well put, Comrade. Maybe some of the success of Moscow's meetings with Pretoria can be attributed to your diplomacy. I feel we are going to work well together.'

That should have put Doblin's wary mind ease. So why did he feel like a snow-hare being circled by minks?

'Comrade Doblin, your work will continue as usual, but all agents are to be directly accountable to me, through you, of course. I want them all active. They are to seek out every de-stabilising influence in the country, especially the UDF, and provide all the assistance they can without direct involvement. Also, they are to follow up every lead on subversive groups working in and around South Africa, whether or not they are linked to a common organisation. They are to report to you daily, and you in turn will report to me.'

These orders were quite contrary to the ones he had been receiving from Moscow since his posting, but it didn't occur to Doblin to question them. It didn't do to interrupt, or to ask questions, especially of the Head of the First Chief Directorate.

They had taken a roundabout route through the outskirts of Pretoria back to the Lombardy poplars. Uri was still delivering orders as he parked the car. He reached into the pocket of his shirt and pulled out a scrap of paper. 'I will be contacting you daily at your office; you will make yourself available. Here is the number at which you may contact me at in an emergency. Memorise it and destroy it. And don't try to trace it.'

Doblin stepped from the car. Uri leant over and spoke through the window, 'What we are working on, Comrade, will be of major benefit to Mother Russia. You will be justly rewarded.'

The BMW drove away, leaving Doblin with a mixture of patriotic pride and unease. He felt like a child left alone on his first day of school trying in vain to believe his mother's parting promises. He was numb and hollow inside.

He looked down at the scrap of paper in his hand. It was a Johannesburg number.

CHAPTER 31

'Ahh, Mrs de Lout, it's already quarter past ten. Your board meeting is due to start about now.' Susan had consulted her diary and was looking at her watch as she walked towards Karen's rosewood desk.

Karen didn't seem to have heard. Her full attention was fixed on the reports before her, and she groped towards her ever-present coffee mug with her free hand.

But just as Susan was about to repeat the reminder, Karen spoke. 'It won't hurt them to wait. It's a woman's prerogative to be late.'

She rose and stepped from behind the desk, smoothing down her pleated charcoal grey skirt. The high ruffle-edged collar of her blouse and her hair piled high on top of her head emphasised her long graceful neck, and the elegant gold locket round her neck added a finishing touch. Simple and business-like, just like the way she chose to conduct her board meetings.

'By the way, what's got into you the last few days?' Karen asked playfully. 'You've been like a cat with two tails.'

'Oh, just a new man in my life,' Susan answered, beaming with pride.

'Lucky you.' Karen tried to keep the envy out of her voice.

Susan's cheeks pinked. 'I do believe, Mrs de Lout, that your brother-in-law will be annoyed if you delay much longer.'

'Speaking of being annoyed, Susan, whatever happened to that journalist from the American lifestyle magazine? Did you manage to get rid of her?'

'Sandy Thomson. Believe it or not, ma'am, she's still sitting in reception. She arrived early this morning.'

'Still waiting to see me? I'll give her full marks for persistence. Have any of the other directors given her an interview?'

'She's been quite a sensation with them all. Even Mr de Lout gave her half an hour.'

This was starting to push at Karen's tolerance. 'Yes, he spoke to me about it,' she said crisply. 'He suggested her article might raise our public profile.' Look, Susan, I don't care what you have to do, answer her questions for me if you have to, but I don't intend to be interviewed by any American magazine.'

She gathered the files from her desk and marched purposefully towards the boardroom.

'Thank you, Carl, but I'll want a more in-depth report for my personal files. We certainly don't want any cost overruns with this venture, like we had with the last.' Karen ignored the man's faint grimace; her attention had already shifted towards Peter, at the other end of the long wooden table.

'Next item on the agenda. We know we're in a healthy position at home. Peter, you've been back from Europe and America for more than a week now; how are we faring overseas?'

The hanging silence said clearly that most of the board members were glad they didn't control the foreign sector.

Peter used the silence like an actor. He purposefully arranged his notes, creating an atmosphere like a judge about to pass an unfavourable verdict.

'As we know, Europe, indeed the entire western world, is moving towards something that could equal the depression of the 1930s. It appears that the Soviets and her allies are experiencing a similar challenge.'

He was priming them for the worst, Karen thought. Because of South Africa's self-sufficiency the world's economic rout had hardly affected it. In fact, de Louts' current position was stronger than it had been for decades. Their profits actually exceeded the board's most optimistic views. The real question was how much the parent company would have to prop up its worldwide subsidiaries. Mentally Karen was already tallying available cash reserves, accessible lines of credit and easily saleable assets. Where possible she intended to turn the situation to profit.

What Peter said next didn't seem to make sense. 'Profits in all western subsidiaries are up by twenty per cent.'

Karen, along with all the other directors, was understandably stunned into silence. This wasn't what they had expected to hear at all. 'I beg your pardon?' she said as if somebody had uttered an offensive oath.

'From the figures I received from our accountants, our turnover is up and our profits have increased, as I said, by twenty per cent.'

'Well, I'll be... Who would've guessed that?' came from one of the directors on Peter's right.

Since Karen had taken over the presidency of de Lout Investments, she had concentrated her own efforts in and around the Republic of South Africa; all other activities had been Peter's responsibility. Thoroughly sceptical, she asked, 'How on earth has that been achieved?'

Peter extracted a thick bundle of papers from the folder in front of him and gave them to his secretary to be distributed. He let the directors have five minutes to peruse the reports, and as he spoke again the triumph in his voice rang as clear as the bells of Notre Dame.

'As you'll all remember, much to the concern of my brother and most of you, I set up a trust account we labelled the number two account. This was to be used as our indemnity fund. As you see from the figures over the last few years, it has been used quite extensively, but this cash reserve has put us in a far stronger position than any of our competition.' Peter paused and confidently swept a gaze around the room. 'This account, and the initial foresight my brother had shown by dealing only with consumable commodities throughout the western world, has enabled our company to profit where others have failed.'

'So where exactly did the millions go to from the indemnity fund?' Karen asked as she consulted the screed of figures before her.

'Well, as you are all aware, the account is held by a shelf company in Jersey. The island's favourable tax laws and banking policies mean that the transactions from this account are entirely confidential. This allowed the majority of the funds to be passed to influential people that were favourably disposed towards de Louts.'

'In other words,' Karen said icily, 'the account was used for bribes.'

'Not to put too fine a point on it, yes.' Peter said. 'So, the small amount we were able to invest has paid us some handsome dividends.'

Karen recalled why de Louts had been lured to St Helier, Jersey's largest town and bustling financial centre. Its status as a tax haven had obvious attractions, and its proximity to London while remaining outside Britain's jurisdiction was a bonus. Yet probably the major advantage was Jersey's self-governing political system, which ensured long-term stability. Of course, de Louts wasn't the only company that had discovered the benefits of this financial centre; Karen knew St Helier bristled with banks. And of course, with the banks came the associated services which discerning clientele could avail themselves of. As de Louts had elected to do.

Karen hadn't been in agreement when the fund was first set up, but now she had to admit Peter's idea had saved them tremendous financial embarrassment. She realised pay-offs were an all too present part of business; it was something she would never truly accept, but she knew she'd have to live with it. 'Well, Peter, I'm sure I speak for all of us when I offer you my congratulations.'

There were nods and murmurs of agreement.

Karen hadn't looked into the figures in depth, but she felt she could safely assume her company was in a more than enviable position. The question was, how were they going to capitalise on this advantage? Looking at Peter she asked, 'You've obviously done your homework. How do you propose we convert this situation to greater profit?'

Everyone was alert, eager to hear the response. Each director could see the tremendous advantages, both personal and professional, of the company's current position.

It was as if Peter was able to read their thoughts. 'When I was first presented with these figures, I too thought we should expand our holdings. But after due consideration, I feel it might be prudent to consolidate.'

Karen was surprised; that wasn't like Peter. He was thorough, but a conservative approach wasn't usually his style.

Before she was able to query his proposal, Peter produced another thick bundle of papers. This time he gave them little more time to consider their contents.

'These reports have been compiled by our European and American analysts. They predict a further decline throughout Europe and American. From these figures you'll realise it's wise to consolidate our position; in a few months the new opportunities will more than offset our wait.'

As the other directors discussed the figures and their implications, Karen continued to study both reports. The profits were more than she had ever hoped for. She wasn't questioning the figures, but for some reason she couldn't fathom, something wasn't quite as it seemed.

Were Peter's assessments logical, or should they begin to capitalise now while they had the chance? Tom hadn't built the company up by logic alone. It would take some time to decide, but Karen felt some move towards expansion should be considered. She needed to analyse the full set of reports in depth, and speak to her European directors before making any decision.

When Karen didn't join the discussion, the other directors gradually fell silent and waited for her lead.

'Once again, congratulations Peter, and I propose we do as you suggest... for now.'

Triumph flitted across Peter's eyes. Then, fleetingly, it was replaced by something far more sinister; Karen could have sworn it was unbridled malice. She chose to ignore it for the time being, and addressed herself to the next item on the agenda.

All eyes around the table were fixed on Etienne Kruger, the director in charge of government joint ventures. Etienne was an Afrikaaner, but not cast in the true Afrikaaner mould. He could appear to be at home in the boozing, brawling atmosphere of the sports-mad Afrikaner world, and was equally comfortable in delicate negotiations with the most cunning of men. His apparently uncompromising façade masked a shrewd and perceptive mind.

'Members of the Board, it gives me great pleasure to announce that the government joint venture on our border with Namibia is entering its final phase. The military oil refinery at Pump Station Omumbo is nearly complete.'

Ten years ago, Pump Station Omumbo had been little more than a hole in the ground. Standing derelict above this gaping wound in the earth was the mining headgear that had helped plunder the vast store of precious minerals from the subterranean reserve.

The Omumbo Mine had been described as a freak; Mother Earth had again stunned the scientific world with another unsolvable mystery.

It had been one of the richest diamond reserves in the world. The theory was that that millennia ago a channel had descended into the molten magma of the Earth's core, and a river of molten lava slowly oozed up the channel, carrying concentrated orbs of pure liquid carbon. As the river met the plug of unyielding bedrock, a pressure built intense enough to crush mountains, and eventually ruptured an opening. Once the Earth's crust was breached, the deluge of molten contents eventually found its way to the coastline of southern Namibia. This caused a massive shift which closed off the channel, leaving a deposit of lava which mutated into a deposit of blue marbled diamond-bearing kimberlite.

At its height, the Omumbo Mine had nearly three times the output of the renowned Jagerfontein, previously one of the richest diamond mines. For several decades, men selfishly plundered it until the reserves came to an abrupt halt. What was left was a subterranean cavern, invisible from the surface.

The mine's isolation, and it's almost non-existent water problems because of its location in the Kalahari Desert, made it ideal for Tom de Lout's partnership with the South African government for the storage of excess crude oil. After the interior surfaces were coated with a sealing compound, it served the purpose for many years. The converted mine's isolation also made it an ideal location for military operations; the only drawback was the vast quantity of refined fuel and oil required to run the base. This problem was solved when de Louts negotiated a contract to build and service a military refinery, fed from the cavity of the old mine, which was now the largest man-made oil reserve of its kind, eclipsing many natural reserves.

'So, Etienne, when is the planned completion date?' Karen asked.

'Believe it or not, the contractors have guaranteed completion ten weeks from now. Otherwise the penalties will eat up every last cent of their profit.'

'Why is the date so important?'

'That is when the Ministry of Defence and the government have requested the opening.'

Karen thought for a moment; she'd have to check the dates, but if that deadline was met it would be yet another civic ceremony she'd have to attend, and in a location that held no interest for her. 'How big an occasion?' she asked flatly.

'The biggest – no expense spared. The president himself will crack the refinery's main gate valve. It will be the military's most important facility, after all – our PR team thinks we can really make a splash.'

No way was Karen going to cut her safari short. If need be, a word in the right ear could get the ceremony cancelled, or at least changed to a more civilised venue.

'We'll see about that,' she said grimly.

CHAPTER 32

Dave and Sandy sat side by side with the photographs of the directors of de Lout Investments spread out before them.

'So you managed to interview all the directors?' Dave asked, staring at a photograph.

'Almost all.'

'Karen de Lout said no?' Dave raised an eyebrow.

'It was short notice,' Sandy protested. 'And I did talk to her personal secretary, at some length.'

Sandy reached down for her notes, and Dave picked up the photo of Peter de Lout. Staring at it intently he asked, 'What's your impression of this guy?'

'Small, but shrewd, and as cool as ice. A man who doesn't suffer fools, and knows how to spot them. He seems well suited as chairman of the board. A worthy adversary for any of de Louts' competitors.'

'Other than chairman, what's his role?'

'He's a qualified accountant, and seems to be in charge of security, does most of the company's feasibility studies, and controls their north American and European subsidiaries.'

Dave fell silent, his eyes fixed on Peter de Lout's face. 'Europe and North America,' he said quietly.

'In my interview he didn't place much emphasis on the overseas side. He does spend time there, but from what he said, he'd prefer not to. As long as the numbers stack up, I believe he'll leave his managers to their own devices. But if things start to go bad, he'll cut and slash, even axe whole plants to turn the books around.'

'OK, what are his major weaknesses?'

Sandy shrugged. 'None that I saw. He's never married, and is very security conscious. I drove past his home – it was done up like Fort Knox.'

For the next hour and a half, they discussed all the other directors, their positions in the company, their responsibilities and of course their weaknesses. Dave had already received a lot of information from Vulcan, but Sandy's penetrating mind and intuition had given him far more than Vulcan's bare facts.

He picked up the last of the photographs. Staring at it, he saw the intelligent eyes and attractive face that had stared back at him many times before.

'Karen de Lout. Tell me about her.'

'I don't have much, I'm afraid, only what I was able to get from her secretary and the other directors. She is president of the corporation, and a formidable woman. She controls the company's activities in and around South Africa. She's shown extraordinary skill and achieved remarkable results. Tom de Lout was something of a genius in business, but since she has taken over de Louts is in a far stronger position than ever before.'

'Weaknesses?'

'None I can establish. But I suspect, hurt the company and you hurt Karen de Lout. She lives and breathes de Louts, especially since the death of her husband.'

'OK. What about movements, routines, friends, family, that the personal stuff?' Dave placed her photograph back on the table.

'She seems to be a loner, and the company takes up all her time. But her secretary did let slip that she is taking an extended holiday soon.'

Dave's interest quickened. 'What and where?'

'Three and a half weeks on safari through Namibia and Botswana to Zimbabwe.'

Dave's brow creased. 'A private one?'

'No, that's the puzzling thing. It's with a travel company based here in Jo'burg. Afro Ventures.'

Dave's instincts flared as if somebody had struck a match. This was the break they had been waiting for. 'Right, I know it's short notice, but I want you to book me on that safari. I don't care how you do it, buy somebody out if you have to, but make sure you get me on it.'

Dave's mind wrestled with the new development, and Sandy's quiet, almost petulant comment almost passed him by. 'I thought that's what you'd say,' she murmured, gathering up the reports and photographs. She was hardly aware of it herself, but her personal feelings were starting to cloud her professional judgment.

'I know we both have a lot to keep us busy, but do you remember the detective who investigated us after that chemical plant business?' he asked.

'James Pearson. I'm not likely to forget him, am I?'

Dave glanced at her, surprised at the vehemence in her tone. What had the man done to her to provoke such a strong reaction? He was obviously missing something here. He tucked the observation away for future attention. 'Well, as it turns out, he has been investigating Vulcan as well. I want you to find out what he knows, who he's spoken to and why. This time his probing mind may work in our favour.'

CHAPTER 33

Karen returned to her office after a lunch in blessed solitude, refreshed but slightly bemused.

She had opted for the Carlton Centre, a fifty-two-storey complex encompassing a hotel, shops and entertainment as well as numerous cafés, and an easy place to elude her ever-present security entourage.

She was in need of the peace after a particularly frustrating morning. Peter had stonewalled her attempts to expand their interests overseas, a ploy she found most annoying.

But what had bemused her was the brief glimpse she had caught of Susan and her new male companion, walking hand in hand through the underground plaza. Susan had been staring adoringly into the man's expressionless face. But the man certainly wasn't Karen's type at all.

Susan wasn't a small woman, but even she looked petite beside his massive proportions; his huge hand had engulfed hers to the wrist. The spade-shaped beard he wore hid most of his face, but to Karen he still looked like an Afrikaaner.

Karen still hadn't figured out what it was that had left her so amazed. It didn't help that seeing her secretary so smitten had clawed at her own bruised emotions and reopened the wounds she thought had begun to heal.

Before the memories succeeded in clouding her reason, a light tap at the door refocused her mind.

Her brother-in-law stood in the doorway. 'Yes, Peter, come in,' she said frostily, indicating one of the leather settees with an outstretched arm.

She launched in right away. 'Peter, I can't tolerate this. You're going against the direct wishes of both myself and the board.'

'The board always goes along with your wishes. Only once since you've taken office have they voted against you.' This was clearly a sore point with Peter.

'Don't be ridiculous. If any member considered any of my proposals ill-judged, they would say so,' she retorted.

Peter continued doggedly. 'Ever since you bullied your proposals through when you were elected president, the board has done your bidding. I concede that you've achieved tremendous results here in southern Africa, but...'

'Oh, how magnanimous,' Karen cut in.

Peter didn't miss a beat. 'But I have achieved just as admirably in Europe. I feel it only fair I'm given the same courtesy.'

'The board has made a decision.'

'Look, I'm not recommending there should be no expansion. What I am saying is *not right now*, and for perfectly valid reasons.'

'I know what your reasons are, and you know why I've disputed them. The board's decision is final,' she declared firmly.

'I see,' Peter responded gravely. Karen was expecting him to come back at her with a different argument, but instead he changed the subject completely. 'When are you proposing to leave for your safari?'

His tone was casual, but she was all too familiar with his calculating mind.

'You know bloody well when I am leaving,' she retorted. 'Don't you dare try to use that as a bargaining tool.'

'Well, I do control the security for the company, and the safety of all the directors is my responsibility.' He held up a hand, and Karen bit back the sharp comment that sprang to her lips. 'You may be interested to know there has been a late booking on your proposed safari, for a man known to our security arm.'

Karen's spirits slumped. She'd been so looking forward to her trip. But her suspicions flared. 'Why exactly are you telling me this?'

Peter spoke deliberately. 'It's just that the end of your safari coincides with the date I've recommended we hold off till, before considering any expansion.'

'So, correct me if I'm wrong, if I recommend that we postpone our planned expansion until after my return, you won't use this so-called late booking as an excuse to make me change my plans?' Karen asked cautiously.

'If that's how you choose to see it. I'll even make sure the opening of Omumbo won't upset your arrangements.'

Karen locked her gaze on Peter's uncompromising façade. A compromise, then. 'OK, you've obviously realised this safari means a lot to me. If you ensure there's no interruption to my trip, you can have your delay. Agreed?' She extended her hand.

Peter accepted it. 'Completely.'

Karen could have sworn she saw relief flicker behind Peter's guarded eyes, but the thought was fleeting. Her safari was safe; allowing him his small victory was a small price to pay for that.

Peter stood up and headed for the door, but Karen stopped him. 'This late booking. Who was it?'

'You mean who is it.'

Karen was confused. She had assumed the late booking meant trouble, and that Peter would have dealt with it.

Peter eyed her, clearly thinking he had scored another victory. 'I think you must've misunderstood me. He's one of the reasons I'm happy for you to take your safari, a totally unexpected bonus really. Without my having to do a thing, you and the company's interests are protected. You'll probably be safer out in the bushveld than you are right here. He's one of the most effective security consultants in Africa, if not the world.'

CHAPTER 34

Dave's eyebrows knotted briefly as he glanced through office window at the sound of a vehicle pulling up the driveway. He recognised Sandy's VW Golf, and glanced at his watch. He wasn't expecting to see her until late this evening. His curiosity turned to alarm when he saw her face as she burst through the door.

'Thank god you're still here. I didn't want to use the phone. James Pearson's dead.'

Dave stilled, as if he was cast in stone. 'How?'

Sandy crossed the office, breathing hard. 'I persuaded the police to show me their report. He was shot down in cold blood, through the back of his head.' She shivered slightly.

'Vulcan,' Dave whispered. 'When?'

'About three months ago.'

'About the same time as Jaunus Zamba was killed in Botswana.'

'I suppose so, yes. But what's that got to do with it?'

Dave sat down heavily. 'You remember me telling you how I was contacted in Melbourne and Perth.'

Sandy nodded.

'What I didn't tell you was by who. My instructions were dropped off by an agent of Vulcan's. His name is Kane Van der Zwet. He's a Dutchman living in the States, and a very dangerous man, I've worked with him in the past. I found out he'd dropped the instructions off in Perth before he flew to Melbourne. And it all happened round about the same time as Zamba was killed. And it appears James Pearson too.'

'But the Botswana government and the UDF accused the South African security forces of killing Zamba,' Sandy cut in.

'That may even be what they really believe, but I was already pretty sure it was Vulcan, and now I'm positive. Vulcan sent in Kane to do the job. All the jobs. Vulcan must've got wind of Pearson's investigation.' Sandy was staring at him, clearly baffled. 'This is how I see it. Kane was sent in to kill Zamba and to turn the UDF's allegiance firmly back to Vulcan. Then he silenced Pearson to put a stop to his investigation. And finally, he was the courier who passed Vulcan's instructions on to me. The timing's so precise, it had to be Kane. And he acts on Vulcan's orders.'

'Well, you'd know Vulcan's methods better than most. So now we've lost Pearson as a possible lead.'

'No, not entirely. I have somebody else working on Pearson's movements. My bet is, he must've been getting uncomfortably close to Vulcan.' Dave looked at his watch. 'Look, I'm running late for a meeting. What I want you to do is chase up everything you can find on Pearson: his movements and recent contacts, and also where he lived, his friends and family, hobbies, and anything else you can lay your hands on. He may yet be able to give us a clue.' He laid his hand on her arm. 'I have to go. Look, Sandy, I know I don't need to tell you this, but be careful. If Kane isn't actually in the country, he can' t be far away.' He closed his eyes briefly; should he tell her? Yes; it was only fair. 'There's something else you need to know. He thinks he has a score to settle with me, and I don't want you to get caught in the crossfire.'

He dropped his hand and began to walk away. Sandy's voice followed him, as firm and fearless as ever. This woman was amazing, he thought.

'I'll need some sort of information on this Kane. I don't even know what he looks like.'

'I'll see what I can do. I can probably get a photograph, but his profile will have to be verbal. Now I really do have to go.'

Amazing, he thought, digging in his pocket for his keys. Truly amazing.

The lift ascended in silence, neither man acknowledging the other's presence. It glided to a cushioned halt at the fourth floor. Just before the doors opened, the shorter of the two stepped forward, turned his head slightly and, hardly moving his lips, murmured, '431.'

Dave rode up two more floors and returned to the fourth floor by the stairs. The corridor was deserted, and it didn't take him long to locate room 431. His knock was quickly answered.

'Hello, Richard. Good flight?'

'Had better.' Richard stepped back to allow Dave to come in. He locked the door and followed him.

It was one of the Holiday Inn's basic double rooms, with a double bed, table and two chairs.

Dave sat at the table with his back to the curtained window. 'Who knows you're here?' he asked.

'In theory, only Johnny and you, but I'm pretty sure I was recognised as I went through passport control.'

'In that case it's probably wise you contact Athol Jansen. We'll be needing as much help as we can get.'

Dave had no intention of telling Richard about his own arrangement with Athol and the South African security service; he had informed Athol of Richard's imminent arrival himself, and knew the South African would give nothing away.

Richard pulled out the seat opposite Dave, unsurprised at the way Dave had effortlessly assumed command. 'I've already contacted him. I'm meeting with him tomorrow.'

'Good. In that case, before you update me on what's happened since we last met, I'd better tell you what I've found out since my arrival. It'll probably help your meeting with Athol.'

He outlined his theory about the motive behind the death of Jaunus Zamba, and more importantly, the UDF's ensuing activities. He expanded on the current situation with de Louts, and briefly touched on James Pearson's investigation and his murder.

Richard listened without interrupting. When he was sure Dave had finished, he leant back and clasped his hands over his belly. 'If you're right, Vulcan's plans are far grander and further advanced than we imagined.'

Dave looked at him for a long moment. 'What do you mean, we?'

Richard returned his gaze. It didn't do to underestimate Dave Old, he reminded himself. 'It's important you know that I haven't been working alone. I've been operating in conjunction with the CIA...'

'No surprise there.' Dave shrugged.

'...and the KGB.'

Dave drew a sharp breath. 'Now, that is a surprise. Jesus, the three of you, together. Don't tell me the Cold War is finally thawing.'

'Maybe, but a lot depends on the outcome of this operation. Although they want Vulcan destroyed as much as we do, they also want to capitalise on the situation. And although we pooled our resources, it was still one step forward and two back. Remember the three teams of watchers at Heathrow waiting for somebody to pick up the computer disks?' Dave nodded. 'We assumed one would've been Vulcan's. But since we've been working together the CIA and KGB have stepped up all their surveillance on agents, couriers and drop-off points. The other two teams were more than likely the Russians' and the CIA's.'

'OK, so that explains the watchers. But does it really make much difference to the way we proceed from here? Surely, if you use their resources properly, something we can use will eventually surface.'

'I suppose that's what I am getting to,' Richard said pensively. 'It's not necessarily what has been uncovered, it's more the lack of it. Since our first meeting neither of them have come up with anything much at all, and it's beyond belief that they've failed to uncover something useful.'

'So they know more than they're letting on. But taking advantage of each other's weakened position doesn't really affect the Vulcan situation,' Dave reasoned.

'Initially that's what I thought, But the men I've been dealing with are at the very top of their organisations. They have huge resources and manpower to draw on. They should have had something to contribute to our common goal. But now—' He slapped the table. 'Now they've both disappeared. Effectively that means they've terminated our arrangement, and are acting independently. We know one is in southern Africa, and we're pretty sure the other isn't far away. And each running his own operation. Now do you see my concern?'

'Yeah, point taken.' Dave began to drum his fingers on the table. 'So, are they trying to hinder Vulcan, or help him?'

'Don't get me wrong, their rhetoric points towards trying to destroy him, but my feeling is they each think they can take over his operation. Vulcan has nearly achieved what both those countries have been trying to do for decades, one through capitalism, the other through communism. If either of them succeeds, we're back to square one.'

Neither man knew what else to say. The situation seemed to be escalating by the week. What had started as a mammoth seek and destroy operation was magnifying into something far more complex. Originally they had been fighting a single adversary; now they seemed to have multiple foes.

Richard was the one who broke the silence. 'If it's any consolation, your hunch looks correct. De Louts' overseas subsidiaries have been siphoning off capital to obscure sources around the world.' Richard reached down to his satchel and extracted a scroll of computer printouts. He flopped them on the table in front of Dave. 'All evidence points to de Louts being where Vulcan derived his original finance from, before his operations became self-sustaining. We may even find they are still his major backer.'

Dave cast his eye briefly over the printouts. 'At least it looks as if I'm right to concentrate on de Louts. I still think Karen de Lout is the key and will lead us to Vulcan.'

'I hope you're right.' Richard shook his head sadly. 'Quite frankly, Dave, Britain and the rest of Europe aren't faring well. The European politicians are refusing to budge on trade restraints. Vulcan must have promised them the earth; either that, or he has them terrified. He reached for his satchel again. 'I brought as much information as I could on the two men running the CIA and the KGB operations.' He extracted two profiles with several photographs attached, and tapped the first one. 'The big man is Uri Ferkatovich, no guesses where he's from. The other one's Brendan Oechsli, Deputy Director of the CIA. He seems to run their show.'

Dave quickly glanced at the photographs. He knew neither was a face he would forget, Ferkatovich because of his size and steely expression, Oechsli with those hypnotic eyes. He put the two photographs aside and pushed everything else back towards Richard. 'I've seen all I need to,' he said. 'It's not information I'd want to be found with.'

Richard gave a small smile. The information was already impressed in Dave's memory; he'd be able to call it up at a moment's notice.

'One last thing. I need a photograph of Kane Van der Zwet.' Dave fumbled for his wallet and drew out a small blank card. He scribbled a number on it and handed it to Richard. 'Post it to this PO Box. It's untraceable.'

Richard slipped the card into his satchel. 'Bit of a tall order, but I'm sure Johnny'll come up with something. All other messages he'll put through the usual channel.'

Both men stood up. Dave stretched out a callused hand and Richard shook it. 'I don't want to sound pessimistic, but it looks as though I may be unable to give you much help from here on in.'

Dave dropped his hand to his side. *'C'est la vie.'* With that, he left the room.

CHAPTER 35

S he must have cried out in her sleep again. She had woken with a start, bolt upright in bed, her chest heaving, terror coursing through her body. The duvet on her king-sized bed was in complete disarray. Karen began to scan the room wildly, seeking the hidden demons from her dream. She never recalled the nightmare in full, but somehow she knew it was the same one: the one that had plagued her long before her marriage with Tom.

What had made her cry out and woke her up was the sensation of plummeting helplessly through the air. The part she did remember was feeling completely alone as she was chased to the edge of a bottomless void by a hunting leopard. It crouched, laid its ears back and snarled, and she tripped and plunged into the dark abyss. Still etched in her mind was the leopard with tortured eyes that seemed to speak of a tormented past.

She would be unable to sleep again, so she slipped out of bed and crossed to the closed French doors that led onto a second-storey balcony. The bedroom had once felt secure, an oasis of peace. It was large, the size of a small apartment, and furnished with beautiful antiques, some pieces Queen Anne, others Chippendale and the odd piece of Sheraton. The walk-in wardrobe was large enough to hang a separate set of clothes for every day of the year, one side for him, the other for her. Both sides were full; Karen hadn't yet been able to bring herself to dispose of Tom's clothes. The en suite, like the bedroom, was tastefully decorated in gold and black, with shining brass and polished black marble. Two separate mirrored vanities faced the huge bath, and like the wardrobe Karen hadn't been able to clear Tom's things away.

She threw back the French doors and stepped lightly onto the balcony of white plastered cement, where she was met by a cool morning breeze. She left the doors open, and the chintz curtains billowed about in the breeze as she stood in front of the waist-high parapet. She lifted her chin and faced into the wind, eyes closed and long brown hair tousled.

It was almost dawn. One moment the light was dim and grey; the next, the sun burst over the horizon and ten hectares of beautifully designed lawns and gardens leapt to life before her eyes. But it gave her no joy. Karen's love for the magnificent house and grounds had died with her husband. To her it was just a place to eat and sleep; a place empty of love.

Tom and Karen had chosen the site in the countryside just north of Johannesburg with great care. It had been her dream home, her bastion while Tom was alive. The house was in the classical Italianate style, modelled on Queen Victoria's beloved Osborne House on the Isle of Wight, but the resemblance was superficial.

The house was finished in brilliant white cement, and was made up of a central two-storey block and two single-storey wings. One wing comprised a formal dining-room with seating for fifty, the main kitchen and service area, and the servants' quarters; the other had two private studies, a library and the informal private living rooms.

The main entrance of the central block was adorned with a finely proportioned portico leading into the main lobby, which was a work of art, with a splendidly vaulted ceiling, white marble floor and massive wooden doorways to the wings. What first caught the eye, though, was the sweeping marble staircase to the bedrooms on the second floor.

It was not only a palatial mansion, befitting the dignity and status of the de Louts; it was also a comfortable home.

Or it had been once, Karen thought as she left the balcony. She bathed and dressed quickly; she had no intention of spending the full day at work on the day before she was due to leave on safari.

She ran briskly down the sweeping staircase, hoping she was the only member of the household awake so early. She was disappointed; one of her bodyguards was sitting at the long wooden kitchen table. As she approached he whisked his feet off the table and snapped shut the novel he was reading.

'Good morning, Mrs de Lout. I didn't expect to see you yet,' he said guiltily.

She gave him a curt nod and crossed the kitchen to a side door that led into a large enclosed cobbled yard in front of the five-car garage. She chose her white BMW convertible, and had backed it out on to the meandering driveway before the bodyguard appeared in her rear-view mirror, She allowed herself a little smile as he reeled to a halt with his hands thrown up in despair. They were a necessity, but how they irked her at times!

There was no real need for her to go into the office today; she had worked long and hard to clear her desk over the last week. But what else was there to do?

The nightmare was still playing on her mind, and without quite realising what she was doing, she turned off the highway and drove into the suburbs.

It wasn't until the beginnings of a panic attack grabbed at her that she recognised an all too familiar street. She pulled into the kerb, heart racing and breath coming in gasps. She hadn't been back to the house at the far end since the day she finished school.

Karen's white suburban upbringing should have been an enviable one in a country that for years beset by the restraints and regulations which affected the majority of the population. But her mother had died giving birth to her, and her father blamed her for the loss of his loving wife. The abuse was not physical, but no less debilitating for that.

She craved love, but experienced only discipline and frosty hostility. Every waking moment of her childhood was spent in a fruitless quest for a sign of affection from her father.

Karen finished school at the top of her class, with a scholarship to Witwatersrand University. She travelled home with her head held high, full of hope for the praise that now would surely come.

The disappointment was like a knockout blow. Her father had laid her scant possessions on the footpath outside the house, his obligation to her now complete, at least in his own eyes. When she pleaded with him to let her stay, his slashing rebuke cut her to the bone, leaving an emotional scar that still troubled her.

'I have never loved you, I never will. And I hope to god you experience the same lonely life you inflicted on me.'

Karen felt wasted inside. She was abandoned, destitute and naïve totally unprepared for the world.

It was by good luck rather than good management that she survived until the beginning of the university's first semester. But armed with her determination and her scholarship, she applied herself to her studies and achieved an MBA with honours.

Alongside her determination was a fierce independence, and a misguided belief that her academic success would give her what she sought. These qualities helped her to forge a career, but the self-sufficient façade she created only masked her inner fear. As if in obedience to her father's parting wish, she felt alone and helpless inside.

Her world was completely turned around when Tom de Lout shattered her emotional shackles. She learnt to love and be loved, and her drive and energy became a positive force instead of a front.

With Tom Karen had finally felt complete; his death had carried her back to those desolate years. Had she finally come to lay the devil to rest? Or was it the lure of the past, drawing her to crave the love and recognition of the man who had dominated her childhood?

It took a mighty force of will to stop the BMW in front of the house. Her body trembled and her heart pounded as if she had just run a marathon as she walked up the path and stood before the painted door. Her resolve began to crack like a brittle bone; steeling herself, she hammered heavily on the door.Silence. She turned to walk away, but heard the door open. Yet she was too afraid to turn around. She broke into a run, but a woman's voice halted her flight.

'Yes, dear, may I help?'

With a sickly feeling Karen turned. The elderly woman on the step looked like the grandmother she had never had: rosy cheeks, smiling face, a floral apron around her waist.

'I was just... I...' The woman waited patiently, and once Karen had stammered out her story, she shook her head sorrowfully.

'Oh dear, how unfortunate. You see, my dear, my husband and I bought this house from your father's estate. Surely you must've read the will?'

The woman's words hit her like a solid blow. She staggered backwards; it didn't even occur to her to ask when her father had died. Without a word she numbly turned away, leaving the woman standing in the doorway of the house she'd never known as a home. In a daze Karen drove away. Had the devil been finally laid to rest, or was the lonely helplessness of her dreams a prelude to being permanently incarcerated in the past? Only time would tell.

CHAPTER 36

There was a knock at the door. Richard finished drying his hands in the bathroom and went to open it.

'Athol. Good to see you again. Come on through.'

Athol followed Richard and took the whole room in at a glance. 'So how have things been?' He took the seat he was offered at the table, and Richard sat opposite him.

'Could be better.' He decided to come straight to the point. 'Look, Athol, I don't want to waste your time. Vulcan; he's causing more trouble than we can afford.'

Athol appeared unconcerned. 'I know he's been causing you all sorts of trouble at home, but there's nothing we can't handle.'

'Come on, Athol, I was born in this country. I know South Africans are proud, but there's pride and there's arrogance.'

Athol's expression turned frosty. Richard tried another tack.

'Have you figured out yet who had Jaunus Zamba killed?' He let the question hang, and Athol's eyes flickered behind his gold-rimmed glasses. So he had indeed figured it out. 'OK, I'll tell you why, shall I?'

Athol dropped his show of indifference. 'All right, you've made your point. I'm well aware of the situation that's developing. And by the way, how the hell do you know so much about my country's security?'

'Like I said, I was born here.'

Athol was one of the few people outside the British security services who knew the true extent of Richard's influence. Where possible, Richard ran Network's African sector on his own, so the two men had worked together many times in the past, and had formed a reluctant bond.

'Answer the question.' Athol began to drum his fingers on the table.

Richard remained silent for long moments, then replied carefully, 'I have a contact close to Vulcan.'

Athol looked startled. Did he mean Dave Old? 'I find that hard to believe. Our intelligence tells us his organisation is watertight.'

'Look, Athol, I'm not trying to turn this into a competition. Just take my word for it, will you?' Richard said, slightly annoyed.

Athol decided to let down his guard. 'I'm sorry, Richard, it's just that for the last few weeks I've been hitting my head against a brick wall. My superiors are treating my claims with scepticism. All I get is *Facts, Jansen, give us facts.*' He looked at Richard but the Englishman didn't react. 'I have to admit that all I know about Vulcan is how his operation affects South Africa, so if we' re going to work together you'd best give me the bigger picture. I'll try and fill what gaps I can.'

Athol soon realised the situation was far worse than he'd imagined. At one stage he could keep his silence no longer. 'Both the KGB and the CIA here in the Republic? Hell, this is turning into a nightmare.'

Richard continued, leaving out only his association with Dave and the extent of de Louts' involvement. He wasn't prepared to compromise the security services' creed, *protect your agents and contacts at all costs.* Dave's role might yet remain undiscovered.

Athol sat dazed as Richard concluded his account. 'I never realised the full extent of Vulcan's power. The stuff about the UDF and South Africa I already knew, but as to the state of the rest of the world, I had no idea.' He briefly shook his head. 'The thing that really worries me is what the KGB and CIA are doing. If we do manage to stop Vulcan, we've still got them to worry about. Are they government backed, or operating on their own?'

'There's been no response from either Moscow or Washington, not that I expected it. I don't really think it matters one way or the other; they're a law unto themselves. I believe they both see the situation as something they can use to further their own aims. Which we now know are the same as Vulcan's; world dominance.'

'So what action do we take?'

'I don't think there's much we can do. Just sit back and wait for a lead from my contact. If he flushes him out before your government falls, we've got a better than even chance of stopping both the KGB and the CIA. If he doesn't, well, they'll be the least of our worries.'

'I know my government needs a shake up, but I was hoping for something a little less extreme,' Athol said unhappily.

Richard was surprised. He had assumed Athol would take a conservative line; his job was national security after all.

The other man seemed to read his mind. 'You think I'm a bit radical for somebody highly placed in security. Well, something has to change. If we can expose Vulcan's plans, let's hope it'll be a catalyst for reform.'

Richard began to commend him for his insight, but Athol hadn't finished.

'Do you really believe a takeover of South Africa is on the cards? Is Vulcan that well organised?'

'Yes to both. But hopefully it will be his planning that lets him down. His biggest gamble will have to be the destruction of your government. Get in the way of that and he'll stumble.'

'So it all depends on your agent?'

'Unless you've got an alternative.'

'I always leave the best to last,' Athol responded cheerfully. 'You've been honest with me. It's only fair you know that I've also infiltrated Vulcan's organisation.'

Richard sat bolt upright in his chair. So Athol had been hedging his bets. He wondered what else the South African had been holding back. How much more did he really know?

But something didn't quite seem to gel. Richard had been considering telling Athol about de Louts, but for now he too would hedge his bets. The destruction of the investment corporation's leadership would hurt South Africa deeply, yet to save his country it was a price Athol must be prepared to pay.

But would Athol himself find the price too high?

CHAPTER 37

The late morning sun streamed through the windows of the office. Sandy was busy at her desk while Dave studied a pile of files and documents. There was a light knock at the door and Sandy looked up, puzzled; she hadn't seen anyone enter reception.

Dave quickly closed the folder he was reading and went the door.

'I see you, my friend,' he said in Zulu.

He opened the door and Sandy saw him greet a thickset, battered-looking black African. The man stood a few inches shorter than Dave and looked strangely familiar; a rare look of pleasure flashed across Dave's face.

'Of course you remember Sandy?' Dave said in English.

'How could I forget such a spirited lady? Hello, Sandy.'

Sandy leapt out of her seat. 'Timot, you old rogue. So you have conquered your frail male ego and shaved off the last of your hair.' She took a step forward and ran a hand over his scar-ridden scalp, cooing, 'Who's a pretty boy?'

'*Hauw*, such insolence. I see you still need lessons in how to train this woman.' But Timot was clearly loving the attention.

'Alas, Timot, the woman is willing, but I fear the man is lacking,' Sandy teased.

A single snort of laughter escaped from Timot.

Dave scratched his nose. 'Yes, well, best we get down to work.'

Sandy and Timot exchanged mischievous glances as they settled themselves on the settees.

Dave decided he had better take control. 'I know you two haven't worked together since the early days, but while I'm on safari I want you to give each other all the help you can. And just for the record, Sandy, I've been keeping Timot informed since I arrived.'

'Ah, the mysterious friend you went to see. I should've guessed.'

'Timot is how I found out about James Pearson. I want you to compare notes. You first, Timot.'

'OK. I was approached by Pearson at my, ah, place of business. He asked me about Vulcan and the Leopard.' Sandy raised her eyebrows. 'No, Sandy,

189

he didn't know he was asking about Dave, and I've since found out he was no longer with the police force. I can only assume he was investigating for a private party from de Louts. My cousin who works as a chauffeur there saw him leave the building several times.'

'Why a private party?' Sandy cut in.

'Because de Louts have one of the best security services in the republic. If the company was going to run an investigation, they'd use their own resources,' Dave said.

Timot wasn't used to being interrupted. He glared at the two of them.

'Sorry,' they said in harmony, each trying to suppress a grin.

Timot cleared his throat theatrically. 'Now where was I? Ah yes, James Pearson. I managed to find out how he came to talk to me and after some gentle persuasion, the man concerned now understands it's important not to talk too liberally again.'

Dave grimaced; he'd seen Timot's gentle persuasion. Timot went on, 'Before he became unable to speak, he did manage to tell me the names of the two places Pearson questioned me about in Natal.'

Sandy broke in, 'What two places?'

'One is KwaMashu, a black township in the north-western outskirts of Durban. The other is the Valley of a Thousand Hills.'

'Any relevance? Dave asked.

'Only that he visited both places before he died. I take it you know he was murdered?' Dave and Sandy nodded. 'I'm going down there soon.'

Dave turned to Sandy. 'Anything you want to ask?'

'Even though I was excluded from the earlier discussions, I've been able to piece it all together, thank you,' she said haughtily.

Dave rolled his eyes. 'OK. What've you got for us, then?' Best to ignore her bruised pride, he thought.

'Not as much as Timot. Pearson appeared to lead a pretty private life and apparently had no family to speak of, so his lawyer is trying to sell his house, lock, stock and barrel. Nothing has been moved since his murder. I've an appointment with the real estate agent tomorrow. I'll give the house the once over then. That's all so far.'

'I'll leave Pearson to you two, then. You'll have to use your initiative while I'm away, and make sure you work together.' Dave picked one of the folders on the table. 'The developments I've got to report aren't too positive, I'm afraid. We've got two new players in the game…'

He proceeded to tell them about the involvement of the Brendan Oechsli and Uri Ferkatovich, and apprehension descended on the room like a cloud not even the bright sunlight could penetrate. What had started as an already complex seek-and-destroy operation was turning into a horror story.

Dave slipped two photographs out of the folder. 'These are the only two I've got. Commit them both to memory, I'd rather they were destroyed.'

'Not faces you'd forget easily,' Timot rumbled. Sandy murmured in agreement.

'Timot, the Russian's yours; Sandy, you've got the American. But don't ask me where to start looking, I wouldn't have a clue.'

Sandy scribbled shorthand on a notepad. 'What about this Dutchman, Kane Van der Zwet?'

'Within a few days a photograph of him should arrive at our other PO box. Show it to Timot and get rid of it.'

Dave sat back and told them all he knew about Kane: their past association, his strengths and weaknesses, his aptitudes and physical skills.

'Any other questions? Remember I leave on safari tomorrow.' He looked from Timot to Sandy; they both shook their heads. 'OK then, we've all got work to do.'

'Yeah, and some of us get the fun part,' Sandy grumbled.

'So I gather. In more ways than one,' Timot murmured, with a twinkle in his eye.

Maybe this would all be a waste of time. Dave, clad in t-shirt and jeans, was standing outside Afro Ventures' head office near the centre of Johannesburg. There had been no sign of Karen de Lout, and as far as the tall, blond-bearded courier and driver knew, all the party had assembled.

The white Land Rover and the food and equipment trailer were parked just up the road. The luggage had been neatly packed into a large canvas cover-all which fitted into the Land Rover's sturdy metal roof-rack; during the safari it would double as a game-viewing platform. In small racks of their own stood three jerry cans, to be used to supplement the long-distant fuel tanks.

The luggage hadn't yet been covered. Maybe there was still time for her to arrive.

The Afro Ventures' logo was blazed across the door: a leopard's head, fangs bared in a silent menacing snarl. It mesmerised him, and he caught himself running his fingers down the four parallel scars beneath his shirt. With an effort he forced himself to drop his hand, and pushed away the memories.

Out of the corner of his eye he caught a flash of light. He looked up to see a black Mercedes limousine pull in on the opposite side of the road. His instincts flared, and Karen de Lout lightly hopped from the back of the vehicle and walked around to the rear.

A black African chauffeur followed her and unlocked the boot. Dave heard her say, 'Thank you, Moses. Enjoy your break while I'm away.'

She retrieved a scruffy canvas backpack from the open boot and strode across the road into the Afro Ventures office.

The photographs Dave had seen hadn't done her justice. She wore jeans, a light blue cotton shirt and white leather trainers, but what was most noticeable was her striking good looks. It was more than feminine beauty; a radiance seemed to glow from her. Her brown shoulder-length hair, tied in a simple ponytail, bobbed up and down as she crossed the road, with a kind of innocence that seemed to enhance her natural beauty.

Dave almost found himself regretting what he must do to that vibrant creature. Then the snarling leopard on the Land Rover's door seemed to challenge his failing spirit. I must be getting soft, he thought, turning away and walking towards the African still standing at the rear of the limousine.

He made some comment about the vehicle, but the African didn't answer; instead he met Dave's eyes, and seemed to be trying to give him some kind of warning. Dave's senses snapped into alert mode. He was being watched – but by whom? All he could see was his own image reflected off the limousine's tinted glass.

He strolled round the car, casting admiring glances, and as he came alongside the front passenger window, he heard a faint electric whine. 'Hello, Dave. You're looking well.'

Dave hoped his initial surprise didn't show. 'Hello, Kane,' he replied casually. 'Better pop the bonnet, I want to talk to you.'

His mind was racing. How the hell did Kane get so close to Karen de Lout? And what the hell was he up to? With one hand he lifted the limousine's bonnet and peered at the vast array of electronic and mechanical workings. Kane came to stand beside him.

'Well?'

'I'm here to make sure you don't screw up,' Kane said, prodding at something electronic.

'How the hell did you get so close?'

'Replied to an ad for a security guard.' Kane patted the motor's distributor.

'Like hell. It must have been fixed from inside.' Dave dropped his hand to his side.

Kane eased the bonnet down and snapped it shut. 'Never mind, I'm here as your back-up if you need me. But I've got responsibilities of my own, so don't stuff it up. Now, say something nice about the car and push off before anyone gets suspicious.'

'Screw you, pal.'

Back beside the Land Rover, Dave looked through the office window at Karen, who was leaning on the counter, talking to a woman. He hoped she hadn't noticed his brief exchange with Kane.

He was watching the limousine disappear round the corner when she glanced up at him, her eyes thoughtful.

It took them just over six hours to reach the old missionary town of Kuruman, on the edge of the mighty Kalahari Desert. Most of the safari members were surprised to find the temperature nowhere near as oppressive as they expected, but then it wasn't yet high summer.

Dave sat up front with Allan, the driver, the first day. Allan's conversation was interesting enough, but Dave's attention was elsewhere. Throughout the journey he felt a determined stare aimed at the back of his head. He wasn't sure, but he was afraid his cover had been blown. Perhaps Karen knew more about him than she should have, though he had no idea how. Exactly what she knew might determine the success of his mission. This phase of the operation had developed complications he could do without. He needed to act quickly.

They set up camp in the enclosure near the middle of the township, behind the Eye of Kuruman, the reliable source of water that allowed the town to prosper. As the evening meal was cooking, Allan suggested that the members introduce themselves. There were six in the party, including Allan himself. The others were a young German industrialist, a real estate broker from England and a female art collector from Port Elizabeth. Dave tuned out as they gave descriptions of their past and their previous endeavours; what he really wanted to hear was how Karen described herself.

'... and after leaving university, I eventually found a job in marketing for a company here in South Africa.'

Dave nearly laughed out loud. To her credit, she hadn't actually lied, but economical with the truth didn't begin to cover it.

He couldn't resist. 'What company do you work for?'

He expected her to glower at him, but instead she looked embarrassed.

'You've probably never heard of it,' was all the reply she gave.

Dave didn't press her any further. When he gave his own account of himself, he saw from the corner of his eye that Karen was every bit as interested in him as he had been in her.

'I live in Johannesburg. I was born in France and am currently involved in security...'

'You mean you're a security guard?' the German chipped in.

'Something like that. I...' He was interrupted by something that could have been a cough from Karen, though to his practised ear it sounded more like a stifled snort of laughter.

So it was to be a game of cat and mouse. The only trouble was, Dave wasn't sure whether he was the cat or the mouse. Things were not working out as he had planned.

Dave woke with a start. The group had bedded down in the open air of the mild Kalahari night. One of his ubiquitous nightmares had woken him; it was an hour or so before daybreak and he knew he'd be unable to sleep again. He lay staring sightlessly at the clear desert sky as the events of the previous day tumbled like dominoes through his mind. No, it definitely wasn't going as he planned.

Originally, he'd had two options: to arrange an accidental death for Karen, or to cultivate an affair so he could influence her actions. The second option was growing more remote by the day, though it was by far the more appealing; it would only work if she believed it was genuine. It was clear that she knew far more about him than he was comfortable with; it wasn't a happy prospect, but it looked as if Karen wouldn't live to see the safari through to its end.

He contemplated getting up and going for a run. That was when he heard a muffled sob, as if somebody had cried out in their sleep. He lay perfectly still for several minutes, but nothing stirred. Perhaps he was mistaken.

He slipped out of his sleeping bag and reached for his running shoes. As he tied the second lace the back of his neck began to bristle; there was no sound, but he could feel a presence.

Quick as a flash he drove upwards, twisting to his side, elbow cocked. Karen was standing in her own running gear behind him. He dropped his arm, expecting her to look horrified, but instead she stepped backwards and poised herself ready to strike. They both broke their defensive stances and stood back, embarrassed.

Amazed more by her actions than her presence, Dave said the first thing that came to mind. 'I'm sorry, you startled me.'

'I startled you?' Karen purred a deep throaty laugh. 'I promise never to sneak up on you again, just as long as you promise never to do the same.'

Clearly the information he had received on Karen hadn't been complete. There had been no mention of any proficiency in martial arts, and her brief display had shown she was no novice. Now even option one was slipping away from him.

Indicating her clothing, he asked, 'Would you like to join me for a run? Perhaps we both need to work off some pent-up energy.'

Karen inclined her head slightly. 'Thank you. I'd like that very much.'

Allan wasted no time getting them on the road heading towards the Augrabies Falls National Park. As it turned out, Dave and Karen were sitting next to one another on the middle seats of the Land Rover. Dave had to admit he had started to develop a grudging admiration for her. He was starting to identify the qualities that had helped her become one of the most influential women in South Africa.

He already knew she had a shrewd and perceptive mind. The morning's brief encounter and the ensuing run had revealed she also had physical skills and fitness to match. He had taken them further, over tougher terrain, than he originally intended; it hardly challenged him at all, since he was still superbly fit, but Karen surprised him yet again. It was only towards the end that she began to falter. She matched him pace for pace, stride for stride right up to the sharp incline before the entrance of the camping enclosure.

He watched her quietly for most of the morning's drive. Her complexion was smooth and clear, the only visible blemish a small brown mole to the left of her chin. She had relaxed her guard and was sitting quite comfortably, staring for most of the time out towards the expanse desert. She appeared to be transfixed by a certain spot. Dave wondered what on earth merited such keen attention.

He decided it was time to break down the reserve between them. 'You're not at work now, Karen,' he said. He didn't speak loudly, but she was startled; perhaps she had indeed been thinking about work.

'Sorry?' she asked.

'The look on your face. You might just as well be back at work.'

'Oh. Yes, you're right. It's hard to step away from it. Point taken, though, we're supposed to be on holiday.' She looked at him with a quick smile, then surprised him all over again. 'You don't sound French to me, and I've never heard of a Frenchman called Dave.'

What was she up to? Or was it only a casual remark? 'No, I suppose I don't. I haven't spent much time there in recent years. And Dave, well, I picked that up on my travels.'

They chatted until they reached the national park, neither of them giving much away. As each kilometre swept by his respect for her grew.

Karen couldn't remember the last time she'd found it so easy to talk and laugh with someone. She was actually enjoying herself.

Before either they knew it, they had reached the Augrabies Falls National Park. The journey had been too short; neither was ready to break off their conversation.

After they had unpacked the Land Rover, Allan, Dave and Keith the real estate broker went to find some firewood. Karen grabbed her camera and left on her own to explore the national park.

Compared to most African national parks, the Augrabies Falls was small, just under five and a half thousand hectares. It included a section of the Orange River to the west, but its most spectacular feature was the Falls themselves, or *Aukoerebis*, the noisy place. Over the centuries the river's ruthless power had cut a gash, producing nineteen separate waterfalls that tumbled into a ravine nearly eighteen kilometres long. Because of the drought, only one was flowing, but it was still spectacular; a chaotic deluge boiled through a narrow gap to cascade nearly a hundred vertical metres into a sheer-sided void.

Karen explored and photographed the rugged beauty of the gorge on foot, totally absorbed in the scenery. Before she knew it, she was beside the main waterfall. It was as if she was dreaming. Mesmerised, she moved towards the edge, staring transfixed at the perpendicular drop that opened like a massive wound before her.

She sat like a zombie, her legs dangling over the edge, beckoning her into its depths. It was the void she'd seen so many times before; this time it was no nightmare, but still seemed to tear her soul in two. The only thing different from her dream were the sheets of thundering water that crashed into the chasm. This time she hadn't been driven to the chasm's gaping edge; she felt it had somehow lured her to its lip. One thought tumbled through her mind like the water below: where was the leopard? There had to be a leopard.

The leopard was the key: somehow she knew that. If she could conquer the threat it posed, real or imagined, she knew she had the power to overcome her tormented past.

She sat on the threshold of something she was unable to fathom. A new life, perhaps? Or the hideous death she had felt looming at her shoulder like an assassin for most of her life. She felt the pull of the abyss below; it was as if it was enticing her into its depths. Slowly she began to slip down the smooth water-polished rock.

That was when she felt the leopard, stalking her. But she was paralysed, and unable to resist.

When Dave arrived back to the camp, Karen was nowhere to be found. He asked one of the others where she had gone; he indicated with a thrust of his chin that she'd headed in the direction of the falls.

He soon caught up with her, so absorbed in her exploration that he was able to observe her unnoticed. He marvelled at how the smallest things captured her full attention: a small rock lizard with a blue head, orange body and tan coloured tail, or a time-weathered rock sculptured into a peculiar shape. He almost envied her.

As she approached the waterfall which gave the park its name, her whole demeanour changed. She stood as if bewitched, entranced by the rift below her. Then she slowly sank to sit with her legs dangling over the edge of the smooth rock.

This was the chance Dave had been waiting for. The sooner he could get it over with, the sooner he would gain Vulcan's trust and be able to get close to him. A simple shove would send her plummeting like a stone to her death. He looked around; there was no one in sight. He thrust aside the respect and admiration he had developed for her and made his mind blank as he'd been taught long ago.

He began to stalk his prey like a predatory cat, all his training flooding to the fore. He moved in unnoticed: one more step to the point of no return. As he took that step, he saw the her camera propped up on the rock beside her with its huge mirrored 1000mm fixed aperture lens. It clearly reflected her expression of utter anguish. Her agony sent his own crashing like a blast of haunted music through his carefully gathered resolve. For the first time in his life, his emotions stood in the way of the task he had set himself. For like an orphan who had found a long-lost sibling, Dave had found somebody whose inner torment equalled his own. He stopped, appalled and sickened by what he'd been about to do. Then the unbelievable happened. Karen, with no help from him, began to slide into the void.

'No!'

As he dove towards her, his chest crashed against the rock. He stretched out his arm, desperately reaching for Karen's. Just in time his fingers locked like a steel clamp around her wrist. A pain lanced through him like red-hot steel, paralysing his arm, and he cried out as he felt his shoulder pop and muscles and tendons tear. His grip began to loosen, but her pleading face made him hurl aside the pain and use every ounce of strength he had to haul her slowly, so slowly, back from a sure and certain death.

As Karen's knees found purchase, she threw herself at Dave and buried her head against his chest, her body racked with desperate sobs. Dave's injured arm hung limp, and he gently stroked her head with his other hand.

Her gut-wrenching sobs slowly subsided and she withdrew her head from the protection of Dave's chest. When she saw the concern etched across his face, her tears began to stream anew. Dave slowly drew her head back to his chest. His life had just changed somehow, forever.

CHAPTER 38

An air of suppressed optimism seemed to embrace the office and its sole inhabitant. The night sky behind Peter's back tumbled in through the huge picture window at his rear. He was the only one left on the executive floor of de Lout House at this time of night; it was long past midnight, and he had arrived back in his own office minutes before, after prowling like a cat through the other offices. He now sat at his desk studying the daily papers.

The office was a mirror image of Karen's in the opposite wing of the executive floor, but it was furnished entirely differently, with the latest architectural designs and the most modern of furniture. His desk was in the same spot as Karen's, but instead of a carved wooden monument to the craftsmanship of old, it was a symbol intended to replace the relics of the past: a simple structure, yet in its way as ostentatious as Karen's antique work of art. An inch-thick sheet of smoke clouded glass, the size of a double bed, sat upon a curving brace of brilliantly polished chrome.

Peter sat at the desk with his face carefully schooled to blankness. It was his feet, clad in hand-tooled Italian leather, that betrayed his real feelings, twitching and jittering as his eyes absorbed the front-page headline:

WORLD ECONOMIES FALTER.

The article described the economic downturn currently taking place throughout the world, and asked why the various governments were apparently unwilling to respond to the decline.

After Peter had read this, the last of the many articles, his poker-face became smug and his eyes turned cold and hard. He leant back in his high-backed chair of chrome and black leather and gazed out into his office.

Since Karen left, he had felt as if invisible shackles had been removed and he no longer had to keep looking over his shoulder. Their agreement to delay any growth in Europe until her return meant a reprieve for him; the information he had presented to the board was false, and any plans for expansion would expose his deception like an executioner's axe. At least now he had time to think.

The majority of the figures Peter had presented had been correct, factually at least. The corporation's worldwide subsidiaries genuinely had achieved substantial growth in all their markets despite the recession – but the price had been far higher than he had indicated. Peter was a brilliant accountant; not only had his reports shown the actual increases, they had also indicated healthy reserves of cash that didn't actually exist.

As Dave and Richard had discovered, de Louts' European and North American subsidiaries had been siphoning vast sums of capital to unknown sources across the globe. De Lout Investments was still asset rich, but now it was cash poor. One unforeseen anomaly could see the giant corporation come tumbling down like a house of cards.

Peter had judged the resources at his disposal very carefully. The one contingency he hadn't foreseen after his brother's death was that the controlling interest in the company would be handed over to Karen. He had expected shares to be held in trust for her, but not for the entire company to be effectively under her direct control. But now Karen's prying eyes would soon be closed forever and the company would be his, to direct as he saw fit. The plan, Vulcan's plan, which had swallowed up so much of the corporation's reserves would ensure his seat of power.

As Peter revelled in the feeling of delicious anticipation, his office door slowly scraped open over the thick loops of shag-pile carpet. His eyes snapped back into focus and he saw a dark silhouette on the threshold.

The figure was unrecognisable, and strangely sinister. Peter swallowed hard. 'Who's there?' he whispered nervously.

The figure moved into the light.

Peter fear was quickly replaced by intense alarm. 'What the hell are you doing here? We should never be seen together, especially not here. You know how careful we need to be.'

The figure moved closer.

'How on earth did you get past the guards?' Peter stood apprehensively behind his desk.

The man spoke in a distinctive American accent. 'So many questions, Peter. You know I never take risks.'

'Then why have you come?' Peter demanded, sinking back down into his chair and beginning to regain control.

'I've come to check on our progress personally, to see that everything's in place.'

The man's use of *our* strangely irked Peter, but he suppressed his anger. He waved an arm at one of the low-slung leather and chrome chairs in front of his desk, back in charge of the situation. 'If you are referring to Natal, it's done, and if you are referring to the takeover of de Louts, it's imminent. The Leopard is active.'

Never taking his eyes off Peter, the man inclined his head in reluctant admiration. But those eyes, piercingly hypnotic, did not reveal his true feelings.

In theory the NASA base at Southview, Johannesburg, was there to monitor and support the United States space shuttle program. But not all the activities at the base were solely NASA -based. One section of the base was set aside for the exclusive use of the CIA.

Just as the Soviet KGB had begun working directly with Pretoria, the CIA had become the another mouthpiece for the United States with the Republic. Since the United States embassy had appeared to scale down due to the world's condemnation of the country's apartheid regime, the CIA had been moved from the embassy in Pretoria to operate secretly from Southview. South Africa was such an important country, not only because of her wealth, but also her strategic placement in the world, that the United States could not afford to allow Russian influence to operate unchallenged.

During its fledgling years, the CIA's role was to co-ordinate covert action outside the USA. It had a mission to roll back communism throughout the world and protect the country's security, and saw itself as the designated special forces of the western world. But as the agency refined its skills, it adopted a subtler role; it now concentrated its efforts throughout most of the world on investigation, in its capacity as advisor on world affairs to the President of the United States.

Now, because of the strategic importance of South Africa and the danger that she might be taken over by an independent or Soviet-backed regime, the CIA's operations there were something of a last bastion of the doctrines of the past. This was especially true at Southview, which was still entrenched in the old dogmas and committed to the age-old fight for US-led capitalism. The agents based there operated on a need to know basis, often working blindly.

The name etched on the smoked glass door was Daniel Shelby. The man himself was the head of Southview station and the most senior CIA officer stationed in South Africa, directly accountable to the Directorate of Operations at Langley. The glass door was thrown open violently, but he remained unmoved, and slowly laid down his pen, removed his glasses and lifted his head to fix his compelling eyes on the intruder.

Oblivious to the steely gaze, the intruder bellowed, 'What the hell are these goddamn orders?' He brandished a sheet of paper and placed his fists squarely on Shelby's desk, his bull neck thrust forward as he fixed his superior with a menacing glare of his own.

Shelby, as he was known to superiors and subordinates alike, placed his elbows on the desktop and steepled his fingers. 'And what orders are these, Rod?'

'You know damn well what orders.' The man's southern twang robbed his harsh tone of much of its sting. 'You've hog-tied me and everyone else. We have to sit back and watch those damn Russians move into action.'

'Still not with you, Rod.'

Rod Zimmerman's deeply tanned face creased into a scowl. He took a step back from the desk and thrust the sheet of paper at Shelby. 'These orders. The ones on my desk this morning, side-lining me into an observer's role.' He curled his lip. 'You received my report two days ago. The Russians are stepping things up. They're throwing so much money and manpower around, we won't have a cat in hell's chance of stopping them unless we start now and pull out all stops of our own.'

'And how do you propose we do that? Waste more money? You know damn well the natives don't care where the money comes from, just as long as it keeps coming.'

'Hell, we gotta do something. Those commies bastards are stirring up a hell of a hornet's nest. And you know as well as I the South Africans have stopped watching them since they reached that marketing accord over gold and diamonds.' Zimmerman's face was almost purple with rage. 'I'm warning you,' he thrust an accusing finger at his superior, 'if the Ruskies continue as they are the South African government may have so much opposition, an overthrow could be imminent.'

'Orders are orders.' Shelby spread his hands in a gesture of finality.

'Stuff you, pal. I'll be putting a report into Langley.'

'You want to go to the top?' Shelby raised an eyebrow.

'Sure, why not, if that's what I gotta do to get somebody to listen.' The prospect didn't appear to daunt him at all.

'Well, in that case you may as well make your report in person.' Shelby stood up and looked over Zimmerman's shoulder. Zimmerman turned to find another man standing in silence on the threshold.

'I don't believe you have met the Deputy Director personally,' Shelby continued calmly.

The stunned look on Zimmerman's face spoke volumes; Brendan Oechsli was the last person he expected to see here in South Africa.

'You have something you want to say to me?' Brendan asked politely.

For the first time Zimmerman was at a loss for words. He was aware of Oechsli's formidable reputation, but that wasn't what had stunned him into silence; it was the piercing stare of those cold hypnotic eyes. Eventually he composed himself. 'Ah... it's the...' He took a deep breath and straightened his shoulders. 'There's been a massive increase in activity by the Russians, sir, and if something's not done the South Africans may have trouble counteracting it.'

Brendan looked over Zimmerman's shoulder at Shelby, who was still standing behind his desk. 'Has he been fully vetted?' After Shelby nodded. 'And briefed on the Vulcan affair?' Another nod, then Brendan turned back to Zimmerman. 'Then you're aware of the predicament the United States finds itself in. Vulcan has politicians all over the world either on his payroll or running scared; his influence may soon be unstoppable. He is planning one last coup, and I believe he means to control South Africa and its gold production. With that he'll have it all; power, influence and a majority holding in the resource that underpins the monetary system of the entire world.'

'But what has that got to do with the Russians, sir?' Zimmerman asked quietly, his fury dissipated.

This was the question Brendan had expected. He took his time before answering. 'Not until Vulcan has taken over South Africa will he make his true identity known. So you see, Zimmerman, he must be unmasked before that happens, and at any cost. We're going to do that, and the way we'll do it is by sitting, watching and waiting. Vulcan can only achieve his master-stroke by causing the destruction of the present South African government. The Russians know that, and they're helping him. We'll take no direct action. We'll just sit back and... wait for things to happen.'

Zimmerman was intrigued, but still mystified. 'Sorry, sir, I still don't get it. Why are the Russians backing Vulcan?'

'Look at it this way, Zimmerman. The Communist system they have fostered at home and abroad is failing. In fact, it's damn near bankrupted the country. They need a massive boost of power and influence. How do you suppose they are planning on achieving that?'

Light dawned in Zimmerman's eyes as he began to see the magnitude of the problem that faced them. 'My god, they think they can take over Vulcan's operation.' He briefly fell silent as the potential consequences sank in. Then he continued, 'Surely it's more important than ever to stop them now, before it's too late?'

'Oh no. That's exactly why we sit and wait.' Brendan glanced across at Shelby. 'Tell him who else would benefit by taking over Vulcan's operation.'

'Us; the United States,' said the station chief with a smile.

'OK, we watch the Russians, and step in at the critical stage. I still don't get how on earth you plan to do that. Won't we need informants in both the Russians' and Vulcan's camps?' Zimmerman looked unconvinced.

Brendan stabbed a finger at the agent's chest. 'Need to know, Zimmerman, need to know. Maybe they're already in place.' His bearing changed; suddenly he was the Deputy Director again, and the whole of the CIA answered to him. 'Follow orders, agent. Do your job and watch the Russians. You're dismissed.'

Zimmerman marched smartly out of the room, leaving Brendan and Shelby alone. Brendan turned his chilling eyes on the station chief. 'We are at critical phase of the operation and we can't afford any screw-ups. Make sure you keep him on a very tight lead. The rest of your agents too.'

Oechsli left the room as swiftly as he had appeared, leaving Shelby pale and shivering. It wasn't Oechsli's words that invaded the station chief's habitual composure; it was the look in those eyes.

CHAPTER 39

The hotel room at the Holiday Inn wasn't an ideal base, but Richard had found himself in worse. He checked the peephole in the door before opening it to admit Johnny, who had landed at Jan Smuts about an hour earlier.

'Glad you were able to get here so soon,' he said. 'Any problems at passport control?'

'No, I was lucky. They didn't even want to search my hold-all.' Johnny lifted it on to the table while Richard pulled the curtains.

'OK, down to business. We haven't much time before you're due to fly out again. What have you got for me?'

Johnny unzipped the hold-all. 'Scrambler unit for your phone; you must've felt hamstrung without it.' He placed a small black box in the middle of the table. 'And a photo of the Dutchman, Kane Van der Zwet.' He pulled out a small frame containing a picture of a sweet old lady. 'My grandmother, on my mother's side.' He turned the frame over and slipped off its cardboard back. Behind the picture were two more: small photographs of Kane, one full face, the other in profile. 'I hope they're for a worthy cause, they cost a pretty penny.'

'They'll be put to good use. Dave Old asked for them. Van der Zwet works for Vulcan; he must be marshalling his troops.'

Johnny replaced the picture frame in the hold-all, which he dropped at his feet. He laid the photographs of Kane beside the scrambler unit. 'I had our first decent lead on Vulcan just before I left.'

Richard sat forward in anticipation, and Johnny related what Dave had already alluded to about Vulcan's methods and his organisation.

'Well done. It's what we suspected, but it's good to have it confirmed. Let's hope there's a lot more to come.' Johnny looked pleased. A little praise goes a long way, Richard thought. 'What else have you got for me?' he inquired.

'OK, you asked about Oechsli and the Russian, Ferkatovich. Nothing on the American; since our little encounter in London, nobody has seen hide nor hair of him. For all we know he may be here in Johannesburg. Uri Ferkatovich is definitely in southern Africa. Our steward friend from Aeroflot confirmed the first sighting as positive, and a man of his description was seen at Windhoek in Namibia. It was a chance sighting by a contact up there, a local barber, which was useful, as it happened. He passed Ferkatovich on Windhoek's main street. I'd only just sent the bulletin through and followed up with a photograph a couple of days later. Perfect timing; Ferkatovich could've passed straight through without detection.'

'How do you mean, useful?' Richard cut in, confused.

'Ferkatovich has grown a beard, but the barber still recognised him. He says Ferkatovich is the spitting image of an Afrikaaner.' Johnny reached down into the hold-all again and took out a large manilla folder. 'I had these identikits drawn up from his photograph on file.'

Richard looked at the two drawings Johnny had placed either side of Ferkatovich's photograph. 'Hell, chance sighting you say, damn lucky one if you ask me. I'd have never picked him out. I'd better send one of these to Dave with the one of Van der Zwet; at least he'll know what to look for. Is that the lot?'

'Last but not least, I know you didn't ask for them, but I brought a couple of the latest London dailies. I thought you would be interested.' Johnny flopped the Sun and the Daily Mail on the table in front of Richard. The inch-high headlines hit him in the eye:

JAPAN CALLS IN LOANS.

Japan was in a precarious situation, owed so much money that her economy was unable to meet its commitments. She was attempting to call in most of her overseas loans.

The article also touched briefly on the breakdown of Japan's talks with the USSR, who had asked Japan for economic aid. They had been set to go ahead, but as country after country began to default on their interest payments, Japan cut off negotiations. Japan's excuse was an unresolved territorial dispute, but the article made it plain that that wasn't the real reason.

A quick glance told Richard the other paper told much the same story. Johnny would have to leave shortly to catch his flight home, and there was still work to be done. 'I don't envy you the task I'm about to give you,' he said, squatting by the cabinet beside the bed. He pulled out a thick document, bound between two plain sheets of manilla, and dropped it on the table in front of Johnny. 'That's my latest report to the PM. Sorry, but you'll have to present in my place. I can't leave South Africa, not at such a critical stage.'

Johnny pulled a face. 'Thanks a lot,' he said flatly.

'It's vital that at this stage no rash moves are made. The mission against

SCARS OF THE LEOPARD

Vulcan is so delicately poised that things could fall either way. A lot is riding on how the PM takes this report. And that depends on you.' He laid a reassuring hand on his shoulder. 'Sorry. I know I'm asking a lot. I've itemised it all, but it'll need the personal touch.'

'Oh well, I've always wanted to see what it's like inside number 10,' Johnny said lightly. Then more seriously, 'But I suppose it's Sir Colin Bleach you're really concerned about?'

'I've already got enough on my plate with Vulcan. I don't want have to worry about Bleach's bumbling incompetence.' Richard looked at his watch. 'You'd best be going.'

Johnny tucked the PM's report safely into the hidden compartment at the bottom of his hold-all. When Richard had seen him on his way, he allowed himself a few minutes' pause for thought. He felt like a blind man fumbling along an unstable and treacherous mountain path.

He reached for the phone and began to dial a number, his mind racing. Where the hell was Brendan Oechsli? And what on earth was Uri Ferkatovich doing disguised as an Afrikaaner?

CHAPTER 40

Doblin was panting heavily. He should be fit by now, with all the running to and fro to the phone kiosks near the office. The Head of The First Chief Directorate of the KGB never spoke more than a few terse words when he rang on the office phone; each time he was to answer one of the public phones, always a different one, and he always only just got there in time.

He grabbed the receiver, out of breath as usual. He'd had to run the down the street before it stopped ringing.

The familiar gravelly voice came down the line. 'Comrade, you only have a few moments to give your report. I hope it's better than the last.'

Doblin winced. The news he had been giving the chief hadn't been bright. All his agents had been active since their first meeting, and until now they hadn't been able to get a substantial lead on any subversive groups working around southern Africa. Nor had any of their offers of support been accepted by the UDF.

This time Doblin felt confident his report was more acceptable. 'We've made some headway.' He paused, but Uri made no comment. He continued, 'One of our teams has just got back from Northern Transvaal. The UDF have caches of arms and ammunition, waiting to be distributed to small units of guerrillas currently being trained all over South Africa.'

'Where did this information come from?' Uri growled.

'Two of our operatives tracked down a known UDF sympathiser. He gave away very little, but a rather large bribe proved persuasive.'

'His name?' Uri demanded.

'Du Preez. He's an Afrikaaner.'

'Did they actually see any of this weaponry, or evidence of these guerrillas?' Uri asked, almost pleasantly.

'Why, no, Comrade, but they are sure the information is accurate,' Doblin answered, uncomfortable at Uri's unusual tone.

Uri barked, 'Doblin I'm not interested in rumours, only facts. Is there anything else?'

'Ah, no, Comrade, no further developments.' Doblin had begun to sweat, and it wasn't from exertion. He hoped his chief would soon end the call.

'I want you to write this report up and file it with the others. I'll want to see it at a later date.'

It took Doblin a few moments to realise the phone was dead. He carefully replaced the receiver and wiped his hand on his trousers. This is the worst project I have ever had to supervise, he thought.

As Uri slammed down the phone he heard a key rattle in the door of the comfortably furnished apartment. He was still scribbling notes on a scrap of paper as the living room door opened and a well-built blonde walked in.

'What are you doing, honey?' she asked, nuzzling his neck and peering over his shoulder. She caught a brief glance of the note before he slipped it into the breast pocket of his shirt. All she noticed was the name du Preez. Uri stood up and enveloped her in a huge bear hug. The girl looked tiny in his arms.

'So, what has my baby been up to today?' he asked in Afrikaans.

'You know, this and that,' she answered in the same language, looking adoringly into his eyes.

'Hey, come on, I'm interested. I really want to know. What has been happening at de Louts today?'

'You know I'm not allowed to tell you,' Susan scolded. 'Even though Karen de Lout is away, I still get a lot of classified reports across my desk.' Susan tried to twist out of Uri's arms. but he pulled her close to his broad chest, making her wheeze slightly as the air was driven from her lungs.

'I'd like to know.' Uri said quietly.

'OK, honey, whatever you say.' Susan knew she shouldn't, but she couldn't resist the raw power Uri exuded. What harm could it do, after all? She was only a secretary, and Uri was a university lecturer; what could be more respectable?

Besides, she was so entranced by Uri that she didn't really care why he wanted all the information he had prised out of her over the last year or so. Susan, for the first time in her life, had found somebody who truly seemed to care about her.

Susan had had a sheltered upbringing, and little contact with members of the opposite sex until she had been in the workforce for several years. Uri had swept her off her feet. Sometimes she didn't see him for months on end, and when they did meet it was often only for a short time, sometimes a night, other times only an hour of two. This was the longest period they had spent together. He travelled around a lot, giving lectures around the world, he told her. These past few weeks had been like living as husband and wife. Susan certainly didn't mind why he wanted the information, just as long he was always there for her.

Uri released her and guided her to the settee. He paid close attention as she told him of the day's activities at de Louts, occasionally asking a question, but for the most part sitting silently, absorbing everything she said.

He had trained her well. She was never to take notes, but memorise information and repeat it back to him hours later. She was so eager to please, Uri had been able to turn her into an accomplished operative without her noticing.

Susan lived for the praise she knew she would receive after her daily reports. This is what it must be like to sit down with a real husband and go over the happenings of the day, she told herself.

When she had finished, Uri said, 'Good, you have done well,' and gave her a single kiss on the lips. 'Now, run along to the bedroom and I'll join you shortly. I've a phone call to make.'

Susan's face turned bright scarlet in anticipation of what was to come. She hugged herself as she obeyed him. For the first time in her life she was completely happy.

CHAPTER 41

It had taken the safari party five days to trek the fourteen hundred and fifty kilometres from the Augrabies Falls to the town of Swakopmund, nestled on the bleak Atlantic coast, halfway between Namibia's southern and northern borders. Allan had set up camp at the town's semi-deserted windswept camping ground, close to the sea.

When the party arrived, they were struck by the town's cosmopolitan air. It was a contrast of two different worlds: sedate German culture and the exuberant spirit of Africa, with African palms standing alongside quaint German architecture. It was a town uniquely African yet influenced by a country a hemisphere away.

After they had made camp Allan drove them out to the Welwitschia Flats to find one of the ancient desert plants, *Welwitschia mirabilis*. Dave stood beside Karen, examining the plant that resembled a visitor from another planet.

'They say it's a living fossil.' Karen murmured.

'It'd need to be, looking like that,' Dave teased.

'Don't insult it.' Karen elbowed him playfully in the ribs.

Dave winced, grabbing at his newly healed shoulder.

'They say this one was alive before the birth of Christ,' Karen went on. 'Even the young plants are five to six hundred years old.'

Their relationship had changed gear since Dave had saved her from falling to her death, but neither of them had spoken of it since it happened. All the same, a bond had begun to develop between them.

'Correct me if I'm wrong, but isn't *mirabilis* Latin for marvellous?' Dave asked.

'Yes it is. I'm impressed; when did you learn Latin?'

Dave hunched his shoulders. 'One of my many hidden talents.'

You can say that again, Karen thought. Dave had continually surprised her since the first day of the safari. His knowledge, his physical dexterity, everything about him seemed to speak of hidden qualities. She had been suspicious of him right from the start, and had asked herself many times, was he a plant, or was it just coincidence that he was there?

After the incident at the Augrabies Falls she had given him the benefit of the doubt. Her whole personality had seemed to change, as if she had thrown away a dark cloak which had shrouded her life. She became witty and whimsical, carefree and unhampered by the burdens of her everyday life.

Dave dropped to his haunches beside the monstrous plant, which stood just over a metre tall. It looked like an old-fashioned camel saddle, with a flat centre and flaring pommels at either end, from which grew a single leaf shredded into a tangled mass. Only the newest growth was green.

He stood up and touched the tattered disarray of leaf with the toe of his running shoe. 'They say it has a huge woody taproot thrust deep underground.'

'A bit like you then,' Karen said, with a challenging stare.

'Sorry?' At times Karen's comments were disconcerting.

'You and your hidden depths. When you open up you're like a walking encyclopaedia. Where did you learn so much?' Karen took a step towards him and looked intently up into his face, her expression serious. 'We've been talking for days, yet I know so little about you.' Karen reached out and grabbed the sleeve of his shirt. 'But I know this much; you're searching for something.'

All the expression drained away from Dave's face, like water through sand. Only his golden eyes showed any sign of the emotions Karen had aroused in him. He appeared to be steeling himself for a decision, and looked down at her. But the blaze of emotion faded, and he turned away. 'Come on, we'd better be getting back to the others. They're all heading back towards the Land Rover.'

Karen's arm fell to her side, disappointment evident on her face. As they left the curious *Welwitschia* behind, that had stumped botanists for over a century and a half, her own curiosity flared. At times over the last five days, walking or just sitting alone with Dave, she'd felt so close to him, yet at the same time so very far away. What was he really after? she wondered.

When Dave and Karen had arrived back at camp after Karen's brush with death at the Augrabies Falls, they had caused quite a stir. It was obvious Karen had been crying, her eyes still red with tears. But it was Dave, white with pain from his injured shoulder, who caused the most commotion.

Karen hadn't even realised he was injured until they were halfway back to camp. She quickly forgot about her own shocking ordeal as she tore a strip off the hem of his already ripped shirt to create a makeshift sling to ease his pain.

At the camp, she anxiously hovered around him while Allan attended to his shoulder.

'I'm going to have to take off your shirt for a better look,' Allan explained.

'Here, I'll do that.' Karen jumped in. She pushed past Allan and began to unfasten the buttons.

Dave locked his free hand around her wrist. His apparent embarrassment intrigued her, but before she noticed the fiery look in his eyes, she said with a hint of humour, 'I promise I'll close my eyes.'

'All right.' Dave released her wrist and stood up. 'I suppose now is as good a time as any.' Karen quickly undid the buttons and gently peeled away what was left of the shirt.

Dave heard the chorus of gasps which followed, and slowly turned around to face Karen. She covered her mouth in horror, realising his chest was just as gruesomely scarred as his back. 'Oh my god,' she exclaimed.

Every member of the group was transfixed, unable to tear their eyes away.

It was Allan who broke the silence. 'Hey,' he called, 'haven't you all got something better to do?'

With mumbled apologies, everyone but Karen turned away. She was still having trouble lifting her gaze from the four parallel scars running down Dave's muscular chest and abdomen, but with an effort she met Dave's flinty glare.

'I thought you said you were going to close your eyes.' Allan said. 'But since you're still here you can help. Full marks on the first aid, but can you grab a proper sling from the first aid kit in the trailer and get a clean shirt from his gear? This one's only fit for recycling.'

'What? Right, yes, of course.'

Allan quickly examined the shoulder. 'It's going to hurt for a day or two and ache for a couple of weeks, but you'll survive.'

Karen ran back with the sling and a shirt, firmly in control of herself again. 'I hope this one's all right, it was at the top of your pack,' she said, helping Dave on with the shirt.

Around the campfire that night everyone was subdued. Dave didn't say a word; he was determined not to show it, but his shoulder hurt like hell. Everybody avoided talking about what had happened during the day. Then, like uncomfortable mourners leaving a wake, they all slowly drifted away to bed.

As Karen lay in her sleeping bag staring up at the star-riddled southern sky, she felt deeply indebted to Dave. Not only had he saved her life; he had offered her a glimpse into a hidden past by exposing his scars. And in some way she didn't understand, it felt as if that past was aligned to hers.

Dave's thoughts were very different. Unable to sleep because of his painful injury, he chased a series of questions around his mind. About Karen de Lout.

Had she really slipped back there at the falls? Why had he saved her, when her death had been the means by which he had planned to take a step closer to Vulcan? And the anguish in her eyes: had he imagined it, or had he witnessed the same feeling he saw reflected so often in the mirror?

Until today, Dave had been consumed by the need to destroy Vulcan. Now everything had changed. In the past nothing had been allowed to stand in his way, and he had never failed to find his mark, but this time he had lost his way. Exposing his scars had been the first of many tentative steps he would have to take.

Karen took it upon herself to be Dave's private nurse. She began in the early hours of the next day, when she caught Dave returning from an early morning run.

'Exactly what do you think you are doing?' she demanded sternly, hands on hips.

Dave was unsure whether to laugh or tell her to mind her own business. Before he could reply, she was by his side, reaching up to ease his arm back into the sling which dangled loose around his neck. 'If you want your shoulder to heal properly, you'll have to keep it completely still for the next few days,' she warned. 'You can't run without moving it, so – no running for a while.'

Only his mother had ever spoken to him like that before. A smile tugged at the corner of his mouth, and he clicked smartly to attention. 'Yes, ma'am,' he managed to say, before his body began to quiver with mirth.

Soon Karen was laughing too, a woman transformed. That was how she continued, no longer quiet and reserved but bright and good-humoured, as if she had shed a constricting skin. A bond had formed between them, and Dave had no idea what to do about it.

An occasional bush, tree and crumbling rock were the only features that relieved the stony desolation of Namibia's arid southern plains. Clouds of dust marked their north-westerly advance and coated the Land Rover a ghostly grey.

They stopped briefly for supplies at Karusburg, then it was north again towards the rugged beauty of Fish River Canyon. They followed the eastern edge, with brief glimpses of the majesty ahead. At the lookout point where they planned to set up camp, they feasted their eyes on the menacing grandeur of the canyon itself.

Over one hundred and sixty kilometres long, it was stunning in its desolation, mesmerising in its silence. The Fish River, nearly six hundred metres down between jutting buttresses of rock, coiled like a sluggish python to join the Orange River on its way to the sea.

When they woke the following day a magnificent vermilion sun illuminated the twisting crags and revealed their full glory. The morning silence hung in the air like a peaceful song: Africa, showing them another of its contrasting moods.

They were to spend a day and a night at the bottom of the canyon. Allan led the party down a steep, unstable trail to a sandy beach. Dave had more difficulty than he expected with the treacherous descent, and not only because of injured shoulder. Like an anxious mother hen, Karen darted around him, trying to guide him to the safest parts of the track, and more than once Dave had to prevent them both from falling. Eventually clasped her around the waist, hauled her off her feet and swung her round; she stood in stunned silence, their faces only centimetres apart. For a few seconds the air between them seemed electrically charged; then Karen muttered, 'OK, you've made your point.'

But it was no easier without her clumsy attempts to help; his eyes kept wandering to her well-shaped body. He caught up with her at the bottom of the canyon, and apologised.

'I was only trying to help,' she said quietly.

'I know. I didn't want to take you down with me. And I'm used to looking after myself.'

'Me too.' A tentative smile curved her lips. 'It's nice to know someone is watching your back, though.'

'Yes. Yes, it is.' Dave was surprised to realise that he meant it. 'So why don't we explore together, watch each other's backs?' he heard himself say.

'I'd like that,' she replied.

'Me too.' He meant that too; another surprise. This day was already full of them, and it was only mid-morning.

Dave and Karen spent the day exploring the cascading cliffs and steep ravines. At times they sat in silence, absorbing the canyon's tranquillity. Mostly they walked and talked, hands not quite touching, each acutely aware of the other's presence. They explored each other's intellect and opinions too, and found in many respects they were very much alike. They were both fiercely independent, driven to reach the goals they set themselves. Karen was amazed by Dave's phenomenal memory, he by her ability to cut swiftly through to the heart of an issue.

Although they avoided the topic for most of the day, they eventually touched briefly on one another's professions. It came as no surprise to either of them that the other already knew; Karen told him honestly that she had used her company's security arm to have him thoroughly checked out as soon as she found he had booked a place on the safari. Dave managed to avoid lying, by telling her he'd recognised her from a photograph and read about her somewhere.

As the day wore on Karen found she felt totally at ease in his company. Dave felt the same, but his senses remained on full alert. The situation wasn't working out at all as he had planned. The more attracted he became to her, the more his emotions would dictate his actions, and he couldn't afford to let that happen. He still had a job to do, though now he was going to have to rethink his entire strategy. Which meant he couldn't let his guard down for a moment, especially when he was this close to Vulcan. He exerted some of the iron discipline he prided himself on, and backed off. Karen sensed his change in mood, and wondered what she had done to drive away this man whom all her instincts told her she could trust. She tried to revive the camaraderie they had found, but Dave remained unmoved; a barrier seemed to have risen between them.

Next day Dave's mind was no clearer. His normally impregnable resolve was in tatters. His fierce attraction to Karen threatened to overwhelm him, and swamp both the professional and the personal impetus towards Vulcan's unmasking and destruction. The plans he had worked out so meticulously at the Wemyss Estate had turned to dust, and for the first time in his career he had no idea which way to turn.

He had always known Karen and de Louts had an integral part to play in his mission; so how could it possibly feel so right to have her standing beside him, gazing at the most awe-inspiring sand dunes in the world?

They had been travelling for a day and part of a night along the edge of the Namib, the oldest unchanged desert in the world, to arrive at the dunes at dawn. The sun was just breaking over the crest of the largest dune, colouring it in shades of violet and peach and emphasising the forbidding beauty sculptured by the relentless wind that the Nama tribe of the south call *Soo-oop-wa*. The dunes towered over three hundred metres into the vibrant desert sky, and their unparalleled beauty seemed to be dissolving Dave's carefully reconstructed reserve.

'They say the Namib is unlike any other desert,' he said, still transfixed by the awesome sight.

'Yes. It's like an iceberg. Most of it is hidden below.'

As the light strengthened, Dave's eyes feasted on the ancient trees, dwarfed by the dull orange mountains of sand. Karen quietly watched him out of the corner of her eye, her thoughts as charged with emotion as his. Since the death of her husband, any time not spent at work had felt like trudging through darkness and desolation. But over the past few days she had seen a glimpse of sunlight shining through the gloom. Dave was the only man since Tom's death who had quickened her interest. When he drew away and began to brood in silence, it was as if that shaft of sunlight had been whisked away. Now his mood seemed to have lifted, a sense of calm washed over her like a warm breeze.

The Land Rover rocked and swayed, finding its own path through the still, silent valley of Tsauchab, allowing Karen her first sight of the outer reaches of the Namib. The towering dunes of Sossusvlei formed a spectacular backdrop, shimmering in the rising heat of day, as the wide stony pan took on a personality of its own.

Karen and Dave took their turn on the edge of the game viewing hatch at the back of the vehicle. As the dunes began to peter out, she touched his shoulder and pointed across the featureless terrain. Partially distorted by the shimmering heat stood a solitary gemsbok.

'They say the gemsbok's blood can get so hot out here that if it reached its brain it would die,'

she said.

Dave was intrigued. 'How does it survive?' he asked.

'It has a network of capillaries that cools the blood before it reaches the brain.'

His eyes twinkled with humour. 'I must say, young lady, you are a mine of information.'

'One does one's best.' Her tone was light, but her relief went deeper;

217

whatever had caused his morose mood, he seemed to be coming out of it. They continued to gaze at the large spiral-horned antelope that had adapted so well to the oppressive desert heat. She hoped Dave would continue to make adaptations of his own.

CHAPTER 42

S he had driven him into a frenzy on the last two occasions they'd met; she had seen fervour then agitation burn in his pale blue eyes. Tonight maybe she'd make it different. Tonight, Sandy planned to see how far she could push the big blond Dutchman.

A week earlier Sandy had gone to Dave's secret post office box in a suburb in the north of Johannesburg, taking particular care to ensure she wasn't followed. She waited until the post office was far behind before pulling to the side of the road to examine the two items she had taken from the box. The first was a postcard from Dave, sent from Kuruman; she easily deciphered his cryptic code, and learned that Kane was in Johannesburg, working as a bodyguard for de Louts. Another example of Vulcan's ability to use his influence, she thought wryly; as if they needed any more. The postcard also briefly mentioned that Dave's plans were on track; he'd made contact with Karen.

I bet you have, Sandy thought jealously.

It was the second item that really caught her interest. It was a plain white envelope, its Johannesburg postmark giving away nothing of its true origin. Inside were two pictures: a photograph, and an identikit drawing. The photograph was of a white male, in his early to mid-thirties, with long flowing blond hair and high cheekbones; on the back was written *Kane Van der Zwet*. Dave had omitted to mention that van de Zwet was so handsome, Sandy thought with a hint of relish. Some parts of this job were more enjoyable than others.

She slid the photograph back in the envelope and extracted the identikit. She didn't think she'd seen the face before, yet it was vaguely familiar. She looked at the name on the back and a frown creased her brow. 'Well, who'd have guessed?' she muttered under her breath. 'I'd better get this to Timot quickly, or he'll never have a hope of finding him.'

The drawing was of the Head of The First Chief Directorate of the KGB – but the beard made him look completely different.

CHAPTER 43

This was only the second time Kane had met Vulcan in private; on all other occasions he had been surrounded by bodyguards. Initially Kane had no idea who he was to meet. He had been summoned to an exclusive suite in the Carlton Hotel in downtown Johannesburg; it wasn't until he recognised the three burly bodyguards standing outside the door that he knew who was waiting for him inside.

He hardly noticed the suite's lavish décor. Vulcan was standing with his back to him, staring out of the picture window across the vast city. Kane respectfully waited just inside the door until his presence was acknowledged.

With no preamble Vulcan turned and spoke. 'Du Preez, how important is he?'

Kane was taken off guard; how did Vulcan known about du Preez? He answered quickly, 'He could be replaced, but it'll set back our plans in Transvaal. Unless it's necessary, I would advise against it.'

'He's been speaking to people he shouldn't. So far not enough to upset our plans, but, well, it's a lapse in security we can ill afford.' Vulcan began to walk into the middle of the room. 'If it's unwise to have him replaced, can you control him?' he demanded.

Kane was still intrigued to know Vulcan had found out, but he pushed the thought aside. 'Yes. I have his measure.'

'Do you now?' Vulcan raised a sceptical eyebrow. 'Then why the hell are we having trouble with him?'

Kane had no answer. As usual Vulcan was several steps ahead of him.

Vulcan waved him into one of the comfortable armchairs in the middle of the room. He sat down opposite, and began to issue his instructions. 'Speak to him, discipline him if you have to, but make sure we have no more trouble with him before the weapons and orders have been distributed. Then get rid of him.'

The pleasure is all mine, Kane thought.

Kane was all too aware of his main failing. He could tolerate any amount of physical pain, but verbal abuse clawed at him and festered like a septic wound until he found a way to crush its source. First Dave in New Zealand,

and now du Preez by bringing Vulcan's displeasure down on him, had caused him extreme mental distress. He needed to destroy them both in order to restore his sullied dignity.

Vulcan hadn't finished with him. Leaning forward slightly, he asked, 'And tell me, Kane, how is our Mr Old progressing with his side of the operation?'

Could the man read his thoughts? Kane wondered, gritting his teeth. And 'our' Mr Old, as if he had sought him out personally. 'I have spoken to him once since his arrival here in South Africa, and by all accounts he seems to have everything under control. He was just leaving on safari with Karen de Lout. But of course, that's something you'll already know.'

'Oh yes, Kane, I know exactly where he is. But I would like to hear your view of the situation. After all, you of all people know how brilliant he can be. And how deceitful.'

Kane struggled to control the burst of anger that leapt up. With an effort he kept his emotions from ruling his tongue; Vulcan needed facts, not feelings. Keeping his tone clinical and impartial, he replied, 'From what I know of Dave Old, and from the brief conversation we've had, I'm certain his side of the operation is running smoothly.'

'Let's hope not too smoothly,' Vulcan said absently.

'Sorry? I'm not with you?' Kane asked, puzzled by his employer's uncharacteristic loss of focus.

But Vulcan's customary self-possession was back. 'What else do you have to report?'

Kane relayed all the arrangements he had made for the storage and distribution of weapons, and itemised the training, progress and readiness of the UDF guerrillas who would use them to create anarchy throughout South Africa.

'So everything's in place. Excellent. All that's left is for the leadership of de Louts to be placed in the right hands, and of course the destruction of the South African government, which will trigger the revolt.' Vulcan paused briefly, turning his penetrating gaze on Kane. 'Now it's time you knew your next and most important task.'

Kane was not easily impressed, but he was overawed by the enormity of Vulcan's plan to destroy the government. As Vulcan outlined the plan, and his own role in it, the hairs on his forearms and the back of his neck begin to twitch with nervous energy. Never before had he been involved in a plan so devastating. A plan he would implement, which would not only ensure his place in history but also initiate a chain reaction that would enable Vulcan to influence the power structure of the world.

Kane left the suite still awestruck by Vulcan's ingenuity. Euphoria began to build as he stepped into the lift. He felt invincible, his veins charged with anticipation for what lay ahead: lofty heights of honour, acclaim and riches, the like of which he had only dreamed of.

As the lift glided to a stop, he looked down at his watch. Forty minutes before his date. This one would end as the last two should have. But before anticipation of a different kind flooded his mind, Dave Old's face, like a ghost from the past, invaded his thoughts. Like a violent change in the weather, a silent rage consumed him. But his time would come.

The rage subsided as he walked from the lift. A quick phone call, he thought, then a bit of sport with Old's frigid assistant. And when he returned from his jaunt, she would be set up as bait.

Du Preez's hand shook as he carefully replaced the receiver. How the hell did he find out? he wondered for the hundredth time since Kane had accused him of opening his mouth. It had been a close call; thank goodness he hadn't told the Russians much. There was a queasy, hollow feeling at the pit of his stomach. That Dutchman had shaken him badly.

The warning he had received was short, but clear. 'Open your mouth again, to anybody, and I'll close it permanently.'

The threat was bad enough, but it got worse. Kane had said he would be coming up to make sure he understood. Du Preez fingered his newly healed nose, and wondered how much death would hurt.

Kane had also told him to start shipping the weapons and ammunition to the guerrillas. 'The destruction of the government is imminent,' he'd said. 'It'll be the signal to begin the uprising.'

Du Preez plucked up enough courage to ask, 'But how will I know when it's happened?'

All he heard before the phone went dead was, 'You won't be able to miss it.'

Sandy had already met up with Kane twice, both times in public places. She wasn't yet prepared to meet with him in private. At least this much of Dave's advice she was prepared to heed.

Her stubborn streak had driven her to undertake some active investigation of her own. From what Dave had said, Kane was a tangible link with Vulcan. So, she surmised, if they could come at Vulcan from two different directions, they would surely have a better chance of successfully tracking him down. In theory she was right, but her annoyance with Dave had clouded her normally sharp mind. Sandy had vastly underestimated the man she was dealing with.

It hadn't taken her long to find what Kane was doing at de Louts, but she was stunned to discover that he was working as one of the personal bodyguards of none other than Karen de Lout.

In her journalist role, she had asked to interview one of the company's bodyguards, and had chosen Kane. She planned to use the interview to find out who had given him the job.

The first time they met was over a long leisurely lunch. Their second meeting was over dinner several days later.

She had chosen the location of this evening's third date with care. Kane was to meet her in the ladies' bar at the Pirates Sports Club; she had booked a table for two at the adjacent restaurant. Sandy often played squash at the courts across the road, so she knew the layout and was well known herself. Her careful preparations made her feel safe.

She was already sitting in an alcove when Kane walked in. God, he's handsome, she thought; I'm going to enjoy this. Nothing like mixing business with pleasure.

He spotted her, raised a hand in greeting and with a beaming smile that showed his perfect white teeth, he walked towards her. He was a full head taller than she was, and exuded a type of magnetism that many women would find hard to resist. But Sandy wasn't many women.

The evening went remarkably well. Kane was so courteous and good-humoured that Sandy found it hard to believe what Dave had said about him was true. She accepted his offer of a nightcap back at his apartment, looking forward with reckless anticipation to what lay ahead. Damn you, Dave Old. she thought. I know what I'm doing, and I'll do as I please.

She refused Kane's offer of a lift back to his apartment, politely but firmly at first, but more assertively when he became insistent. 'Listen, buster, either I take my own transport, or you'll be drinking that nightcap on your own.'

Like the gentleman he'd been all night Kane backed off and held his hands up in a gesture of mock submission. If Sandy had seen his face as he turned away, she might have had second thoughts about how the evening was ending.

Sandy followed the taillights of Kane's Ford Granada out of the club's car park, passing an old Volkswagen Beetle parked out on its own near the entrance. A small part of her mind registered the driver, slumped over the wheel, asleep, but the thought was a fleeting one. She had other things on her mind tonight.

Timot shook his head in silent admiration as he started the Beetle and tucked it in a couple of cars behind Sandy. He had no idea how Dave knew, but as usual, he was right.

CHAPTER 44

A drab grey day saw the Afro Ventures safari head off on their leisurely trek inland towards the Namibian capital. Against all his instincts and better judgement, Dave was starting to enjoy Karen's company. She not only stimulated his mind with her bright, perceptive take on the world around them, she could also do something very few others had achieved – she made him laugh.

Before they set off for Windhoek, Karen had told Allan and the rest of the group that she was less than impressed that there was no time to see the flamingos at the Walvis Bay lagoon. She understood they couldn't fit in everything, but as they left Swakopmund she amused herself by pretending to be in a huff, sitting beside Dave with her arms folded and an exaggerated pout on her face.

Dave was trying to keep a grin off his face, and when Karen turned to face him, she couldn't resist playing her charade out a little bit more.

'Did you know that flamingos are pink because of the carotene in the tiny saltwater shrimps they eat?' she asked, 'Not that I've seen any recently.' She jabbed an accusing finger into Allan's back.

'Really?' Dave exclaimed, feigning a look of fascination.

'Yes.' She nodded vigorously. 'If they were unable to feed on them, after their next moult they would go white.'

Dave gazed at her. 'Karen, you are a veritable fountain of useful knowledge,' he said with heavy emphasis.

She sniffed loudly, and turned away. 'Well, if you're going to be like that...'

Dave was amused and impressed by her in equal parts. He had already seen a glimpse of the negotiation skills she probably used every day as president of de Lout Investments. It was inevitable that she would need to pay a visit to the de Louts office at Windhoek, and he had watched her persuade Allan that an extended stop in the Namibian capital would be a good idea. Allan had been reluctant, but she wore him down with a mixture of wheedling and hurt silence.

'Three hours, and that's my best offer. I don't even know why I'm giving you that,' Allan conceded, trying to suppress a grin.

When he were out of earshot, Karen turned to Dave. 'He was tough. You should see how fast my directors give in when I use that approach.'

'Incorrigible. That's what you are.' Dave shook his head at her, trying not to laugh and not quite succeeding.

Windhoek was a city with a flavour of Europe mingled with the mood of Africa, founded at the beginning of the twentieth century by German colonialists, who created an impressive settlement with a unique multicultural spirit.

'Are you sure you want to come with me?' Karen asked as they walked down the main street. 'You'll have to wait in reception. I'll be busy with some rather sensitive material.'

'Well, I was hoping I could make a few phone calls? If you don't mind? I assumed your phone lines would be more secure than most.'

'I don't mind at all. And you're right, of course. We've some large mining concerns here in the south west, and there are things we need to keep private.'

Dave could have made his calls from any number of locations in Windhoek; he didn't intend to say anything that would leave an eavesdropper any the wiser. His main reason for accompanying Karen was to observe her in work mode, a different side of her from the carefree woman she had blossomed into on their journey.

For such a large company, the de Louts Namibia office was quite unobtrusive. As the thought crossed Dave's mind, Karen seemed to read his thoughts.

'It's really only a branch office. The majority of the work is done at de Lout House in Jo'burg.'

Karen had dressed up as best she could, in her tidiest pair of jeans and a khaki shirt with a beige scarf knotted at her throat. 'How do I look?' she asked, as the lift ascended.

Dave was unsure how to respond. The simple clothes enhanced her natural beauty, but she didn't look at all like the president of a huge multi-national corporation and one of the most powerful women in southern Africa.

'Perfect,' he answered. Did all women need reassurance about their appearance? he wondered.

As if to save him further embarrassment, the lift cushioned to a stop and opened into the reception area of de Louts' Namibian office.

The offices took up this floor and the one above, conservatively styled reminiscent of an old-fashioned legal firm, with dark wood panelling and frosted glass. The stern receptionist behind the solid wooden counter seemed to match her surroundings, Dave thought. Karen, like a desert flower that received its first drop of rain, was a woman transformed. She walked erect, head held high, her whole bearing exuding power and control. Dave could hardly believe his eyes.

It took the receptionist a few moments to acknowledge their presence. 'Yes?' she snapped eventually, looking distastefully down her nose at their casual attire.

'My name is Karen de Lout. I have come to assess this office and its staff.'

The receptionist's jaw dropped.

'Well, don't just sit there,' Karen continued briskly. 'I have a schedule to keep. I need to see the branch manager, Mr van der Merwe.' The receptionist was still staring open-mouthed; Karen's tone grew more impatient. 'Please tell him I'm here. No, don't bother, I'll tell him myself.'

She marched across the small foyer to the frosted-glass door marked with the manager's name. Without knocking, she wrenched the handle and pushed it open. Dave was fascinated, and couldn't stop himself from following.

'What the...?' greeted Karen as she barged into the room. A man in his late forties rose, a half-eaten sandwich in one hand and a document in the other. He was as stunned as the receptionist when he recognised Karen, but he recovered a lot more quickly. 'Mrs de Lout, what a pleasure.'

'Well, the greeting I received at your front desk was no pleasure at all. The mission statement on the wall in your foyer states, "Throughout the world de Lout Investments prides itself on good service to its clients." You have a problem, Mr van der Merwe. Remedy it, or get rid of it.'

A thunderstruck Van der Merwe was speechless.

Karen waved a dismissive hand at the sandwich, dangling forgotten from his hand. 'When you've finished your lunch, I'd first like you to make an office and telephone available for Mr Old, and then we've some work to do.' She eyed him, lips pursed. 'I do hope everything's in order.'

As Dave sat down in the office he had been allocated, he was amazed and impressed at the change in Karen. Gone was the woman in relaxed holiday mood; in its place was with a tough businesswoman exuding such force and power that her staff couldn't help but treat her with deference and respect. He could hardly believe it was the same person. The profile he received from Vulcan had been sadly lacking.

His own respect and admiration for her was growing day by day, and he felt he was sailing in completely uncharted waters. He only had one more trick up his sleeve; he just hoped he would be able to carry it through.

He sat, his thoughts racing, for several minutes, then came to a decision. He picked up the phone and dialled a Johannesburg number, thinking how ironical it was that he was making the call from a de Louts office.

The call was answered immediately. 'Timot, Dave,' he said, and the line went dead.

He waited five more minutes, then dialled another number. Timot answered again, this time from a public phone box just around the corner from his office. It was a technique they had perfected in the past.

The two men's minds worked in such accord that no code was necessary; keeping their exchanges brief was security enough. Dave began, 'The Dutchman, what of him?'

'She made contact.'

'Damn!' Dave whispered. He had hoped he was wrong, and regretted again having told Sandy about Kane. 'Do what you have to, stick to them like glue.' Dave changed topics. 'And Natal?'

'I was lucky. I got back just before she made contact with the Dutchman. Too much to tell. It'll wait until you're back.' Timot answered.

'Anything important?'

'Not to speak of, a lot of activity. Maybe you'll make something of it.' It was clear Timot thought it was a wasted trip.

'The American and the Russian?' Those two really bugged Dave. They'd thrown a real spanner in the works.

'Nothing. Couple of ghosts.'

'OK, just do what you can.'

'And how are things with you?' Timot asked. 'I thought you'd be home by now.'

'Yeah, so did I. I'm going to need some help.' In as few as words as possible, Dave told Timot of his decision.

Dumbfounded, Timot stood and stared at the phone once he'd cradled it.

Dave was his closest friend, and not once had he seen him lack the skills to complete a mission. What was more, he would never have guessed that this was an area in which Dave would need help.

CHAPTER 45

The bush telegraph works better than most other forms of communication in Africa, and it had been working overtime.

An envelope began its journey at Jan Smuts International Airport, to Gaborone, the capital of Botswana. When the flight landed, the hostess handed it to one of the ground crew, who ran to a Cessna preparing for take-off to Maun on the edge of the Okavango Delta. From Maun it travelled two hundred and fifty kilometres to Shakawe, the northernmost fishing camp in the Delta, where the head tribesman of the Hambu entrusted it to his eldest son Narmu.

The young man continued the journey by dugout canoe to the opposite bank of the delta, where he hid his canoe and set off towards the Namibian border. His loping strides ate up the ground as far as Angola, and Mucusso National Park. Now he was in unfamiliar territory, but he scanned the land for the trail his father had described; he was to wait there and give the envelope to its final recipient. Narmu squatted in the middle of the trail; he was scared, but would never have admitted it. His father had told him of a breed of animal far more dangerous than the hippos and crocodiles in the delta – a group of guerrillas whose way of life was death, brutality and destruction.

Despite his fear, he slept like a dog, curled up in the dirt with only his monkey skin *kaross* to cover him. He woke with a start to find he was unable to move. A hard object was rammed into his temple and a foot in a worn boot crushed his neck. He cut off his scream and tried to look up.

All he saw was another pair of scuffed boots and the dull metal barrel of a rifle.

One of the men spoke in a language he didn't understand, and he was rolled over with the flick of a boot. The same boot landed on his chest and the barrel of the rifle hovered above his face. The man barked a question, and another came into view. dressed the same as the other two. Narmu recognised their boots, tatty jeans and scruffy t-shirts as the uniform of the African guerrilla. The second man's air of command marked him out as the leader, and one side of his face was scarred, his whole face was twisted out of shape.

Scarface barked again and Narmu was hauled to his feet and stripped. One of the guerrillas found the envelope and gave it to Scarface, who recognised his name printed on it. He slit it open and found two photographs and a printed message it would take him some time to decipher. He slipped everything back into the envelope and looked at Narmu, who was quaking with terror. He made a shoo-ing motion, and when the lad didn't move, he yelled, 'GO!'

Unable to believe his luck, Narmu scooped up his *kaross* and ran like an antelope. Relief washed over him; he would be home safe by the end of the day.

The three guerrillas watched dispassionately as the youth settled into his stride. Scarface nodded, and one of his companions casually lifted his AK 47 and shot from the hip. The bullets ripped into Narmu's back, shattering his spine and tearing his intestines out through a cavernous exit wound in his stomach. As the bullets hacked into his body, he fell shuddering to the ground. The last thing he saw was the hideous stare of the man with the shiny scar-ravaged face.

When Scarface saw the youth's body go limp, he turned to the man with the gun, whose name was Trigger. 'Bring the bearers through, while I read the message.'

The message from Johannesburg was short and clear, and he was mouthing through it again as the third man approached. He was the tallest of the three, and because of his height was called J'Long.

'The bearers have nearly all gone,' he said. Scarface understood the hidden question: were they to go with them or did the message give different orders?

Scarface looked at the procession of bearers winding down the tree-lined trail, long rectangular boxes balanced on their heads. He noticed with grim satisfaction that none of them looked down at the lifeless youth.

He had a decision to make. His initial orders regarding the bearers had been very clear: they were to escort them and the weapons all the way to Transvaal. But the message in the envelope had come from a different source. He considered his options carefully and looked up at J'Long.

'We will stay with the porters and weapons until we reach the Zambian border. Then we have real work to do.' He saw his own brutal gleam of anticipation reflected in his comrade's eyes, and called Comrade Trigger to join them. He gave them each a photograph, and they studied them intently.

'The white woman we kill, the white man we are to be careful of,' he told them.

Trigger licked his lips. He hadn't had a white woman since the end of the Rhodesian bush war, when he and a group of five others had taken a white farmer's wife for sport.

Scarface was speaking again. 'We see the weapons across the border, and then we must go across the Corridor into Botswana and wait for this white woman at Third Bridge, in the Moremi Game Reserve.'

'I know that area well,' J'Long said. 'But something troubles me, Comrade. The white man. I have seen him somewhere before. But I cannot think where.'

Scarface slipped the photographs back into the envelope. 'If it is important you will remember,' he told his comrade.

CHAPTER 46

Windhoek and Namibia were left behind as Allan guided the safari through soft yellow-beige sand on its way to Maun in Botswana. The Kalahari wasn't like the desert Dave had imagined; the stalky grass and scattered stunted bushes of the thornveld stretched from one horizon to the other.

After a night outside a bleak farming oasis, they headed for Lake Ngami in the southernmost corner of the Okavango Delta, renowned for its bird-life, but far from the wildlife extravaganza they expected, what they found was a shallow dustbowl littered with bones. The prolonged Botswanan drought was much worse than they expected.

Dave laid a sympathetic hand on Karen's shoulder. 'David Livingstone described the lake as a fine sheet of water,' he said sadly.

He wore only a pair of shorts; everyone had grown used to his scars. Karen was acutely aware of his bare skin so close to her. She stood motionless, unwilling to risk driving him away again. But the intimate moment faded as he turned away, apparently oblivious to her feelings. 'I think we'd better get back,' he said. 'Looks like Allan wants to press on.'

What an enigma this man was, Karen thought. An invisible barrier seemed to surround him.

Maun was the tribal capital of the Batswana people and a gateway into the game parks and wildlife reserves. Allan made a brief stop for fuel among the hodgepodge of circular huts, European style houses and scattered umbrellas of mopane trees. They were on the edge of one of the world's last true wildernesses, the largest wetland in Africa: the Okavango Delta. Karen's excitement was infectious, and Dave couldn't help but be drawn in.

The safari party made their base at Crocodile Camp twelve kilometres north of Maun, and travelled back in the early morning to be ferried by light aircraft into the middle of the Delta. They crossed the Buffalo Fence, erected to prevent the spread of foot and mouth disease from wild buffalo to domesticated cattle, and prevent cattle from over-grazing the delta as they had their own range.

Nothing had prepared Karen for the constantly changing pattern of greens, yellows and browns and the shimmering light reflected off the lagoons and waterways. There was no sign of human life, just a sheet of shallow water stretching as far as the eye could see over, creating a lush oasis laced with hundreds of islands, some studded with clumps of trees, others fringed with reeds and rushes and garnished with mats of rich vibrant green. The larger islands supported open grasslands, others stately baobab trees, Africa's arboreal monarchs.

The flight took fifteen minutes. Karen's dismay showed on her face; surely the runway was far too short?

Allan laughed. 'I wouldn't worry. The pilot's been bush-flying for years.'

The plane skimmed the top of the vegetation and landed squarely on the very tip of the runway. Karen was still convinced he was trying to land far too fast; the plane was careering headlong towards the lagoon. But at the last moment the pilot used the plane's own momentum by applying one wheel-brake to send it back the way it came; when it stopped, he turned and gave her a wide, self-satisfied grin.

Delta Camp was idyllic. The lodge, built around two mopane trees with reed-thatched roofs and walls, exuded peace and tranquillity, and everyone was struck by the cheerful chorus of bird life. The scene was set for an unforgettable journey.

Allan assembled the group at the water's edge in front of the open-air restaurant. A group of local tribesmen were loading their belongings into the *mekoro*, the canoe-like craft which would carry them through the delta's enchanted world. Karen was amazed at how quickly Dave picked up the local language.

When he removed his shirt and they saw his scars, at first they treated him with diffidence, but he broke down their reserve by teasing them in their own dialect.

'How far to tonight's camp, Nbwane?' he asked the head guide.

Nbwane, grey-haired and slight of build, stared silently at him. Receiving no answer, Dave tried another approach. 'Maybe it is true, then, what I hear from your cousins the Tswana. It is said that because you spend so much time in the water, you can only converse with something that resembles a hippo. Like the women you take as wives.'

Dave spoke in such a deadpan tone that Nbwane was clearly at a loss – then he gave them all a beaming smile, and soon they all were hooting with laughter, even the hapless Nbwane. He clapped his hands and bobbed his head. 'I would be honoured if you and your woman would ride with me,' he said.

Dave shot a look at Karen, who asked suspiciously, 'What did he say?'

'He'd like us to ride in his *mokoro*,' Dave said quickly.

Well, it was half true, Karen thought. She also understood the dialect, though not as well as Dave. She decided not to let on.

With Nbwane leading the way, the file of canoes began a four-hour journey to their campsite for the night on one of the islands. Nbwane chattered away, giving them a rare insight to the delta. Karen coasted through emerald carpets of water lilies, and beds of papyrus tipped with green and golden brown tassels. Once in a while they rounded a corner and sent a herd of aquatic sitatunga antelope splashing through the shallows. They even witnessed a strikingly handsome fish-eagle on its hunt for food. Swooping with talons raked to strike the surface of the water and snatch its unsuspecting prey.

The sunset was the most brilliantly vivid they had ever seen. The magnificent orange orb dipped into the horizon in a cascade of fiery reds, smouldering apricots and burnt browns, the blaze of colour reflected in the gleaming waters of the delta. All day Karen had witnessed beauty she had never experienced before; and the distant moan of a lion, the occasional whoop of a hyena and the cough of a nearby leopard lulled her off to sleep.

Almost.

'This woman of yours, she is a little skinny.' Nbwane spoke in dialect, but she understood most of it.

'To you perhaps. Me, I prefer a slim woman to the hippos you marry,' Dave replied. Nbwane guffawed. 'And she's not my woman,' Dave added.

Karen would have preferred her first compliment from Dave not to involve hippos, but this was a step in the right direction.

'There is a saying amongst my people,' was Nbwane's next sally. 'Even the bravest man's courage leaves him when he is rejected by a woman. Surely a brave and scarred warrior such as you does not suffer this distress.'

'Just watch where you're going, you silly little bugger,' was the only riposte Dave could think of.

The truth suddenly dawned on Karen. Dave had backed off because the prospect of getting too close to her unnerved him.

Earlier, when most of the group went on a game-viewing walk through the grasslands, Dave and Karen had hiked off on their own. With the skill of a native tracker, he showed her barely visible animal signs and taught her to stalk game with extraordinary skill and patience, through the long grass towards a grazing herd of zebra, until she was close enough to reach out and touch a sleeping youngster basking beside its mother. Dave clearly had a deep affinity with this ancient land – and an attraction of a very different kind came to fruition. An almost electric energy passed between them whenever they touched. The bond that had developed was so easy, so natural, that Karen couldn't ignore it, and knew Dave would have to confront it sooner or later.

Under the sweeping umbrella of a lone acacia tree they both fell silent. Karen knew the first move would have to come from her; she reached for his hands, looked up into his face and lifted her face in invitation. But his eyes flicked to the side and she felt him flinch; he dragged her roughly to her knees and silenced her with a finger to his lips. Karen could have sworn she saw him sniff the air. Then a sawing cough ripped the air. The acacia was the leopard's tree and they had invaded its territory.

Dave slowly guided Karen behind his back, and she realised in horror that he was steeling himself to attack. In a fluid movement, he sprang forward with a blood-curdling roar. Karen screamed and he disappeared into the grass. There was a flurry of movement, a piercing squeal, then all movement stopped and a deathly quiet descended.

But against all reason, Dave's voice rang out. 'Got ya, you little bugger.' In a different tone he called, 'Come and see our fearsome leopard.'

Karen moved forward tentatively. Dave was kneeling in the grass. No, not *in* the grass; *on* something, which squirmed and struggled beneath him. He stood up and announced, 'Meet one of Africa's most dangerous animals.'

Karen looked down at the creature. Its beaming smile showed perfect white teeth, contrasting with gleaming black skin. The figure began to giggle, and pushed itself to a sitting position. Karen could hardly believe her eyes. 'Nbwane, you wicked, wicked little man.'

It was easy to laugh when it was all over. Sitting upright in the *mokoro*, gazing down the narrow channel of papyrus, Karen indulged in a quiet chuckle. Then everything seemed to stop. Dave froze: he had sensed something outside her range. Nbwane dug the pole into the riverbed and stopped the canoe.

'What is it?' Karen whispered. Dave briefly shook his head to silence her.

'Can you see it yet, Nbwane?' he quietly asked in dialect.

Nbwane swallowed hard. 'To the right, through the reeds.'

'Just think of it as your wife,' Dave said.

Karen followed his gaze and swallowed a gasp. A pair of piggy eyes stared unblinkingly back at her, above gaping pink nostrils on a grotesque snout.

Karen could even see droplets of water at the tips of bristly whiskers. She was no more than ten metres from one of the most dangerous animals in Africa: a huge, black, scar-ravaged bull hippopotamus.

'What do we do, Nbwane?' Dave asked, still eyeing the beast.

'I think it is the *kubu's* play.' Nbwane was transfixed.

'Stuff him,' Dave said, slowly reaching behind him.

The hippo swung its swollen body towards them and unhinged its cavernous jaw, exposing massive razor-edged teeth. Dave heard a squeak from Nbwane and a sharp intake of breath from Karen.

He tossed the object he had retrieved into the air. Karen's thousand-dollar Pentax camera floated in a perfect arc to land with a splash behind the hippo.

A hippo's hearing is far better than its sight. In a tumult of reeds and water it turned, gnashing at anything in sight. It honked and bellowed, overran the camera and crashed through the mass of vegetation until it disappeared.

Karen rounded on Dave. 'That was my camera, buster. Get in there and find it. Go on,' she insisted, when Dave gave her a disbelieving stare.

Eventually Dave placed a cautious foot over the side. The water came up to his knees. Nbwane began to hoot with glee.

He groped around, and eventually held up a strap attached to what looked like a lump of black oozing slime and rotting vegetation. 'Next time you decide to save my life,' Karen said, 'would you mind using your own camera?'

It was the following morning, and the others had all flown back to Maun, leaving only Dave, Allan and herself for the last flight out of the Delta's enchanted watery world. All their gear had been stowed and Karen was about to board the plane when Nbwane sidled up to her, respectfully bobbing his head, a beaming smile lighting up his face.

Karen placed an affectionate hand on his shoulder. Nbwane and Dave stood open-mouthed as she spoke to the little guide in his own language.

'I am grateful to you, Nbwane. You have shown me a face of Africa that I never knew existed. You have also helped me to understand this man beside you. These things I thank you for, but...' She paused, drawing out the moment. 'I'm afraid you are still a silly little bugger and a pathetic excuse for a leopard.' Then she turned to Dave and spoke in English. 'Now it's your turn, sir. Skinny I may be, but at least I've got the courage to go after what I want.'

All the things he had unwittingly said to Nbwane came tumbling back into Dave's mind. Nbwane was grinning from ear to ear. The hunter in him appreciated the way Karen had set and baited a trap for them. His laughter began to boom and echo around the clearing.

Karen waited until Dave had climbed aboard the plane, then she said to Nbwane, 'I wish you a fruitful life, and beware of those prowling leopards.'

'Ah, but you have it wrong.' Nbwane looked serious. 'It is you who must beware of the Leopard.'

The words struck her like a physical blow. She followed Nbwane's gaze into the plane, but all she could see was the glint of Dave's intense golden eyes. She turned to ask Nbwane what he meant, but he had gone.

CHAPTER 47

'How are things going? Any progress?'

'No different. God, it's frustrating.' Athol was leaning against a block wall, his arms folded across his chest.

Richard and Athol had chosen the Johannesburg Zoo as the venue for their meeting. They had finally come to a stop in front of one of the larger animal enclosures.

A giraffe strolled gracefully past. 'So nobody's prepared to listen?' Richard asked, his eyes following the elegant animal.

'Not a bloody soul,' Athol confirmed.

Richard turned his back on the enclosure, mirroring Athol's stance. 'But how on earth can they justify that?' he asked pensively.

'What did you say to me about South African arrogance? I've been confounded by so much bureaucratic high-handedness, I can't get any support whatsoever. Can you believe they rejected my claims outright?' Athol dropped his head dejectedly.

'So you've gone through all the proper channels.'

'Oh, for Christ's sake,' Athol snapped. The air seemed to crackle with static as if Richard had somehow invoked an electric storm.

He held up his hands in an attempt to pacify his companion. He of all people knew the stress Athol was under. 'I'm just trying to clarify it in my own mind. I realise you'll have followed the correct procedure. I just want to know exactly what you've done.'

Athol let out a long breath. 'OK, sorry, it's starting to wear me down. I've only had a month of this. How on earth have you coped?'

Richard shrugged. 'You get hardened to it.'

When Athol saw Richard wasn't going to say any more, he continued, 'I've spoken to my superiors, and also to the minister, on numerous occasions. But because I've been unable to produce any hard evidence that Vulcan's still controlling the UDF, all my claims have been ignored.'

Richard was speechless.

'My government is playing right into Vulcan's hands,' Athol went on. 'They believe that with our positive balance of trade, plus no apparent threat to national security from the UDF, they're in a stronger position than they've been in for decades.'

'Or certain members of your government are unprepared to act because Vulcan has them on his payroll.'

It was Athol's turn to stare in disbelief. 'My god, that never occurred to me.'

'We can get back to that. What did they say about Vulcan's overseas activities? Surely they have to acknowledge those?'

Athol closed his eyes. 'They stone-walled me there too. They said the evidence was only superficial. Their standard reply was, "What concern is it of ours anyway?" You're right, you know, Vulcan must've infiltrated the government.'

'Did you mention the KGB and the CIA?' Richard asked, already knowing the answer.

'Yes, and again the same response. Not interested, no facts.' Dispirited, Athol turned around and placed his hands on the edge of the wall. Even the antics of two frolicking blue wildebeest down in the enclosure were unable to lift his blackened mood. 'I've really only got one item worthy of any comment. Brendan Oechsli was sighted at the NASA base here in Jo'burg.'

'Well, that's something. It goes some way towards confirming my suspicions about the CIA and KGB. Ferkatovich has been seen up in Windhoek recently.'

'That's all we need.' Athol turned around. 'Vulcan, the CIA and now the bloody KGB, all perched like vultures waiting to pounce on the spoils dished out by an arrogant government.'

'Come on, Athol, that'll only happen if we let it. We've still got a few aces up our sleeve,' Richard said. 'What've you found out from your man close to Vulcan?'

'Not a word. I haven't heard from him for a couple of weeks. He's following his own line of investigation. I don't expect to hear from for another week or so. What about yours?'

'Nothing more as yet. But I'm in contact with him.'

Athol took off his glasses and held them up to the light. He huffed on both lenses and polished them with his handkerchief. 'So what's our next move?'

Richard knew it must have taken a lot for Athol to swallow his pride and ask for help, however indirectly. He reached into the inside pocket of his jacket and produced an envelope. He handed it to Athol. 'Two photographs, one of Brendan Oechsli, the other of a Dutchman called Kane Van der Zwet. There's also an identikit of Uri Ferkatovich. We need them located and followed. That may produce a few leads.'

Athol slit the flap of the envelope. 'We've got one of Oechsli and, shit, I was going to say of the Russian, but not looking like this.' Athol stared at the drawing. 'The beard changes his appearance completely. We'd never have located him. Is this recent?'

'Very.'

'I won't ask how you got it. Who's the Dutchman, Van der Zwet? He shouldn't be too hard to spot.'

'As long as he doesn't spot you first. He's a nasty piece of work. He's the one that caused you all the problems with Zamba up in Botswana.'

Athol's gaze flicked to Richard's. 'Was he now?'

'He's one of Vulcan's hit men. You'll have his photograph on file at your Department of Home Affairs for his employment visa, possibly under an assumed name. He's a direct link to Vulcan, but we can't afford to spook him. If you do look for him make sure you use your best men, or you'll probably never see them again.'

'Right, besides these three, what else?' Athol asked, pocketing the envelope.

'Only one thing left: the UDF. We need an inside story on what's really happening.' Athol was about to cut in, but Richard held up a hand. 'I know that's what you've been trying to do, but it doesn't alter the fact we've got no leads.'

'Yeah, OK, point taken,' Athol conceded. 'I'll have all our informants questioned again.'

There was little more to be said. They turned to go their separate ways. It didn't occur to Richard to tell Athol that he already knew exactly where the Dutchman was.

CHAPTER 48

The phone was making the empty living room vibrate. Kane was still shrugging on his white towelling robe as he ran towards it. 'Yes?' he said snapped irritably, then more respectfully, 'Yes, sir.' He guiltily pulled the robe closed across his naked body and sat down at the breakfast bar.

'We're moving into the last phase, Kane,' said the familiar voice. 'It's time to pick up the shipment from the Valley of a Thousand Hills, and make sure you tidy up any loose ends while you're there. Deliver and install it, check up on the preparations and the readiness of the UDF groups throughout the country. And make sure you're back here within a couple of weeks. There may be other loose ends to tidy up. Finish whatever you're doing, and get on with it.'

Without another word Vulcan ended the call. Kane replaced his receiver too, a surge of adrenalin tingling through his body. He gazed unseeingly at the phone, enjoying the anticipation. *Finish whatever you're doing*, he thought. *Better do as the boss tells me.* With a lustful gleam in his pale blue eyes, he returned to the bedroom, where Sandy was sprawled naked on her back on the double bed.

Kane ran his finger along her shapely leg, and leaned over to admire the picture she presented: an ankle caught under a fold of tousled sheet, an arm tossed out over the pillow, the other hand resting comfortably on her tanned thigh. Her mouth was slightly open, showing a glimpse of even white teeth, and with each breath her breasts rose and fell.

The bed lurched as it took Kane's weight as well as hers, and her eyes flew open. Good, she was awake. Kane liked his women co-operative, or at least be aware. She looked at him with questions in her eyes, as if she was trying to remember where she was; then her gaze snapped into focus and she raised her hands to grip his bunched shoulders. He moved on top and drove hard into her; she threw her head back and screamed, then cried 'Yes!' as pain and pleasure melded. She hollowed her back and curled her fingers into his shoulders as she met every frenzied thrust.

A cruel smile crept over his face, and he withdrew. Sandy struggled on to her elbows and looked up at him with a moan of protest. But he wasn't done with her yet. He scooped her up and flipped her over, and guided his still erect member between her buttocks. Her back hollowed and a gasp escaped her lips as her whole body shuddered. He pushed her head into the pillow with a hand on the back of her neck, and they became like two animals rutting. Kane roared as wave upon wave of pleasure consumed him; Sandy's shrieks told him she was out of control. He was hardly aware of collapsing on top of her as they both finally spiralled back to earth.

CHAPTER 49

Karen and Dave were both lost in their private thoughts. Since leaving Delta Camp they had distanced themselves from one another; Karen was disturbed by Nbwane's comment about the Leopard, and Dave had his own reasons.

It was mid-morning; the trailer had been replenished with supplies, and they were on the road again, heading for the Moremi Wildlife Reserve. Karen sat in the middle seat of the Land Rover, next to Dave, a jumble of thoughts churning around her mind. At least back in Jo'burg she was able to immerse herself in work; out here there was too much time to brood.

The barren terrain they were crossing did little to soothe her roiling mind, but she had no desire to let herself fall into the kind of gloom that sometimes descended at home. She turned to Dave, who was reading the Botswana daily newspaper.

'Don't tell me you ran twenty-four kilometres into Maun and back this morning, just to get that?' she asked, tapping the paper as he folded it and laid it on his lap.

'I needed the exercise after the inactivity in the delta,' he answered with a quick smile.

'Exercise!' the German chipped in from the seat behind. 'That's nearly a marathon.'

Allan glanced briefly over his shoulder, disapproval in his eyes. Catching up on world news was no way to leave the rigours of modern society behind.

'If you've finished with it, do you mind if I have a look?' Karen asked, reaching out a hand towards the paper.

That was the last thing Dave wanted.

The newspaper was the main, in fact the only, reason for his daybreak run into Maun. Because of the delicate nature of the mission, Dave and Richard Black needed a simple, unobtrusive method of communication. To this end, they placed coded advertisements newspapers wherever he was working. They had used it quite successfully in New Zealand, right under Kane's nose at the airport in Perth, and were using it again in Africa.

Inside this paper there were several messages to keep Dave up to date with developments. It was unlikely Karen would recognise them if she happened to read them, but given her perceptive, probing mind, Dave wasn't prepared to take the risk.

Karen reached for the paper, and as her fingers began to close on it, he whipped it away from her grasp and held it above her head.

A trace of a smile sneaked across Karen's lips as a playful mood washed her mind clean of gloom. This was just what she needed. She snatched at the paper again, but Dave still held it out of reach.

'I'd like to give it to you, but I can't. On safari, you see, we leave the real world behind. Isn't that right, Allan?'

While Dave's attention was on the party leader, Karen pounced. She made a show of reaching for the paper, and as Dave reacted, she jabbed a finger into his unprotected ribs. He winced, she grabbed the paper and a playful tug-of-war ensued.

'OK, you win,' Dave said, pushing the paper into Karen's lap. His subtle ploy worked. Almost disappointed that Dave had given up so easily, Karen loosened her grip; at the same moment the Land Rover lurched into a sandy hollow, and with a quick flick of his wrist Dave regained possession. He quickly threw the paper over the front seat where it landed at Allan's feet. 'I think you'd better look after that,' he said. 'We don't want Karen ruining her holiday, do we?'

The short bout of childish playfulness achieved two objectives for Dave. The distance that had begun to open up between himself and Karen had closed again; and Karen wouldn't be reading the newspaper. As for Karen, her gloomy mood had lifted, and she was looking forward to the sights and mysteries that lay ahead. Next on their itinerary was the Moremi Wildlife Reserve.

The scenery was quite unlike anything they had seen so far. They passed through the south gate along a meandering track of thick whitish-grey sand. Savanna-type woodlands, mopane forests and the flood plains of the nearby delta existed side by side in this unique region.

The warm colours of the landscape formed a background for a banquet of game and wildlife. There were spiral-horned kudu; zebra, their camouflage stripes nearly invisible among the trees; giraffe, the tall and stately giants; sleek roan tsessebe; and fleet-footed impala, entertaining the visitors with their frolicking.

The campsite at Third Bridge was only distinguishable from the surrounding bush by the rough-hewn log bridge which gave it its name.

There were no facilities, only recesses in the bush running down to the small river. Allan chose a shady, secluded alcove a hundred metres from the bridge.

Dave woke with a start, unsure what had disturbed him. Not a nightmare, not this time. Holding his breath and lying quite still, he heard the distant roar of a lion and the rustle and creak of insects, but they would not have invaded his sleep. Only a human noise would do that. He slowly let out his breath, but the only other sound was the slow thump of his heart.

He lay quietly for a few more minutes, but heard nothing out of place. He found himself thinking about Karen, and chose not to push the thoughts aside.

She was probably the most desirable woman he had ever met, and not because of her wealth or beauty. It was her intelligence and perceptive mind that attracted him, coupled with her love for life and the drive and confidence she seemed to exude. There was something else too, some hidden quality that he had so far been unable to fathom.

If only... he began to think; but that was one sentiment not to be explored. He had a job to do and there was no place in what lay ahead for emotional distractions, especially here at Third Bridge.

His head snapped up as his acute hearing caught the noise again. This time he identified it as a muffled cry of pain. Again he heard it, this time louder.

He threw off his sleeping bag, grabbed the pen-light torch beside his head and reached for the zipper of the tent. He stepped into the cool night breeze wearing only a pair of black briefs. His tanned body reflected the fragments of light scattered by the wash of the pale moon. The cry came again, this time unmistakeably from the tent beside him. Karen's tent. He bent down, drew the zipper up and stepped inside.

The first thing that hit him was the slightly acrid scent of human perspiration. He flicked on the torch. Karen was lying on her back with her head rolling from side to side, her hair plastered to her scalp. He knelt down beside her and lifted the sleeping bag from her sweat-lathered body. She was gripped by some all-consuming turmoil; he tried to wake her, but to no avail.

Dave's heart began to break, tears prickled at his eyes. This was what she kept hidden: like him, she was tormented by nightmares from the past.

He laid the torch down beside her and left the tent. He quickly returned with his own sleeping bag and a towel, and peeled her bag away from her shivering body. He tried not to stare as he gently lifted her arms and slipped her nightdress off, but he couldn't help himself; he was only human, and a red-blooded man. She was sleek and lean, and the sheen of sweat emphasised her finely muscled, feminine physique.

Karen groaned feebly, but still didn't wake. Feeling like a Peeping Tom, Dave guiltily averted his eyes and covered her with his sleeping bag. He spread the towel and let her roll on to it.

She was quiet now; the nightmare must have played itself out. Dave knelt beside her, his mind completely numb, gazing down at her now peaceful face. He tenderly brushed the damp strands of hair from her eyes. He was about to go when she called out, 'Tom? Don't leave me, not again,' and clamped a hand around his wrist.

Dave felt something burst inside him. He was looking down at somebody whose pain was just as real, just as agonising as his own. Gently prising her fingers open, he said, 'Tom has gone, Karen. You'll have to settle for me.'

He eased her on to her side and lay down behind her. Her whole body had stiffened; she was awake now. But as he wrapped a protective arm over her, the tension flowed away like hot water through ice. Her body softened against him and her breathing slowed to the rhythm of peaceful sleep – something which Dave knew would elude him tonight, and on many more nights.

Karen woke slowly. She felt rested and relaxed, and realised she'd slept soundly through most of the night, something she hadn't managed for a long time. The sun illuminated the inside of the tent, and she smelled the musky male scent beside her. She stretched out a hand, seeking for the man lying at her side – but there was no one there. The sinking sense of loss she woke to every morning was quickly displaced by a warm soothing glow. The space beside her was still warm and strangely reassuring; he had only just left.

Karen sat up, and as the cover fell to her waist, she realised she had slept naked. Maybe next time I'll stay awake, she thought with a smile.

She ran a hand through her hair, and found a mass of knots. I must look a sight, she thought self-consciously, reaching for her bikini top and a pair of white running shorts. She needed to go down to the river and bathe.

As she stepped out of her tent an invigorating morning chill licked her tanned skin. She looked around, expecting to see Dave, but he was nowhere about. There was neither movement nor sound from the rest of the camp.

Karen gathered up her towel, and instead of heading down the road to the water-hole beside the bridge she decided to cut through the bush and find a secluded stretch of water where she could wash unseen. The river was farther away than she anticipated, but the cooling breeze and the morning chorus heightened her mood. She stepped out of the bush onto a small stretch of sand, with walls of tangled reeds forming a secluded bay.

Karen cautiously scanned the area; the coast appeared to be clear. Allan had warned that the water was infested with crocodile, so she had no intention of wading in more than a couple of metres. She unclipped her sports bra and bent down and scooped handfuls of cool water over her hair and upper body. Goosebumps formed on her skin as she scrubbed away the dried sweat with handfuls of coarse white sand.

A vibrant energy flowed through her body, and she felt wide awake and thoroughly alive as she vigorously washed her long brown hair.

Suddenly the atmosphere seemed to change. Her hands stilled, and she flicked her wet hair away from her face and crouched in the water.

Something had alarmed her, but what? She scanned the river and the reed beds, but saw nothing. The bush had fallen silent: no birdsong, no rustling in the undergrowth.

Karen cautiously backed towards the beach, her internal alarms screaming like a siren even when she reached the water's edge. No tell-tale ripples disturbed the surface of the river; whatever the danger was, it wasn't a crocodile.

In the water at her feet, a distorted reflection shimmered. Her heart leapt into her mouth, and she tried to scream and jump away, but a callused hand closed around her mouth. She smelled the stench of human sweat and unwashed clothes; her instincts told her to struggle forward, but her self-defence training had taught her otherwise. She took a nimble step back and drove her elbow into the attacker's stomach.

With grim satisfaction it sank into the man, and he buckled forward, wheezing. She followed the movement by flipping her other hand over her shoulder and around the back of her assailant's neck, then she lunged forward and tossed him over her back. When he landed, she savagely twisted his head to the side and raised her other hand to drive a stunning blow into his temple. But before the punch landed, another hand locked around her wrist. Karen flicked her head to the side, pivoted on one leg and snapped a side-kick into the new man's chest.

Karen looked around wildly, her mind racing. Only the two attackers were in sight, but both were quickly recovering. Time seemed to stand still; she needed to warn the others, especially Dave. He would know what to do.

She had never heard of terrorists operating this far south.

She wheeled round to race for the bush, but her way was blocked by the man she had kicked. She gasped in horror when she saw his face, hideously scarred and disfigured. For the first time she hesitated; his eyes fixed her with a brutal, murderous stare.

Until now she had been following her instincts; now her courage was in tatters. She spun around, her only escape route the crocodile-infested water.

Fleeing like a gazelle, she sidestepped the first attacker, who was kneeling in the river. She sprang into the air, diving for deeper water, but as she hit the surface, a hand clamped like a metal shackle around her ankle. She kicked and flailed her legs, landing some telling blows, but the man maintained his unrelenting grip. She knew she was doomed when the scar-faced man waded into the water, grabbed her arm and twisted it savagely up her back. She stifled an agonised moan as he began to speak, and through her pain Karen recognised the language. It was Zulu, or a dialect very similar.

'Get the white whore's other arm, J'Long, before she tries to get away again.'

J'Long released Karen's leg and grabbed her other arm, twisting it up her back. They hauled her to her feet, and this time she failed to suppress her cry.

Half-naked and trapped, Karen knew when she was beaten, but that didn't stop her kicking and thrashing like a frightened animal. But she was held securely, and the terrorists' inhuman laughs told her the worst was still to come.

That was when a figure seemed to materialise from the bush. The man with the hideous face reached for a pistol tucked in his waistband. Karen gasped in relief, and yelled in warning. Dave stood stock-still, his face empty of expression, his hands dangling limp at his sides.

The man called J'Long hissed a warning. 'Comrade Scarface, I know this man. He is the Leopard.'

The truth crashed over Karen like an avalanche. 'Beware of the Leopard,' she whispered. She had been blind all along. Dave was the Leopard.

She should have known; the evidence was all there. His last-minute booking on the safari; his stand-offish demeanour; Nbwane's warning in the delta. She even remembered sensing the presence of a leopard at the Augrabies Falls. It had been a setup from the start. Dave had been sent to kill her.

She let her body go limp; she no longer cared what the band of cut-throats chose to do. She thought she had finally found someone she could respect, and who truly seemed to care for her, and the previous night was a prelude to better things. How wrong could she be?

Less than half an hour earlier, Dave had been jogging down the sandy track towards the camp, gradually warming down after one of his better morning runs. Slowing to a walk, he shrugged off his damp t-shirt and used it to wipe the sweat from his neck and shoulders. As he did so, he briefly glimpsed Karen disappearing into the bush, a towel dangling from her hand. She was obviously going off to bathe.

Dave's stomach lurched. His sixth sense was working overtime again, and he felt decidedly uneasy. If his intuition served him correctly, now would be the time. With his t-shirt bunched in his fist, he followed her into the bush.

He used his long-ago training to track her. She hadn't taken the straight longer route to the river, and had travelled a long way from camp. He heard splashing; she must be close.

A few paces from the edge of the bush, he noticed another set of footprints overlaying Karen's; the new prints were familiar, similar to some he had tracked many years ago. His head shot up as he heard a painful cry, before he was able to react, his nostrils caught the scent of rancid human and the barrel of a gun probed his back.

'My name is Comrade Trigger,' a voice said quietly. 'We have been waiting for you. Come and see what we have been asked to do.'

Dave recognised the language as Sindebele. He also knew the man behind him, at least the type of man. He walked a few more paces and stopped just beyond the bush on the beach, his t-shirt still bunched in his hand beside his leg.

The sight that met him came as no surprise. Two more Matabele, one taller than average, the other with a grotesquely scarred face, were struggling with Karen at the water's edge. Her arms were forced behind her back, her chest was bare and her sopping white shorts clung to her hips.

How dare they humiliate her like that, was Dave's first thought, but he forced it aside. This was his world and he had a job to do.

Relief and elation suffused Karen's face, and she shouted a warning as the man on her right raised a gun and pointed it at his chest. The tall black man on her other side hissed a warning. Dave clearly heard the words, *Comrade Scarface*, and *The Leopard*. Yes, he knew these men.

Karen's face drained of colour. She stared at him, and her whole body slumped, and she hung limp in her assailant's arms.

The tall terrorist spoke again, and this time Dave heard every word. 'He fought against us during the *chimurenga* with the dung-eating jackals, the Selous Scouts. He is the one we took across the border into Mozambique. Remember, look at his scars.'

Scarface thought for several seconds before he spoke. 'It is no concern of ours. The message was very clear.'

'Well, come on, what are you waiting for?' Dave snapped at the black men in a commanding voice. 'Let's get it over and done with.'

Silent tears streamed down Karen's face. She understood everything now. Coarse laughter seemed to erupt all around her as she was dragged towards the beach.

Then there was a scurry of movement in front of her. She slowly raised her head, and stared in disbelief at the scene that met her eyes.

Dave took a step forward and seemed to stumble. Karen saw for the first time that a third man stood behind him with a rifle levelled at the small of his back. Dave was on one knee with his hands splayed on the sand. The taunting laughter still resounded in Karen's ears, reminding her of an amusement park's house of horrors. But when she looked across at Dave's eyes, they were no longer dull and lifeless, but burning flames of raging gold, consumed by fury.

He appeared to push himself off the sand, raising his buttocks first, keeping his back parallel to the ground. In a fluid movement he straightened his leg and kicked backwards; there was a meaty thud as his foot landed on the sternum of the terrorist behind him. Comrade Trigger flew spread-eagled to land on his back, dazed, the wind driven from his lungs. Dave snapped his head around to look at Scarface, who was levelling his pistol, ready to fire.

With a well-judged underhand throw, Dave tossed his sweat-soaked t-shirt into the man's hideous face. Scarface's aim was spoiled, but his pistol still snapped off two shots in Dave's direction.

He had to release Karen's arm to drag the t-shirt off his face. Blinking the big white man's sweat out of his eyes, he saw his shots had missed. But the man had thrown himself back towards the fallen Comrade Trigger. Scarface wouldn't miss a second time.

Dave landed on the ground beside the man he'd kicked in the chest. Scarface's pistol would soon be in action again; thankfully the t-shirt ploy had worked and the previous shots had landed between his legs. He counted off seconds in his mind: one, two, three. Time was running out; another two seconds and the pistol would be aimed at his chest. He grabbed for the AK 47 beside the fallen man.

Karen bit down on her lower lip as Scarface released her arm and the pain from her arm and shoulder subsided. He lifted his handgun again and aimed at Dave, who was grappling for something beside the prone figure lying on the sand. Her other arm was still painfully locked behind her back, but she gritted her teeth and let fly a punishing side-kick, catching Scarface at the base of his skull. Again the pistol barked; again it didn't find its mark.

Dave winced as the bullet whisked past his head. He silently applauded Karen for her courage and skill, and picked up Comrade Trigger's AK 47. Still on his back, he flicked a back-handed punch into the base of Comrade Trigger's nose. He heard the bones around the nose splinter as they were driven into the frontal lobes of the Matabele's brain.

Karen popped another snap-kick at Scarface, this time in the middle of his face. As it connected with a satisfying whack, she screamed; J'Long was viciously twisting her arm, almost to breaking point.

Her scream galvanised Dave. He swung the rifle and touched the trigger. Most of the black man was hidden behind Karen, but the bullet struck, throwing both Karen and the terrorist over backwards. Sickly apprehension dragged like a claw at Dave's gut, had he missed his mark? Had the bullet thumped into Karen's chest? He had to force the thought aside as Scarface struggled to take aim again. He eased the rifle round and tapped the trigger once, twice, three times. This time there was no doubt. One bullet hit Scarface in the chest, the next in his throat, the third through the bridge of his nose.

Scarface lurched and reeled as if he was seized by an epileptic fit. Before the man stopped twitching, Dave swiftly moved with the butt of the rifle poised to ram into his hideous face. But it wasn't necessary. He dropped the AK and retrieved the pistol. In a murderous rage he swung around and waded into the river to finish off the guerrilla who had caused Karen's death.

He levelled the gun, and with his forefinger trembling on the trigger, he swivelled to find Karen, kneeling at the water's edge, gaping wide-eyed back at him.

'Thank god,' he breathed, lowering the gun. Karen pointed down. The dead figure of Comrade J'Long lay in the water in front of her. Half his head was missing.

Dave and Karen sat in the water staring dumbly at one another. Karen eyes began to swell with tears. 'I thought you'd come to kill me,' she sobbed, holding out her arms.

But Dave looked away, his eyes flaring again. He raised the gun, and everything moved in slow motion again. Dave turned the gun towards her face, and her stomach seemed to plummet. So it had all been a cruel and callous game; Dave had saved her life so he could be the one to snatch it away again. The pistol barked. It was over.

There was a loud splash behind her. She jumped, and looked over her shoulder. The third man, the one she thought Dave had killed first, was lying in the water, a knife in his outstretched hand. He had stumbled into the water and tried to drive it into her back. Karen lurched at Dave and threw her arms tightly around his neck. This time he didn't demur.

They clutched one another for endless minutes, rocking back and forth. Eventually he said, 'Come on, we can't stay here. We need to go an explain to the others – they'll have heard the shots. And the crocodiles will soon smell the blood.'

He picked up his t-shirt and held it out to her. 'Best to cover yourself up,' he grinned.

Karen had forgotten she was almost naked. She thanked him, but he had already turned away. His manner had changed completely; he was brisk and business-like, as if what had just happened was all in a day's work to him. He grabbed the terrorist with the knife by the shoulder and flipped him over to search him, but found nothing. He floated him out into deeper water and gave him a hefty shove. He returned to search J'Long; again nothing. His lifeless body received the same treatment.

Karen was watching him in slightly horrified fascination. 'Shouldn't we, well, tell somebody?' she asked nervously.

'Tell who what?' Dave continued about his gruesome business.

He searched Scarface, and this time he found what he was looking for. Men like this always carried their orders with them.

Karen tried again. 'Tell somebody they tried to kill us.'

Dave still wasn't listening. He pushed Scarface's body out into the deeper channel to join his companions. He took her hand and together they waded to the shore. Placing his hands on Karen's shoulders and looking down at her with compassionate eyes, he said, 'You'll have to trust me. We're in my world now, playing by different rules. I understand them; you don't.' He held up the sodden envelope he'd retrieved from Scarface. 'If I'm right, this'll show you what I mean.' He opened it and pulled out two photographs, which he handed to her.

Karen gasped. One was of herself, the other of Dave. He also handed her a note printed in large, easily legible script. This time her mouth dropped open. It was a contract for her murder; but it was the name scrawled at the bottom of the page that shocked her the most. It was the name the private detective James Pearson had given her, weeks ago. The one that was somehow connected with her husband's death.

Dave pointed to the name. 'Vulcan. He had your husband killed, and he sent those thugs after you.'

Karen was in a state of shock. She hardly noticed Dave gather up all the weapons and throw them into the water, and cover the signs of struggle and the splashes of blood with sand. The crocodiles would soon take care of the bodies in the water. He took Karen by the hand and led her back into the bush and towards the camp.

Eventually Karen recovered her wits. 'You have to tell me. Who on earth is this Vulcan?'

Dave stopped and looked into her emerald eyes. 'He's my employer.'

CHAPTER 50

A muted growl like that of an angry lion roared from the great diesel engine, shattering the silence of the surrounding desert. With a blast of billowing black fumes from the shining chrome smoke-stacks, the hungry engine burst into life, only to have its roar of power bled off as the driver repeated the practised rhythm of changing down through the gears. As he hit the exhaust brake for the last time, the huge articulated truck slowly pulled to a stop with a great hiss of air, in front of the barbed-wire-topped security fence. The driver sat in his cab, looking indifferently past the army corporal who stood guarding the wire-mesh gates.

A sign hanging on the fence beside the gates blazed at the driver:

PUMP STATION OMUMBO
MILITARY PROPERTY
NO ADMITTANCE

Behind the fence lay eighty hectares of tall shining towers, tanks and criss-crossing pipes that twisted and turned in every direction, resembling a lifeless maze. Dotted around this metal jungle were squat buildings of brick and concrete block.

What once had been a derelict redundant mine had been transformed into a state-of-the-art oil refinery, capable of processing fifty thousand barrels a day, all earmarked for military consumption.

The corporal, a snub-nosed sub-machine gun slung across his stomach and a clipboard in his hand, approached the laden truck. 'You from de Louts?' he asked wearily in English. He wiped the sweat from his brow; another half-hour and his duty would be over. He was looking forward to getting to the canteen.

'That's what it says on the side of the truck,' the driver retorted in heavily accented Afrikaans.

The corporal let out a heavy sigh. 'We can make this easy or hard, the choice is yours, Dutchie,' he retaliated in English. 'Is this the last shipment from Natal?'

The differences between the English-speaking South Africans and their Afrikaaner countrymen had festered like a malignant wound for nearly a century. Without answering the corporal's question, the driver scowled and hooked a thumb to the rear of his vehicle. A large white van had pulled up on the verge behind the truck in a cloud of dust, and a man was getting out. The corporal took a final look at the truck driver, shook his head in irritation, then walked towards the newcomer, paying no attention to the gleaming lengths of pipe, metal flanges and numerous other pumping accessories securely tied to the truck bed. For the last year he had seen countless identical loads ferried into the military refinery. He met the van driver halfway along the truck.

'You in charge of the load?' he asked respectfully. The blond-haired man stood a full head taller than him.

'Sure am, Corporal. I take it you'd like to see my clearance.' Kane reached into the pocket of his shirt.

'Well, procedure is procedure,' the corporal said lightly.

Kane handed over the documents, his eyes fixed on the corporal's weapon. Israeli manufactured, blowback-operated 9mm Uzi, rate of fire six hundred rounds per minute. The refinery must be pretty important, then. No soldier on normal guard duty would be given a weapon with such overwhelming destructive power.

The corporal studied Kane's clearance for several seconds. Everything was in order. 'I'll have to check the van; all small vehicles have to be searched. Sorry.' He hunched his shoulders self-deprecatingly.

The orders appeared not to worry Kane in the slightest; he didn't even accompany the corporal to the van, but walked towards the driver instead. But if the soldier had seen the nervous look in his pale blue eyes, he might have checked the van more closely.

The corporal opened the rear doors. Sitting in a shallow wooden crate was a huge metal gate valve, without its circular handle. The mass of metal must have weighed well over a tonne, and took up most of the van's cargo space. He was about to jump up into the van to give it a closer inspection, then thought better of it; the equipment was obviously for the refinery. He closed the doors and walked back towards the gates.

Kane was talking to the driver. 'Everything in order?' he asked the approaching soldier.

'Sure. What's it for?' The flicked his head at the van, not really caring if he got an answer.

'The gate valve? It's the tap to go over the main feed from the reservoir, to regulate the flow of crude,' Kane lied.

The corporal nodded, ticked his clipboard and went to open the gates.

255

Kane let out a sigh of relief. Phase one, complete.

'Well, where the bloody hell's the handle?' the construction overseer barked. 'How on earth are we supposed to test the blasted thing?'

'It's not to be used until—' Kane began. He was cut off by the overseer.

'I don't give a shit. The gate valve has to be checked before the refinery's opening.'

Upon entering the refinery, Kane had followed the truck through the maze of interconnecting pipes, walkways and towering circular structures and pulled up beside the reservoir's main outlet feed. A huge pipe with a circular flange stuck waist-high out of a concrete pad; above that flange and below another was a large gap. This was where the gate valve was to go. Once it was in place, in theory it would regulate the flow of crude drawn by the refinery's massive pump, which would pipe the crude throughout the refinery.

Kane was standing beside the gap. He took a step towards the overseer and dealt him a resounding open-handed blow across the face. The man's head snapped to one side and he was thrown off balance. Kane struck another blow, backhanded this time.

Before the overseer regained his bearings, Kane grabbed him by the collar and hauled him off his feet. 'If you touch that gate valve before the opening, I'll personally throw you off the site piece by fucking piece. If you get my meaning.'

A thin line of blood was trickled from the overseer's nose. He curtly bobbed his head, and Kane lowered him to the ground.

'Well then, if you would be kind enough to bolt the gate valve in place, I can leave you in peace.'

With a nervous glance at Kane, the overseer hustled his men into action. The sooner the big blond thug left, the better.

Kane watched as the crew deployed a crane, and manhandled the gate valve into place. The sheen of sweat on his face had nothing to do with the fierce heat of the Kalahari sun. With a heavy sigh and a shake of his head, he was relieved to see it in place. As the last bolt was tightened, he spoke to the overseer again, his voice quiet but edged with venom. 'As was previously arranged, the gate valve's special handle will be delivered with the government and company guests for the opening. Until then it is not to be opened. That honour has been reserved for the president himself.' He turned to walk away.

'Screw you, mate,' the overseer mouthed. He had no intention of following orders.

As if Kane had read the man's mind, he stopped and turned around, a murderous glare in his ice-cold eyes. 'By the way, you'll have noticed the shaft has been specially coated and sealed. I'll be here to check that seal hasn't been broken before the ceremony. Please make sure it isn't tampered with. It's your responsibility.'

Kane drove through the security gates and left the refinery behind. He had no intention of being anywhere near when that handle was turned. Phase two, complete.

The plan for the destruction of South Africa's key government and army officials was in place. World history was about to change

CHAPTER 51

Karen was speechless. Dave's hands were still on her shoulders; she shrugged them off and turned away.

'All I can say is please trust me,' he said. 'Look, we'll talk later, I promise. For the moment, we need to get back to the camp before Allan sends out a search party.'

They made their way back through the bush in silence, and were greeted by a concerned gathering.

Allan was the first to see them. 'Thank god you're all right. Did you hear the gunfire?' Anything else he said was swamped by a barrage of questions from the others.

Dave waited patiently for them to fall silent. 'Yes, we heard it,' he said calmly. 'It seemed to come from further north. Probably rangers culling excess game.'

'Not here in Moremi they wouldn't—' Allan began. Dave cut him off in the same even tone.

'No, Allan, we're pretty sure it was game rangers. That's right, isn't it, Karen?'

Karen gave a quick nod and looked away. She had composed herself remarkably well, but her usual vibrancy was muted.

Allan looked at her, then at Dave. 'Oh, I see. Yes, of course, I'm sure you're right.'

The glance that passed between him and Dave revealed that he knew damn well something had happened out there in the bushveld, but he wasn't going to push Dave into an explanation.

'Shouldn't we go and investigate?' one of the party members asked.

'No, I don't think so,' answered Allan, still looking at Dave. 'Sometimes a man with a gun, game ranger or not, can kill an unexpected target. Isn't that right, Dave?'

'It's been known to happen, yes,' Dave said. 'This game viewing drive you're planning this morning – Karen and I have decided to stay behind.'

'Right, yes, OK.' Allan looked at Karen for agreement and received another brief nod. 'We were just about to leave. We'll see you both when we return?' More question than comment.

'You can count on it.' Dave took Karen's arm and led her away.

They both went to their tents to don fresh clothes, and by some unspoken agreement met on a grassy bank beside the river, close to the bridge. They both sat in silence for a long time. It was Karen who broke it.

'Well? Are you going to tell me what's going on?'

'What exactly did my file say?' Dave asked, evading the question.

'OK, we'll play it your way. But you'll have to tell me sooner or later. It said you were one of the most effective security consultants in South Africa, and probably the most expensive. You run a small organisation, but guarantee results. It listed your previous contracts with de Louts' associated companies, and with the other companies you have worked for throughout the Republic. Your references, South African and international, were impeccable, and your personal details were verifiable. All most impressive. Now are you going to tell me about Vulcan?'

Dave took a deep breath. 'Karen, what I'm about to tell you, you may have trouble believing. But I'm going to be entirely honest, something that for the last seventeen years hasn't come naturally for me. I really am employed by Vulcan—' He let the statement hang, but there was no response from Karen other than the level gaze she had directed at him as soon as they sat down. He continued, 'I also work for the British SIS and your own country's National Security Service. Vulcan is a man I've been tracking for many years.'

'So you're a double-agent?'

Dave snorted. 'You could say that.'

'But what's it all about?' Karen looked part suspicious, part mystified.

'Nobody knows who Vulcan is. What they do know is that he leaves a blaze of destruction in his wake, and he's as elusive as a flame. He's taken the name of the Roman god of fire, which sums him up to a T. Tell me what you know about him.'

Karen shrugged. 'I've only heard of him recently. I hired a private investigator to investigate my husband's death. He was the one who dug up the name, before he was...'

'Killed,' Dave finished. 'So it was you who hired James Pearson.'

'You know him?' Karen asked, startled.

'Vulcan had James Pearson killed as well as your husband. Yes, I knew him. What else did he tell you?'

Karen told him of her association with James Pearson and the information he had uncovered. '... so you see, I thought you'd come to kill me, when those... those men called you the Leopard.'

'No wonder you went sheet white.' Dave spread his hands in an apologetic gesture. 'Look, I'm sorry you had to go through that, but it shows you how Vulcan works. When he wants a job done, he'll cover all possible contingencies.'

Tears suddenly filled Karen's eyes, and she grabbed Dave's arm. 'Why did he have Tom killed? If you know, please tell me!'

'Please bear with me, I know it must be hard, but I am getting to it.'

Karen withdrew her hand and made an effort to compose herself. When he was sure he had her full attention, Dave asked about the detective again. 'The note, the one the police inspector showed you, do you think you can remember everything that was on it? It could be important.'

'Of course I can,' Karen said indignantly. 'I've an excellent memory for detail.'

'Don't tell me now – it may complicate what I have to tell you. But I'd like you to write it out.' Dave closed his eyes; it was important to strike the right note if he wanted her on side. 'Right, tell me why the whole world's experiencing an economic decline.'

Karen raised an eyebrow in query, but did as he asked, taking a few seconds to ponder. 'I take it "whole" excludes South Africa?' Dave said nothing. 'OK. Without getting too technical, I'd have to say it's because of mismanagement by the larger economies and the trickledown effect on the smaller ones. Also market restraints, trade embargoes and general mismanagement of funds by people in positions of power.'

'I agree with all that – but don't you think it's all a bit of a coincidence?'

Karen shrugged. 'Maybe. But how does that involve Vulcan? And what does it have to do with Tom's death?'

'Vulcan has orchestrated it.' Karen looked astonished, and opened her mouth to speak, but Dave held up his hand. 'If you'll just let me explain.'

For the next half-hour Dave methodically told Karen everything he knew about Vulcan's activities and achievements all over the world. Then, closer to home, he told her of Vulcan's intention to install the UDF as his puppet government in South Africa, thus influencing the power structure of the world. Karen didn't once interrupt. She listened, fascinated and appalled, until he had finished.

'And yet you work for him. Why?'

'No, Karen. I'm employed by him. There's a big difference. And why? Somebody needs to get close to him. He has to be destroyed.'

'There has to be more to it than that. Why are you really after him?'

Karen's instincts were clearly in full working order, but Dave wasn't prepared to share the whole truth. 'I've told you why. It's your choice whether to believe me or not.'

Obviously disappointed, Karen tried another tack. 'All right, then, tell me this: how is he planning to oust the current government? That'll be no mean feat.'

'I don't have a clue, but I guarantee it'll be violent, and very final.'

'So where do I come in?' Karen asked, feeling like an innocent bystander being drawn into a web of deceit. Though her mind was spinning like a top, she was aware Dave still hadn't told her why Tom had been killed. But the question remained unasked; Dave was speaking again.

'OK, there are two, maybe three reasons you're involved. First: Vulcan needs an infrastructure in place in every dominant country throughout the world. He needs an organisation that will not only supply him with ready capital in the short term, but will also be large enough to launder massive amounts of extorted revenue, and exert his brand of economic repression. Name me one company that's intertwined with the economy of South Africa, and also has major interests and holdings throughout the world?'

Karen stared at Dave, transfixed. The answer was out before she could stop it. 'De Louts,' she whispered.

'Exactly. That's why Vulcan had your husband killed. Afterwards he commissioned me to de-stabilise your company still further. He needs de Louts, in order to secure South Africa and execute his worldwide plans. Now that Tom's dead, whether you like it or not, you're the key to the stable running of de Louts, and to a large degree the economy of South Africa. Without you as president of the corporation, Vulcan's job would be that much easier.'

'The second reason?' Karen was stunned, but determined to follow this through to the end, however bitter it proved to be.

'It follows from the first. You and de Lout Investments are the key, either to me destroying Vulcan, or Vulcan succeeding with his worldwide plans.'

Karen's thoughts reeled as her revulsion for everything he had told her turned to anger. 'You're implying I'm somehow connected to Vulcan,' she flared.

'Yes, that's exactly what I'm implying. How subtle or tenuous the link is, I haven't yet been able to fathom.' Before Karen was able to defend herself, Dave shot another question at her. 'How do you think Vulcan was originally financed?'

Karen was still seething with anger. 'Quite frankly, I don't give a damn, but no doubt you're going to tell me.'

'I have evidence that your company is siphoning huge amounts of cash to hidden sources throughout the world. Either your European and north American subsidiaries are financing Vulcan, or he's robbing you blind.'

Colour began to suffuse Karen's face. 'Now you've gone too far. I've seen the reports that state...'

'That your overseas subsidiaries have made substantial profits,' Dave finished. 'Try this for size...' He recited from memory virtually the same figures presented to Karen. Everything from turnover and expenditure, to company profitability.

She stared at him, aghast. 'That's all confidential. Where on earth did you get...'

Dave held up an impatient hand. 'From Vulcan, and probably a hell of a lot earlier than you received them. Now listen to this – it's from a different source...'

If Dave's first recital had amazed her, the second left her visibly perplexed. The turnovers were the same as the first time; what made the difference was the distortion of expenditure against income. Karen started to see the discrepancies that he'd noticed all those months ago.

'Karen, only you can tell me if the second set of figures are correct, but you should know that the source that supplied them has never been wrong to my knowledge. Answer me this: if those figures are right, why are companies similar to yours struggling, when de Louts' overseas subsidiaries are enjoying massive increases in turnover, yet no visible boost in profits?' He didn't wait for an answer. 'Could it be because your company is being given preferential treatment by crooked politicians, so that that increase in capital can finance Vulcan's organisation?' Dave fell silent. Karen's stupefied expression told him she knew nothing of any involvement Vulcan had with her company. He laid a compassionate hand on her arm. 'If you want your company saved, and if I'm to put a stop to this... this monster, I really need your help.'

Karen's heart had sunk to her toes, but she knew Dave was telling the truth. It was all down to Peter. For reasons she didn't yet understand, he had presented the board with falsified information. And before she left for the safari the two of them had struck that deal effectively hid his fraudulent activities. His words came blaring into her mind: *It's just that the end of your safari coincides with the date I've recommended we hold off till, before considering any worldwide expansion.*

That was when she knew all Dave's assumptions were correct. Not only had the company activities Peter controlled gone unchecked since her husband's death, Peter didn't intend that she would get back from the safari at all.

It took a while, but Karen eventually composed herself.

'Before I'm prepared to give you my support, I've got a few questions. You said you were prepared to be entirely honest with me, and I believe you have been so far. I hope that you'll continue to be so.' She paused, and looked him straight in the eye, assuring herself that he knew his answers would dictate the extent of her future involvement. Then she asked her first question. 'Who gave you that second set of figures?'

It was a question Dave knew she would ask. He had no wish to compromise Richard Black and Network, but Karen would sense it if he lied. Even half-truths wouldn't be good enough. 'OK. But you keep this to yourself. The British SIS is associated with an information-gathering agency called Network. They gave me the figures. It's actually Network that I work for.'

'So would you have used me, killed me even, to ruin my company as a means to destroy Vulcan?' Her eyes hadn't left Dave's face. Dave closed his eyes. Whatever he answered, it would be wrong. 'Karen, one way or another you should be dead.' What else could he say?

Her expression didn't alter. 'Who are you?' she asked. 'What are you really doing here?'

Dave's shoulders slumped. The lie he'd been living for so long had begun to appal him. He gave Karen his true history, his voice mechanical, his face blank.

'Dave Old is my given name, and I suppose I'm half French. I do have a French mother, but I was born in New Zealand just over thirty-six years ago. For fifteen of the last seventeen years my life has been a lie. I've forgotten more about deceit and destruction than an army of people could learn. Barring the colour of my skin, because of the gift I possess for languages I can pass as a native in virtually any country in the world.' He paused, unsure where to go next. 'After leaving school I spent five years in the French Foreign Legion, and because of certain qualities the Legion recognised, I was given special training. Needless to say, they made sure I was used effectively. At the end of my term, because of the knowledge I'd acquired they tried to execute me. It backfired, and I ended up extorting them. I walked away with a vast sum of money, a French identity and a reference from the French Army. I then spent several years fighting in Rhodesia with the Selous Scouts, before moving south and setting up my private consultancy in Jo'burg. While I was in South Africa I was approached by both Network and South Africa's National Security. That's when I made myself available to Vulcan. The rest you know, and for what it's worth, you're the only other person who knows the whole story.'

'Thank you for your honesty.' But Karen wasn't entirely satisfied. 'Earlier you said there were three reasons I was involved, but you only gave me two. You also said I should be dead. If destroying Vulcan means so much, why am I not?'

This was the question Dave had been dreading most. He swallowed hard, and looking down at the ground. After a few moments he raised his head and looked evenly at Karen. His eyes seemed to change to a softer shade of gold, and she saw naked truth blaze from them.

'I had training while I was in the Legion that helped me to win over members of the opposite sex. In all other aspects of my life I have skills most people envy. I was taught, take emotion out of the situation and anything becomes possible. With you, I can't. The third reason you're involved is the same reason you're not dead. Karen, you're the most extraordinary woman I've ever met. I could never bring myself to harm you in any way, much less kill you.' He lowered his head again. 'I've wanted to tell you for days, and had actually chosen today to do it.' He raised his head and stared out across the river. 'You remember I asked to use the phone at your office in Windhoek?' Karen nodded, her eyes soft.

'I phoned a friend, on the pretext of finding out what was happening in Jo'burg, but mainly to get his views on taking you into my confidence and asking for your help. He gave me some advice, which I must say was next to useless. So I made up my own mind, and decided to approach you here at Third Bridge. That's what I had come for when that guerrilla sneaked up behind me in the bush. Normally, nobody would be able to get that close to me without my knowledge. My instincts told me something was wrong this morning, but I didn't listen. I was too concerned with what you'd say.'

'Did you have anything to do with my husband's death?' Karen held her breath.

'The head of Network and I set a trap for Vulcan. We assumed, rightly as it turned out, that I was a valuable part of his African organisation. I lay low back in New Zealand for two years, with Network subtly feeding information to anyone who inquired about my whereabouts. We let Vulcan find me and appear to lure me back. Karen, I can prove I was in New Zealand when Tom was killed.'

Karen let out her breath. She stretched out a hand and touched Dave's. 'All right. You've answered my questions as best you can. I'm prepared to help you, but I've a hundred more questions I need to ask.'

'Karen, if you're prepared to help me there are a hundred things I still have to tell you. I told you earlier Vulcan had your husband killed, but I'm sure I know who actually murdered him. And I'm afraid you know him.'

'Know him? Who?' Karen breathed.

'In a moment. First, I need more answers. How could your company pay millions out to finance Vulcan without your knowledge?'

Karen knew exactly how, yet some distorted loyalty stopped her mentioning Peter's name without first giving him a chance to explain. Surely he couldn't be involved with a tyrant like Vulcan.

Dave noticed her hesitation, but he didn't need an answer; Sandy had already given him that. He asked another question. 'Who's in charge of your company's security?' He knew the answer to that too.

This time Karen didn't hesitate. 'My brother-in-law, Peter de Lout.'

'So he'll be the one who hired your new bodyguard. The one who was with you when you were dropped off at Afro Ventures' office.' Dave hated what he was doing to her, but it was necessary to bait the trap.

'That's right, a big fellow, Kane Van der somebody.'

'I believe it was Kane who killed your husband,' Dave said quietly. 'Your brother-in-law hired him for Vulcan, as well as siphoning millions into Vulcan's war-chest.' He only paused for a second. 'Peter de Lout is somehow involved with Vulcan, as well as the murder of your husband, his own brother. I'm sorry, Karen.'

After the morning's close encounter and everything that had happened since, the dam that held Karen's emotions in check came tumbling down. Dave opened his arms and drew her close.

Tears welled up and sobs racked her body, but somehow Karen knew this was the last time she would mourn Tom. In Dave she had found somebody she could truly respect; the strength she drew from him buoyed her flagging courage. He had laid open his soul for her frank and searching inspection, and shown himself to be a man who was prepared to keep no secrets. If she could help him track down Vulcan, then maybe, just maybe they would have a chance together.

Karen's healing was nearly over. Dave's had hardly begun.

As the sun drifted through its leisurely arc, Dave remained motionless. When Karen's racking sobs wore themselves out, she had fallen asleep, and he had gently lowered himself on to his back with her head on his chest. The morning's ordeal, the realisation of the grisly truth behind Tom's death and her company's involvement with Vulcan, had exhausted her.

She stirred, and raised her head to gaze blearily up at him. 'Hello there. I must've dozed off.'

'If you call two hours a doze, yes, I suppose you did,' Dave responded with a chuckle. 'Come on, let's go for a walk.'

They strolled over the bridge, away from the camp, and it didn't take Karen long to come fully awake. She found it quite natural to slip her hand into his. They walked on for several minutes in silence, content, enjoying each other's company. It was Karen who broke the silence.

'You'll have my complete co-operation, and all the resources of de Louts, to find and destroy Vulcan.'

Dave stopped and looked down at her. 'Thank you, Karen. We're going to need all of that. But I think we've both had enough of Vulcan for one day. How about we pretend we're on safari?'

Karen laughed. 'Shouldn't we get back to Jo'burg? I have questions for a certain brother-in-law.'

'I know I've said it before, but you'll have to trust me. Peter's another link to Vulcan, and so is Kane. Me too, for that matter. If we sever one of those links, Vulcan will go to ground and we'll never be able to find him. One thing I've learnt about him is his timing is always precise. He sent in those guerrillas today, but he'll have set aside the full twenty-four days of the safari for me to finish you off, or at the very least to exert some measure of control over you. The guerrillas were a pretty solid indication that Vulcan wants you dead.' He slipped an arm around her shoulders, trying to soften the morbid truth. 'It's only been a week or so since the safari started, so we've still plenty of time to make a move. Besides, I need a few more days to find out what else you know. I'm sure a bit of gentle probing will reveal a lot.'

'I bet it will,' Karen said seductively, watching his eyes twinkle.

For the next few days neither Dave nor Karen mentioned Vulcan's name. The mood that wove itself around them was infectious. Everyone in the safari party seemed to sparkle with the sheer joy of living.

They were like a young couple who had just discovered love for the very first time. At times they were oblivious to those around them. Once when Allan asked a simple question, they both broke into laughter that went on unabated for several minutes. They lived in an enchanted world, wishing it could last forever. They explored each other's minds, talking and arguing playfully throughout the day. At night they would sit by the campfire, half-listening to the conversation around them, sometimes taking part, but mostly enjoying a silent intimacy.

The night brought a closer bond of trust. In quiet murmurs they would share hidden thoughts, and when the fire had eventually burnt down to an amber glow, Dave would lead Karen to her tent and give her a lingering goodnight kiss before returning alone to his own tent. They yearned for one another, but respectfully gave each other time, waiting for the right moment.

Through those idyllic days, the safari moved on. The Moremi Reserve was an unspoilt wonderland with an amazing concentration of game. It felt as if they were in the real Africa of old. North of Third Bridge they were treated to a brief view of a large herd of elephant, swaggering across the golden grassland. As they watched the great beasts fade into the distance, they seemed to illustrate the fate of the shrinking wilderness.

The sedate gold and auburn tinted woodlands around the north gate were a fitting conclusion to their visit. A clattery log bridge over the dry Khawi River took them towards Southern Chobe, mostly yellow winter grass scattered with clumps of bush and stunted trees: just as diverse and bountiful, but entirely different.

At Chobe's Savuti Marsh, aptly named the Marsh of Predators, they parked on top of the banks that circled the pan close to the campsite. Karen stood in front of Dave, his arms draped around her, looking down at the vast display of game drinking or at rest by the water.

'Gosh, look at them all,' Karen marvelled, her eyes wide with wonder.

'You lot are so lucky,' said Allan. 'In all the years I've been coming here, I've never seen such a variety. But most of all, see those two sable down there. What a privilege.'

A pair of majestic, chocolate brown sable antelope were drinking, similar in size to their equally rare fawn cousins the roan which stood nearby, but with one difference: their long, curved rapier horns. Sable are known for their aggressive nature, so they enjoyed little attention from the other predators.

'I can see why lion are lured to Savuti. They've got rather a large choice of game to choose from,' Dave said, watching a small herd of wary giraffe, towering above the other game. One of the stately giants had decided it was safe to drink, and adopted the customary awkward stance with forelegs splayed wide.

'It'd be like getting caught with your pants down if a pride of lion came over the horizon now,' Dave said.

As if somebody had a flicked a switch, the whole array of animals flinched. The giraffe raised its head. One glossy-coated impala gave a high-pitched snort and jumped a couple of metres in the air. The rest stood motionless, eyes riveted on one spot, trying to identify the source of agitation. A grey waterbuck was poised ready for flight, while two warthogs trotted with tails erect and manes waving over the bank and out of sight. A small, skittish herd of Cape buffalo closed ranks. Even the stolid Burchell's zebra, stiff manes pointing skyward, were ready to bolt.

The swiftest of all African antelope, the gregarious copper-coloured tsessebe, relaxed first. Seven bachelor elephant bulls appeared over the bank, trumpeting. The release of tension was visible. A pair of spiral-horned kudu bulls turned to one another and appeared to comment on the pointless antics of the other game, which of course they were never stupid enough to join in.

The elephants proceeded to dismantle the peaceful setting. One pair crashed noisily into the middle of the cooling pan, scooping mud and water in their trunks and flinging it at the animals still in range. Those close by shied away in comical exasperation. Three more bulls cavorted about the pan chasing the other game. The sable antelope stood their ground; the zebras indignantly strutted away. The fun-loving impala stole the show, joining the elephants in their game.

Soon the riotous activity died down and the elephants had the pan to themselves. Dave led Karen to a shady spot and they watched the elephants enjoy the refreshing water. The creatures seemed to realise they were on show and regarded the couple with happy indifference.

In the afternoon they took a slow game-viewing drive. Allan guided them to their first pride of lion, five lionesses and two young cubs, all sleeping, or sunning themselves.

'Look at them, they're like big cuddly cats,' Karen said.

'Yeah, and I spent five years in a monastery training to be a monk,' Dave snorted.

'Well, we know that,' Karen replied. 'But how did that lot get the title of King of the Beasts? They look so peaceful.'

'Don't let their appearance fool you,' Allan said seriously. 'They are beasts of the night. That's when they're dangerous.'

The Savuti Campsite was a large unfenced area of bushveld, and for the guests it proved a dry and thirsty night. Elephant had been through the camp and ripped up the water pipes. It was pointless to spend more than one night there; they took a vote: the Chobe Forest Reserve on their way through to Serondela in the north, or east towards the campsite at Tjinga. Tjinga won.

'Stop!' Dave laid a determined hand on Allan's shoulder. Dawn had just broken, they had risen early and were on the road again. Allan recognised Dave's sixth sense and complied without hesitation. Dave slowly turned his head as if trying to place a noise.

'That mound to the right.' He hustled them up on the platform on top of the vehicle. In front of them lay a small open grassy plain, studded with clumps of bush and ringed by a thin woodland. Expectancy hung over them like an electric mist.

What appeared was one of the most dangerous animals in Africa: a massive black Cape buffalo bull, head down, chomping on the dewy grass. Its colossal boss of jet-black horns stretched just under a metre and a half around its curve from point to point. It moved forward like a living excavator, shoving continuous clumps of grass into its mouth without a break.

The group watched unacknowledged for nearly ten minutes. Its body was black as night, its balding coat criss-crossed with scars and claw marks from unsuccessful lion attacks. It was a giant, a bull amongst bulls.

Dave slowly lifted his arm. Out of the woodlands emerged a pride of lions, four females and a huge golden-maned male, returning home after an unsuccessful night's hunt. They walked in a staggered line, while the bull grazed, blissfully unaware of any intruder's presence. Suddenly the lion froze, and the lionesses followed suit. With a subtle flick of his black-tipped tail he gave his orders. Two lionesses circled left, the others right, blending with the plain.

The bull stopped moving; only his shining black eyes darted around. Then he slowly lifted his head and cupped his tattered ears forward. The lionesses had soundlessly encircled him, trying drive him into a headlong rush. When he ran, two would pounce from the rear and collapse his hindquarters, while the other two attacked from the sides.

But the bull knew the predator's tricks. It was four against one, but he had tank-like strength and cunning accumulated over many years.

The lionesses charged in, but the bull gave as good as he got. The safari party watched, totally absorbed, as he lashed and tossed his attackers into retreat and planted his rump firmly in the nearest bush. The battle turned into a stand-off.

The cats hissed and snarled, coiled like springs and ready to explode into action at his slightest mistake. But the bull ducked his head and flicked his horns, easily keeping his assailants at bay. The lionesses formed a semicircle at his side and in a flash of tawny light from the other direction, two hundred and fifty kilograms of solid lion collided with his mountainous frame. The great beast had waited for his chance; he lodged his jaws around bull's bulging throat. A spilt second later, the lionesses charged; sheer weight of numbers swiftly overwhelmed the bewildered bull.

The tension that had crescendoed among the human spectators was matched only by their fascination. Even Dave could not fail to be affected.

As the lions tore at the dying beast, a window appeared in the tangle of thrashing bodies and they saw the lion rake four parallel bleeding lines down the bull's muscular shoulder. Dave gasped, and Karen turned towards him. His hand clutched at the almost identical scars beneath his shirt, and his eyes reflected his own long-ago ordeal.

The drive from the Savuti to Tjinga beside the dry course of the Ngwezumba River, through golden grasslands interspersed with forests and thick bushlands, was less spectacular, but presented some fine game viewing opportunities. Here they experienced the high spot of the entire trip: a pair of white rhinoceros.

Dusk was falling and they were nearing the campsite, when in the middle of the track, barring their way, stood two titanic monsters, four tonnes each of armour-plated muscle, their massive horns curling in front of them. Normally their cousins the black rhino are the aggressive members of the family, but one of this pair forgot the rules.

With passengers shrieking in amused consternation, Allan hurriedly put the vehicle in reverse and steered a corkscrew course between clumps of vegetation and the lumbering beast. The comical chase ended after a few minutes when the rhino puffed to a halt. It lowered its huge head, huffed through flaring nostrils and pawed the ground to warn against further intrusion before strutting confidently into the bush, honour satisfied.

Rudimentary didn't begin to describe the Tjinga campsite. It was set in the sparse cover of mopane woodlands, beside a dry sun-baked pan, and had no facilities beyond a single water-tank. The long drought had long since dried off the water-hole. They set up camp under the sweeping cover of two large mopane trees, and it had been a tiring day; silence soon fell over the tents.

Karen woke during the early hours of the morning. Her first thought was for Dave. He had fallen quiet after the lion kill, which had affected him deeply; even the lively chase with the rhino had barely lifted his spirits. She grabbed her torch and headed for his tent.

He was thrashing from side to side, his body coated in sweat. Karen gently tried to shake him awake, but only succeeded in increasing his distress. She persisted, and after a little gentler persuasion his eyelids fluttered opened, revealing a dull, lifeless stare. He lay for several minutes looking dolefully at her.

When Karen could stand it no longer, she asked, 'Please, what is it? What happened today?'

With an effort Dave roused himself. 'If you really want to know you'd better get your sleeping bag before we both catch our death of cold.'

By the time Karen had returned Dave had dried himself down and thrown his damp sleeping bag aside. They settled down together under Karen's, he on his back and she nestled close against his side.

Dave began to speak. 'Those three guerrillas at Third Bridge, I've fought against them and others like them before.'

'Yes. Something about Mozambique and the Selous Scouts.'

'Yes, that's right,' Dave looked at her, surprised. 'I didn't think you'd remember. Well, when I was fighting in Rhodesia, our main job was to locate the nationalist guerrillas in the bush and relay information to the main body of Rhodesian troops. We gained quite an accurate picture of their activities inside and outside of Rhodesia.'

He fell silent for a few moments, then went on, 'We had another role too, a clandestine one. We needed to eliminate the guerrillas' leadership, and we started digging up some pretty disturbing stuff. We heard about someone who was helping the guerrillas, not with money, but with training and direction. Their tactics started to confirm that. They started fighting with real purpose.'

This was starting to sound familiar to Karen, though she wasn't sure why.

'We were still getting good results, but the guerrillas had upped the tempo. They started hitting soft targets further into Rhodesia, and they were getting better at causing damage and outrage.'

Dave fell silent again, and Karen found his hand and wrapped hers around it.

He took a breath and picked up the story. 'At the beginning of '77 we'd just arrived at Salisbury and had been given leave – but before we even had a chance to change, we were back in action. A group of guerrillas had hit a Catholic mission about sixty kilometres to the north. God, it was barbaric. They'd massacred seven white missionaries, all in the name of freedom.' He shuddered. 'The men got away lightly, they were shot outright. But guerrillas raped the nuns and when they'd finished, they used their bayonets to violate them. They left three of them to bleed to death. If it was meant to provoke us, it worked. We set off in pursuit. But instead of the guerrillas heading north, the shorter route to Mozambique, they went east. We thought it was their first mistake. It turned out to be ours.'

He paused again, and Karen felt his heart rate increase.

'They left a trail a blind man could have followed, and we were positive we'd catch them. That was our second mistake.

'We were lifted by a chopper and dropped on their trail about fifty kilometres from the border, only hours behind them. That was when we found out it had been a setup from the start. We ran headlong into an ambush just before the Mozambique border. We must've been outnumbered ten to one. I saw the other three go down just before something was rammed into the back of my head. Next thing I knew I was trussed up like a pig, tied to a pole and being hauled through the jungle inside Mozambique. I presumed all the others were dead, and it wasn't long before I wished I was too.

'During the next few days I faded in and out, but when I was conscious I heard Vulcan's name for the first time.'

Dave felt Karen's body stiffen, and remembered what he had told her about Vulcan's methods. In Rhodesia he had helped mould a group of dissidents into a fighting force that had eventually won a country – and now he was doing it all over again, this time on a far greater scale.

Dave turned his head in the torchlight and looked down into her eyes. 'I'm going to tell you why I'm really tracking Vulcan – how it became personal. He stole something from me, and only his death will bring it back.'

For two days the guerrillas worked on him, until his flesh hung in ribbons. Dave was suspended like a living crucifix, bound hand and foot, and each time he failed to answer a questions, they lashed him with a *sjambok* whip. Soon he ceased to feel it, and fell into semi-consciousness.

'It is hopeless. Vulcan will not be pleased,' said the guerrillas' commanding officer in Sindebele. What kind of white man could endure such punishment?

The officer and his ZAPU men had just been relocated from the forests of Botswana, to re-intensify guerrilla activity on the war's eastern front. He hoped that interrogating members of the Rhodesian Security Forces would supply reliable information to help Vulcan. What he hadn't anticipated was that the first man they captured would be a member of the infamous Selous Scouts.

'He is a man,' the interrogator said. 'He will break.'

'He should have broken already, Comrade. We need to supply Vulcan with useful information.'

'And if I cannot make him talk, Comrade?'

'Work on him some more. If he still does not talk, take him to the rondavel. He is no more use to us.'

Again, the pain didn't register. With wrists shackled, Dave was driven to one of the crude rondavels scattered around the camp. He was quickly bundled inside and the door was slammed shut.

At first he lay oblivious to his surroundings, grateful to rest his ravaged body. Then a stench slowly pierced his half-conscious mind: squalor, carnage – and the unmistakable odour of a predatory cat.

He sensed the movement before he saw it. Crouched on a platform beside the barred window was a huge leopard, two and a half metres long and close to seventy kilograms. Its dappled golden coat glowed even in the dull light, and its tail dangled, swishing rhythmically. He made out long white fangs and fiery golden eyes. Its ears flattened, and its huge body seemed to swell.

Dave remained motionless; any sudden movement could be his last. He surveyed the room for a weapon, or protection. Nothing. Just him and the leopard.

He slowly rolled over, biting back cries of agony. He forced his hips and legs through his manacled hands so they were in front of his body. Then a steel rod probed through the window and its sharpened tip lunged into the leopard's shoulder. The big cat exploded in a ball of fury, and Dave knew death was certain.

The leopard is the most cunning of animals. They attack silently, jaws clamped on their victim's throat, and claws unsheathed to yank away the top of the skull. As if this wasn't enough, like a kitten playing with a ball of wool, they disembowel their stricken prey.

Dave's body went cold with horror. He looked frantically around and spotted a thigh bone that looked human. The leopard had tasted human flesh before. As he lunged towards the bone, the leopard pounced, and claws raked down his chest and stomach; pain hit him like a splatter of molten metal, and he lost consciousness.

Timot had watched the camp for two days from the dense undergrowth, biding his time. Two hours earlier a large body of men had marched from the compound, leaving only a skeleton crew. Now was his best hope.

He knew exactly what lay in the rondavel. Did he leave the friend he cherished to his fate, or risk his own life trying to save him when he was already as good as dead? There was only one choice.

Timot killed two sentries soundlessly, added their weapons to his own cache, then marched into the camp. With an automatic weapon in either hand he swept the compound clean, then ran towards the rondavel. He charged like a bull, sending the rough door flying and startling the leopard. Fear galvanised him; he bellowed at the beast, and dealt it a stunning blow. It collapsed senseless; he swung an arm under his unconscious friend and heaved him to his shoulder.

Timot marched for many hours oblivious to his fatigue, to put as much distance as he could between them and the guerrillas. He headed into the Mozambique jungle deep inside enemy territory; if they were to survive, he couldn't afford to blunder into hostile forces.

Luck was on his side. The heavens opened, washing away their tracks, and he stumbled on a cave in an outcrop of rocks. He laid Dave's broken body down, gathered some dry vegetation and made a bed for his wounded friend.

He was mortified by Dave's injuries; surely not even he could survive the four lacerations from chest to stomach. The festering bacteria on a leopard's claws could cause a deadly infection, and the wounds were already red and swollen. Timot was dog-tired, but his work had just begun.

He ventured out, returning sometime later with several bark containers. The first held cobwebs, which he laid along the lacerations to stop the bleeding. The next was filled with mould and fungi which he ground it to a paste and smeared liberally over the cuts.

The inside of the final container appeared to be alive. Timot put a hand into the writhing mass and took out an inch-long reddish-brown ant with pincer jaws. He pinched the edges of one laceration together and poised the insect above it. The ant sensed human flesh and its jaws clamped shut; with a quick twist Timot severed its body. He repeated the exercise along all four wounds, until four neat rows of black stitches closed them. Timot grunted.

Dave now had a fighting chance of survival.

The turning point came several days later. Dave's flesh had wasted from his body, and he began to struggle for breath; Timot tried to restrain him, and in exasperation he grabbed Dave by the hair and shouted, 'Don't die, damn you, you're the only friend I've ever had.'

Dave's Adam's apple began to bob, and Timot thought he was trying to gasp some final words. He laid his ear close to his friend's lips.

'For Christ sake, let go of my hair, you're hurting my head,' was what he heard.

Timot dropped Dave's head as if it was a live mamba. Relief rolled over him. Dave was going to make it.

The last thing Dave saw as he drifted into his first natural sleep in days was the huge Zulu's face beaming a smile of genuine joy.

They stayed there for just over four weeks. Dave's body healed quickly, thanks to his own resources and Timot's natural remedies. His flesh was wasted and his features gaunt, but his spirit was strong.

Darkness was falling, and Timot was preparing a sumptuous meal of worms and flies. Their diet varied, but was always nutritious and packed with protein. Tonight Timot decided to test Dave's mental agility.

'It is whispered amongst the kraals of Zululand there is a man as swift as a gazelle and as strong as an ox,' he said.

Dave nodded sagely and played along. 'I have heard it said there is such a man. It also said he is as brave as a lion.'

Timot nodded and clicked his tongue. 'He must truly be a man.'

Dave responded, playing his part. 'Tell me, my learned friend, how would I know such a man?'

Timot looked serious. 'A man saved from death, who would choose to bed down beside a sleeping leopard, would only ever know this man as his guardian angel.'

'And I'm so privileged.' Dave joined in his friend's burst of raucous laughter.

'Ah, but there is another man you must also now be aware of. A man just as courageous, just as a hardy,' Timot continued.

'And how would I know this man?' Dave asked.

This time Timot did not laugh. 'You would know this man by the scars he will carry. This man will be known as the Leopard.'

CHAPTER 52

'What do you mean, who? Kane Van der Zwet, that's who!' Richard Black was sitting at the table in his hotel room, screeds of paper littered in front of him, the phone clamped to his ear, trying very hard not to lose his temper.

'OK, OK, I know you're doing your best. But he's been away from Johannesburg for five days now, and we haven't got a clue where he's gone, or what he's doing. Remember he is a direct link to Vulcan, and his main hitman here in South Africa.'

The other person spoke, and Richard tucked the phone between his neck and his shoulder. 'Just hang on a minute.' He began sorting through the papers in front of him. 'Yes, you told me that. I've got it here in front of me. "Said he'd be back within a couple weeks",' he read. 'No, you didn't tell me that.' He began to write. 'So he said he had to spend some time in Natal. Is that all?'

He held the receiver away from his ear. 'I just told you I knew you were doing your best. But you did make contact with him about two weeks ago, and we're no closer to Vulcan now than we were then.'

Richard listened some more before butting in. 'Look, just keep me informed, and the minute Van der Zwet appears, let me know. And be careful.' Richard hung up and leaned back in his chair. Hell of a feisty one, he thought.

He pushed the thought aside and reached for two large pictures on the table, one a photograph, the other an identikit drawing. 'And where the hell have you two got to?' he said aloud. He was no closer to finding Vulcan, or Uri Ferkatovich and Brendan Oechsli, and gathering information about the UDF's current activity was a non-starter. He just hoped Dave was faring better. He reached down and held up the photograph of Brendan Oechsli.

'Athol Jansen. Who is he?' Brendan Oechsli asked, holding up a handwritten memo. 'You say he asked for me by name?'

'Of course, the receptionist denied all knowledge of you,' Daniel Shelby began to say, but was abruptly cut off.

'I hope to hell she did. She shouldn't even know I'm in the country.' Brendan spoke quietly, fixing his menacing eyes on Shelby. 'In future, make sure your agents keep all classified information to themselves. And you haven't answered my question. Jansen, who is he?'

'Sorry, sir. I'll talk to the agents.' Shelby reached for a file in the bottom drawer of his desk. 'Jansen's with South Africa's National Security, and he appears to have got wind that something isn't quite as it seems. I had to speak to him myself, he was most persistent. He's suspicious, thinks the Russians are upping their involvement, trying to increase funds to the UDF. He wanted to know why we hadn't informed them earlier.' Shelby looked expectantly at Brendan.

'And,' Brendan expostulated, 'if I want to know something I'll ask.'

'Sorry, sir. After all, this is his country. I implied we were unaware of any increased activity. He kept on insisting he wanted to talk to you personally. Which of course I said it would be impossible, as you rarely left the States.'

'Of course.' Brendan's sarcasm wasn't lost on Shelby. 'What's actually happening with the UDF?'

'It appears they may be the vehicle Vulcan will use to take over control of the Republic. It's all in my report.'

'Did he mention Vulcan at all?'

'No, sir. But one thing does puzzle me. If he is so concerned, why hasn't he taken any action against the Russians and the UDF himself?'

Brendan let out a brief chuckle. He took a seat on one of the visitor's chairs in front of Shelby's desk. 'Because, my dear Shelby, none of his superiors believe him. Compared to the rest of the world the Republic's economy is buoyant, and with the UDF's leadership in disarray the government believes they're solid as a rock. No, we won't have any more trouble from him, and if we do, just stonewall him again. Better still, cite political harassment and threaten to contact his superiors. That'll keep the bastard off our back.'

'Aren't we taking a bit of a risk. What happens if Vulcan succeeds? Or worse still, the Soviets take over his operation before we have a chance to?' Shelby asked tentatively.

'You just leave it to me,' Brendan said, stabbing a finger at Shelby's chest, 'and make sure you keep your agents under control. We can't afford the slightest screw-up. Anything else?' Brendan rose, ready to leave.

'Just this. It came in only yesterday.' Shelby handed a sheet of paper to his superior. 'It looks as if this one's English.'

'Damn!' Brendan crumpled the sheet.

It was one of the few times Shelby had seen Brendan show any real emotion. 'Is he important?'

'Important? He really could screw everything up. How long's he been in the country?'

'Sorry, sir, wouldn't have a clue,' Shelby said wincing inwardly. Richard Black, whoever he was, certainly didn't please his superior, especially if he was here in South Africa. 'What would you like me to do?'

Brendan raised an impatient hand. 'Nothing, nothing at all. Just leave it to me.'

'Comrade, Comrade, when I say I want our operatives to give the UDF assistance I mean real assistance. I don't want them to pay lip service to my request.' Uri Ferkatovich appeared very calm. He and Doblin sat in the quiet of Pretoria's public library pretending to read.

Doblin was quaking in his shoes and having trouble hiding it. He swallowed heavily. 'I believe our operatives are doing the best they can.' It was true, though in some ways he wished it was not. He could almost hear his heart racing; his ulcers were definitely burning.

'Oh, you do, do you? Then why haven't I seen any results? The UDF still seems to be resisting our offers.' Uri tilted his craggy head towards Doblin.

'It seems, Comrade Colonel, that we... we... haven't got enough funds,' Doblin gabbled. 'All we've been able to learn is that they may be poised to launch a massive strike against the South African government, sometime soon.' Doblin always had difficulty looking directly at his superior; today all he wanted to do was run as far as possible from him, especially now he had mentioned the forbidden topic: the extra demands on his already tight budget.

'If money is the only thing hampering your operatives, why didn't you say so before?' Uri said. The menace had left his tone, and he sounded almost pleasant.

'I... I... thought we... we...' Doblin eventually stammered to a halt, stricken dumb by disbelief.

'In future you will be entirely open with me about the problems you encounter. You know how important this is to me.' Uri got up to leave. 'I shall double your budget. Use it wisely. Oh, and one other thing: have you heard of someone named Vulcan in connection with the UDF?'

'No, it is a name I would remember. Is it important?' Doblin asked, his interest quickening.

'It could be.' Uri looked away. Information about Vulcan was on a need to know basis. For now, Doblin would remain in the dark. 'Just keep me informed.' He began to walk away, a smile dancing across his face.

Doblin's next remark wiped the smile clean away. 'There is an Englishman here in the republic named Richard Black. He's asking a lot of questions, including some searching ones about the UDF.'

Uri scowled, his back to Doblin. 'Keep me informed,' he repeated gruffly as he walked away. He had a few important phone calls to make.

CHAPTER 53

Vulcan had only just put down the phone when it rang again. 'Kane. Your timing is impeccable. Yes, the line is secure.' He sat back comfortably in his chair. 'I trust all is going according to plan. Omumbo first?'

He listened for several minutes as Kane delivered his report.

'So everything is in progress in Natal? The gate valve is in place? Good.' He listened again for several moments. 'Ah, the overseer at the refinery. No, no, Kane, not your problem. I'll handle it from here.'

Kane was disappointed. He was looking forward to dealing with the overseer himself. But Vulcan had moved on to another topic.

'The UDF guerrillas? I've just left the camp here in Orange Free State; they're far more advanced than I expected. They'll be ready in plenty of time. No, sir, I only have the groups left near Cape Town and the ones in the Transvaal to visit. I inspected the one in Natal before I picked up the consignment. Yes, they'll certainly be ready. All they need is their orders, and of course the signal to start the uprising.'

'They will receive their orders in good time. Inspect the last few groups and get back here as soon as possible. I have another job I need you to do.' Vulcan retrieved a handwritten message from his desk.

'There is a certain Englishman who requires your attention. Oh, and Kane, when you get to the base in Transvaal, let me know how our three friends got on in Moremi.'

CHAPTER 54

'Now you see how the two fit together, why I'm determined to bring Vulcan down, and how I became known as the Leopard,' Dave said quietly.

It was mid-morning. They had risen at the first glimmer of daylight and walked away from the camp as Dave told his story. Now they were on their way back to Tjinga, down a sandy, bush-fringed track.

'This man Timot must mean a great deal to you.' Karen was still awestruck by what she had heard.

'More than my own brother.' Even that was no reward for the debt he owed his friend.

'Did you remain in Rhodesia afterwards?' Karen asked, still intrigued.

'I spent several months recuperating in South Africa. My wounds had healed, but I was a mess inside. There was only one way to sort myself out, and that was to return to the bush and start fighting again. While the guerrillas were beating me, I kept hearing the name over and over again. Vulcan, Vulcan, Vulcan.' There was such venom in his voice that Karen almost backed away. 'It gave me something to focus on, a target for the rage inside me. When I got back to the Salisbury, I started tracking him down.'

Once again her heart went out to him; it must have been unimaginably hard to share those gruesome memories.

'If the Rhodesian Army hadn't been so desperate for able-bodied fighting men, I'm sure I would've been discharged. I was out of control. I began taking needless risks to get the smallest clue about Vulcan. Only Timot was prepared to fight with me. We left a trail of destruction in our wake; for twelve months we wreaked havoc amongst the guerrillas.

'I don't know how it happened, but the name Leopard stuck, not with the Scouts, but with the guerrillas. Some of them probably still remember the name. There were huge bounties on our heads; that never stopped us, but we couldn't find the slightest lead on him.'

Dave began to rub his scars, only stopping when he realised Karen was watching him curiously.

'The futility of what I was doing hit home one day when Timot and I were deep inside Zambian territory. We'd just stopped for the night after pursuing ten guerrillas who had hit a farm just across the border. They'd set up another ambush, but luckily we'd stopped on the fringe of it. That didn't stop them opening fire. They shot Timot's belt off his waist. I'd nearly got my best friend killed. They chased us for hours. That was when I saw that war had no meaning for me. I had to find a better way to bring Vulcan down. And the rest you know.'

They walked on in silence for several minutes. 'No wonder you've been so obsessed with wanting to track down and destroy Vulcan,' Karen said.

Dave stopped. Obsessed? he thought. Is that what I am?

'What is it?' Karen asked.

'You're the second person to call me obsessed,' he said. 'I'm starting to wonder if you're right.' He gazed out over the dry bushland. 'Is this all I'm living for, to destroy Vulcan?'

Karen spoke quietly. 'If that was true, I'd be long dead.' She slipped her arms around his waist and he drew her close. They stood for several minutes before moving on again.

'There was a look in your eyes that day at the Augrabies Falls,' Dave said after a while. 'It told me there was something in your past too, something that still tormented you. I had no idea how bad it was, or what it was, but there was something, and from that moment I felt drawn to you. Then the other night at Third Bridge, well, I knew you felt the same.'

Karen couldn't help herself; it all came spilling out, her childhood and early years with her father, deprived of anything resembling emotion, the few years with Tom which had been a kind of reprieve, and finally the living hell after his death.

'Until you came into my life, I never felt safe, and now I do. And in a way I can't explain, I feel fulfilled. At last I've put the past behind me, where it belongs, and that's thanks to you. And no matter what happens, I hope I'm able to help you do the same with yours.'

Dave felt as awkward as a teenager on a first date. 'Thank you,' was all he could think to say.

'So all we have to do is track Vulcan down. Then we can set about finding some a semblance of order in our lives?'

'If only!' Dave replied with a wistful look. 'There are a few other things you should know.'

'Oh no,' Karen groaned, not knowing whether to laugh or cry. 'There's more?'

'Just a little. Ever heard of the CIA and the KGB?'

It took Dave a few minutes to explain what he knew about the two security organisations, their involvement in the current situation and their plans for the future. Karen wasn't a happy woman when he had finished.

'Well, isn't that great?' she said. 'Not only is Vulcan trying to use my company to take over South Africa and god knows what else, but now I have the bloody CIA and KGB breathing down my neck. How much more bizarre can it get?'

'If you put it like that, I suppose there's only one thing left for you,' Dave responded, trying to hide his amusement at the absurdity of it all.

'And what the hell's that may I ask?' Karen asked, her tart tone masking the edge of hysteria.

'Trust me,' Dave said flippantly. 'I do this sort of thing for a living.'

Karen didn't know whether to laugh or cry, and crying was favourite. 'What are we going to do? I'm going to lose my company, aren't I?'

Dave, serious again, lifted her chin. 'For a start, tears aren't going to help.'

'It'd make me feel a hell of a lot better.'

For the first time in days Dave's mind clicked back into focus. 'OK. We need a new plan. The first thing we have to do is get back to Jo'burg undetected. I've already been out of circulation far too long.'

Karen's sharp intelligence also snapped back into action, and her despondency fell away like a badly secured load. 'If you've been involved with Vulcan's previous company takeovers, can't we track him down through their ownership?'

'I've tried, and Network's tried. He must have one hell of an accountant working for him. They're just a maze of foreign ownership, dummy companies, nominees, trustee holdings, you name it and he's got it. It's such a complicated...' Karen had fallen quiet. 'What is it?' he asked.

'Give me a minute. Something you said... Dummy companies, trustees...'

Dave knew her well enough to wait without distracting her. It was the right thing to do; after a minute or two she snapped her fingers in triumph. 'Accountant and trustees. I think I might just be able to give you that break.' She grabbed Dave's arm. 'You said Vulcan must have one hell of an accountant working for him. Well, we know my brother-in-law is somehow involved with Vulcan, and there's no better accountant than him.'

'OK, but we already know...' Dave began, but Karen hadn't finished.

'The other word you used was trustees. Peter has exclusive control over a trust account we set up in Jersey. We use it as our indemnity fund in Europe.

He set it up when Tom was still in control, and I never liked it. Peter has always controlled that account.'

'So the account was used for bribes?'

'It's an everyday part of corporate business.' Karen shrugged indifferently. 'Some companies like to call it something less pejorative, but basically yes, it was used for bribes.'

Dave was almost afraid to ask. 'What sort of balance did the account normally hold?'

'In relation to our total European turnover, it was insignificant, but still many millions of pounds.'

'Enough to finance Vulcan until his organisation became self-generating, then a supplementary pot to dip into when the need arises.' Dave was starting to feel excited. 'Do you have the authority to have the account audited?'

'Of course I do. I have a mandate over any part of de Louts' operations worldwide.'

'Well, you said it. You may well have given us our first major break. Possibly solved your own most pressing problem at the same time.' Dave held up a finger 'One, we may have identified where Vulcan got his original finance from.' A second finger. 'Two, you may be able to stop the outflow of cash from your European and North American subsidiaries. That's if this is the account that the funds were channelled through...'

'It must be,' Karen butted in. 'Peter wouldn't be able to set up another account without my consent.'

'And three,' a third finger, 'with an audit, even if we have to go back years, we may find that's where Vulcan got the cash to finance his early takeovers. If that's the case, we may be able to track him from a different angle.'

Karen realised Dave was already way ahead of her, but it didn't take her long to catch up.

'Oh god,' she said, her own excitement matching his, 'one of the prerequisites for the account, in fact the only safeguard built into it, is that funds can only be transferred to recognised, legitimate sources, either individuals or companies. I never checked up on it, but Peter would've had to stick to it, or the bank would have raised an encoded tag. I'm not sure what system Tom put in place, but the only person authorised to remove that safeguard is the current president of de Louts. Me.'

'What do you mean, raised a tag?' Dave asked, unfamiliar with the banking term.

'In this case it would probably mean both a manual and computerised check. No matter how big the transaction, if it didn't go to a recognised source or if the procedure was altered in some way, I'd be asked for verification before the transaction could be cleared.'

'So you're saying all funds transferred so far must have gone somewhere traceable?'

'Exactly. And if they have gone into an associated account, I'll be able to have that audited too.'

This could lead to a major breach in Vulcan's normally impermeable security, Dave thought. What was more, there was only one organisation that had the resources for the type of audit they needed. Now more than ever it was imperative they to get back to Johannesburg. He needed to talk to Richard Black.

'Where the bloody hell have you two been?' Allan flared. 'No, on second thoughts, I don't want to know.' Concern was etched heavily across his face.

Compared to the problems they faced back in Jo'burg, Allan's worries were small fry; Dave grinned, and Karen stifled a laugh.

'I don't know what's so funny,' Allan growled. 'This is the African wilds, people get hurt out here.'

'We know,' Karen said, still trying not to laugh. She lifted Dave's t-shirt and pointed at his scars. 'Some of us more than most.'

Her gesture defused Allan's temper; he knew Dave was well able to look after them both.

'All right. Just don't disappear without telling anyone, OK? Look, we're just off for a game viewing drive. Are you coming?'

Without consulting Dave, Karen answered, 'Thanks, but no thanks. We'll see you when you get back.'

'That was a bit mean, wasn't it?' Dave said, as Allan walked away, still indignant. 'We should have apologised for worrying him. Anyway, what's got into you? There's nothing we can do until we get back to Jo'burg. A drive would've been quite pleasant.'

'Oh, I've got something a lot more pleasant in mind.' Karen took Dave's hand and led him towards the tents.

They knelt before each other naked. Dave couldn't keep his eyes off her, and to Karen it seemed like the most natural thing in the world.

She ran her fingertips down his chest and over his firm belly. Dave gasped; her touch seemed to light a fire inside him. He leaned forward and delicately kissed her mouth, then scooped an arm around her and gently lowered her to the floor.

They took it slowly, touching, stroking, exploring each other, and when their bodies joined Karen rose to a place she had never been before. Dave filled a need deep inside her that she hadn't known existed. Wave after wave of pleasure consumed her, each a crescendo only to be transcended by the next.

Still coupled together, they drifted down into a semi-conscious state of peace and harmony. For them both, there was a sense that this was where they were meant to be. Of completeness.

When Allan and the other safari members returned, Dave took Allan aside. After a brief but persuasive discussion, they set off for Victoria Falls in Zimbabwe. From there Allan headed back to Botswana, and Dave and Karen boarded a flight for Johannesburg, a Gulfstream jet piloted by an old friend of Tom de Lout's. It hadn't take them long to decide how to disappear, and hopefully fool Vulcan into thinking Dave had fulfilled his mission.

'An intercontinental jet for the short hop back to Jo'burg?' Dave cocked a teasing eyebrow, casting an eye over the around the eight-seater's plush interior.

'Big is best,' Karen answered, tartly. 'Anyway, it was the only aircraft available.'

'At least it's fast — we don't have time to waste.' Dave was serious again. 'Better get down to business. I want you to write out exactly what was on James Pearson's note. The one the police inspector showed you.'

Karen left her seat and found a pen and paper in the galley. After only a few minutes she had written it out just as it had been presented to her.

Dave read from the piece of paper she proffered. 'Watch those close to you. Beware the Leopard, U235, Valley 1000, Reflecting shield, Hot and Cells. The first two are self-explanatory, they'll be referring to your brother-in-law and me. But the last four. Mean anything to you?' he asked, bemused.

'Not a thing.'

Dave stared down at the words. Something seemed to flutter like a moth caught in a spider's web, just below the surface of his mind. If he tried to force it, he would drive it further away. He folded the note and put it in his pocket. 'Well then, I've already made the arrangements, but we'll have to wait until we get picked up at Jan Smuts.' Making a play of consulting his watch, he continued, 'That still leaves us just over an hour to kill. Any suggestions?'

Karen stood up and went to lock the cabin door.

An hour and a half later she looked across the tarmac. 'It looks as though your ride hasn't turned up.'

'Really?' A long black Mercedes limousine glided out of the night towards the Gulfstream's retractable steps.

Dave led the way down the steps towards the waiting vehicle. A tall black African was holding open the passenger door. Karen was dumbfounded.

'I see you, *Nkosi*,' the man said in Zulu.

'I see you also, Moses.' Dave accepted the compliment with a slight inclination of his head. Moses turned to Karen and spoke again in Zulu.

'You are privileged, *Nkosikazi*, to have such a man as this to protect you.' Thunderstruck, Karen stammered, 'But he's my... Moses, you... Dave, this man works for me.' She climbed into the familiar interior of her own limousine and stared at Dave, waiting for an explanation.

'He's also Timot's cousin,' came the reply.

That was when it really struck home. Her company really could be controlled by others, and she wouldn't have the slightest knowledge.

Meanwhile, back in Kasane, Botswana, a black police constable, dressed smartly in a khaki uniform, pushed his chair back across the wooden floor and walked up to the counter. 'Yes, may I help you?' he asked in heavily accented English.

'Yes, Constable, I'd like to report the disappearance of two foreign tourists.'

The constable sighed. It was going to be a long, weary night. He rummaged under the counter for the appropriate forms, then with his tongue stuck out the side of his mouth, he waited with his pen poised. 'Your relationship to the missing persons?'

'I was their tourist guide. I'm a driver with the safari company Afro Ventures.'

After his trip back to Kasane from Victoria Falls, Allan knew it was going to be a long and weary night.

CHAPTER 55

'Room 228? I think it would be Mr Peter Hindes you're after. He's in room 431. I believe he hasn't been down today. If you let me sign for the package, I'll make sure he gets it,' the hotel receptionist said politely.

The courier from DHL just shrugged, placed the package on the counter and turned away. He didn't hear the receptionist turn to the night porter and comment on his size, his good looks and his flowing blond hair.

Dave pulled his BMW into the Holiday Inn car park just behind a DHL courier van. The buoyant mood he had carried with him from the safari was shattered. He recognised Kane immediately; he was dressed as a courier and appeared to be taking a package into the hotel. There could be only one reason he was here. Vulcan had got wind of Richard Black and his investigation, and had sent in his chief fixer to put a permanent stop to it. Dave needed to warn Richard; the head of Network was no match for a man like Kane.

Dave was about to leave his car when Kane reappeared and walked to the back of the van, looking around carefully before stripping off the courier jacket. A dull flash of metal confirmed Dave's hunch; there was a pistol inside his belt at the small of his back. Dave only had minutes to warn Richard.

Kane walked back into the hotel and Dave followed. He found a phone in the lobby and impatiently waited to be connected. It seemed like an eternity, but at last he heard Richard's voice.

'Richard, Dave Old. You've got sixty seconds to pack the essentials and get the hell out of your room. Van der Zwet's in the hotel and on your trail. Use the stairs and meet me down in the car park. I'll be in the white BMW. Make sure you're not seen. Fifty-five seconds.'

Richard didn't ask questions. He slammed down the phone, unplugged the scrambler unit and scooped the material littering the table into the travel bag he always kept ready. Everything else he left. He peered cautiously round the door; the coast was clear. Heart pounding like a locomotive, he ran down the hall to the stairwell. As he pulled the door behind him, he heard the soft chime of the elevator. As he raced headlong down the stairs, a door crashed overhead. It had to be Kane thundering down behind him. I'm getting too old for this, he thought.

After endless moments he was on the ground floor. He wrenched open the door and nearly died of fright. Dave stood there, a gun in his hand. He flicked a thumb over his shoulder. 'The white BMW, get in the back on the floor. I'll slow him down.'

As Dave stepped into the cool interior of the stairwell, he heard Kane on the landing above. He pointed the pistol skyward and emptied its magazine up the middle of the spiralling stairs. Bullets ricocheted off metal banisters and concrete walls as he left as quietly as he could. It was unlikely the barrage of shots would injure Kane, but it would slow up any sane man.

In the BMW, he heard Richard panting heavily behind him. 'Out of condition, aren't we?' he said, amused.

'What the hell was all that shooting?' Richard gasped.

'Keep your head well down, at the moment you're the last person I want to be seen with.'

Dave glanced into his rear view mirror and saw Kane skid to a halt outside the hotel entrance, his gaze sweeping wildly from side to side. He must have continued down the stairs through his hail of bullets. But for the moment at least, his prey had eluded him.

On the way to his place, Dave updated Richard on the developments since they had last spoken: Karen de Lout's offer of support, their disappearance in Zimbabwe, and most important, the audit they needed on the de Louts trust account in Jersey.

'So where is she, Karen de Lout?' Richard asked as the car drew to a halt. He was barely able to conceal his excitement at the new turn of events. 'I'll need to talk to her at length.'

'She's here. I'm including her in the team. Her input will be vital.'

'Is that wise?' Richard was clearly concerned.

Dave misread his meaning. 'She'll be safer here than anywhere else. Come on, we'd better go in, they'll be waiting.'

It was just as he expected. The room bristled with tension as Sandy and Karen stood like two gaming cocks. Richard almost expected to see a blaze of feathers erupt. Without Dave's knowledge, Sandy had been on Richard's payroll for years. He had found out long ago about Sandy's fierce loyalty, and her feelings towards Dave.

It was worse than he had imagined. Karen gave Dave a lingering kiss and hug, he suspected more to rile Sandy than out of genuine affection, and if Sandy's eyes had been daggers, they would have been embedded in the other woman's heart. Both women had the situation summed up: one had somebody the other wanted, and that somebody was totally oblivious to the volcano he was sitting on.

Totally ignorant of any impending disaster, Dave turned to Richard. 'I'll introduce you around.'

'Ah, the man from Network,' Karen said as she was introduced. A cool, firm handshake told Richard he had met a fellow professional.

Next Dave introduced Sandy. 'This is my personal assistant, who I don't believe you've met. Sandy Thomson, Richard Black.'

'I believe you're right,' Richard lied, as Sandy demurely shook his hand. 'And this is the man who named me the Leopard. Richard Black, Timot Ngema.'

Hell, you're an ugly brute, Richard thought looking at the hulking Zulu's bald, scarred head. But nothing showed on his face as he extended his hand.

Timot accepted the handshake with surprise; it was executed in typical African fashion. 'So, this Englishman is well travelled,' he said approvingly.

'Better than that, he was born in South Africa,' Dave explained. 'We've all got a lot to cover, so let's get on. I'll grab myself a chair.' He headed into the reception area, closely followed by Timot.

'There are a few things you should know,' Timot said. 'I don't know how, but Richard and Sandy know each another. It was obvious from their body language.'

Dave thoughtfully rubbed his chin. 'OK, I'll watch them closely.'

Timot was relieved Dave had accepted his first observation so readily; the second was a different matter, and he might not be quite so open to persuasion. Tact was not the big Zulu's strong suit, but he did his best to suggest that Dave might want to tread carefully around Karen and Sandy. At first, his friend was intrigued, but his expression slowly changed to disbelief.

'Sandy? No, you've got that wrong. Sandy's a bit of a tease, but... no, you've misread it. Come on, we've got work to do.'

With a dismissive wave, he returned to the office. Timot followed, hoping Dave was right, but pretty sure he wasn't. Two women with designs on the same man was a recipe for trouble.

Dave's council of war was in session, in more ways than one. Sandy and Karen were engaged in a silent battle of their own.

They were sitting round the table in the main office, Dave next to Karen, Sandy opposite. Dave had taken heed of Timot and was discreetly watching Sandy and Richard.

'Kane Van der Zwet: where is he, and what've you found out from him?' he asked his assistant.

Sandy blushed bright red; how on earth had he known about her relationship with Kane? She glanced fleetingly at Richard, but dismissed the thought before it was properly formed; he was far too professional, and anyway, how would *he* have known? If Dave knew she had slept with Kane, it wouldn't help her case, especially with that woman tucking herself in so close to him.

In fact, whatever she had done with Kane, it didn't concern Dave in the slightest. He looked upon Sandy as a professional, and sometimes professionals had to behave in ways other people might find disturbing. What did concern him was the glance Sandy shot at Richard. Without a doubt Timot was correct. And if that was the case, was it so unlikely his other assumption was correct too?'

He decided to test Timot's theory, and moved his hand to rest it on Karen's knee. As Karen covered it with hers, Sandy's colour rose and the skin of her face seemed to tighten. He had seen that expression before: it signified silent rage.

Dave was flabbergasted, it had never crossed his mind that Sandy had feelings for him. He would need to tread very carefully indeed around both women.

He began to look at Sandy in a totally new light. He caught himself comparing her with Karen but managed to thrust the thought firmly aside. Personal sentiments would just have to wait; right now, they all had a job to do.

Sandy still hadn't answered his question about Van der Zwet. Forcing his attention back to the issue they were discussing, he said, 'Let me refresh your memory...'

He listed all of Kane and Sandy's meetings, from the time they had first met, right through to the intimate hours at his apartment. Timot had kept him well informed.

This hadn't come from Richard, Sandy thought. He had reluctantly agreed to her cultivating a relationship with Kane, but he knew nothing of their meetings; this information was far too detailed. Dave had had her followed, probably by Timot.

'Anyone would think you didn't trust me to get the job done,' she accused him.

Dave realised, a little guiltily, that she was right, at least sometimes. All the same, he didn't question her loyalty, though he did wonder why, and for how long, she'd been working for Richard. He couldn't help a brief knowing glance in his direction before returning to Sandy.

'I'm not interested in how you feel about being followed; you made a decision you thought correct at the time, and which I'm sure we'll profit from. But Kane's a dangerous man, and a valuable link to Vulcan. Now can you please answer the question?'

Sandy felt vindicated to a certain degree. She pulled herself together and began her report. 'As yet, I've been unable to find out anything useful. All I know is, he's still in the employment of Karen's company...' she swallowed hard '... but at the moment he's away from Jo'burg. Said he had some business to attend to in Natal.'

'Not anymore. We had an... encounter this morning.' Dave flicked his head at Richard, and there were a few surprised murmurs. He looked at Sandy. 'If I'm any judge, he'll soon be making contact with you again, and don't think he doesn't know you're my assistant. Remember, he bears me a grudge, and if repaying it means using innocent people he won't think twice. You'll be meeting him again, but this time on my terms.'

Karen was impressed by how effortlessly Dave was controlling the meeting. She found herself comparing him with Tom when he'd been alive. They were alike in many ways, the power they exuded and the way they attracted and embraced responsibility. If Dave were to choose the business world to exercise his many skills, few others could match his talents.

Yet in other ways they were totally different. Dave was so perceptive of her needs, something Tom had never been. He not only anticipated her thoughts and stimulated her mind, but also his touch could play a full orchestra concerto on her body. On the safari she had even begun to hope there might be a chance they could build a relationship that would enhance their separate lives – but now, sitting opposite her, she sensed a threat to that possibility. Less than a month ago, Sandy's blonde, willowy good looks and feisty temperament would have left Karen feeling entirely inadequate; though now her new-found confidence assured her that was not the case, she still felt vulnerable. It was ironic, she thought; here they all were, fighting a common enemy far greater, yet her own chief fear was of someone far closer at hand.

Dave was speaking again. 'Also, Sandy, did you come up with anything more on James Pearson, after you'd inspected his house?'

'No, not really.' Sandy was more than happy that the topic of Kane had finally been dropped. 'He did have rather a peculiar hobby, but that's all.' She hurried on, 'One wall of his study was lined with books on nuclear physics. It didn't seem that important.'

Again, Dave felt something flutter just below his conscious mind, but again it wouldn't surface. 'OK, we'll think about that later. For the moment, you'd all better take a look at this.' He handed round Karen's reconstruction of James Pearson's note.

It met with blank looks from the two women, but Timot raised a finger. 'Valley 1000. Could that be the Valley of a Thousand Hills? We do know he visited there.'

Dave responded, 'When I spoke to you from Windhoek, you said there was too much to tell me about your trip to Natal. I got the impression you thought it was wasted. Why? Surely he must've found something of interest down there?'

'Why he went, I don't have a clue, though he did find something of interest. But what it was I have no idea.' He nodded towards Karen. 'Maybe Mrs de Lout can shed some light?'

'Please, Timot, it's Karen. Mrs de Lout is my mother-in-law. I don't see how I can...' Karen's brow creased. 'Wait a moment, though. The Valley of a Thousand Hills. We have a huge engineering plant there; it manufactures all our drilling, mining and pumping equipment.' She looked across at the big Zulu. 'Is that where he went?'

'Yes, he spoke with one of the workers there.'

Dave asked, 'What's the significance of the engineering shop to your current operations? Is there anything big on the go that involves the shop?'

'Not really, not that I know of. It's supplying the new military oil refinery being built in the Kalahari. Pump Station Omumbo; you've probably read about it. That's about all.'

The group fell silent. Perhaps there was no connection with Vulcan after all, and Timot's trip to Natal had been wasted.

'We'll leave it for now,' Dave said. 'I can't see where it fits in, but let's all give it some thought.' Something was still niggling in the back of his mind.

'It's all too much of a coincidence, especially in the light of Pearson's murder. Let's assume Kane visited the engineering shop too, and see if anything else comes up.' He turned back to Sandy. 'Have you and Timot come up with anything on Oechsli and Ferkatovich?'

Their blank expressions were response enough, but Richard interjected for the first time since the meeting began. 'I think I might be able to help there.'

He had been sitting quietly, absorbing everything that had been said, impressed by the way Dave was running the operation despite the lack of progress.

'I can tell you they are both in the country. I take it you all understand why?' He looked at Karen; she was an unknown quantity to him. But he needn't have worried; her expression told him she was well up to speed.

'As to their whereabouts, I can't help,' he continued. 'But I do know the American is operating out of the NASA base at Southview, and Ferkatovich, well, he must be controlling the KGB agents through their Resident in Pretoria.'

'So where are the KGB and the CIA channelling their energies at the moment?' Sandy asked. 'It's clear they're both active.'

'The KGB, certainly. They're targeting any group that opposes the present government, especially the UDF. The CIA are a different matter. The KGB are making all right moves, but the CIA are falling woefully short if they want to be in a strong position for the final push.'

'So you're worried.' said Dave. He knew Richard better than the others.

'Brendan Oechsli's too fine a tactician to let something as potentially profitable as Vulcan's organisation slip through his fingers.'

As he finished speaking, Richard placed pictures of both men on the table. They all heard Karen's sharp intake of breath as she laid a finger on the identikit of Ferkatovich.

'I've seen this man,' she whispered, visibly disturbed, 'He's my personal secretary's new boyfriend. Oh my god, I think he recently moved in with her.'

Silence.

Dave broke it. 'Well, it looks like we've found the Russian. How long has she been seeing him?'

'For quite a while.'

Karen's stomach knotted. Not only did Vulcan have inside knowledge of her company through Peter; now it seemed the KGB were in there too, through Susan. It was getting worse by the minute. 'God, all that privileged information. She slumped back in her seat. 'I'm starting to wonder exactly who is running de Louts.'

'I think we need a break,' Dave said after a long pause.

Sandy stood up and moved to the coffee machine. 'I can manage, thanks,' she said sharply when Karen began to lay out mugs.

Karen stepped away and joined the men. 'I think we'll have to include Athol Jansen and the South African's National Security,' Dave was saying. 'We just haven't got the manpower to track Oechsli and the Russian, as well as Kane. And Kane is the one who's linked to Vulcan – that's the main issue here.' He looked at Karen. 'Can you supply us with your secretary's address?'

'Of course.' She had slumped back into her seat, still dismayed at the extent of the foreign incursion into her company.

Dave began to issue instructions. 'Richard, can you contact Athol? Timot, as we've located the Russian, I want you to concentrate all your efforts on finding the American. And Sandy, you and I have a little business to attend to with a certain Dutchman.'

Sandy nodded, still busy with the coffee.

'What about me?' Karen sat up, alert and positive again.

Dave gave her an appreciative smile. This woman was like a rubber ball, bouncing back ready for the next battle. 'You'll be busy enough with Richard. There's more than enough to do getting National Security on side.' He looked at Richard. 'I take it as de Louts are a major influence in Europe, you'll want to know what sort of damaging information has been passed to the Russians.' Richard nodded briefly. 'And there's the audit on the bank account in Jersey to organise.'

'What bank account?' Sandy pounced, determined not to let Dave cut her out in favour of this de Lout woman. She was disappointed.

'I think it's best I let Karen explain,' he said. 'It could be the break we've been waiting for.'

The more Karen had to say, the more impressed Richard became with her. It was easy to see how she controlled one of the most powerful companies in Africa.

Sandy was trying to feel sorry for her. Her husband had been murdered, the KGB were siphoning off any useful information they could, and as if that wasn't enough, her own brother-in-law was diverting cash from the company to Vulcan, and worse, knew there was a plot to have her killed. It was appalling and fascinating in equal measure. But all was fair in love and war, so she didn't quite succeed in feeling sympathy for Karen.

Once Karen had explained about the indemnity account, and the safeguards which might prove to be Peter's fatal mistake, Richard couldn't help asking the question they were all thinking. 'Why? Why would your brother-in-law help Vulcan? What does he get out of it?'

This was something Dave and Karen had discussed; he took up the baton. 'He may not know what's going on. But that's not really the point. Whatever the connection, we know Vulcan needs de Louts and will go to any lengths to gain control, including murder. But Peter and this account may lead us to him.' He pointed a finger at Richard. 'And you and I both know that if there's anybody who can track him down through the vast screed of figures and transactions the audit will bring, it's your man Johnny.'

The meeting was almost over. Dave turned to Timot. 'As well as tracking the American, I need you to gather as much information as you can about the UDF. They have to be preparing for a massive push to destabilise the country. The way I read it, if we can determine their state of readiness, it might give us a clue on how soon Vulcan will implement his plans to destroy the government.'

'If the country is to be prevented from falling into the hands of the UDF, the security must be tightened up at Parliament,' Timot mused. 'That's the only place all the influential politicians can be destroyed in one fell swoop. Then again, even if Vulcan does achieve that, surely the army will still be powerful enough to step in and take control. Unless he's—'

He was stopped by a gasp from Karen.

'Oh my god! Pump Station Omumbo!'

They all turned to look at her.

'In three days' time Pump Station Omumbo has its grand opening. Now I know why I wasn't supposed to come back from the safari.' She blew out a long breath; the others continued to stare at her, puzzled. 'The ceremony will be attended by all the top brass from the army, as well as the president and most of the cabinet. I was against such a big affair from the start, but Peter...'

Everything fell into place; the whole sequence of seemingly unrelated events meshed into a coherent picture, not only to Karen, but to the rest of the group as well. Her planned death, James Pearson's and Kane's trips to Natal, the engineering shop in the Valley of a Thousand Hills: they were all linked. Vulcan was planning the destruction of South Africa's most powerful men three days from now, at Pump Station Omumbo.

It was Dave who eventually broke the silence. 'So that's where it all begins.'
'But how?' Sandy asked.

'Given the number of dignitaries involved, it'll have to be a series of explosive devices, or one massive one.' Dave looked at Timot. 'I hope you haven't forgotten what they taught you in Rhodesia. We may need those skills.' He didn't wait for a reply, or explain what those skills were. His mind was already worrying the new problem like a dog with a bone.

'Hell, this changes things completely. We've got so little time. Richard, I think I'd better be the one to talk to Athol; I've worked with him in the past. You and Karen better get started on the audit. Timot, stay with the American. Sandy, you have a Dutchman to find.'

'But shouldn't we warn the government?' Karen asked, clearly horrified.

It was Richard who answered. 'That may drive Vulcan further underground, and this is the closest we've ever been to him.' He turned to Dave. 'But it's your play, you're calling the shots. And if it's any help, I've already spoken with Athol. His superiors don't believe they have a thing to worry about, so he may not be much help at all, and since we're so short on time...'

Everybody looked at Dave, glad the decision was his.

'OK,' he said after a few moments. 'We'll cross that bridge when we come to it; nothing's ever achieved without some risk. Maybe this is the bait we'll have to use to lure Vulcan out.'

CHAPTER 56

'What do you mean, they never turned up?'

Kane was in the lounge of the same exclusive suite in the Carlton Hotel where several weeks before Vulcan had outlined the ambitious plan which would give him not only sovereignty over South Africa but also enormous influence over the power structure of the world. He stood respectfully by the door; he hadn't yet been offered a seat.

'Well, sir, the three guerrillas left the main party soon after they crossed into Zambia, and appeared to head down into Botswana as they were instructed. That's the last that has been heard of them.'

This was clearly a contingency Vulcan hadn't foreseen. He huffed out a breath, whether in frustration or disappointment Kane couldn't be sure. He fixed Kane with a stare that could have cut through ice.

'I hope the weapons arrived safely at least,' he challenged.

'Safely, just a little late. I had to break...'

'I'm not interested.' Vulcan held up a hand to emphasis. 'It would appear Dave Old resented the help we gave him.' Vulcan's glare softened, and he waved Kane into a seat. 'It's of little consequence,' he continued. 'It appears the main objective has still been achieved.' The icy glare in Vulcan's eyes became a chilling smile. 'A pity really. I've heard stories of how the guerrillas treat a white woman before they kill her. She would have deserved that.'

'Sorry, I'm not actually with you?' Kane was confused. Vulcan so rarely showed emotion of any kind.

Like a dog shaking off a wet coat, Vulcan threw off the alien sensation. He took the seat opposite Kane, remote and calculating again.

'I have just heard both Karen de Lout and Dave Old have disappeared from the Chobe National Park,' he went on.

Kane was surprised. 'No disrespect, sir, but are you sure he's killed her? It's not his normal style. And I've never known him to take so long over a mission.'

He should have known better than to say anything, he quickly saw. Vulcan was a man who resented being challenged, however subtly. He rounded on Kane. 'Unlike you, with your fiasco over Richard Black, Dave Old hasn't once let me down. How he chooses to implement and his plans is his business; yours not to reason why. Or ask questions.'

Humiliation and fury blazed behind Kane's blank expression. Dave Old again, he thought bitterly. Whenever he least expected it, Dave's superior skills rose to taunt him. He had to wrench his attention back to Vulcan as the man began to speak again.

'When he makes contact, which he will, be assured, you're to call me immediately. Then you can relay his next orders.' Vulcan paused, well aware of the seething emotion behind Kane's deadpan gaze, and pleased to have been the cause of it. He continued in an appeasing tone.

'Kane, we are at a critical phase, not only with our plans for South Africa, but with the rest of the world as well. Karen de Lout's influence has been destroyed, de Louts is now free to be used as I judge fit. Her death was just one of many objectives that have been fulfilled. Because this one was so important, I foresaw the need for two contingency plans; as it happens, only one was needed. But in your case with Richard Black, I felt no back-up would be required because of the normal calibre of your work.'

Vulcan paused, letting the compliment gain a fleeting hold before bringing Kane crashing back to earth.

'Yet it appears I miscalculated. You fell dismally short, something I never usually tolerate. I'm giving you a second chance. Make sure you use it wisely, for it will be the only one you get.' He paused again, letting the warning cleave a wound in Kane's already fragile ego. But the man was far too useful to alienate; he wanted to scare him into submission, but needed to keep him on side. 'But of course,' he continued, 'as we both know, that is all you'll need.'

Part of Kane knew Vulcan was a master manipulator. Another part didn't know whether he was coming or going. Now, as Vulcan finished speaking, he felt strangely honoured, and like an errant son trying to impress his father, he became determined to prove his worth again. He listened carefully to Vulcan's new instructions.

'Across the passageway in the suite opposite are all the members of the UDF's inner circle. We have brought them into the country in dribs and drabs. Once the heads of the Republic's government and army have been destroyed and all the media outlets are secured, their voices on radio and faces on television will initiate a popular uprising.'

'What am I to do?' Kane asked, hunger burning in his eyes. He was already beginning to feel the euphoria that he knew was to come.

'How can I put this?' Vulcan began. 'Kane, you command a certain respect from these people, your last demonstration saw to that. I'd like you to talk to them again and impress the importance of their roles during the coming events. But make it clear they know exactly who is controlling the coup.'

The suite was a mirror image of Vulcan's. Six black men lounged in various poses about the sitting room. Most of them had been staying in the hotel for several days, and if anybody had happened to peruse the guest register, they would have found that this suite and six other rooms had all been booked in the name of an American company. The company had requested that their executives be allowed privacy during their stay; accordingly, they had been given a special Double A status: all meals were to be served discreetly in the rooms, which were to be only serviced when requested, usually in the absence of their guests.

Kane entered the suite unannounced. He walked straight over to the huge plate glass window and peered out with hands behind his back, as if intrigued by the scene that sprawled before him. It was a gesture carefully chosen to intimidate; none of the men had seen him since their last meeting in Gaborone.

He had assessed the room's occupants as he walked towards the window. The whole atmosphere seemed to change from relaxation to all-consuming fear. Such was the tension that his arrival created that one of the six men jumped in fright when he eventually spoke.

'I take it, Mr Gamon, that your wife's finger has healed.' Silence. 'Sorry I didn't quite catch that.' He turned around. Still no answer; the man was paralysed. 'And Mr Tombo, I trust your niece is no longer using crutches? Good.' He acknowledged the man's fearful nod.

Kane began pacing about the room. Six pairs of eyes were fixed on him. He stopped and sat down casually on the arm of a vacant chair. 'I want to leave you in no doubt as to the importance of the next few days. You, gentlemen, will soon be forming the new government of South Africa, or whatever you choose to call it. You will be briefed on the individual roles Vulcan has chosen for you. My own role will be to ensure you abide by his wishes.'

He glanced round the room. It had been a master-stroke to execute Jaunus Zamba before their eyes. Not a shred of defiance, much less contempt, was evident on their faces. He continued, 'If any of you who choose to, shall we say, misinterpret your roles or your new-found power, I'll always be there to help you self-correct.'

Their sombre expressions told him Vulcan would always have their complete co-operation, at least until another demonstration became necessary. He looked round; one of the men was trying to make himself as inconspicuous as possible.

'Mr Ngeate, I understand your second daughter looked most attractive at her white wedding...'

The veiled threat had the desired effect. All the members of the UDF's inner circle were in no doubt what would happen if any of them chose to ignore Vulcan's requests, no matter how powerful they appeared to have become. It was firmly embedded in each of their minds who would really be controlling their destiny and South Africa's future.

None of them had said a word, and Kane felt he had made his point and firmly re-established the inner circle's loyalty. It was prudent to end this brief meeting to give them time to reflect. 'You will be taken separately aside and told in detail what your future responsibilities will be. For all our sakes, I urge you to use them wisely. If it becomes necessary for us to meet again, believe me when I say I will enjoy the encounter more than you will.' With a final sweeping glance around the suite, Kane took his leave.

Kane felt invincible, like a lion. He lived to see the fear that had shone in each of the black men's eyes. Not even Vulcan's earlier cutting remarks could dull the consuming lust for power that had grown with the fear he had instilled so effortlessly. He needed a release an outlet to vent the hunger that burned inside him.

Like a shark drawn by the smell of blood, his thoughts turned to Sandy; she would easily fulfil that absorbing need. His mind played with the pleasurable ways he would use Sandy to quench his craving; but then his thoughts switched to Dave Old. He came to a decision. The time had come once and for all. He would strike back and inflict some pain of his own.

Sandy lay naked on the bed. Her whole body tingled with a mixture of anticipation and fear. She should never have left without telling Dave.

Kane ripped the sheet from her body, as he had her clothes,. He towered above her, dressed only in boxer shorts, his wild hungry eyes roving over her defenceless body like a pair of hunting dogs. She had fooled herself, believing she had Kane's measure. Dave was right after all. Now she was seeing for the first time how powerful and cruel he was, and had always been.

Kane loomed over her, like a hunter who had finally trapped his prey. Sandy's usual confidence had faded into a dim memory. She knew it was hopeless trying to resist him as he laid the flat of his hand on her heaving chest and pushed her down into the bed. Her terrified eyes were riveted on his savage blue ones. Sandy pleaded, 'Please Kane, what are you going to do?'

Kane wasn't listening. His other hand glided lightly over her body, a touch that used to heighten her desire but now intensified her fear. That fear served only to inflame Kane's barbaric lust.

The hand prowled over her breasts, and her body betrayed her; her erect nipples aroused Kane even further. The hand ran down her stomach, whispered over her mound of blond, velvet-smooth hair and parted her thighs.

Sandy lay mesmerised, unable to resist. She had never seen that wild, corrupt look in his eyes before.

'How's Dave?' he whispered.

The words seemed to lick about her face as if spat from the mouth of the devil himself. Her fear took on a life of its own, like coiled ropes knotted tight about her abdomen. She froze, unable to answer, then—

'I'm fine, now get your filthy fucking hands off her.'

Dave's tone was even, tinged with the lightest trace of malice, but sparks flashed in his golden eyes.

He had entered Kane's apartment soundlessly, like his namesake the leopard, and stood in the open doorway levelling a silenced Beretta at Kane.

With reflexes like a cobra's Kane clenched a stranglehold around Sandy's throat. 'Drop it or she dies,' he hissed.

'Don't be ridiculous,' came the response. 'Let her go, or lose your elbow.'

Sandy's face began to turn purple and she fixed huge pleading eyes on Dave. Her hands plucked ineffectually at Kane's vice-like grip and she gasped desperately for air.

Dave's hand jerked, and a bullet slammed into the wall behind the bed, carving a shallow furrow through Kane's arm as it flew. 'Next time the joint,' he said calmly.

Kane released Sandy and covered the bleeding gash with his hand.

Sandy threw herself at Dave in relief. It almost proved their undoing as she obscured his line of fire for a split second. Kane didn't need a second chance, but Dave roughly peeled Sandy to the side and met him with a silenced barrel between his eyes.

'Try it, you animal. I won't hesitate to oblige.'

Despite himself, Kane backed away.

Now that Sandy was safe, Dave's fury erupted. Disgusted, he flicked the pistol. 'Put your hands behind your head, turn around and face the wall.'

Kane obeyed, blood from the wound running down his arm. Dave's expression softened as he looked down into Sandy's frightened eyes. She was still badly shaken, but she had something to tell him.

'I think he's come straight from Vulcan. It was like he was crazed with power. Maybe he's been given new orders.'

They both saw Kane's body stiffen. Sandy was correct.

'He wants me to relay your next orders,' Kane ventured, knowing the situation was delicately poised. He cursed himself inwardly; again he had underestimated Dave.

Dave loathed Kane and would happily have put a bullet through his head, but the more information he got about Vulcan the better. He would have to try and string him along. But before he had said a word, Sandy cut in.

'You and Vulcan can both go to hell. It'll be a pleasure to see you burn together.'

She only realised her mistake when Kane's torso stiffened.

'Now it's all beginning to add up,' he snarled. 'You're not working for Vulcan at all, you're on the other side, the bastards who want him destroyed. Well, you'll get no help from me.'

'We'll see about that,' Dave murmured under his breath.

'Sorry,' Sandy muttered.

'Oh, I think you earned it,' Dave said, not without sympathy. He lifted an eyebrow and glanced over her naked body. 'Might be wise if you found some clothes.'

Sandy suddenly realised she was stark naked. Recovering quickly, she found her still wearable underwear and slipped it on. Dave hid a smile, but couldn't help admiring her shapely body.

Despite the circumstances Dave found himself comparing her with Karen. They were very different: Sandy slim and willowy, Karen finely sculptured. The pistol still pointed at Kane's exposed back, he found his thoughts wandering to the two women's other qualities. Sandy was lively, sometimes tempestuous; Karen was determined and compassionate. He briefly wondered how different things might have been if he had let Sandy develop their relationship as she must have been trying to do.

But Timot was right; he couldn't keep them both. But neither did he want to drive one of them away. He would have to make a choice.

Sandy had discarded her shredded dress and grabbed Kane's shirt from beside the bed. 'I'll be in the bathroom. I have to tidy up.'

Dave and Kane were left alone. He longed to pull the trigger, but there was work to be done. 'Back up,' he said. 'Over here, towards me, then into the lounge.'

'Turn around and sit on the floor. Crossed legs and hands behind your head.'

Kane obeyed, and was entirely defenceless. But undaunted, his only thought was for how he was going to get out alive.

'Where have you been, Kane? They tell me you've been out of town?' Dave had taken a seat on one of the stools beside the breakfast bar, and held the pistol loosely in his lap.

'Screw you, pal,' was the only answer.

Kane was unsure what to do. He knew Dave was ruthless, and would want revenge for his little tart. But if he was trying to destroy Vulcan the thing he needed above all else was information. Dave wouldn't want me dead, Kane thought.

'I'll tell you what, why don't you tell me what I want to know? If you don't, I suppose I'll just have to pull the trigger.'

It was said so casually, yet Kane felt his uncertainty flare. He had seen the savage beast that raged behind Dave's eyes. He managed to swallow his doubt and decided to call the man's bluff.

But it wasn't from Dave that the real threat would come.

Sandy entered the room and stood beside Dave, her arms folded. 'If somebody's going to shoot him, let it be me,' she said. She was dressed in Kane's shirt, and had washed her face and brushed her hair. Sandy was back to her normal feisty self.

'Fair enough.' Dave hooked his index finger through the pistol's trigger guard and held it out to her. 'I can't begrudge you that.'

Kane was horrified. Sandy was a loose cannon, and she was eagerly reaching for the gun.

'Where, Dave? Where will it hurt the most?'

'Where do you think?' It was all the answer she needed. She lowered the weapon and pointed it at Kane's groin.

Jesus, she was actually going do it. Kane stared into her vengeful eyes. During their torrid affair, he had seen a similar hungry look. At those times nothing would stop her until her craving was fulfilled.

'Stop, I'll talk!' he shouted in desperation.

Sandy's mouth twisted. 'Screw you, you've had your chance.'

Phut.

Kane cried out. He felt no pain, yet the floor beneath him had erupted. Confusion reigned.

'What the hell did you do that for?' Sandy rounded on Dave. 'I missed him completely.'

'Shut up.' Dave grabbed the gun and turned to face Kane. 'Next time I won't stop her,' he barked. 'Where the hell have you been, and why?'

Kane spoke without thinking. 'Valley of a Thousand Hills, Vulcan sent me, I...'

'Why?' Dave demanded when he faltered.

Silence. Kane had already said too much. If Vulcan found out, he was as good as dead.

Dave saw his eyes go blank and his muscular jaw set rigid. No amount of bullying would make him say any more. Time to try another tactic.

'You don't like me, do you, Kane? You know I've always been better than you.' Dave slashed him with the truth like a *sjambok* whip. Again there was silence. 'Well, I'm going to give you a chance to even the score. Stand up.' He flick the pistol barrel. 'But make sure you do a good job. Sandy'll have the gun.'

The odds were stacked against Kane. His arm hurt like hell, but at least he had full use of it. His only chance was to eventually get in close to Dave, secure a fatal hold and force Sandy to give him the gun. The thought of killing them both galvanised him.

With the gun still levelled at Kane's chest, Dave took a notebook from his pocket, opened it and pointed to a name and number. 'Call him,' he said to Sandy, 'give him this address and tell him to come right over.' She obeyed, and Dave turned his attention back to Kane. 'You are going to tell me two things: what you picked up from the Valley of a Thousand Hills, and who Vulcan is.'

'Go to hell. This time it's just you and me. You haven't got your attack dog to protect you.'

While Dave waited for Sandy to finish the call, he considered what Kane had said. Clay, his canine friend at home in New Zealand, hadn't crossed his mind in months. 'You know, you're right, I hadn't thought of that.'

Time to even the score.

'Did I ever tell you I never liked you either?' He shot Kane in the hip, a glancing blow. That was worth at least a Labrador. he thought.

Two flesh wounds would hamper Kane enough to give Dave an edge. He handed the pistol to Sandy, not taking his eyes off the other man. 'Don't shoot him unless you have to,' he told her.

'Awww, spoil sport,' she grumbled.

Kane clutched his injured hip, clearly in pain but determined not to show it. Dave had learnt long ago never to fight when consumed with rage, but after what Kane had almost done to Sandy, he was unable to keep himself in check. He snapped a brutal side kick, catching Kane square in the face. As Kane staggered backwards, he hounded him with kicks left and right, pushing him up against the apartment's door.

The two gunshot wounds and the barrage of kicks had indeed given him his edge. Kane was stunned. Dave used his forehead like a battering ram and smashed into the bridge of Kane's nose. He drew his head back for another strike, but instead drove a knee into the Dutchman's groin. As Kane uttered a strangled cry, Dave hissed into his bloodied face, 'That's for Sandy, you prick. And any others who didn't deserve your treatment.'

Dave grabbed a handful of hair, rammed his face down into an upraised knee, then dragged him, stumbling, back to the middle of the room, where he pole-axed him with a double-fisted blow. Kane hadn't had a chance to defend himself, much less retaliate.

Sandy stood open-mouthed, the pistol dangling from her hand, not sure whether to be horrified or exultant. This was a side of Dave she hadn't seen before. Kane didn't stand a chance.

Kane lay on his back, his face a mask of blood, red welts covering his chest and upper body, but still his ice-blue eyes betrayed his cold fury. Dave drove his knee into the fallen man's solar plexus, and his lungs emptied in a single shuddering breath.

'Why did you go to Natal?' Dave demanded through Kane's gasps.

'OK,' Kane croaked. He heaved a few breaths and looked up into Dave's smouldering eyes, and saw something that bit deeply into his wounded pride. His defeated expression changed. 'Go to hell,' he whispered.

Dave had totally misjudged his powers of recovery. With the speed of a mamba, Kane cupped his hands and clapped a resounding blow over both his ears. Caught totally off guard Dave tried to jump up, but his balance was awry. Before he knew it, Kane had kicked his feet from under him. As he fell to the ground, he was met by a flurry of blows.

Kane was oblivious to everything except his need for revenge. The flesh wounds hardly handicapped him as his rage drove him on.

Dave had ignored all his training, had thrown caution to the winds and launched into battle while still consumed with fury. The old Foreign Legion adage came blaring into his mind: a good man thinking rationally will nearly always beat a good man consumed with rage. He regained his balance and pushed the anger away with the cold determination that had become his watchword. As Kane's brutal volley of blows rained about his body, he hoped he hadn't left it too late. Again, it was Sandy that galvanised him into greater effort.

Phut.

'Shit, I missed!' Sandy cursed. She danced above the two thrashing men, aiming recklessly, seeking her own retribution.

Phut.

'Shit, again!'

Dave bellowed, 'No, Sandy!'

Sandy couldn't resist a powerful kick that just missed Kane's bloody head. She backed away as the men separated and rolled to their feet, pain and injuries banished by the adrenalin coursing through their veins. Kane had the height and weight advantage, but Dave had a few tricks of his own.

Kane's violent onslaught appeared to wear Dave down, and he raised his fist and braced himself to strike a final blow. But the punch never found its mark. Dave put all his weight and energy into a blow that landed squarely on Kane's jaw. He reeled backwards, briefly losing consciousness. When he came to, he was face down with Dave's knee in his back and the pistol rammed into his temple.

'Where did you go after Natal?' Dave demanded.

'You'll never know. Pull the trigger, if you've got the guts.'

'With pleasure!' He pumped Kane's knee and upper thigh full of lead and jammed the silencer into one of the wounds. 'Where did you go?' he yelled.

Kane couldn't help himself. 'Omumbo and the UDF's guerrilla training camps,' he screamed.

'Who is Vulcan, and where can I find him?' The gun twisted further into the wound.

Kane's body stiffened, and collapsed into unconsciousness.

'Damn,' Dave whispered. He rose gingerly to his feet, his own pain now making its presence felt.

There was a barrage of thumps on the door. Dave's exhaustion dropped away and in a blur of movement, he leapt away from Kane's prone body and raised the pistol. The door caved in, and Athol Jansen's face blundered into his sights.

Athol's mouth gaped open as he took in Dave's battered wounded face, a defiant Sandy dressed only in a baggy shirt, and Kane's blood-splattered, broken body. Blood pumped from one of the wounds in his thigh, and Dave waved the pistol towards him.

'I don't really care, but you might want to stop the bleeding. He's worth interrogating. He just told me the UDF are training up guerrillas.' He held out a hand to Sandy. 'Come on, let's go home.' As they passed the flabbergasted South African and his dazed entourage, he added, 'I'd keep a lid on this if I were you. We still have Vulcan to find.'

Leaning on Sandy, he limped from the room. He couldn't help but feel they were still no further ahead. Vulcan was still at large, his identity still unknown and Kane hadn't given him anything they hadn't already worked out for themselves.

Tomorrow's grand opening of the oil refinery was rapidly approaching. It looked as though Pump Station Omumbo would be their last hope.

'You told Athol about Kane's involvement with the UDF. Why not about Natal and Pump Station Omumbo?' Sandy asked, slightly confused. She helped Dave lower himself on to a settee. He winced as stiffness seized his whole body.

'We still have to find Vulcan, and Omumbo may be our only chance. Athol's hands are tied; if he knew that was where Vulcan planned his big gesture he'd have the opening cancelled...'

'But I don't see how we can...' Sandy began, but Dave was in no mood for interruptions.

'I don't either,' he said abruptly, 'All I do know is that Omumbo will lead us to Vulcan. I can feel it. If we have to, we'll stop the opening ourselves, but—'

Before he could continue Richard and Karen walked in.

'I'm glad you two are back,' Richard said. 'We've just finished... good god, what the hell happened to you?'

Karen's hands flew to her mouth. Ignoring Sandy, she ran forward and dropped to her knees in front of Dave. She didn't say a word; something told her she wouldn't like the answers to the questions bubbling to her lips.

'Looks worse than it is,' Dave offered, well aware that it wasn't quite true. 'Believe it or not, most of the blood's not mine.' But one eye was half-closed, both cheeks were swollen and beginning to blossom with purple bruising, and while a multitude of smaller cuts and bruises festooned the rest of him. Nothing was broken, but that was the best that could be said.

Richard looked down at him, almost as concerned as Karen. 'I suppose you're going to say, "you should see the other guy".' He looked from Dave to Sandy and back again, but neither volunteered an explanation.

'Let's just say there was a slight altercation with Kane.' Dave shifted awkwardly. 'After one of us tried to take him on her own.'

Sandy stroked her own bruised throat, an unconscious protective gesture. She opened her mouth to speak, but the words deserted her. The whole episode had shaken her badly; it had stemmed from her misguided attempts to get close Kane, and she felt as if the ordeal they had just been through was her fault. She realised she was still wearing his shirt, and it filled her with disgust. She jumped to her feet. 'I think we'd both better go and tidy up and change.'

'So, what did you find out? 'Richard demanded. The sun had set, and the time for sympathy and concern was over. It was down to business again. 'Are we any closer to finding Vulcan?'

Dave felt a hundred per cent better after a wash and a change of clothes, and some gentle first aid on his abrasions from Karen. 'Nothing we hadn't already pieced together,' he said ruefully. 'Kane confirmed he'd been in Natal and did pick up something for Omumbo from the Valley of a Thousand Hills. He also mentioned visiting UDF guerrilla training camps.'

That quickened Richard's interest. 'So what happened to Kane after your... altercation? Where is he now?'

'He's still alive, or was when I last saw him. Athol Jansen's got him. I didn't say a word to Athol about Omumbo; he doesn't know Kane is involved there, or how important it is, at least not from me. I did tell him Kane knew the locations of the guerrilla camps.'

'How do the guerrillas fit in? 'Karen asked, keen to get everything straight in her mind.

'Probably to strike at vulnerable targets to destabilise the government. Whatever's been planned at Omumbo will probably be their signal to launch those attacks. If Athol's any kind of interrogator, he'll have the location of their camps out of Kane before they have a chance to move.'

'That's if Kane survives to be interrogated.' Sandy looked grimly at Dave. 'He was in a pretty poor state when we left.'

I bet he was, Karen thought, remembering with a shudder how brutally effective Dave had been at Third Bridge. 'But at least that's one less worry,' she said.

'He'll survive, but the timing will be critical. If the camps are raided too soon before Omumbo's opening, Vulcan will go to ground. If we can let the opening play out right up till the very last minute, maybe, just maybe, Vulcan will show himself.'

'OK, what have we got in our favour?' Richard asked. 'What's our current position?'

'One, Kane's out of the way. But we need to be aware that it may make Vulcan suspicious,' Dave said. 'Two, if Athol does his job properly, we may not have to worry about the UDF. That may also slow up the CIA and the KGB, but again that depends on Athol. Three, we already know Peter de Lout is involved somehow, so he could be a useful source of information when the time is right. And four, Johnny and the audit on the de Louts trust account.'

'A fair bit going for us, then,' Richard said.

'But a hell of a lot that's not,' Dave shot back. 'The fact remains, we still don't have a clue who Vulcan is, or where to even start looking. We're still running blind.' Mindful of his bruises, he turned carefully to look at Karen. 'What's happening with the audit?'

'We spoke to Johnny, and it's all set up at his end. We were able to also contact the bank manager in Jersey, and after we'd gone through all the correct procedures he was very helpful indeed. Johnny's already made contact. That's about as much as we can do. It's up to Johnny now.'

'Anything else?' Dave looked back at Richard.

'Johnny says things are looking grim all over the world. It's even affecting the United Nations. Eighteen of the member countries, notably the USA and the USSR, are withholding part of their contributions; we can only assume it's because of the financial straits they're in. Other than that, Karen has pretty well summed up where we're at. We were just going over what her secretary might have passed to Ferkatovich when you two arrived back. By the way, any word on the Russian? Has Athol located him?'

Before Dave could answer, the phone pealed shrilly. Sandy went to answer it.

'Hello, yes, he's right here.' She put the call on hold. 'Speak of the devil, it's Athol.'

Dave picked up the extension on the coffee table. 'Athol,' he said in an expressionless voice. 'Before you start, this is an open line.' He listened

310

for several minutes, chipping in with occasional one-syllable responses. 'The AIDS virus?' he eventually asked, surprised. 'Could work, he's pretty promiscuous. It'd eat at his ego, and yeah, definitely scare him.' Silence again. 'Right, just keep me informed.' He replaced the receiver and looked up at Sandy. 'You may just be right that Kane won't live to tell the tale. He's in theatre at the moment, and the doctors aren't committing themselves. Athol had a lot of trouble stopping the bleeding. But if he's allowed to, he'll try to question him later this evening.'

Karen couldn't prevent herself. 'What on earth did you do to him, Dave?'

Sandy met her eyes and answered for him. 'I don't think you'd really want to know.'

Richard decided he would also rather stay ignorant, but Karen persisted. 'So what was that about the AIDS virus?'

Sandy looked up sharply. 'AIDS? Is this something I need to know about?'

'What? Oh, I see. No, no need to panic. Kane's getting blood transfusions. They're pumping him full of healthy blood at present, but Athol's going to threaten to use AIDS infected blood. I expect that will get quite a response.'

'Surely he wouldn't really do it, would he?' Karen asked, horrified. 'I've heard of some dirty tricks in business, but nothing quite as...'

She trailed off and looked at the other three faces. They all wore the same steely expressions. Dave shrugged. 'Desperate measures for desperate times,' he said.

There was silence for a few moments, then Richard decided it was time to change the subject. 'What about Ferkatovich? Has Athol located him?'

'He didn't mention him just then, but I talked to him several times yesterday. The security agents who tracked him down got a positive ID, but then he disappeared.'

'You mean he knew somebody was on to him?'

'Looks that way,' Dave said. 'But I really think we need to concentrate on Vulcan, at least for the time being. We're just so short of time and manpower...'

The phone interrupted him again. 'Ah, Timot,' he said abruptly. 'Keep it short, it's an open line. Ah, you've found him, that's great.' He listened for a moment, then, 'Moses? Yeah, leave him there and come back here as soon as you can. I need you to head out into the Kalahari.'

Karen's interest quickened when she heard the name of her chauffeur. She knew he was working for the right side, and ultimately for her benefit, but it still irked her slightly that he was taking orders from somewhere else.

'Timot's found Oechsli?' she asked.

'Yes, but you're not going to like it,' Dave responded. 'He's just entered de Lout House, and not for the first time.'

'What do you mean?' Karen demanded in dismay.

'Moses saw a man go into the building late one night, a day or so after we left on safari. He's just recognised the same man again'

'What was he doing there late at night?' Karen blurted.

'Who?' Dave asked.

'Moses, no, Oechsli, no, oh I don't know, both of them?' Karen stammered, confused and discomposed.

Dave tried to still her racing mind. 'Moses was instructed to watch the office block a month or so back. And Oechsli, well, it looks as if he's wired into your company in some way. Timot's left Moses there, with instructions to follow Oechsli when he reappears.'

'Wired into my company,' Karen muttered. 'What the hell's going on?'

Moses had been working for Timot for a month or more, and she had no idea. But there was so much she had no idea about. First Vulcan, then the Russian, and now the Deputy Director of the CIA, all with access to god knew what information about her company. *Her* company, or so she used to think. The list of intruders didn't even include Dave and Network; at least they were on her side. Karen was angry now, seething inside. She would use all her power, to fight for what was rightfully hers. She would either destroy these interfering trespassers, or be destroyed herself in the attempt. Karen de Lout did not give up without a fight.

Dave saw the determination in her eyes, and was heartened by it. While they were on safari he thought he had found a real partner to share his life. He thought he knew himself pretty well, but she had uncovered feelings he was unable to explain, and opened a passage through his stony façade into his soul.

But forcing himself to examine his inner self had also opened his eyes to someone else. He had always regarded Sandy as a colleague and a helpmate – but she too had dug a path into that part of him that he barely recognised. A life without her in it was unimaginable.

Both women had been with him in potentially life-threatening situations; both had exhibited enviable strength of character, and triumphed against appalling odds. Both were ambitious, driven and determined, each in her own way. But at some point in the future, a future he had not even contemplated, he had a choice to make. It could turn out to be the hardest one of his life.

For now, though, there was Vulcan. Not only the havoc he was about to wreak on the world's economy, but also the power he still wielded over Dave himself. Until Vulcan was destroyed, everything else belonged in the realm of fantasy.

That thought brought Dave's mind back into focus. He held out a hand to Karen. 'I can't imagine how it feels to know so many outsiders are manipulating your company, but our priority is Vulcan. He has to remain our primary target – our only target for the time being. If we're unable to stop him everything else becomes incidental.'

Karen nodded. 'Agreed – but why the Americans, for god's sake?'

Dave gave her a small, humourless smile. 'Both the Soviets and the Americans obviously know your company is vital for Vulcan's plans for the wider world. We can only surmise that their own plans are no different.'

Richard cut in. 'Have you read today's addition of the *Star*?' He flopped the Johannesburg paper down in front of Dave. The headline blared:

UNREST SWEEPS REPUBLIC AS ANNIVERSARY OF SOWETO APPROACHES

Even though he loathed Vulcan and everything he stood for, Dave couldn't help some grudging admiration of his timing. 'He couldn't have pitched it better. With emotion running at an all-time high, if he does succeed in destroying the leadership, the UDF will be swept into power. And it's his UDF.' The humourless smile flicked over his face again. 'Then it's goodbye world as we know it.'

They all fell silent. Dave wanted nothing more than to sit back and scan the rest of the paper.

But they all had work to do. 'Sandy, I have a job for you.'

She looked up. 'Talk to Timot about Omumbo?'

'Not just talk. You're going as well.'

'Me?' Sandy shrieked.

'Yes, you,' Dave responded calmly. 'He'll need back-up. And it will mean both of you are in good hands.'

Sandy ignored his wry smile. 'But why? What can we do there?'

'Well, you know better than most about Timot and explosives.' Richard and Karen looked at him with questions in their eyes, and he explained, 'Timot has a knack with most kinds of munitions, something he picked up during the Rhodesian war. He can assemble and dismantle pretty well any weapons and explosives, and even better, he has an instinct for the best place to position or find a bomb. We've come to the conclusion that Vulcan is planning to destroy the gathering with explosives. If we're right, Timot's the man to sniff them out before they can go off.'

'Surely they'll have security wrapped it up tight as a drum,' Richard cut in. 'The bombs are probably in place already – that's the only way they could do it. And Timot won't stand a chance of getting in.'

'Oh, he will. All we need to do is get them to the area.' Dave looked at Karen. 'We'll need to borrow your company pilot friend again, with a helicopter this time. I take it de Louts can oblige?'

'We certainly can, but it'll have to be another pilot. The man that flew us in from Victoria Falls only flies fixed wings. It won't be a problem, though,' she assured him. 'I'll get straight on to it. They can probably pick Timot and Sandy up from here.'

'Great, that'll save a lot of time. They'll need all they can get.'

There was a long night ahead and an awful lot to cover. It was just as well Dave had resisted the temptation to flick through the rest of the newspaper. Vulcan's plans were bigger than he would ever have imagined.

CHAPTER 57

The twilight was fading quickly behind the huge plate glass window, and a faint orange glow bathed the sprawling city beyond.

Peter de Lout sat contentedly behind his huge modern desk. He had dismissed his secretary, and for the first time today was sitting quietly, rejoicing over what he had heard this morning. Of course, throughout the day he had had to appear distressed, as befitted the news of his sister-in-law's disappearance. But now that the executive floor of de Lout House was empty, his true emotions could surface like water from a bubbling spring.

She was gone, and the company was his. He could mould it, shape it, use it as he chose. There was nobody, nobody at all, to dictate to him, or rob him of what was rightfully his.

'Good evening, Peter.'

The voice bounced from the darkness of his office, momentarily shattering his mood.

Peter started, but managed to keep the surprise off his face. He looked up towards the silhouetted figure on the threshold.

He recognised the intruder, but was still disturbed as to how the man was able to get past the bodyguards and through the tight security.

'Brendan, please come in.' Peter waved an arm to offer his uninvited guest a seat.

Brendan Oechsli spoke in his distinctive southern twang. 'I heard this morning your sister-in-law has gone missing. A terrible shame.'

Peter ignored his ironic tone. 'A contingency that should never have been necessary.'

'Ah, but a task the Leopard was more than equal too. I'm most impressed.' Brendan sat with his legs crossed, carefully straightening a creases in his trouser leg. 'What other progress has been made?'

Peter said eyebrows raised, 'You already seem to know as much as I do.'

Brendan fixed him with a penetrating glare, but Peter seemed undaunted.

'Has our friend Van der Zwet been in touch since this morning?' As Brendan asked the question he could have sworn the faintest flicker of concern danced behind Peter's eyes. 'Are there problems?' he asked suspiciously.

'I expected to hear from him earlier this evening. It's most unlike him to go quiet. Unless...' Peter trailed off into silence.

'Unless what? 'Brendan challenged, concerned himself now. The operation was at far too critical a stage for any unforeseen glitches.

'Unless of course he has located the Englishman, Richard Black. Then I wouldn't expect to hear from him until he's completed the job.'

The tension left Brendan's body. Then it occurred to him that Peter might have feigned concern in order to play on his emotions. Not for the first time, Brendan was having difficulty working this man out. He abandoned the attempt in favour of practicalities. 'So, at your end, all is in place for tomorrow?' he asked instead.

'All is in place,' Peter confirmed with a slight inclination of his head. 'I've already arranged transfer of the last of the extra funds from Jersey this morning.'

'Rather a sizeable amount, I take it,' Brendan said with a small frown. 'Doesn't that mean it will take far longer to clear?'

'Normally that would be the case, yes. However, the funds will be available in good time,' Peter stated, confidently. 'I've short-circuited the transfer procedure. With Karen de Lout out of the way, it's no longer necessary to go through such lengthy channels.'

Brendan nodded, though it was a side of the operation he preferred to keep at a distance. He knew he could rely on Peter to have it under control.

It was Peter's turn to ask a searching question. 'And the CIA agents here in the Republic, I take it they have been doing their job as instructed?'

'Very much so,' Brendan said with a satisfied smile. 'They've done their job admirably. They're quite inactive, exactly as we want them.' His expression became serious. 'But I understand the KGB are uncovering...'

Brendan was interrupted by the soft ringtone of Peter's private phone. He waited as Peter answered the call.

Helen was nervous. She had never had to ring the number before and had been avoiding making the call for most of the day.

Helen was an international banking clerk at Chase Marlow International, in their office in St Helier. She loved Jersey's towering cliffs, solitary beaches and temperate climate. Most of all she loved St Helier; it combined a relaxed way of life with a sophistication provided by the prosperity brought by the finance industry and its popularity as a centre for tourism.

For six years a large sum of money had been credited monthly into a savings account in her name. All she had to do in return was ring the number in South Africa if there was any unusual activity around a certain account. She bit her nails nervously. Nobody had asked why she was working late. Her boss had even praised her dedication. It was now or never. Helen swallowed her nerves, picked up the phone and dialled.

Her anxiety level leapt when someone actually picked up. She had forgotten the correct identification procedure long ago.

'Hello,' Helen began, surprised at how calm she felt. 'I have information regarding a bank account here in Jersey.' The man seemed to know exactly what she was talking about. 'There has been some unusual activity,' she ventured. The man seemed to know all about that too.

She took the receiver from her ear and looked at it indignantly. How rude. He hadn't even given her a chance to tell him about the audit.

Brendan watched with interest. Peter was clearly keen to end the call. Valuable information, Brendan decided.

Peter replaced the receiver and looked up, slightly irritated. 'A safeguard, set up to protect our activities in Jersey,' he said. He made a mental note to have the woman disciplined for incorrect procedure. As he looked at Brendan again, the American's face told him he was unconvinced.

'The shortened procedure I used to set up the transfer will have triggered a tag, a check, to verify that the funds can be cleared. It would normally need authorisation from my sister-in-law. However, as I have emergency control, and am acting president of de Louts, there isn't a problem.' As far as Peter was concerned, that was the end of the matter; he changed the subject. 'You mentioned the KGB. Are there problems there?'

Brendan thought for a moment. Peter had more than enough to do; he could deal with this himself. 'It's of no concern,' he said. 'After tomorrow we'll have little to worry about.' He rose to his feet. 'Speaking of tomorrow, I'll see you in plenty of time. We must finalise the addresses our friends of the inner circle will give to the nation after the guerrillas have launched their attacks.'

Peter remained seated. He was irked by the America's use of "our", and despite the work he still had to do before tomorrow, Brendan's nonchalant dismissal of the KGB hadn't convinced him. He decided to make a few inquiries of his own.

As he watched Brendan leave, his mind was already elsewhere. The funds from Jersey had to be allocated to various influential but susceptible sources throughout the world. For now, the KGB would just have to wait.

Although the night air was cool, Sergei Doblin had to take his handkerchief from his pocket and wipe the sweat from his brow. At times he didn't understand the Head of the First Chief Directorate of the KGB at all. Again, he had to run to answer the public phone on Pretorius Street, but this time instead of the usual cutting tone Uri had been in the most jovial of moods. Doblin didn't know which was worse. His superior's words still echoed through his mind.

'Congratulations, Comrade, the mission has been a resounding success. Thank you for your support. I will not be bothering you further.' What did he mean, resounding success? And why would he not be bothering Doblin further?'

The agents had received no support at all from the UDF. Admittedly over the last few days information had been trickling through, but nothing substantial, nothing anyone could quantify as a resounding success. No, at times, Doblin just didn't understand Uri Ferkatovich.

Doblin turned away from the telephone kiosk, still bemused. Tomorrow was another day. Somehow he knew it would bring more than an explosive rebuke.

CHAPTER 58

Dave and Karen rode up in the elevator alone and in silence. The meeting with Richard and Sandy had lasted into the small hours, and now dawn was breaking.

The meeting had been long, and when it drew to a conclusion, Karen and Dave had drifted off to bed. Unsurprisingly, Dave was almost asleep before his head hit the pillow. Karen had gently laid her head on his chest. The slow rhythmic thump of his heart was curiously reassuring.

Thoughts chased each other around her mind, mainly about this man breathing beside her. He had changed her life completely, and opened her eyes to a world she hardly knew existed. And although she'd been exposed to a barbaric underworld that threatened to destroy the company she cherished in memory of her husband, she had also experienced a kind of companionship she had never had with Tom. Although Dave hadn't yet made a commitment to her, Karen was unperturbed. If that commitment came, it would be after he had overcome Vulcan and the demons of his past. With that thought in mind, Karen drifted off to sleep.

They had risen early, well before dawn. Karen dressed in her business clothes, from a selection Moses had discreetly retrieved from her house. She had chosen a navy-blue suit and a plain white blouse, power-dressing at its most powerful. For today was D-day.

Karen faced the prospect of the ruination of her world; she could lose everything, even the man now at her side. Or, like a gambler betting everything on the final throw of the dice, by risking it all and helping Dave to expose and annihilate Vulcan, her company and life would become hers again. Karen hoped if that end was achieved, she would still have Dave at her side.

She marvelled at how quickly Dave had recovered from his injuries. All that remained of his swollen cheek and bruised eye was a slight puffy smudge in the soft tissue. Other than that, only a few dry scabs around his face showed the titanic struggle with Kane.

Dave was tapping a folded newspaper against his leg. Compared to Karen, he was simply dressed; he wore an open-necked shirt and casual trousers with light rubber-soled shoes, and looked comfortably relaxed. He also wore a lightweight jacket to hide the gun Karen had seen, holstered on his belt. Dave was also dressed for business, but business of a very different kind.

The lift slid to a halt in the magnificently decorated reception area of de Lout House's executive floor. Neither of them gave the pastel-hued walls and natural wood a second glance. They were here to work.

It was too early for the front office staff, and the hush absorbed their footfalls as they walked down the carpeted corridor to Karen's office.

It didn't surprise Karen to see her secretary sitting at her desk beside the main office door. Susan didn't hear them approach until they were almost on top of her. With a start her hand flew up to her open mouth.

'Mrs de Lout, I... we... we all thought...'

Karen cut her off in mid-sentence. 'My office, five minutes,' she commanded, her voice laced with venom. Without stopping, Karen and Dave walked past the flabbergasted secretary into the office.

Susan couldn't believe it. First to see Karen alive, and then to be ordered into her office in such a forbidding tone. It was as clear as the blazing sun, Karen *knew*.

When Karen had disappeared from the safari, Susan had plucked up the courage to talk to Uri, though to no avail. She didn't want to believe he was involved, but she had given him the details of the safari. Nobody else had known Karen's itinerary, except of course Peter de Lout.

Why had Uri wanted the timetable, as well as all that other information? she found herself asking, not for the first time. She found she didn't really want to know. The next five minutes would be the longest she would ever have to wait. And who was that tall man with Karen? She felt guilty enough, already, and he made the fear twisting the pit of her stomach even more snake-like. Susan shuddered; that man meant trouble.

'Very nice,' Dave observed, taking in the rich dark panelling and tasteful decor of Karen's office.

Together they were drawn to the enormous window behind her carved rosewood desk. He tossed the newspaper he was carrying on the desk, and they gazed in wonder at the scene; tinged by the early sunlight, the city seemed to be built *of* gold as well as *on* gold.

Several peaceful minutes passed before the tranquillity was shattered by a knocking on the door.

'Call her in, but let me handle it,' Dave said, his mind suddenly cold and calculating. Somehow Susan's association with Uri Ferkatovich was linked to Vulcan; he knew it in his bones.

'Enter.'

Dave and Karen presented a united front behind the desk as Susan timidly approached. She couldn't look at Karen, but she was unable drag her eyes away from the malevolent glare of the tall man at her side.

Silence reigned for endless moments. Susan jumped when Dave eventually spoke. 'How's Uri?'

Oh Lord. They did know! Susan began to cry.

This wasn't at all what Dave had expected. This wasn't a hardened Soviet spy, just a confused and frightened woman.

'From the top again, 'Karen said. She wasn't totally without sympathy, but Susan had passed on classified information to the KGB.

She started her story again, her voice barely audible. 'Speak up,' Karen ordered. 'We both need to hear.'

'Uri is the only man that ever showed me any kindness or love, I suppose,' Susan said, more embarrassed than frightened now. 'He told me he was a university lecturer, that he lectured around the world. He said he had a series of lectures to give in South Africa, so he would be here for several months. I knew his interest in de Louts was more than casual, but he made me feel so, I don't know, wanted, I suppose. It's obvious now that he was just using me. I'm sorry, but I just couldn't help myself.'

'How long have you known him?' Dave asked.

Susan peered up at him. 'Two years,' she whispered.

'Tell us again what you passed on about the safari information,' he demanded, far less sympathetically than Karen.

Susan cast a desperate glance at Karen before answering. 'It was that weekend I went up to Zimbabwe. He asked for your itinerary and I gave it to him. Then when you went missing I realised it must be my fault.'

'And you say he's only recently walked out on you?' Dave asked bluntly, ignoring the tears that threatened to overwhelm her again.

Susan painfully nodded her head.

Seeing the state she was in, Karen took over. Time spent consoling the girl was time wasted. 'How did you meet him? I know you don't get out much.'

'Oh, it was here, one evening at an office party, before your... when I was working for your husband. Mr de Lout, Mr Peter de Lout introduced us.'

Karen's heart missed a beat. Peter de Lout was involved with the KGB, as well as with Vulcan and the CIA, and while Tom was alive! So she had never had full control of her company.

Dave was speaking again. 'OK, Susan, you can go now. But make sure you stay available. Don't leave the building, and don't talk to anyone. Somebody else will be here shortly, with more questions for you.'

Susan left the room, still apologising. Karen stood up and rolled her shoulders to release some of the tension that had built. 'Sorry, I should be getting used to it by now. But two years. It's almost beyond belief.' She stretched out a hand and touched Dave's arm. 'Do you think Ferkatovich could be Peter's link to Vulcan? Or perhaps he's Vulcan?'

'It's possible.' Dave allowed himself the faintest glimmer of hope. 'It could explain how Vulcan's been able to infiltrate Soviet security – it's normally impregnable. I think we'd better get Richard over here right away.' He picked up the phone on Karen's desk. 'Mind you, it could be a red herring. The KGB might just be one step ahead of us.' Dave dialled as he spoke, and drummed his fingers on the desk as it rang at the other end.

'Richard, we could have a break. Can you come up to Karen's office? We want you to question someone. No, bring the scrambler unit, you'll have to call Johnny from here. What? Oh, the executive floor. Turn left out of the lifts and follow the corridor to the far end.'

As he hung up, something caught his eye, and he reached for the newspaper he had thrown down.

'What is it with that paper?' Karen asked. 'You've been carting it around since last night.'

Dave didn't reply. Something was tugging at his mind, but this time it was so close to the surface it was making his skin crawl. Whatever it was, it wasn't going to be good news.

Karen looked past him at the headline he was staring at.

CHERNOBYL NUCLEAR DISASTER - A LASTING LEGACY.

Dave had gone still and quiet. 'What is it?' she asked.

He began flicking through the rest of the paper. He had only turned over a few pages when he stabbed accusingly at a small article. The colour drained from his face under his tan. 'Oh god, no!' he breathed in horror. 'What has that bastard done!'

Karen couldn't stand it any longer. 'Come on, talk to me,' she demanded.

The headline above the article read:

AMERICAN NUCLEAR SCIENTIST FOUND DEAD.

Reading on, she learned that the scientist was one of forty Americans hired to help operate the Koeberg nuclear power plant just north of Cape Town. He was found dead in a deep ravine in the Valley of a Thousand Hills. A group of schoolchildren had stumbled across his body while on a botany trip. Police said the American had been murdered, shot through the back of the head, possibly ten days ago.

'I still don't understand.' Karen threw her hands up in exasperation. Dave was leaning against the window, still looking pale and stunned.

'Pearson's note,' he eventually said.

'What about it?' Karen's frustration was growing; Dave had stumbled on to something and wasn't sharing it. The edge in her voice seemed to bring Dave round.

'Timot was right. Remember the last few items on James Pearson's note we didn't understand? U-235, Valley 1000, Reflecting shield, Hot and Cells.' Karen nodded. 'Well, Valley 1000 has to be the Valley of a Thousand Hills.'

'Yes, but what's this all about?' Karen pointed to the newspaper.

'We know Pearson went there before he was killed.'

She opened her mouth to speak, but he carried on. 'OK, do you remember the books in his apartment? Sandy told us – his peculiar hobby.'

'Nuclear physics.' Karen was starting to feel uneasy.

'And we're assuming Vulcan is going to try and assassinate the government and army officials at Omumbo, using some kind of explosive.'

Karen froze. Something told her she didn't want to hear what Dave was about to say.

'Karen, how long ago did Kane go to Natal, to your engineering shop? In the Valley of a Thousand Hills?'

Karen's head was spinning. It was all becoming all too appallingly clear. Kane had been in the Valley of a Thousand Hills to pick up something for Pump Station Omumbo – at the same time as the nuclear scientist was killed.

She was too stunned to speak, but Dave pressed on. 'Remember the last items on Pearson's note? U-235, Reflecting shield, Hot and Cells. You must have misinterpreted. Hot and Cells will be Hot Cells – lead-shielded rooms for the safe handling of radioactive material. Reflecting shield, that's supposed to be neutron reflector. So have a guess what U-235 is? A correct answer could win you a trip to Hiroshima, August 6th, 1945. Only this time it will be at Pump Station Omumbo.'

Karen closed her eyes. She didn't want to believe what she was hearing.

Dave continued, 'U-235 is a chemical symbol – uranium 235. Highly enriched uranium, weapons grade, the kind used for nuclear bombs. Somehow, Vulcan has built a dirty bomb at your engineering plant, and Kane has taken it to Omumbo. He's not just out to destroy the leadership of South Africa; he's planning a demonstration, to establish he's a new power to be reckoned with throughout the world. And Timot and Sandy are sitting right on top of it.'

'I don't care if he's questioning a suspect.' Dave spoke quietly, his voice as cold as ice. 'I need you to get him and put him on the line. I've already told you, it's confidential.' His knuckles turned white as he gripped the phone. 'Just tell him Dave Old is calling. He'll be expecting...'·Dave trailed off into silence; the person on the other end had obviously done as they were asked.

Karen watched as he stared through the window, unable to keep still. He was clearly fuming, but he kept it under control. He began to speak again.

'Athol, at last... Of course it's important!' This time he failed to govern his temper. 'Shut up, Athol,' he barked. 'Everyone in your government is about to be assassinated. So are the commanders-in-chief of the army. I want you in Karen de Lout's office, here in de Lout House, within the hour, sooner if possible. Kane will just have to wait.' He slammed the receiver down and began pacing up and down the office like a caged leopard.

Karen had never seen Dave in such a state before. Not that she blamed him; he must feel as impotent as she did. There was nothing to be done until Athol arrived; only he could supply the answers they desperately needed. Meanwhile, she could only hope to god Dave had got it wrong.

After a while she could stand it no longer; he was driving her crazy. Although it was the last thing on earth she wanted to know, she decided to ask him the question still lurking in the back of her mind. If nothing else, it might take his mind off Sandy and Timot. 'Tell me how he's done it. How has Vulcan built a dirty bomb? I thought it was pretty well impossible for terrorists to build a nuclear device?'

'Oh Karen. Vulcan's no terrorist. He's got a massive organisation behind him, and has colossal resources to draw from.' Dave came to sit beside her; her ploy to distract him had worked. 'Do you know anything about how a nuclear device works?'

Karen nodded. 'Not much, but a little. I know there are two types, atomic and thermonuclear. Both release huge amounts of energy and radioactivity. Atomic works through the splitting of atoms, thermonuclear joins small atoms together. That's about it.'

'OK. I think we have to assume Vulcan has built an atomic device, rather than a thermonuclear one.'

'Why?'

'Because it'd be easier to build, and he can source all the materials he needs here in South Africa.'

'But surely South Africa hasn't...'

Dave cut her off. 'Let me finish, then judge for yourself.' Karen nodded a reluctant agreement, and he continued, 'The power of an atomic bomb comes from the forces holding the atoms together, the huge amount of energy in the nucleus of each atom. A nuclear bomb explodes when the nucleus releases that binding energy. Nuclear fission takes place when a neutron strikes the nucleus of a plutonium atom. Or in Vulcan's case, uranium.'

'You mean like the reaction when the white ball smashes into the rack on a pool table?'

'Hey, good image!' Dave managed a smile. 'When the nucleus splits, it releases two or three more neutrons as well as a lot of energy. These split other nuclei, and a chain reaction starts. Then, when the uranium can't contain the energy any longer, it all erupts.'

Karen couldn't help but be interested. 'But how can the energy in a tiny atom be so powerful?' she asked.

'That's something I don't understand – but put it this way. If the earth were compressed to the same density as the sub-atomic particles in the nucleus, its diameter would only be about half a kilometre. That takes a lot of energy.'

'Hell! No wonder nuclear devices are so powerful.' The distraction technique was working; Karen cast about her mind for something else to ask. 'What about 235? Why has uranium got those numbers after it?'

Dave had to think about that. 'OK, without getting too technical, it's a bit like cars: manufacturers produce different models, but they're all the same make.'

'So there are different types of uranium?'

'Exactly. Usually two types, the heavier 238 and lighter 235. 238 is fairly benign, 235 atoms are the ones that split more readily to trigger the chain reaction.'

'So if you can get your hands on enough uranium 235 you can make yourself an atomic bomb.'

'In theory, yes.'

'In that case, why are they so difficult to make?' Karen found she was morbidly fascinated.

'Because separating the two different kinds of uranium is so difficult.' Dave was immersed in the subject now. 'It's called uranium enrichment. 235 is very rare, and to be weapons grade, the uranium has to be enriched to ninety-something per cent.'

'And somehow, Vulcan has got his hands on enough weapons grade uranium to build a bomb.'

'It's looking that way.'

'So how has he done it?'

'If you're asking where did he get the uranium, I have no idea. How did he go about building the bomb? My best guess is that nuclear scientist. And I believe he built it in your engineering shop in the Valley of a Thousand Hills.'

'I know I'm not going to like it, but how have you worked that out?' By now Karen was just wishing the nightmare would end.

'Remember the Hot Cells in Pearson's note? He meant the lead-shielded rooms at your plant. They have sophisticated remote-handling equipment used for processing radioactive material.'

Karen could hardly breathe. This was worse than she could ever have imagined, but it sounded so simple.

'Maybe Vulcan hasn't been able to get enough weapons grade uranium,' she said, knowing she was grasping at straws; desperate for Dave to be wrong.

'I believe he has,' he said simply.

'But how, if it's so difficult to manufacture?'

'If my hunch is correct, the South African government did it for him.'

'I didn't think South Africa was that technologically advanced.'

'Maybe not, but it's a wealthy country. The Koeberg nuclear power station is operating smoothly. Where do you think they get the low-enriched uranium to power the reactor?'

Karen couldn't answer.

'From the government's so-called pilot-scale uranium enrichment plant at Valindaba,' Dave went on. 'It produces forty-five per cent enriched uranium for its research reactor at Pelindaba; if it can do that, all it needs to do is continue processing the uranium and it'll soon have weapons grade uranium. If I'm right, that's where Vulcan got it. And if there's any missing, Athol will know.'

A commotion at the office door cut short his explanation.

'I'm sorry, gentlemen, you just can't barge in,' said Susan.

Someone pushed the door open, and Dave laid a firm hand on Karen's arm. His other hand moved to the gun in his waistband; he wasn't taking any chances.

He released Karen and dropped his other hand when Athol and Richard walked into the room. Susan followed them in.

'I'm sorry, Mrs de Lout, they wouldn't listen.'

'Thank you, Susan.'

Susan, thoroughly flustered, turned away and quietly closed the door behind her.

'We met in the elevator,' Athol explained. He looked from Dave to Karen and back again, clearly puzzled, but there were more important matters at stake. He rounded on Dave. 'Now, what's all this bullshit about assassinations? I had to leave the hospital just as Kane had started to talk. He's already given up most of the UDF guerrilla camps.'

Richard said nothing. Karen pointed to one of the comfortable settees, and he sat down to listen.

Dave picked up the newspaper from Karen's desk and shoved it under Athol's nose, pointing at the article about the dead scientist. 'Know the man, do you?'

The flicker of recognition behind Athol's gold-rimmed glasses told Dave he did, but he shook his head.

'OK. Let me tell you about a few of our findings, then perhaps you'd like to reconsider.'

Karen joined Richard on the settee, but Dave and Athol remained standing. It was hard to tell which of them was angrier.

'Before I first made contact with Karen,' Dave continued, 'a private investigator was investigating her husband's death. The investigator was killed, probably by Kane. He left behind a note that we've only just managed to decipher. It said Uranium 235, Neutron Reflector and Hot Cells.' Athol's eyes opened wide. 'That's right,' Dave went on, 'they're all used for building a nuclear device. Athol, where do you think was the last place this private investigator visited before he died?'

This time Athol's expression matched Richard's; they were both appalled.

'Right again; the Valley of a Thousand Hills. The same place as the nuclear scientist was found.'

Athol dropped heavily on to the other settee. Not in his wildest nightmares had he expected this.

Dave continued doggedly, 'De Louts have an engineering plant in the

Valley of a Thousand Hills that has supplied all the piping and pumping equipment for...?' He looked at Athol, eyebrows raised.

The South African's mouth fell open. 'No,' was all he could say.

'Oh yes, Pump Station Omumbo. And Vulcan's hatchet man, our friend Kane, delivered the last of the engineering shop's consignments there a few days ago.'

'The big opening's today,' Athol breathed.

'Athol, there's a question only you can answer.' Dave's face tightened into stern lines. 'How much uranium 235 has gone missing from the enrichment plant at Valindaba?'

Silence seemed to fill the room like another presence. Richard muttered an astonished oath. The colour drained from Athol's face. That was answer enough.

'How much?' Dave repeated quietly.

Athol shot a glance at Richard.

'No need to worry about your precious security. Richard already knows most of this. Sandy works for him.'

Now it was Richard's turn to gape in astonishment. And that, Dave thought, covers my back.

'How much?' he asked for the third time.

'A security guard went missing... as well as sixteen kilograms,' came the answer. 'And the opening at Omumbo is only an hour and a half away.'

'What?' Dave leapt forward, shocked to the core. 'It's not supposed to be till this afternoon – another five and a half hours. Who the hell brought it forward?'

'Who do you think?' Athol groaned.' I was in charge of Omumbo's security before you gave us Kane.'

An hour and ten minutes to go, Karen thought gravely.

It was amazing what could be achieved in twenty minutes. She had walked into the security wing of de Lout House like an apparition; the staff could hardly believe their eyes, but they had still produced a photograph of Kane. It was company policy to photograph all new staff, and she was relieved to find procedure had been followed despite his clandestine association with Peter.

Armed with the photograph, Dave and Athol had left for the airport, where the Gulfstream she organised was waiting to take them out to Pump Station Omumbo. It would take a little under an hour in the air to reach the refinery. They would have precious little time to locate and disarm a nuclear device.

CHAPTER 59

Peter de Lout's usual cool resolve had abandoned him. Something had gone desperately wrong, and today of all days. He had been so sure she was no longer a problem, that she'd been taken care of once and for all. Peter had been about to walk into the security wing through a side entrance when he became aware that it was far too quiet in there. He peered around the door, and his heart missed a beat. Karen was there, and the staff were obviously as shocked to see her as he was.

Peter began to back away, but stopped dead when he heard her ask for a photograph of Kane Van der Zwet.

Now, back in his office, a multitude of questions tumbled through his mind. How much did she know? Perhaps she was even responsible for Kane's recent disappearance. He took several deep breaths, trying to relieve some tension and help his mind function. At least he had managed to move the funds from the trust account in Jersey. Or had he?

He looked at his watch; an hour and five minutes to go. His mind clicked back into focus. There was no way anyone could stop today's sequence of events. Just one more loose end to tidy up. With this one he needed help. He reached for the phone.

CHAPTER 60

'Damn, all frequencies are still jammed into Omumbo. I've told the copilot to keep trying all the way there.' Dave dropped into the seat beside Athol, his mind moving in a very different direction from the last time he had travelled on the Gulfstream.

'We'll be lucky to make it.' Athol consulted his watch anxiously. Twenty minutes to go. 'I still don't get why the bloody hell you didn't tell me about all this sooner.'

Dave ignored the question; he had already explained more than once. 'We'll have to hope Timot and Sandy have located the bomb, even if they don't know what it is. If they haven't, we'll just have to show Kane's photo around. Surely a guard or somebody will remember him,' he said.

Athol began thinking aloud. 'We'll have to evacuate the dignitaries as soon as we get there...'

Dave looked at him in amazed disbelief. 'Christ, get real,' he scoffed. 'That bomb is nearly as large as the one that destroyed Hiroshima. It'll create a fireball nearly as hot as he sun, and it's sitting on millions of litres of crude oil. Where exactly are you going to evacuate them to?'

Athol he removed his glasses and rubbed his face. 'Shit, give me a break. How many times have you been twenty minutes from a nuclear blast?' He blew out a breath. 'Do we know how it will be detonated? Could it be remote controlled?'

Dave took a deep breath and composed himself before answering. He needed Athol's complete co-operation.

'It'll have to be manually triggered. All the radio signals are jammed, remember.'

Dave's mind was reeling. Of course he cared about the government and army officials, and even more about what Vulcan planned to do next. But most important to him, Sandy and Timot were down there. Two of the people he cared most about.

Sandy hadn't seen Timot for hours. Not since they left the refinery just before dawn. She was stretched out on the ground, sunning herself next to a camelthorn tree. Boy, she was glad it was winter. She had no desire to experience the summer heat of the Kalahari. Even today it was nearly too hot to sunbathe.

Sandy was taking full advantage of the second part of her personal creed. The first part was *work hard*. She had done that last night, traipsing around every part of the refinery after Timot. They had nearly been caught a couple of times. So it was time for the second part: *play hard*. Or in this case: *do nothing and enjoy it*.

It was so peaceful and quiet, not a breath of wind. The air was clear, and although the ground was harsh and dry, it was clean. Dreamily she closed her eyes again.

A dark shadow fell across her head. She froze.

Whatever it was, it had come from behind the camelthorn tree. She hadn't heard a thing, even though the desert air carried the faintest of sounds. Then her heart missed a beat, as he remembered this was leopard country. Timot had left her at the base of the tree while it was still dark, and not once had she bothered to look up into its branches.

The creature coughed. She had heard the leopard's growl was like a cough. Jesus, now what? Fight or flight were both hopeless. The creature coughed again.

Then a deep rumbling voice said, 'One so skinny should be ashamed to uncover her body.'

Her relief was palpable, but she still managed to retort, 'And one so bald should not be so quick to denounce another. Where the hell did you come from, Timot, I never heard a thing.' Feeling a little foolish, Sandy quickly stood and slipped her shirt back on.

'Some of us are blessed,' Timot shrugged.

Sandy rolled her eyes and buttoned her shirt. 'Where to now, oh gifted one?'

Timot grew serious. 'We've got problems. It looks as though the opening has been brought forward. They're just about to start.'

'Oh no! Dave thinks it won't be for four hours. He's going to be too late to stop them. What the hell are we going to do?'

They both scrambled up the low ridge that hid them from the refinery. They could just make out the opening party taking their seats in front of the raised platform around the main gate valve. The president was stepping up to the podium.

'Have you located the explosives?' Sandy asked.

'No, but they have to be somewhere near the president. A hunch tells me the main gate valve, but I can't see how. We had a good look at it last night, and when I tapped it, it sounded hollow. If they are there, they must be buried.'

'So, what are we...' Sandy nearly died of fright as a silver-bodied jet flashed just overhead.

'There's your answer,' Timot said. 'The cavalry just arrived. Come on, we'll meet him around at the front gates.'

'Regulations be damned. Fly as low over the oil refinery as you can, and make as much noise as possible.' Dave's voice lashed like a whip.

The pilot decided he was serious. 'Where do I land?'

'On the road leading to the main gates, it'll be just as good as the runway.'

The pilot opened his mouth to object again, then remembered Karen de Lout's explicit instructions. "Follow all, and I mean *all*, of his orders."

The corporal at the main gate couldn't believe his eyes. An executive type jet had just touched down, and was screaming down the road at unbelievable speed. His feet felt like lead and his heart thumped wildly in his chest, but the thought that lurched through his mind was how ridiculous he must look, pointing his sub-machine gun at a plane.

The Gulfstream's nose gently rocked up and down as the pilot brought it to a stop. He couldn't keep the wicked smile off his face; the poor soldier on the ground was as white as a sheet.

Dave ran down the Gulfstream's retractable steps with Athol bringing up the rear. Athol flashed his security card at the puzzled corporal guarding the gates, then pulled out the photograph of Kane.

'Have you seen this man before? He brought in the last consignment of goods from Natal. We need to know what he brought and where he took it.'

'No, sir, but I did come on duty just after the goods arrived.' The corporal hitched his thumb over his shoulder. 'The NCO you want to talk to is standing on the left of the guard of honour, in front of the main office block. Geffin's his name.'

'Good man. Dave, you take this.' He handed him a spare security pass. 'Corporal, you run interference for him.' Athol set off at speed, yelling over his shoulder, 'And take him wherever he wants to go.'

Where the hell were they? Surely Timot and Sandy had heard the jet. Looking for an atomic bomb in the eighty hectares of sprawling refinery would be a needle in a haystack without Timot.

The corporal was levelling his Uzi. Dave's arm shot out and grabbed the weapon.

'They're with me.' Timot and Sandy were running round the perimeter fence. When they stopped in front of him, he thrust the Uzi at Timot and demanded, 'Where?'

Timot didn't hesitate. 'Either the main gate valve or under the platform around it. They're in the middle of the refinery.'

Dave began to run., Timot caught up and added, 'I searched the area last night and couldn't find a thing. But the explosives have to be there.'

Dave's reply made him stagger. 'I hope you're right. It's nuclear.'

'I'm sorry, sir. I can't let you come any closer. That's only a National Security clearance and we're under army jurisdiction.'

A sergeant had stopped Dave and Timot some two hundred metres from the assembly of guests, suspiciously eyeing Timot and the sub-machine gun he carried. The president was speaking, gesturing towards the gate valve.

Dave didn't bother to argue. Before the sergeant knew it, he had a pistol pointed to his head.

'You're under my jurisdiction now. We're going to stop the opening whether you like it or not.'

One checkpoint down, one to go.

Dave turned the soldier around, shoved his Beretta in his back, and pushed him into a run. They headed down a wide corridor of towering pipes and walkways towards the final checkpoint.

Even after the low screaming pass of the Gulfstream, the opening was still proceeding. Typical, he thought; the arrogance and pride of South Africa's president wouldn't allow him to interrupt an opportunity to make his presence felt.

He turned his head and spoke to Timot. 'I'm going to try the direct approach and try to run straight through. If I make it, stay there and cover them for me—' He flicked his head at the checkpoint. 'Use the Uzi if you have to, or we'll all be as good as dead.'

It was a huge risk. There were half a dozen soldiers this time, all trained for the job.

As he ran on, the bulky shape of the main gate valve came into view.

It was obvious it was the atomic bomb; he should have guessed sooner. Its centrepiece was globe-shaped; that would house the target sphere of uranium and its outer covering of lead protecting it. A long tubular barrel stuck out horizontally; it was supposed to surround the handle's shaft, but in fact it was the gun barrel, ready to shoot the small cone-like wedge of uranium into the target sphere to cause the nuclear blast.

They were screwing the special handle into place; once it was fitted and the shaft was turned it would detonate the device. He quickened his pace, pushing the sergeant faster. They ran through the final checkpoint, meeting no attempt to block their way. Confusion reigned as Timot bellowed an order and cocked his weapon.

It had worked; there was still a chance. The president stepped up to the gate valve, his arm stretched out. Dave was still fifty metres away as he grasped the handle with both hands. Forty metres; thirty; twenty; fifteen. Dave filled his lungs to shout. Ten metres; Dave screamed a warning, but the handle had begun to turn.

Then all sound was drowned as the air erupted in a shuddering blaze of violence. The ground shook, and there was a blaze of burning metal. He had failed. It was over.

But he was wrong. As the dust began to settle, he saw that the explosion was actually a volley of gunfire from the snipers positioned in the towers around the guests.

The president took the barrage in his stride. Nothing was going to stop him from turning the handle and opening a new chapter in the history books. He looked contemptuously at Dave, reapplied his grip and pushed down on. This time it began to move.

'STOP!'

Athol appeared from behind the president, somewhat out of breath. 'It's a bomb, sir, a rather large bomb.'

As they walked back to the waiting Gulfstream, after profuse thanks from South Africa's president, Sandy heard the whole story. Dave had risked his life for them; she was grateful, but still appalled. He wrapped his arm around her and hugged her close, clamping an affectionate hand on Timot's shoulder. He had never shown such warmth towards her before. Perhaps he was changing.

The four of them climbed into the Gulfstream for the journey back to

Johannesburg. The pilot wasted no time with preflight procedures; Dave told him to get back to de Lout House as quickly as possible, and he was mindful of Mrs de Lout's instructions.

Dave could tell the pilot didn't like him, but he could live with that. He couldn't let feelings interfere with what still had to be done. But his own feelings refused to lie down as his eyes settled on Sandy.

She had so nearly been a victim of the most monstrous of Vulcan's crimes. If he and Athol had arrived minutes later, they would have seen nothing but a massive mushroom cloud, and the turbulence caused by the nuclear blast might have maimed the jet. But worst of all, Dave would have witnessed two cherished lives gone forever.

Timot's death was something they had both faced often in the past. Sandy's was another matter. He hoped he would never have to face that prospect again. They had been through so much together.

Over his years in South Africa, Sandy had become a constant companion and a true friend. They had lived and worked together in a purely platonic way, but he found himself wondering what it would have been like if he hadn't been consumed by his need to seek and destroy Vulcan. Now he thought he knew the answer – at least until the thought of Karen popped into his mind.

Time enough to think about all that later, he thought. There was still work to do. 'Athol, you said back at Karen's office, Kane had started to talk. Was it useful?'

Athol's eyes glistened behind his glasses. 'Oh yes,' he said with relish. 'He was unconscious most of the night and into the morning. When he came to, I threatened him with the AIDS infected blood; his fear was palpable. It worked like a charm. He began singing like a bird.'

'So, you got the locations of the guerrilla camps?' Sandy asked, impressed.

'Not all of them, I was interrupted by Dave, but most. I left my assistant there. By the time I'm back, he'll have milked out every last scrap of information.'

'How are you going to play it, rounding up the guerrillas?' Dave asked with interest.

'It's already started. As Kane revealed each location, contingency plans were actioned. It'll be done in one fell swoop, with the police and the security forces as back-up.' Athol couldn't stop himself from rubbing his hands together with glee.

'Then what?' Sandy again.

'They'll be tried, of course, but hopefully it'll be the catalyst to make the government realise they can either initiate change themselves, abolish apartheid, or have it forced upon them.' Athol shook his head sadly. 'Shit, if they don't, it'll happen all over again, nothing surer. And next time the people of South Africa may not be so lucky.'

Dave broke in. 'Before we actually lay down the Republic's new constitution,' he said sarcastically, 'aren't we forgetting something?' Blank stares were the only response. 'Oh, for Christ's sake!' he exploded. 'Remember our old friend Vulcan? We may have stifled his coup and worldwide demonstration, but we still don't know who he is. In fact, we're probably further away from him than before.'

He had their full attention now.

'If we don't identify him today, he'll be back. And next time he'll be twice as hard to catch.'

Athol was the first to speak. 'OK, what do we do?'

'*We* don't do anything. *You've* got enough on your plate with the UDF and Kane.' Dave wanted to stay in control, and he wanted to keep Athol and Richard apart. Finding Vulcan was personal, but that was no reason to forego the handsome profit he stood to make from both South Africa and Britain.

Athol didn't argue. 'OK, I'll get as much information as possible from Kane and relay to you. How are you going to play it?'

Dave briefly related Karen's involvement, especially the trust account in Jersey how Peter de Lout had been manipulating it for Vulcan's use, and the audit which was now in progress.

'It'll be a long shot, won't it?' Athol asked.

'Maybe, but that's all we've got. So it's agreed, you stick with Kane and the UDF?' Athol nodded. 'Right,' whatever jammed the radio signals before we landed has been lifted. I got the pilot to radio ahead and organise Moses to meet us at Jan Smuts. He'll take Timot and me back to de Lout House.'

'Hey, what about me?' Sandy flared. 'You're not leaving me out, not at this stage of the game.'

'I wouldn't dream of it.' Dave almost laughed; the thought was absurd. 'I want you to catch a taxi back to our office and grab everything we've gathered so far on Vulcan, no matter how irrelevant it seems, and bring it all to Karen's office. We going to work from there.'

'Why?' Sandy asked. 'That's one a hell of a lot to carry.'

'Because now Vulcan knows somebody's breathing down his neck, there's no reason to hide our identity. And de Louts has one of the best security and information gathering services in the world, second only to Network. We may need to use it.'

As the Gulfstream shot through the stratosphere back to Johannesburg, Sandy's attention wavered as Dave spoke to the other two men. He was on the verge of winning or losing the biggest battle of his life. Vulcan was the cause of his scars; if Dave was able to destroy Vulcan, his tormented past would be behind him.

In all the years Sandy had worked with Dave he had never once looked like settling down. He always seemed to be striving for something she could only call success. But now it dawned on her that it wasn't success as she knew it; everything he did was simply to get closer to Vulcan, in order to destroy him.

Sandy's heart went out to him. He was so close, she couldn't imagine what would happen if this chance slipped away.

She knew the answer. He would rise again and trudge another dreary path after his nemesis. But if he succeeded, his life would be changed forever. He might even be ready to settle down at last. Sandy was determined that it would be with her. Karen de Lout might have peeled away the last few layers of his steely reserve, but she was the one who had cracked that façade.

Dave had a choice to make, and Sandy would do all in her power to make sure he made the right one.

The black Mercedes limousine slowly glided down the ramp into the cavernous underground car park below de Lout House. Moses had to swerve violently as an identical limousine flew past in the opposite direction, tinted windows making it impossible to see who was inside. He turned his head slightly once the car had passed. 'Peter de Lout's,' he murmured.

Moses pulled the limousine into Karen's parking space by the elevator, and Dave stepped from its plush interior.

'Our bird, flown the coop?' Timot said.

'We'll know soon enough.' Dave turned to look at Timot. 'Go and see if it was him, and if it wasn't, bring him to Karen's office. I'll meet you there.'

Dave knew something was wrong as soon as he stepped from the lift. The reception staff were huddled together, talking in excited groups. Dave's heart leapt to his mouth, and he ran towards Karen's office.

It was a scene of utter mayhem. The office was a shambles, furniture overturned, books strewn everywhere, paper and debris littering the floor. There had obviously been an enormous struggle. Dave heard a weak groan from under an upturned settee.

It was Richard. He had a huge gash on the top of his head, pouring with blood.

Dave heaved the settee aside, went down on one knee and lifted Richard into a sitting position. He grabbed a cushion and pressed it over the bleeding. Richard was slowly coming around.

'What happened, where's Karen?' Dave asked, close to panic. He clasped Richard's jaw and shook him. 'Come on, come on, wake up, damn you!' Dave was frantic now. 'Karen, where is she?' he demanded again.

Richard groaned and twisted his chin out of Dave's hand. 'Ouhh Christ. Dave. What... where...?' He moved his head from side to side, blinking and grimacing.

It was all Dave could do to hold back from slapping him awake. 'Karen,' he hissed urgently. 'Where is she?'

Richard was slowly recovering. He sat up, rubbing his eyes. 'Karen. You should've seen her.' He moved his head gingerly, and felt around for a few moments before replacing Dave's hand with his own on the cushion doing duty as a pressure pad.

'Keep holding that down. You're bleeding,' Dave advised, trying not to imagine what might have happened to Karen.

'She fought like a wildcat,' Richard said.

Dave was growing more impatient as the seconds ticked by. 'Who did she fight? Where is she?' he demanded.

'They... he took her away,' Richard mumbled, on the verge of lapsing back into oblivion.

Dave was suddenly cold. 'Who? Where?'

This was useless, he thought; Richard was in no state to make any sense. He flipped the fallen settee over and helped his friend to stumble over to it. By some miracle, a jug of water and two glasses remained undamaged, standing on a small table under the window. He half-filled one of the glasses and put it in Richard's hand.

After a minute or two and few sips of water, the Network boss was coherent again. 'I must've got a hell of a whack on the head. They hit me from behind. He dragged Karen off, but she nearly...' He swayed backwards and closed his eyes. 'You won't believe – it was...'

A phone began to ring, stopping him in mid-sentence. As Dave looked around for it, there was a groan from under an upturned bookcase.

Richard pointed at the phone, which was on the floor behind the desk. 'That'll be Johnny, I gave him Karen's number. I'll see who's under the bookcase.' He lurched to his feet, but fell back again, grimacing and clutching the cushion on his head.

Dave ran over and picked up the phone. 'Hello, yes... It's Dave Old, Johnny.' He looked anxiously over at the bookcase. Susan was crawling out from under it. 'Look, Johnny, if it's important, tell me, or he'll just have to ring you back.' He gripped the receiver, his incredulity growing as Johnny spoke. Silence. 'You're kidding me. Never in this world. All right. Leave it with me.' He dropped the receiver on the carpet and looked across at Richard. He had no idea what he was expecting Johnny to say, but it wasn't this.

Susan had extricated herself from under the bookcase and was sitting on the floor, cautiously feeling her limbs for injuries.

'She says she heard where he... Vulcan took Karen,' Richard said.

Dave mind snapped back into focus. He went down on one knee and grabbed Susan's arm. 'Where? Where has she been taken?'

'Home. Her house. He said he wanted to destroy every last trace of her.'

Dave was on his feet and running for the door in a split second. Susan's voice trailed quietly after him. 'All this time he was only using me. Tell her I'm sorry.'

The lift to the basement car park took less than a minute, but it felt like hours. Dave flew towards the limousine; the man leaning up against the car wasn't Moses, but he didn't hesitate. 'Get me to Karen's house. Vulcan's taken her there.'

The twenty-minute drive was a living hell. This was all his fault; he should never have left her, knowing as much as he did about the way Vulcan worked. The prospect of losing her, and by that monster's hand... well, it was unthinkable, that was all.

It crossed his mind fleetingly that he had felt much the same when Sandy's life was on the line at Omumbo, but that was a dilemma for another day. For the moment, he needed to channel all his energy into this, the most daunting challenge he had ever faced. And he had one big advantage: Vulcan had been identified, and was a man he had studied. He knew exactly what he was dealing with.

The limousine glided into the gateway of the de Lout mansion. The huge white marble and black wrought iron entrance was exactly as Karen had described. Dave reached behind his back and drew his Beretta to check its load. He was ready for whatever awaited him: death, or a new life.

The limousine glided almost soundlessly along the meandering driveway, and the gleaming white mansion came into view. There was no noise and no movement, but Peter de Lout's limousine, identical to the one Dave was in, stood conspicuously in front the portico, by the main entrance. It was parked askew, one of its rear doors flung open wide.

Without taking his eyes off the door of the mansion, Dave instructed the man behind the wheel, 'Follow the driveway around to the right. There should be a large garage. Wait for me there.'

Pistol at the ready, Dave was out of the car while it was still moving. He crouched and ran to the other limousine, knelt behind it and counted silently to three. Then in a blaze of movement, he pitched himself through the open door and swept the pistol around the interior. Nothing; it was abandoned.

He leapt from the car and ran towards the massive double doors. He squatted beside the portico; again nothing, no movement, no tell-tale sign of a trap. All he encountered was silence, and a slightly open door that reminded him of an ancient tomb.

He steeled himself; it was now or never. With only Karen's description of the house to guide him, he slipped inside, the gun in a firm double-handed grip.

The stench hit him full in the face like a solid wall as he entered the lobby. He stumbled backwards and snorted, trying desperately to clear his head. He looked around, assessing the situation. It was everywhere, pooling on the floor, running down the walls. The entire vestibule was soaked in petrol. Vulcan, true to his self-proclaimed title, was about to set the building aflame.

Vulcan was here and he had to find him. But where? He made a split-second decision to go left, and silently moved forward, his eyes never settling anywhere for very long. His training kicked in. All his senses were on full alert, his veins were charged with adrenalin, and the gun had become an extension of his arm.

He heard a stifled cry and his head snapped towards the sound. He quickened his stealthy pace, and heard muffled voices, followed by a sound like bone driven into flesh. He came to a pair of solid wooden doors, one of them slightly ajar. His memory told him a private study lay behind them.

The smacking noise sounded again, then a voice.

'You've stolen everything that should've been mine.'

'No-o-o-o, please,' came a desperate cry.

341

It was Karen. Dave's cold resolve shattered. He saw her through the crack between the doors. A closed fist struck her across the face.

Years of pent-up anger boiled to the surface like a raging volcano as Dave barged through the door. His fury was fuelled by Karen's face, purplish red and swollen, bleeding from the corner of her mouth.

'*VULCAN!*' Dave screamed, crouching and aiming the gun.

'No!' Karen shrieked. 'Behind you!'

He was unconscious before he hit the ground.

There was a light, a long, long way away. Dave knew he was meant to move towards it. But he felt so tired, and his legs were as heavy as lead.

The light started to move away, and he blinked. *Karen. Karen.* The name echoed through his mind, and the light raced forward to meet him.

Karen! It all flashed back into his mind: where he was, her battered face. He tried to jump up and raise his gun, but he couldn't move. He looked down and found himself sitting in an upright chair, his hands tied to the back and his feet bound to the legs. He glanced round the room, and was met by a pair of unyielding, almost hypnotic eyes.

'Welcome back, Mr Old. My, we do have a temper, don't we?' The man those eyes belonged to gazed at him with something like awe. 'I always thought I'd hired someone like myself, cold, unemotional. Someone who always got the job done. A rare mistake on my part.'

'Dave, are you all right?' Karen spoke with difficulty, but her voice was full of concern. She sat beside him, bound in a similar fashion.

'I'm touched. Such sympathy for an assassin from his victim.'

Dave wanted to shout, 'You'll never get away with it.' But Vulcan already had.

For the first time he realised there were more than three of them in the room. 'I should have guessed,' he sighed. It was all too convenient. Brendan Oechsli stood to the side of Vulcan, holding his Beretta. 'You. And your Russian pal.' He nodded towards Uri Ferkatovich, who was standing beside the desk across the room.

Brendan neither confirmed nor denied it. Instead he said, 'The name Leopard suits you. We knew somebody was out there stalking us, but who or from what direction we could never tell. It was Karen's sudden reappearance that gave the game away. We never imagined for a minute that it was you. Vulcan here is most upset.'

'How long, Dave?' Vulcan asked quietly. 'How long have you been after me?'

'Screw, you pal,' Dave said with venom.

'Spending two years cooling your tail back in New Zealand was a master-stroke,' Brendan said with grudging admiration. 'That really put you above suspicion.' He waved the gun towards Vulcan. 'You must've wanted him real bad.'

'More than you'll ever know.'

'But why?' Brendan asked. 'I don't get it.'

'I think I know.' Vulcan stepped forward and yanked Dave's shirt open. He and Brendan both drew a sharp breath. 'So you really are the walking legend. I thought your code name was just a coincidence. They should've killed you, you know, that chance they had in Mozambique.' Vulcan laughed humourlessly. 'All that trouble you caused when you went back to fight in the bush.'

Dave could hold his temper no longer. 'You bastard. I hope you burn in hell,' he flared as he strained against his bonds.

Vulcan had moved to the floor-to-ceiling picture windows behind Karen. He cocked his head to one side. 'Hell, you say. Close, but not quite. I took my name for a reason. You have to admit we've done a good job of burning the world's economy. But you couldn't resist upsetting my little demonstration in the desert, could you? Believe me, the hell I'm going to create for you is just about to begin.' Vulcan turned his second accomplice. 'Show them, Uri.'

'With pleasure my friend,' said Uri Ferkatovich. His great paw closed on a large container of petrol and swung it to and fro, cover the walls, bookshelves and floor of the study.

Karen was still struggling to no avail. Dave's anger had subsided, and he was completely calm and ready to meet his maker – but not before he'd had answers to some questions. He looked at Vulcan, all expression gone from his face. Vulcan seemed almost disappointed at his calmness.

'You're an evil man,' Dave began, 'but one thing I don't understand: why kill your own brother and destroy all he's created?'

Vulcan sniffed contemptuously. 'Tom was weak. I had plans that could allow us to monopolise the markets of the world. Slowly, I was winning him over, but then he married this... this *woman*.' He spat the last word at Karen with hatred in his eyes. 'He changed. She turned him soft.'

'That's not true. Our profits increased.' Karen protested.

'Yes, but in all the wrong places. Consumables overseas were never going to bring us real power. That lay in South Africa, with our mineral wealth.'

Dave was appalled, but still fascinated. 'So you recruited two of the most powerful men in the world, one from the KGB the other from the CIA, to work at your side. 'How did you do it?' he couldn't help asking.

'The only real lure. Power.' It was Brendan who answered, his eyes firmly fixed on Vulcan. His respect and admiration for the man were plain. 'It was easy, you see. Uri and I are powerful men, but we were both hamstrung by a lack of vision in both our governments. Peter showed us true power, neat and uncomplicated. Power that will eventually rule the world.'

All three men moved towards the double doors. Vulcan spoke again. 'Uri, if you'd be so kind. Our guests are waiting.'

Uri produced an engraved silver antique cigarette lighter from his trouser pocket, and flicked a flame into life. He held it out in front of him, his intentions clear.

Vulcan looked at Karen, his eyes cold and determined. 'For what you did to my brother, I hope you burn, here if not in hell.'

Dave closed his eyes and waited. But the eruption of noise that followed signalled a new and very different sort of hell.

Karen's limousine had glided to a stop a short while before, in front of the huge garage. It was Timot who sat at the wheel, and he had no intention of obeying Dave's admonition to wait. He wasn't going to have all the fun to himself.

He rechecked the pistol Dave had given him in the Gulfstream, and as he crossed the cobbled yard at the rear of the mansion, he realised he didn't have a clue how many they were up against.

He found himself in the kitchen, and a quick rummage through the drawers supplied him with a long thin-bladed boning knife. He tucked his pistol into the waistband of his trousers and moved stealthily forward with the knife extended.

He made his silent way through the main dining room, and it was when he reached the lobby that he knew they were in real trouble; the petrol fumes were evidence enough. He skirted around the pools of flammable liquid and followed the liquid trail into the left wing to a pair of closed double doors. He listened to the voices in the room beyond, and the final comment chilled him to the bone.

'For what you did to my brother, I hope you burn, here if not in hell.'

Timot didn't recognise the voice, but the threat was clear.

I suppose I could knock, he thought, backing away. Lowering a powerful shoulder, he barged forward and smashed through the doors. They boomed open, crashing back against their hinges.

Timot ran headlong into the back of three men, who were all thrown forward. Dave and Karen were bound upright in chairs, but they would have to wait.

One of the men had a gun. It was the American, Brendan Oechsli. Timot glanced the other way. 'Ouhh shit!' he muttered. It was the Russian, Uri Ferkatovich, and he held a naked flame. He certainly hadn't expected that.

Timot erupted into movement. He threw the boning knife into his other hand and snatched the pistol from his belt. With a back-handed swipe of the knife he slashed Oechsli across the throat, rupturing his jugular and slicing the American's neck to the bone.

Blood gushed from the wound, and Brendan dropped the pistol and slowly sank to the floor.

In the same movement, Timot snapped off a shot off at the immense bulk of the Russian. The antique lighter, still burning, dropped to the floor, but there was no whoosh of flames. Uri stumbled to his knees.

Two down, one to go.

Timot rounded on Peter de Lout, who was running for the door. Timot raised his pistol and crashed it down on the base of his skull. Peter, Vulcan, collapsed unconscious to the floor. Without slackening his pace Timot ran over to Dave and Karen. He dropped the gun and used the knife to cut through the ropes holding Dave's legs to the chair.

Karen screamed, 'Behind you, look out!'

Dave's legs were free. Timot was up in a flash and ready with the knife. Despite the gunshot wound to his lower chest Uri was closing in; Timot swished and slashed at the monstrous Russian, who moved surprisingly fast for a big man who was badly wounded.

Dave was on his feet, his hands still bound to the chair. He ran wildly backwards towards the wall. The antique chair shattered on impact; the pieces fell away but his hands were still tied. He looked frantically around the room. Only the Russian remained a threat; Vulcan lay still as a post and the American's life-blood still poured from his neck.

Dave squatted above the pistol Timot had dropped, then stood with his back to the Zulu, holding the gun behind him.

'Timot!' he yelled. 'Take it!'

In a blur of movement Timot, flung the knife into his other hand, scooped up the gun and began to empty the magazine into the advancing Russian.

Uri's huge frame flinched and bucked as each shot crashed into him, but he didn't falter.

'Christ, shoot him in the head,' Dave bellowed. The gun would soon be empty.

Timot raised the weapon, and with one last thunderous roar Uri's head snapped backwards and exploded. The big Russian teetered and keeled over backwards. Timot didn't see him fall; he was occupied with cutting Dave's bindings, then Karen's.

Karen stood up, rubbing her wrists, and staggered towards Dave and Timot. Dave caught her as she stumbled, then both he and Timot followed her horrified gaze. Uri's body twitched and jerked in his death throe, and one of his hands touched the lighter, which was lying beside a pool of petrol, the flame still alight.

Without a word, Dave and Timot grabbed Karen by her arms and ran at the full-length window. As they hit the glass a great whoosh of scalding air catapulted them to safety in a shower of glass. They had escaped Vulcan's version of hell.

Brushing glass and debris from his bleeding forearm, Dave was the first to speak. 'We better call the fire brigade.'

'No.' Karen laid a restraining hand on Dave's other arm. 'Let it burn with Vulcan. It's only a link to a past we all want to forget.'

Their heads turned as another huge whoosh told them the rest of the petrol had caught. They stood transfixed. It was a fitting end for a tyrant who chose to name himself for the Roman God of Fire.

Timot broke the mood. 'Well, which one was Vulcan?' he asked perplexed, 'I still don't know.'

'There's your answer.' Dave pointed at the shattered remains of the window. A figure staggered to stand silhouetted against the backdrop of flames. Peter de Lout had risen from the floor, and was surrounded by a beast of dancing flames: a beast he had spawned. Oblivious to any pain, he stared at them until another whoosh engulfed his body. He tried to scream but the fire leapt down his throat. It was as if Vulcan, the true Roman God of Fire, had come to claim the arrogant mortal who had tried to steal his name.

Another eruption brought the roof of the study crashing down, obliterating any sign of Peter de Lout.

And with that, Dave's own years of hell were over. Like a shroud that had constantly clouded his life, his tormented past fell away, leaving a sense of freedom he thought he could never experience.

CHAPTER 61

Two weeks after the death of Vulcan, the change in Dave had been nothing less than phenomenal. There were no more nightmares, no more brooding silences, and his quiet resolve was replaced by an infectious energy nobody was immune to. He laughed freely and often for the first time in years. It was like the dawning of a new age.

Every day of the two weeks had been packed with meeting and debriefings with officials and dignitaries from South Africa and around the world. Not only was Dave able to leave the past behind, but the countries Vulcan had manipulated could focus on repairing their economies without fear of outside intervention.

But not all of Dave's reserve was consigned to the past. He still faced a personal dilemma, and spent hours alone, wrestling with this final demon. He had an agonising decision to make, between Karen and Sandy. But now it was made, and with sadness mixed with trepidation, he had chosen today to tell Karen.

He pushed open the door to Karen's office. The noise it made as it dragged across the shag pile carpet grated his already tender nerves. Karen was waiting for him. She looked tired and drawn; she was having to fight tooth and nail to save her overseas subsidiaries.

Her eyes were huge and fearful, almost like a timid schoolgirl wrongly accused of bad behaviour. Neither of them said a word as Dave approached.

He kept it simple and short; that was his way. Then he briefly hugged her and gave her the lightest of kisses on her forehead. No more words were needed.

Karen watched him leave, tears streaming down her face. She made no attempt to prevent them from splashing upon her blouse. Dave had gone. Karen was alone. Again.

As Dave stopped his car outside his office, he looked through the window and saw Richard and Sandy waiting for him. Seeing Karen had not been easy, but now that was over he felt as if a weight had lifted.

He entered the room with a smile on his face. 'Like your bald patch,' he said, standing over Richard and prodding the shaven spot around the neatly closed gash on his head where his stitches had been.

Richard and Sandy laughed. Vulcan's death was far more than the passing of one man; they had all taken on a new lease of life, and this vibrant side of Dave's personality was something they had rarely seen before.

'Been a hell of a couple weeks,' Dave said cheerfully. 'How's everybody bearing up?'

He looked at Sandy and smiled reflectively. Yes, it was the right decision. A painful one, but for better or worse, one he was willing to live with.

He slumped down on the settee opposite Sandy. She saw his smile, met it briefly with a studious one of her own, before turning away and focusing back on business.

This was the first real chance he, Sandy, and Richard had had to talk since Vulcan's death. They had been involved in meetings together, always formal affairs, but for the most part their recent schedules of meetings with government officials and security organisations had sent them miles apart. There was hardly a country in the world which was not keen to gather as much information as possible about Vulcan and his organisation; it was vital to ensure a tyrant like him was never able to rise again.

'I have one question, Dave,' Richard said. 'How on earth did you know Sandy worked for me? You dropped it like a bombshell. I couldn't believe it.'

'No great revelation. Timot figured it out. How long have you been working together?' Dave's gaze swept from one to the other.

'Oh, years, since before I first approached you to track down Vulcan. Sandy had worked for me on a few jobs, and you were her idea. You'd supplied me with information, but I still didn't know a thing about you. I needed to be sure you were genuine,' Richard replied.

'All that time. So you must've known about my deal with the South Africans?'

'Well, I do now!' Richard laughed. 'I suspected, but Sandy has what I'd call split loyalties, so she never said a word.'

'You mean she suits herself.' Dave chuckled; Sandy was the picture of innocence. He changed the subject. 'In hindsight it's obvious, but Peter de Lout, eh? Who'd have believed it? What else has been uncovered on his organisation?'

Richard handed them both two photocopied documents. 'From Johnny,' he explained. 'He's still compiling it. Laying aside the massive environmental disaster, and the enormous radioactive wasteland he would've created in the Kalahari from Omumbo; by gaining control of the South African government, coupled with that devastating show of power, Vulcan's organisation would've attained huge manipulative influence around the world.'

'What's this house on Balboa Island? Isn't that in southern California,' Sandy asked, consulting her report.

'Looks like that was his worldwide headquarters. Johnny's working from there at present. Apparently the computer system takes up a whole room and is state of the art. But once he cracked the access code, it showed the full extent of Vulcan's operations.'

'But how the hell did Vulcan get to spend so much time there?' Sandy asked, puzzled.

Dave answered for Richard. 'He didn't need to. Because Peter de Lout was in charge of de Louts security arm, he was able to set up a direct feed between de Lout House and Balboa.'

'Yes, Johnny's really excited about that, said it was to do with package switching and transmission protocols, whatever they are. He said it was called something like ARPANET, and he wants one.' Richard rolled his eyes in long-suffering acquiescence – Johnny was always after the latest technology. He continued, 'When Peter did need to travel overseas, being in control of de Louts' overseas subsidiaries gave him the perfect cover.'

'But why did he stay with de Louts?'

'Three main reasons. One: to keep his operation small and effective he needed de Louts' security arm to gather information. Two: he needed access to vast amounts of capital to feed his organisation. And three: de Louts was the key to his operation. He needed one organisation with a secure base and subsidiaries in virtually every country in world to spread his brand of economic terrorism.'

'So he had his brother killed so he could take control,' Sandy suggested.

'Yes, but he didn't count on Karen inheriting Tom de Lout's preferential shares.'

'So that's when Vulcan rehired you?'

'I think Kane had already contacted me before Karen took over. I suppose he knew she'd be trouble.'

'But why didn't he get Kane to knock her off,' Sandy cut in, 'like her husband?'

'Give me a chance and I'll explain.' He ignored her tart expression and continued, 'Vulcan rehired me because he had other uses for Kane. As it turned out it couldn't have worked better for the trap Richard and I had set.'

'But wasn't it a risk? Didn't it occur to him you might go after him instead of Karen?' Sandy asked.

'Sure, it was a risk,' Dave answered with a shrug. 'But Vulcan wasn't above taking the odd risk. He could always have called me off if he suspected...'

Sandy chipped in again. 'What about Karen's safari, then?'

'What about Karen's safari?'

'Was that a set-up?' she asked seriously.

'I believe it was her decision, though I suppose Vulcan might have put the idea in her head,' Dave answered. 'Once she'd become president of de Louts he needed her out of the way; she had the power to upset his plans. But I think he had a far more personal reason for wanting her dead. He was jealous. He thought she was using her feminine wiles to influence his brother.'

'But why didn't he just have her taken care of in Jo'burg?' Sandy asked, slightly confused.

'The same reason Tom de Lout was killed in Zimbabwe,' Dave explained. 'Their security in Johannesburg was too tight. There would've been some rather difficult questions to answer. Remember he was in charge of de Louts' security arm.'

Sandy still felt uncomfortable talking about Karen de Lout. She changed the subject. 'So how did Ferkatovich and Oechsli fit in? Did either of you suspect them?'

'Not that they were actually involved with Vulcan,' Richard admitted. 'I knew there was some skulduggery going on, but I hadn't the faintest idea they were actually in cahoots with him until they started showing up at de Louts House.'

'Oh, by the way, thanks,' Dave said sarcastically. 'You could've warned me. I didn't have a clue until I had to face them at Karen's house.'

'Yes, well.' Richard fingered the wound on top of his head. 'I sort of had other things on my mind.'

Dave gave a wry nod. 'Any thoughts on how Vulcan recruited them?'

'A lot of this is only assumption,' Richard began. 'My guess is that he approached Oechsli directly – that would've been easy enough. Ferkatovich was another matter.' He gave Dave an ironic grin. 'They didn't want to admit to it, but the South Africans think Peter de Lout and Ferkatovich made contact during the preliminary discussions between Pretoria and Moscow to set up their joint accord to regulate the world's precious minerals markets.

Peter had been co-opted as an advisor to the official negotiating team.'

'So Ferkatovich helped Vulcan to break through Soviet security?' Sandy asked.

'It appears so,' Richard answered. 'The CIA gave him a foot in the door of the West, and the KGB let him in to the Eastern Block. But they also gave him a far greater advantage he probably hadn't initially foreseen. With the governments of the superpowers up in arms because of the state of their economies, he got Ferkatovich and Oechsli to organise the tri-lateral agreement with me. So any opposition we Brits might have put up was very effectively hamstrung.'

Dave had a question he had been dying to ask ever since he walked into the office. 'How exactly did Johnny track down Vulcan?'

'What took you so long to ask that?' Richard said, amused. He closed his eyes, composing his thoughts. 'OK. We all know about Peter de Lout's wizardry with figures? Well, Johnny's initial audit of the de Louts trust account turned up nothing; all the transfers were either to affiliated bank accounts or to recognised sources. The recognised sources turned out to be shelf companies in either Jersey or Guernsey, with their shares held by nominees, so that's where the trail ended.'

'Until...?' Dave prompted.

'Until Vulcan tried to transfer a sizeable amount, short-circuiting the normal procedure and triggering a tag which would usually have alerted Karen. Because she was away, or as he thought, dead, he thought there was no risk. The transfer's recipient was a holding company solely owned by Peter de Lout.'

'But that still doesn't prove...' Dave began.

Richard held up his hand. 'Johnny, genius and lateral thinker that he is, decided to do some cross-referencing with the list of companies you gave him, the ones Vulcan had taken over with your help. That led him straight to the back door of one of the companies on your list.'

'Hell, Johnny must've been busy.'

'He was, and will be for some time yet.' Richard sat back. 'You tell me something now. How's de Louts shaping up? They must've lost one hell of a lot of money.'

'Not so good abroad, though it's still too early to tell,' Dave answered. 'But the parent company here in the Republic is faring quite well, all except for the engineering shop in the Valley of a Thousand Hills.'

'Yeah, about that,' Sandy cut in. 'What on earth led James Pearson to the engineering shop in the first place?'

'We're at a bit of a loss on that one,' Dave admitted. 'Best guess is he had good contacts in the black community.'

'And what about the UDF?'

'Well, it's still legal,' Dave replied. 'It will probably survive; it's closely aligned with the ANC, after all. This whole business has given the government a hell of a shake-up. They're already talking about serious reform.'

'So what's happening in the rest of the world?' she asked.

'The moderates in the Kremlin are happy,' Richard answered. 'Ferkatovich's death means the KGB is as good as dead too. We might even be heading for real democracy, not only in the Soviet Union, but behind all of the Iron Curtain.'

Dave whistled in amazement. 'Do you think so?'

'Oh, we have our sources! It appears an anti-corruption campaign has been initiated, and there's been a spate of imprisonments among high-ranking officials. My contacts are talking about continued hardship, but also definite reforms.'

'Sounds impressive,' Dave commented. 'What about the States and Europe?'

'Europe needs to halt the economic decline, or they could be looking at a major monetary crisis in a few years. The United States is already having difficulty containing the federal budget. They're looking at a massive balance of payments deficit and are looking forward to becoming the world's largest debtor.'

'So even though Vulcan failed, the repercussions could be felt for years to come.'

'Huge understatement, Dave. If I were you, I'd consider very carefully where you place your future investments.'

EPILOGUE

The countryside was veiled in darkness. There was no moon. It was one of those jet-black nights that even the multitude of shimmering stars adorning the southern hemisphere's sky was unable to penetrate. For miles around the only light was a bright, narrow shaft, like a knife blade. It shone like a beacon, escaping through the smallest of cracks between the heavy velvet curtains of a single-storey country homestead built of Summerhill stone and surrounded by open farmland.

It was cool outside the house. Winter gripped the land, but inside the house it was warm. A log-burner glowed on the hearth, and the living room radiated warmth and tranquillity.

On a sheepskin rug on the parquet floor a huge yellow Labrador was asleep. A middle-aged woman, also asleep, sat in a green leather chair, laughter lines etched around her eyes and a half-finished book open in her lap.

The dog's eyes snapped open. He had sensed somebody approaching the house. He lifted his head and cocked it to the side as he heard the crunch of gravel. Somebody was walking up the drive.

The Labrador growled, and the woman stirred. The dog flicked a glance at her, then fixed his eyes back on the door. Again, he growled, and this time the woman woke with a start.

'What is it, Clay boy? You gave me a fright,' she said in French, rubbing the sleep from her eyes.

Clay was standing now, hackles raised. The handle of the back door turned.

Anne, still heavy with sleep, struggled out of her chair. A tall dark shadow stood in the recess in front of the door. She gasped in shocked disbelief.

Clay flew at the man, and they met in the middle of the kitchen. A brief struggle ensued, then the man began to speak. 'Easy, boy, it's good to see you as well.' He broke into an affectionate laugh and went down on one knee to hug the excited dog.

Clay whined and wagged his tail. The man stood up and looked at Anne, standing bewildered beside her chair. 'Hello, Mum. I told you I'd be back,' he said in French.

'*Cheri*, you could at least have written.' She did her best to look severe, but was betrayed by the tears in her eyes. 'Sometimes, Dave Old, I could...' But her son's crushing hug robbed her of the breath to finish.

Clay pranced excitedly around the reunited mother and son, but after a few moments he stopped his antics and cocked his head curiously at another figure standing hesitantly in the open doorway.

Anne followed his gaze. 'Hello, who do we have here?' she asked.

Dave broke away and turned to the figure, holding out an arm to draw her to his side.

She was tall, and strikingly attractive, dressed in jeans and a simple white blouse. As she walked into the light, Anne saw long brown hair falling about broad, elegant shoulders.

Dave spoke again. 'Mum, this is my fiancée, Karen de Lout.'

Karen couldn't help herself. Tears of joy began to stream down her face, as they had done on the day Dave had left her at her office, to consider his marriage proposal.

Anne greeted her in English. 'Well then, welcome to the family.'

INDEX

Baba - Zulu/Sindebele: sir.
Bakkie - Afrikaans: pick-up truck.
C'est la vie - French: such is life.
Cheri - French: darling.
Chimurenga - Zimbabwean: war of independence.
FRELIMO - Mozambique: Mozambique Liberation Front.
Impi - Zulu/Sindebele: regiment.
Kubu - Seyei: hippopotamus.
Madala - Zulu /Sindebele: friendly form of address for old man.
Mekoro - Setswana/plural: shallow dugout canoes.
MLPA - Angola: The popular Movement for the Liberation of Angola.
Mokoro - Setswana/singular: shallow dugout canoe.
Moped - English: light motorcycle fitted with auxiliary pedals.
Nkosi - Zulu/Sindebele: lord or sir.
Nkosikazi - Zulu/Sindebele: chief's principle wife.
RENAMO - Mozambique: National Mozambique Resistance.
Sjambok - Afrikaans: a whip made from the hide of a hippopotamus or rhinoceros.
Smoko - New Zealand English: afternoon or morning tea.
Unita - Angola: National Union for the Total Independence of Angola
Voetsek - Afrikaans/impolite: go away.
ZANU - Zimbabwean/Shona: Zimbabwe African National Union.
ZAPU - Zimbabwean/Matabele: Zimbabwe African People's Union.

Website - Get personalised book information and up-to-date news about the author and his works:

DavidMarkQuigley.com

Email – Be the first know about the author's new releases, awesome giveaways and news by signing up for his VIP mailing list:

books@davidmarkquigley.com

Reviews - Did you enjoy this book? If so, I would love to hear about it. Honest reviews help readers find the right book for their needs.

To leave a review, please head to the Book's page on Amazon, scroll to the bottom of the page under "More about the author" and select "Write a customer review".

I hope you enjoy reading this book as much as I did writing it; it has been a pleasure having you as one of my readers. Thank you.

Printed in Great Britain
by Amazon